MODERN   MASTERPIECES
OF   SCIENCE   FICTION

MODERN MASTERPIECES
OF SCIENCE FICTION

Edited by
SAM MOSKOWITZ

THE WORLD PUBLISHING COMPANY

Cleveland and New York

Published by
The World Publishing Company
2231 West 110th Street
Cleveland 2, Ohio

Published simultaneously in Canada by
Nelson, Foster & Scott Ltd.

Library of Congress
Catalog Card Number: 65-18008

FIRST EDITION

Copyright © 1965 by Sam Moskowitz

HC166

To
Wallace Exman

*Who saw
the possibilities*

G rateful acknowledgment is given to the following for permission to use the copyrighted material appearing in this anthology: Forrest J. Ackerman—"The Enchanted Village" by A. E. van Vogt, from *Other Worlds Science Stories*, July, 1950. Copyright 1950 by The Clark Publishing Company. Reprinted by permission of the author and the author's agent, Forrest J. Ackerman.

Harry Altshuler—"The Strange Flight of Richard Clayton" by Robert Bloch, from *Amazing Stories*, March, 1939. Copyright 1938 by Ziff-Davis Publishing Company. Reprinted by permission of the author and the author's agent, Harry Altshuler.

Isaac Asimov—"Liar!" by Isaac Asimov, from *Astounding Science-Fiction*, May, 1941. Copyright 1941 by Street & Smith Publications, Inc. Reprinted by permission of the author.

Lurton Blassingame—". . . We Also Walk Dogs" by Robert A. Heinlein, from *Astounding Science-Fiction*, July, 1941. Copyright 1941 by Street & Smith Publications, Inc. Reprinted by permission of the author and the author's agent, Lurton Blassingame.

L. Sprague de Camp—"The Command" by L. Sprague de Camp, from *Astounding Science-Fiction*, October, 1938. Copyright 1938 by Street & Smith Publications, Inc.

Fritz Leiber—"Coming Attraction" by Fritz Leiber, from *Galaxy Science Fiction*, November, 1950. Copyright 1950 by World Editions, Inc.

Will F. Jenkins—"A Logic Named Joe" by Murray Leinster, from *Astounding Science-Fiction*, March, 1946. Copyright 1946 by Street & Smith Publications, Inc.

Scott Meredith Literary Agency, Inc.—"Night" by John W. Campbell, from *Astounding Stories*, October, 1935. Copyright 1935 by Street & Smith Publications, Inc. Reprinted by permission of the author and the author's agents, Scott Meredith Literary Agency, Inc. "Before Eden" by Arthur C. Clarke, from *Amazing Stories*, June, 1961. Copyright 1961 by Ziff-Davis Publishing Company. Reprinted by permission of the author and the author's agents, Scott Meredith Literary Agency, Inc. "Kindness" by Lester del Rey, from *Astounding Science-Fiction*, October, 1944. Copyright 1944 by Street & Smith Publications, Inc. Reprinted by permission of the author and the author's agents, Scott Meredith Literary Agency, Inc. "Mother" by Philip José Farmer, from *Thrilling Wonder Stories*, April, 1953. Copyright 1953 by Standard Magazines, Inc. Reprinted by permission of the author and the author's agents, Scott Meredith Literary Agency, Inc. "Requiem" by Edmond Hamilton, from *Amazing Stories*, April,

CONTENTS

INTRODUCTION

Modern science fiction, among the insiders in the field, is a phrase that refers to a readily identifiable change in the format of the science fiction story, which was begun in 1938 and was readily apparent by the middle of 1939. The revolutionary was John W. Campbell, who not only forcibly moved this branch of fiction in the direction in which he wanted it to go but under the name of Don A. Stuart had previously written prototypes of the kind of stories he had in mind.

Campbell's "Modern" * science fiction laid special emphasis on certain things:

---

*When "modern" is used in quotes at certain places in the text it is not intended to denigrate, but to recognize that "modern" science fiction is more than a quarter of a century old.

1. The *way* stories were written. He demanded a much higher degree of sophistication in the *average* story he published than had generally been true of science fiction. This applied not only to the stylistic proficiency but also to the manner in which ideas were introduced. Indirection became a characteristic of the literary method of modern science fiction. It has been said, with some justice, that what science fiction called "good writing" merely followed the mainstream vogue of the thirties and that even today, 26 years later, "modern" science fiction reads more like the SATURDAY EVENING POST and COSMOPOLITAN of the depression era than avant garde fiction.

2. Greater emphasis on the psychological. How would the people of tomorrow's world be affected by the inevitable technological and social changes? What would their everyday behavior be like under such radically changed circumstances? What situations would provide drama in the innumerable fabricated futures to come?

3. The importance of philosophy on cultural action. Every civilization lives according to a certain firm or diffuse philosophy. Evaluation was to be given not only to the future philosophies *of man*, but to the bizarre and infinite hypothetical philosophies of alien creatures.

4. The exploration of the possibility of strange powers in various members of the human race. Most directly involved were humans who were a physical or mental mutation, but comprehensively telepathy, levitation, teleportation, telekinesis were embraced as well as the entire gamut of what has become known as Fortean phenomenon —the catalogue of inexplicable happenings which Charles Fort believed disobeyed the "laws" of science.

5. A broadening of the policies of science fiction to include not only social protest of politics, business, war and Western civilization's mores (to which it had always been receptive) but protest and criticism of *religion*, which had been, like sex, carefully side-stepped. Modern science fiction later extended its scope to cover sex, but not through

Campbell, who did not care to run stories on that subject in the pages of his magazine.

This did not rule out the exploration of future technology, particularly atomic power, but such themes proved to be in the distinct minority. Science fiction became less interested in illuminating the road of science than in circling like a trapped moth around the hypnotic lure of literary pretension.

All these elements had been present in science fiction previously, but their appearance was haphazard. Campbell knew what goals he had in mind and the circumstances made it possible for him to get authors to conform to his desires.

Though there were many markets opening up for science fiction writers in 1939, as new titles multiplied, the country was still very much in a state of financial depression and an editor could command many willing typewriters. ASTOUNDING SCIENCE-FICTION was the leading magazine in sales and prestige when Campbell took over. It consistently paid top rates (which was one cent a word and slightly up). While other science fiction magazines also listed one cent a word as their rate in WRITER's DIGEST, it often was less for the longer lengths, particularly novels, and payment was not always on acceptance.

Campbell tirelessly fed writers ideas, not only for plots, but for unique approaches to a theme. He demanded and got elaborate rewrites. He also represented the largest monthly market for wordage, purchasing between ASTOUNDING SCIENCE-FICTION and a fantasy-oriented companion magazine, UNKNOWN, nearly 200,000 words. Pleasing Campbell was good business.

Campbell also had the good fortune to assume editorship at the very onset of a new wave of popularity for science fiction. The profitable sales of a magazine titled MARVEL SCIENCE STORIES, whose first issue, dated August, 1938, (it appeared on the newsstands May 9, 1938) caused the pulp companies, who by and large were convinced that science fiction was not properly commercial, to take special notice. When AMAZING STORIES, the field's first magazine, beginning publication with its issue dated April, 1926, was sold to Ziff-Davis (June, 1938 issue), and quickly began to climb in circulation, the rush got underway.

All these factors made it possible for one man to shape the nature of the stories the science fiction writers would produce and thereby command the direction of the field. He gathered round him in only two years, a cadre of crack talent that a quarter of a century later would still be dominating the world of science fiction.

His loudest gun, however, was still the old-time favorite Edward E. Smith, Ph. D., who had created a sensation with *The Skylark of Space* in 1928, a story which moved science fiction out of the confines of the solar system, and whose *Grey Lensman* for ASTOUNDING SCIENCE-FICTION in 1939 presented a thrilling picture of an entire galaxy patrolled by a very special type of police.

The adaptable Jack Williamson, who had initially gained popularity imitating A. Merritt, proved he also belonged in the forefront of changing science fiction, but other than these veterans, the early phase of the science fiction revolution was predominantly the work of new recruits.

Campbell had been hired as editor of ASTOUNDING STORIES by F. Orlin Tremaine in 1937. Tremaine had taken control of the virtually defunct title in late 1933 and, in a brilliant drive, had made it the indisputable field leader by 1935. However, through 1936 and 1937 the average quality of the material not only declined, but frequently verged on dullness, though three authors discovered in 1937 and 1938—Eric Frank Russell, L. Sprague de Camp and Lester del Rey—were to play an important part in the revival of science fiction. In 1939 Campbell discovered A. E. van Vogt, Robert A. Heinlein and Theodore Sturgeon, and took Isaac Asimov under his wing. These were to prove the real sluggers in his literary batting lineup.

While an occasional work by these men appeared elsewhere, Campbell generally got first look at everything and to all practical purposes had exclusive use of their talents. This scarcely disturbed the competition who had the bulk of previous favorites to draw upon. If Campbell wanted to hold his fledglings to his bosom that was his affair. Other directions in science fiction were proving at least as profitable for them without all the effort Campbell was expending.

Leading contemporary science fiction magazines included AMAZING STORIES, now under the editorship of Raymond A. Palmer, hewing to a policy of elementary science fiction, simply told, with virtually no attempt at sophistication or a high order of originality. There was a market for such a magazine and it pushed ahead of ASTOUNDING SCIENCE-FICTION in circulation.

When taunted by this fact, as a counter to the wisdom of his editorial stance, Campbell, instead of becoming disturbed, asserted that he was highly pleased. His claim was that ASTOUNDING SCIENCE-FICTION was tailored for a more mature audience. It no longer published the elementary type of science fiction that could attract the youngsters. It was therefore essential that such magazines as AMAZING STORIES existed and prospered, he contended, because they would graduate readers to ASTOUNDING SCIENCE-FICTION. Just as medical specialists needed general practitioners to refer patients to them, ASTOUNDING SCIENCE-FICTION needed publications featuring elementary stories with wide appeal to recruit new readership.

If Campbell's theory was correct, the science fiction field was ideally set up for him, because while AMAZING printed the most basic science fiction, Standard Publications, with THRLLING WONDER STORIES, STARTLING STORIES and CAPTAIN FUTURE, provided a stepladder effect by appealing to the teenagers. Their mainstays were the big names of the thirties: Eando Binder, Manly Wade Wellman, John Russell Fearn, Frank Belknap Long, Jack Williamson and Edmond Hamilton. STARTLING STORIES ran a complete novel each

issue as well as a hall-of-fame reprint, and on an action
level was an excellent value for fifteen cents. CAPTAIN
FUTURE was a character magazine, doing for science fiction
what THE SHADOW did for the detective story, and was
pegged for average ages of 14 and below.

There was also a sense of nostalgia and a collecting
instinct among science fiction readers that had not been
generally catered to until Munsey issued a magazine of
reprints titled FAMOUS FANTASTIC MYSTERIES, devoted at
first to famous fantasies from the old ARGOSY, ALL-STORY
and CAVALIER. Big name authors of an era preceding the
first science fiction magazine in 1926 paraded across the
contents pages of its issues: A. Merritt, George Allan
England, Austin Hall, Charles B. Stilson, Victor Rousseau,
Homer Eon Flint and Ray Cummings. Their style and
their plots were in the Edgar Rice Burroughs tradition of
the scientific romance. They represented pure escape, with
adventures on other worlds, in lost valleys and unknown
dimensions with rich and colorful thrills and a strange but
lovely princess frequently the reward of heroic exertions.
This magazine also found a solid audience.

As titles proliferated within the science fiction field,
specialization became further evident. One of the most
interesting such magazines was PLANET STORIES, a quarterly
experiment of the Fiction House pulp chain, made up
entirely of *interplanetary* stories. The quality was very
uneven, but the magazine began to take a direction completely different than the others. It wanted action, but it
also wanted the romance and wonder of the spaceways.
It began to develop a type of science that had the feel of
the old ARGOSY-ALL-STORY scientific romances featured by
FAMOUS FANTASTIC MYSTERIES, but was written in a faster
style and with more scientific window dressing. Its editor,
Malcolm Reiss, also proved receptive to the off-trail science
fiction and frequently printed stories that were not only
unique, but of exceptional literary quality.

The only new magazines that to any degree followed

Campbell's policy were two edited by Frederik Pohl for Popular Publications titled ASTONISHING STORIES and SUPER SCIENCE STORIES. ASTONISHING STORIES had the distinction of being the first science fiction magazine to sell for as little as ten cents. SUPER SCIENCE STORIES published short novels complete, and competed with STARTLING STORIES. The only problem here was that Pohl could pay only a half-cent a word. He got the other magazines' rejects, and of these he found Campbell's authors most acceptable. Practically from the first issues, Isaac Asimov, Robert A. Heinlein, L. Sprague de Camp, Clifford D. Simak, as well as lesser lights from Campbell's coterie, appeared in his publication.

When the editorship of Pohl's publications was assumed by Alden H. Norton in the summer of 1941 the policy was continued with the addition of scientific fantasies similar to those found in PLANET STORIES. It was openmindedness to stories of this type that led Norton to discover Ray Bradbury, buying his first story *Pendulum* written in collaboration with Henry Hasse for the Nov., 1941 SUPER SCIENCE STORIES. In common with PLANET STORIES and the Standard Magazines group, he shared the swashbuckling literary talents of Leigh Brackett and the Merritt-like fantastes of Henry Kuttner.

Many other titles came and went, but the foregoing comprised the most influential and represented the types of science fiction most popular at the time the United States entered World War II. The effect of the draft and special industrial assignments of the specially qualified affected Campbell severely. His mainstays were predominantly of draft age, and certain of them such as Heinlein, de Camp, Asimov, had occupational specialties which war industry needed.

The other magazines had a far higher percentage of older and draft-exempt authors, who continued to write, and all, throughout the war years, had publishing frequency and wordage requirements far less demanding than ASTOUNDING SCIENCE-FICTION. One new outstanding author, Fritz Leiber, was added to the roster by Campbell during the war years and Clifford D. Simak came into his own during this period, contributing the stories that made up his justifiably famous book, *City*. Murray Leinster, a veritable patriarch among writers, also helped fill the war gap nobly. Henry Kuttner, under the pen name of Lewis Padgett, was recruited to write for Campbell a series of remarkable stories in the vein of John Collier, while his wife, C. L. Moore, cloaked in the alias of Lawrence O'Donnell, was hailed as an extraordinary discovery by the gullible readership. Jack Williamson for a brief time played the role of the promising young writer, Will Stewart, writing heavy-science stories about anti-matter until the lure of adventure found him enlisting in the armed services and getting more than he bargained for in the Pacific air war.

Just as the Jews for centuries sustained themselves with the slogan "Tomorrow in Israel," John W. Campbell sustained his readers with a blinding vision of what they might expect when "the boys come marching home."

The appearance of the first post-war major science fiction anthology, *The Best of Science Fiction*, edited by Groff Conklin in 1946 proved a triumph for John W. Campbell. The book became a best seller in the true meaning of the term and the bulk of the wordage in the volume was modern science fiction from Campbell's magazine. In a preface written by Campbell, the basic differences between "modern" and previous forms of science fiction were spelled out.

First, the writing method:

> In older science fiction—H. G. Wells and nearly all stories written before 1935—the author took time out to bring the reader up to date as to what had happened before his story opened. The best modern writers of science fiction have worked out some truly remarkable techniques for presenting a great deal of background and associated material without intruding into the flow

of the story. That is no small feat, when a complete new world must be established at the same time a story is being presented.

Secondly, the content:

But the modern science-fiction writer doesn't merely say, "In about ten years we will have atomic weapons." He goes further; his primary interest is in what these weapons will do to political, economic and cultural structures of human society.

A few months after the issuance of *The Best of Science Fiction*, an even more impressive monument to Campbell's brand of science fiction collected as *Adventure in Time and Space* and sub-titled "An Anthology of Modern Science-Fiction Stories," edited by Raymond J. Healy and J. Francis McComas, rocketed to equally impressive sales figures. Of the 35 stories in the book, all but three were from Campbell's magazines, and of the 32 from his magazine, only four had not been purchased under his editorship and one of these was his own novelette *Forgetfulness!*

Such science fiction magazine publishers who were not impressed by the sales reports were properly impressed by the reviews. Both anthologies received widespread praise in the most respected newspapers and magazines. Previously, serious literary consideration of the products of the pulp science fiction magazines had been disappointingly infrequent. This current attention was certainly heady wine. Perhaps there was more to the Campbell brand of science fiction than it had been given credit for, it was conjectured. All those sales and glory, too!

Slowly the masters of modern science fiction returned from the wars, but not necessarily into Campbell's open embrace. Not too long after the appearance of the two major science fiction anthologies, L. Sprague de Camp, Theodore Sturgeon and Robert A. Heinlein showed up in THRILLING WONDER STORIES. Soon A. E. van Vogt was in the enemy camp, as were a number of other writers who generally had been considered Campbell exclusives such as L. Ron Hubbard, Cleve Cartmill, George O. Smith and Raymond F. Jones.

More science-fiction anthologies appeared, with heavy representations by "modern" science fiction authors from ASTOUNDING SCIENCE-FICTION. Specialty book companies were formed, issuing famous novels and short stories of science fiction in hard cover. A disproportionate percentage of these also came from Campbell's magazines, and when the books were reviewed, those with the "modern" stories always seemed to get preferential treatment.

When the post-war paper shortage began to ease towards the end of 1948, the long-delayed spate of new science fiction magazines arrived. The first was the revival of SUPER SCIENCE STORIES under the editorship of Alden H. Norton, dated January, 1949. It was obvious that the previous policy of using stories both of Campbell's modern science fiction, and action adventure fantasy would be continued.

The editor of another new periodical, THE MAGAZINE OF FANTASY AND SCIENCE FICTION (Fall, 1949) was Anthony Boucher, well-known detective story writer, critic and a former contributor to ASTOUNDING SCIENCE-FICTION. He was completely sold on Campbell's bill-of-fare, most particularly the emphasis on skillful writing. All of Campbell's top-notchers who could cleverly turn a phrase eventually turned up in the pages of his magazine.

The most costly raid came with the appearance of GALAXY SCIENCE FICTION (October, 1950) edited by H. L. Gold, who had previously written and edited science fiction. Up until now, Campbell had gotten first look at a substantial part of the stories by his favorites that appeared elsewhere. However with his rates matched by THRILLING WONDER STORIES and THE MAGAZINE OF FANTASY AND SCIENCE FICTION and *topped* by GALAXY SCIENCE FICTION, that situation ended. In its introductory issue GALAXY SCIENCE FICTION carried Campbell's heavy guns, Clifford D.

Simak, Theodore Sturgeon, Fritz Leiber and Isaac Asimov.

Campbell raised his rates and creatively continued to develop new talent, but whereas before he could exercise severe discipline in building them into top-notchers by reason of his commanding economic and prestige position in the field, now he found that after a single good story they would often begin showing up elsewhere. GALAXY SCIENCE FICTION's policy was but an extension of Campbell's, but with greatest emphasis on the psychological aspects of science fiction, as introduced by ASTOUNDING SCIENCE-FICTION in such masterpieces as Clifford D. Simak's *Huddling Place*.

Outside of Campbell's sphere of influence, the action school of science fiction as exemplified by PLANET STORIES and THRILLING WONDER STORIES had published the emotion-packed space parables of the stylistic virtuoso Ray Bradbury. Scores of his best stories were bought and published at but a penny a word, and new anthologies rarely appeared without a Bradbury story, solidifying transient pulp popularity into recognition and prestige. This laid the foundation for his successful career. Equally as honored, Arthur C. Clarke was one of the upcoming young British literary lions, influenced by Campbell's *writing* and first published in ASTOUNDING SCIENCE FICTION in this country, yet, like many other likely prospects, quickly lured away to contribute his best work to the competition.

By 1952 the science fiction tide was cresting. At one time 32 different titles were on the stands simultaneously. The earlier boom in 1939 had healthily stabilized with science fiction magazines aimed at different strata of readership. This boom took the cue of "follow the leader." THRILLING WONDER STORIES and STARTLING STORIES, once the bastions of teen-age action, under the successive administrations of editors Sam Merwin and Sam Mines, in content had become indistinguishable from ASTOUNDING SCIENCE-FICTION. GALAXY SCIENCE FICTION and THE MAGAZINE OF FANTASY AND SCIENCE FICTION. Not only had the stories been lifted to a new height of sophistication, but in August, 1952, like a bombshell they exploded a novel, *The Lovers*, by Philip José Farmer which proved a milestone in the history of science fiction, opening up the various manifestations of sex to writers of modern science fiction, breaking a taboo which had been rigidly inflexible before.

It was not that the incorporation of sex into science fiction proved unhealthy—the field would be much poorer without the contributions of Farmer—it was the *completeness* of the usurpation of the strongholds of scientific wonder, action, and romance by stories of a philosophical, psychiatric or sexual bent that posed a danger.

A number of forces contributed to the switch by most of the remaining holdouts to the publication of "modern" science fiction to the virtual exclusion of any other type. Predominant was the weight of new titles, far too burdensome to be supported by the existing readership. As the complete pie of audience was sliced ever thinner by the accumulation of new titles, publishers attributed their circulation problems to *editorial policy*. On every hand (even in their own pages) reviewers praised the polished works of the modern masters and ridiculed any other form. To publish and read "modern" science fiction had also become a status symbol, a badge of prestige and maturity. Was that not the logical direction to take?

AMAZING STORIES, which had been the circulation leader the entire decade between 1940 and 1950, abandoned its policy of elementary science fiction and with the April-May, 1953 number converted from pulp to digest size with slick stories by Robert A. Heinlein, Theodore Sturgeon, Murray Leinster and Ray Bradbury.

FAMOUS FANTASTIC MYSTERIES, symbolic of those magazines publishing reprints of escapism for 14 years, folded with its June, 1953 number. PLANET STORIES did not abandon its policy but found a declining pool of usable material at its low rates. It perished in 1955 as did THRILLING WONDER STORIES and STARTLING STORIES. At the onset of 1956, "modern" science fiction was all there was. All other forms had vanished. For better or for worse, science fiction stories with the emphasis on the turn of phrase, with the plot twists pivoting on various aspects of psychology, philosophy, psychiatry, religion, sociology and sex dominated the field.

One man in particular bitterly deplored the changeover —John W. Campbell. It had never been his intent to supersede the other forms of science fiction. He had set out to add a new, more mature dimension to the existing body of the literature. The field needed the elementary types. Now there were many universities but no grammar schools.

Actually John W. Campbell had already taken a divergent tack. He had always been interested in the exploration of hidden powers in the human mind. This first took the form of what he called mutants and led to the writing of such stories as *Slan* by A. E. van Vogt, of a human species with flesh-and-blood antennae called tendrils, that can read other minds. This approach was followed by Henry Kuttner under the pen name of Lewis Padgett in a series about the "baldies," a mind-reading group attempting to integrate into the populace.

The theories of Charles Fort regarding strange events that seemed to defy the tenets of scientific theory, also fascinated him, and it was his interest in this phase that led to publication of Eric Frank Russell's novel *Sinister Barrier*, in which it is discovered that the human race is nothing more than the kept cattle of a superior culture.

Stories based on intellectually superior mutants and various ramifications of Charles Fort's presentation were to become frequent in Astounding Science-Fiction. When new competitors appropriated most of the tenets he had promoted in "modern" science fiction, John Campbell moved his authors further in the Fortean direction. The kick-off piece was an article titled *Dianetics: The Evolution of a Science* by L. Ron Hubbard (Astounding Science-Fiction, May, 1950). Hubbard was a prolific pulp writer, who made a good record on naval duty during World War II and claimed to have been the actual inspiration for the title character of the play *Mr. Roberts.* He had done some remarkable writing of science fiction for Campbell, his novel *Final Blackout* without question ranking as one of the finest future war stories ever written.

Dianetics proposed to be a system of self-help therapy that could cure all forms of insanity where there had been no brain damage; a technique for curing non-germ diseases such as ulcers, arthritis and asthma; a method of giving a man a perfect, error-free memory, among other things. A book titled *Dianetics* proved a best seller and launched Hubbard on a career that eventually found him living in a great English mansion, unabashedly wealthy.

Campbell, with considerable vigor, attempted to get stories based on Dianetics (Hubbard wrote a fantasy involving Dianetics, *Masters of Sleep,* for FANTASTIC ADVENTURES, October, 1950). He also pushed forward a search for evidence of the existence of extra-sensory motivated equipment (which he termed psionic machines) and new principles of dynamics which led him to champion a prototype of an "anti-gravity" device called the Dean Drive.

Some very clever and entertaining stories did result from this divergence, though they were actually sheer fantasies based on hypothetical, imaginary sciences. The better rejects trickled down to the lower paying markets and by this method, "psi" stories become an integral part of what is today called "modern" science fiction.

"Modern" science fiction has been criticized for many things. The most damning has been the charge that its casual narration, its stress on indirection and its interweaving of background as part of the story flow has deleted a great deal of what has been euphemized as "sense of wonder" from its context. Another major criticism has been that with the emphasis on psychology, philosophy, psychiatry, sociology and psi, there has been a lag in new concepts, and scientific advances have been rapidly turning many tried and true gambits into history. A consequence of this

is that backgrounds in "modern" science fiction stories tend
to be props, standardized so as to make it easier to make
a point in a plot in which the science and technology are
merely incidental.

Even if all the foregoing are acknowledged, it still must
be admitted that "modern" science fiction has recorded unprecedented achievement. There is not a major reference
work on English literature produced in the past 10 years
without material on science fiction, and it is rare that such
a volume does not assign at least minor status to certain
science fiction writers.

A quarter of a century ago, any science fiction writers
developed by the magazines who could boast even a single
hard-cover book to his credit, was regarded by his fellows
with awe. Today, one would be sorely pressed to find a
published magazine story by a ranking science fiction writer
that had not gone into book form or at least been included
in an anthology.

Every technologically advanced non-Communist nation
in the world today regularly publishes science fiction, and
the majority of it is reprints of America's "modern" science
fiction. Almost anywhere in the world it is possible to secure
a selection of outstanding American authors. Behind the
Iron Curtain, American science fiction is translated and reprinted. Science fiction is as much a cultural export of this
nation as jazz and has resulted in the formation of con-
vention-sponsoring clubs even as far away as Japan.

The twenty-one authors anthologized in this volume are
beyond doubt the major shapers of "modern" science fiction.
These are the writers who gave it substance, contributed
something distinctive and have written a disproportionate
share of the landmarks in the format. Two authors, who
had a monumental influence on the development of "modern" science fiction are not included here, because they
belong to an earlier era. They are Olaf Stapledon and Stan-
ley G. Weinbaum. From Stapledon was derived the emphasis on philosophical concepts as a plot basis for science

fiction. From Weinbaum the methods of combining narrative, dialogue and background in a non-interrupted flow.

Edward E. Smith is presented first, because in *Galactic Patrol* and *The Grey Lensman,* he offered the formula of science fiction on a galactic scale; John W. Campbell is second, because Smith was his inspirator and because he wrote the prototypes of what today has become "modern" science fiction. The Campbell story is the only one in this collection published before 1938.

The next four, Murray Leinster, Edmond Hamilton, Jack Williamson and John Wyndham, had made reputations in the field long before the popularity of modern science fiction and were the old guard that most successfully converted to and contributed to the development of the new form. One author who initially appeared in 1930, Clifford D. Simak, is not presented in this group because his was only a secondary figure until the forties.

Eric Frank Russell, L. Sprague de Camp and Lester del Rey are a trio of transitional discoveries made while ASTOUNDING STORIES was becoming ASTOUNDING SCIENCE-FICTION. Russell was to be the prime popularizer of Fortean themes; de Camp, an extremely able satirist in the Mark Twain tradition; and del Rey, a trail blazer in the incorporation of both sentiment and realism into science fiction.

The five that follow, Robert A. Heinlein, A. E. van Vogt, Isaac Asimov, Theodore Sturgeon, Clifford D. Simak and Fritz Leiber, most purely symbolize what is referred to as "modern" science fiction. Heinlein is the supreme master and primary stylistic influence of the art of weaving the background into the progression of the story, as well as the popularizer of many outstanding gambits including the thousand-year space ship; A. E. van Vogt, in addition to his classic on mental mutations, incorporated semantics as successful plot material; Isaac Asimov not only gave the field the "Three Laws of Robotics" which, by limiting the action of robots, offered authors unprecedented story opportunities, but wrote the most successful of all detective stories in a science fiction context; Theodore Sturgeon, an inspired stylist, exploited the theory of gestalt relationships within science fiction; Clifford D. Simak fathered the psychiatric story in science fiction, by writing *Huddling Place*, which appears in this collection; and Fritz Leiber popularized the device of explaining the supernatural scientifically.

C. L. Moore, Henry Kuttner and Robert Bloch have one fact in common. They were all discovered by WEIRD TALES magazine, and gained their first reputations in tales of science fantasy, the supernatural and the horrifying. C. L. Moore is probably the most outstanding of modern women writers of science fiction. Her tales of Northwest Smith, space rover, won her first reputation and she gained another writing as Lawrence O'Donnell, for Campbell; Henry Kuttner excelled at the John Collier type of short story under the name of Lewis Padgett, but he was one of the best of the parallel school that combined the scientific romance with action. The story in this collection is from that area of his work, to provide an example of what was being written and read at the same time as "modern" science fiction gained popularity. This story came from SUPER SCIENCE STORIES and was similar to much of the material featured in PLANET STORIES and THRILLING WONDER STORIES. The C. L. Moore story has been taken from FAMOUS FANTASTIC MYSTERIES to provide a sample of the romantic scientific fantasies with which they held in thrall many loyal readers for 14 years, to contrast with other stories in this collection. Robert Bloch has become one of the cinema masters of horror and terror and the tremendous impact of those elements in *The Strange Flight of Richard Clayton*, a space exploration story, shows where he developed his facility as a master of shock.

Finally, the most recently acclaimed masters of "modern" science fiction—Ray Bradbury, Arthur C. Clarke and Philip José Farmer—have broken with the traditionalists of their school and scored in uniquely individualistic fashions. Bradbury was equally adept at horror or science fiction in a high-powered literary sense. We offer his short story, *Wake for the Living*, which combines both elements. Clarke has most effectively combined valid scientific insight with poignant poetry and *Before Eden* ranks as one of his finest. Philip José Farmer, in his legitimate use of Freud and sex, turns in a stunning work of symbolism and entertainment in *Mother*.

This anthology is in every sense a companion to the editor's *Seekers of Tomorrow*, which is a webwork history of modern science fiction, presented in the form of in-depth studies of all the authors featured in this book, plus certain others who made outstanding contributions. This book is intended to give superior examples of the actual fiction of the twenty-one most influential practitioners of modern science fiction.

Together with *Seekers of Tomorrow*, this collection forms a basic two-volume reference of a literary phenomenon of our time.

Sam Moskowitz

Newark, New Jersey

THE

VORTEX BLASTERS

by

EDWARD E. SMITH, Ph.D.

Safety devices that do not protect.
The "unsinkable" ships that, before the days of Bergenholm and of atomic and cosmic energy, sank into the waters of the earth.

More particularly, safety devices which, while protecting against one agent of destruction, attract magnet-like another and worse. Such as the armored cable within the walls of a wooden house. It protects the electrical conductors within against accidental external shorts; but, inadequately grounded as it must of necessity be, it may attract and upon occasion has attracted the stupendous force of lightning. Then, fused, volatized, flaming incandescent throughout the length, breadth, and height of a dwelling, that dwelling's existence thereafter is to be measured in minutes.

Specifically, four lightning rods. The lightning rods protecting the chromium, glass, and plastic home of Neal Cloud. Those rods were adequately grounded, grounded with copper-silver cables the bigness of a strong man's arm; for Neal Cloud, atomic physicist, knew his lightning and he was taking no chances whatever with the safety of his lovely wife and their three wonderful kids.

He did not know, he did not even suspect, that under certain conditions of atmospheric potential and of ground-magnetic stress his perfectly designed lightning-rod system would become a super-powerful magnet for flying vortices of atomic disintegration.

And now Neal Cloud, atomic physicist, sat at his desk in a strained, dull apathy. His face was a yellowish-gray white, his tendoned hands gripped rigidly the arms of his chair. His eyes, hard and lifeless, stared unseeingly past the small, three-dimensional block portrait of all that had made life worth living.

For his guardian against lightning had been a vortex-magnet at the moment when a luckless wight had attempted to abate the nuisance of a "loose" atomic vortex. That wight died, of course—they almost always do—and the vortex, instead of being destroyed, was simply broken up into an indefinite number of widely-scattered new vortices. And one of these bits of furious, uncontrolled energy, resembling more nearly a handful of material rived from a sun than anything else with which ordinary man is familiar, darted toward and crashed downward to earth through Neal Cloud's new house.

That home did not burn; it simply exploded. Nothing of it, in it, or around it stood a chance, for in a fractional second of time the place where it had been was a crater of seething, boiling lava—a crater which filled the atmosphere to a height of miles with poisonous vapors; which flooded all circumambient space with lethal radiations.

Cosmically, the whole thing was infinitesimal. Ever since man learned how to liberate intra-atomic energy, the vortices of disintegration had been breaking out of control. Such accidents had been happening, were happening, and would continue indefinitely to happen. More than one world, perhaps, had been or would be consumed to the last gram by such loose atomic vortices. What of that? Of what real importance are a few grains of sand to an ocean beach five thousand miles long, a hundred miles wide, and ten miles deep?

And even to that individual grain of sand called "Earth" —or, in modern parlance, "Sol Three," or "Tellus of Sol," or simply "Tellus"—the affair was of negligible importance. One man had died; but, in dying, he had added one more page to the thick bulk of negative results already on file. That Mrs. Cloud and her children had perished was merely unfortunate. The vortex itself was not yet a real threat to Tellus. It was a "new" one, and thus it would be a long time before it would become other than a local menace. And well before that could happen—before even the oldest of Tellus' loose vortices had eaten away much of her mass or poisoned much of her atmosphere, her scientists would have solved the problem. It was unthinkable that Tellus, the point of origin, and the very center of Galactic Civilization, should cease to exist.

But to Neal Cloud the accident was the ultimate catastrophe. His personal universe had crashed in ruins; what was left was not worth picking up. He and Jo had been married for almost twenty years and the bonds between them had grown stronger, deeper, truer with every passing day. And the kids. . . . . . . .It *couldn't* have happened . . . . . fate COULDN'T do this to him . . . . but it had . . . . . it could. Gone . . . . *gone* . . . GONE.

And to Neal Cloud, atomic physicist, sitting there at his desk in torn, despairing abstraction, with black maggots of thought gnawing holes in his brain, the catastrophe was doubly galling because of its cruel irony. For he was second from the top in the Atomic Research Laboratory; his life's work had been a search for a means of extinguishment of exactly such loose vortices as had destroyed his all.

His eyes focused vaguely upon the portrait. Clear, honest

gray eyes . . . lines of character and humor . . . sweetly curved lips, ready to smile or to kiss. . . . .

He wrenched his eyes away and scribbled briefly upon a sheet of paper. Then, getting up stiffly, he took the portrait and moved woodenly across the room to a furnace. As though enshrining it he placed the plastic block upon a refractory between the electrodes and threw a switch. After the flaming arc had done its work he turned and handed the paper to a tall man, dressed in plain gray leather, who had been watching him with quiet, understanding eyes. Significant enough to the initiated of the importance of this laboratory is the fact that it was headed by an Unattached Lensman.

"As of now, Phil, if it's QX with you."

The Gray Lensman took the document, glanced at it, and slowly, meticulously, tore it into sixteen equal pieces.

"Uh, uh, Storm," he denied, gently. "Not a resignation. Leave of absence, yes—indefinite—but not a resignation."

"Why?" It was scarcely a question; Cloud's voice was level, uninflected. "I won't be worth the paper I'd waste."

"Now, no," the Lensman conceded, "but the future's another matter. I haven't said anything so far, because to anyone who knew you and Jo as I knew you it was abundantly clear that nothing could be said." Two hands gripped and held. "For the future, though, four words were uttered long ago, that have never been improved upon. 'This, too, shall pass.' "

"You think so?"

"I don't think so, Storm—I know so. I've been around a long time. You are too good a man, and the world has too much use for you, for you to go down permanently out of control. You've got a place in the world, and you'll be back—" A thought struck the Lensman, and he went on in an altered tone. "You wouldn't—but of course you wouldn't—you couldn't."

"I don't think so. No I won't—that never was any kind of a solution to any problem."

Nor was it. Until that moment, suicide had not entered Cloud's mind, and he rejected it instantly. His kind of man did not take the easy way out.

After a brief farewell Cloud made his way to an elevator and was whisked down to the garage. Into his big blue DeKhotinsky Sixteen Special and away.

Through traffic so heavy that front-, rear-, and side-bumpers almost touched he drove with his wonted cool skill; even though, consciously, he did not know that the other cars were there. He slowed, turned, stopped, "gave her the oof," all in correct response to flashing signals in all shapes and colors—purely automatically. Consciously, he did not know where he was going, nor care. If he thought at all, his numbed brain was simply trying to run away from its own bitter imaging—which, if he had thought at all, he would have known to be a hopeless task. But he did not think; he simply acted, dumbly, miserably. His eyes saw, optically; his body reacted, mechanically; his thinking brain was completely in abeyance.

Into a one-way skyway he rocketed, along it over the suburbs and into the transcontinental super-highway. Edging inward, lane after lane, he reached the "unlimited" way—unlimited, that is, except for being limited to cars of not less than seven hundred horsepower; in perfect mechanical condition, driven by registered, tested drivers at speeds not less than one hundred and twenty-five miles an hour—flashed his registry number at the control station, and shoved his right foot down to the floor.

Now everyone knows that an ordinary DeKhotinsky Sporter will do a hundred and forty honestly-measured miles in one honestly measured hour; but very few ordinary drivers have ever found out how fast one of those brutal big souped-up Sixteens can wheel. They simply haven't got what it takes to open one up.

"Storm" Cloud found out that day. He held that two-and-a-half-ton Juggernaut on the road, wide open, for two solid hours. But it didn't help. Drive as he would, he could not outrun that which rode with him. Beside him and within him and behind him. For Jo was there. Jo and the kids, but mostly Jo. It was Jo's car as much as it was his. "Babe, the big blue ox," was Jo's pet name for it; because, like Paul Bunyan's fabulous beast, it was pretty nearly six feet between the eyes. Everything they had ever had was that way. She was in the seat beside him. Every dear, every sweet, every luscious, lovely memory of her was there. . . . and behind him, just out of eye-corner visibility, were the three kids. And a whole lifetime of this loomed ahead—a vista of emptiness more vacuous far than the emptiest reaches of intergalactic space. Damnation! He couldn't stand much more of—

High over the roadway, far ahead, a brilliant octagon flared red. That meant "STOP!" in any language. Cloud eased up his accelerator, eased down his mighty brakes. He pulled up at the control station and a trimly-uniformed officer made a gesture.

"Sorry, sir," the policeman said, "but you'll have to detour here. There's a loose atomic vortex beside the road up ahead—

"Oh! It's Dr. Cloud!" Recognition flashed into the guard's eyes. "I didn't recognize you at first. It'll be two or three miles before you'll have to put on your armor; you'll know when better than anyone can tell you. They didn't tell us they were going to send for *you*. It's just a little new one, and the dope we got was that they were going to shove it off into the canyon with pressure."

"They didn't send for me." Cloud tried to smile. "I'm just driving around—haven't my armor along, even. So I guess I might as well go back."

He turned the Special around. A loose vortex—new. There might be a hundred of them, scattered over a radius of two hundred miles. Sisters of the one that had murdered his family—the hellish spawn of that accursed Number

Eleven vortex that that damnably incompetent bungling ass had tried to blow up. . . . Into his mind there leaped a picture, wiresharp, of Number Eleven as he had last seen it, and simultaneously an idea hit him like a blow from a fist.

He thought. *Really* thought, now; cogently, intensely, clearly. If he could do it . . . . could actually blow out the atomic flame of an atomic vortex . . . . not exactly revenge, but . . . . By Klono's brazen bowels, it would work—it'd *have* to work—he'd *make* it work! And grimly, quietly, but alive in every fiber now, he drove back toward the city practically as fast as he had come away.

If the Lensman was surprised at Cloud's sudden reappearance in the laboratory he did not show it. Nor did he offer any comment as his erstwhile first assistant went to various lockers and cupboards, assembling meters, coils, tubes, armor, and other paraphernalia and apparatus.

"Guess that's all I'll need, Chief," Cloud remarked, finally. "Here's a blank check. If some of this stuff shouldn't happen to be in usable condition when I get done with it, fill it out to suit, will you?"

"No," and the Lensman tore up the check just as he had torn up the resignation. "If you want the stuff for legitimate purposes, you're on Patrol business and it is the Patrol's risk. If, on the other hand, you think that you're going to try to snuff a vortex, the stuff stays here. That's final, Storm."

"You're right—and wrong, Phil," Cloud stated, not at all sheepishly. "I'm going to blow out Number One vortex with duodec, yes—but I'm *really* going to blow it out, not merely make a stab at it as an excuse for suicide, as you think."

"How?" the big Lensman's query was skepticism incarnate. "It can't be done, except by an almost impossibly fortuitous accident. You yourself have been the most bitterly opposed of us all to these suicidal attempts."

"I know it—I didn't have the solution myself until a few hours ago—it hit me all at once. Funny I never thought of it before; it's been right in sight all the time."

"That's the way with most problems," the Chief admitted. "Plain enough after you see the key equation. Well, I'm perfectly willing to be convinced, but I warn you that I'll take a lot of convincing—and someone else will do the work, not you."

"When I get done you'll see why I'll pretty nearly have to do it myself. But to convince you, exactly what is the knot?"

"Variability," snapped the older man. "To be effective, the charge of explosive at the moment of impact must match, within very close limits, the activity of the vortex itself. Too small a charge scatters it around in vortices which, while much smaller than the original, are still large enough to be self-sustaining. Too large a charge simply rekindles the original vortex—still larger—in its original crater. And the activity that must be matched varies so tremendously, in magnitude, maxima, and minima, and the cycle is so erratic—ranging from seconds to hours without discoverable rhyme or reason—that all attempts to do so at any predetermined instant have failed completely. Why, even Kinnison and Cardynge and the Conference of Scientists couldn't solve it, any more than they could work out a tractor beam that could be used as a tow-line on one."

"Not exactly," Cloud demurred. "They found that it could be forecast, for a few seconds at least—length of time directly proportional to the length of the cycle in question —by an extension of the calculus of warped surfaces."

"Humph!" the Lensman snorted. "So what? What good is a ten-second forecast when it takes a calculating machine an hour to solve the equations. . . . Oh!" He broke off, staring.

"Oh," he repeated, slowly, "I forgot that you're a lightning calculator—a mathematical prodigy from the day you were born—who never has to use a calculating machine even to compute an orbit. . . . But there are other things."

"I'll say there are; plenty of them. I'd thought of the calculator angle before, of course, but there was a worse thing than variability to contend with. . . ."

"What?" the Lensman demanded.

"Fear," Cloud replied, crisply. "At the thought of a hand-to-hand battle with a vortex my brain froze solid. Fear—the sheer, stark, natural human fear of death, that robs a man of the fine edge of control and brings on the very death that he is trying so hard to avoid. That's what had me stopped."

"Right . . . . you may be right," the Lensman pondered, his fingers drumming quietly upon his desk. "And you are not afraid of death—now—even subconsciously. But tell me, Storm, please, that you won't invite it."

"I will not invite it, sir, now that I've got a job to do. But that's as far as I'll go in promising. I won't make any superhuman effort to avoid it. I'll take all due precautions, for the sake of the job, but if it gets me, what the hell? The quicker it does, the better—the sooner I'll be with Jo."

"You believe that?"

"Implicitly."

"The vortices are as good as gone, then. They haven't got any more chance than Boskone has of licking the Patrol."

"I'm afraid so," almost glumly. "The only way for it to get me is for me to make a mistake, and I don't feel any coming on."

"But what's your angle?" the Lensman asked, interest lighting his eyes. "You can't use the customary attack; your time will be too short."

"Like this," and taking down a sheet of drafting paper, Cloud sketched rapidly. "This is the crater, here, with the vortex at the bottom, there. From the observers' instruments or from a shielded set-up of my own I get my data on mass, emission, maxima, minima, and so on. Then I have them make me three duodec bombs—one on the mark of the activity I'm figuring on shooting at, and one each five percent over and under that figure—cased in neocarballoy of exactly the computed thickness to last until it gets to the center of the vortex. Then I take off in a flying suit, armored and shielded, say about here. . . ."

"If you take off at all, you'll take off in a suit, inside a one-man flitter," the Lensman interrupted. "Too many instruments for a suit, to say nothing of bombs, and you'll need more screen than a suit can deliver. We can adapt a flitter for bomb-throwing easily enough."

"QX; that would be better, of course. In that case, I set my flitter into a projectile trajectory like this, whose objective is the center of the vortex, there. See? Ten seconds or so away, at about this point, I take my instantaneous readings, solve the equations at that particular warped surface for some certain zero time. . . ."

"But suppose that the cycle won't give you a ten-second solution?"

"Then I'll swing around and try again until a long cycle *does* show up."

"QX. It will, sometime."

"Sure. Then, having everything set for zero time, and assuming that the activity is somewhere near my postulated value. . . ."

"Assume that it isn't—it probably won't be," the Chief grunted.

"I accelerate or decelerate—"

"Solving new equations all the while?"

"Sure—don't interrupt so—until at zero time the activity, extrapolated to zero time, matches one of my bombs. I cut that bomb loose, shoot myself off in a sharp curve, and Z-W-E-E-E-T - POWIE! She's out!" With an expressive, sweeping gesture.

"You hope," the Lensman was frankly dubious. "And there you are, right in the middle of that explosion, with two duodec bombs outside your armor—or just inside your flitter."

"Oh, no. I've shot them away several seconds ago, so that they explode somewhere else, nowhere near me."

"*I* hope. But do you realize just how busy a man you are going to be during those ten or twelve seconds?"

"Fully." Cloud's face grew somber. "But I will be in full control. I won't be afraid of anything that can happen— *anything*. And," he went on, under his breath, "that's the hell of it."

"QX," the Lensman admitted finally, "you can go. There are a lot of things you haven't mentioned, but you'll probably be able to work them out as you go along. I think I'll go out and work with the boys in the lookout station while you're doing your stuff. When are you figuring on starting?"

"How long will it take to get the flitter ready?"

"A couple of days. Say we meet you there Saturday morning?"

"Saturday, the tenth, at eight o'clock. I'll be there."

And again Neal Cloud and Babe, the big blue ox, hit the road. And as he rolled, the physicist mulled over in his mind the assignment to which he had set himself.

Like fire, only worse, intra-atomic energy was a good servant, but a terrible master. Man had liberated it before he could really control it. In fact, control was not yet, and perhaps never would be, perfect. Up to a certain size and activity, yes. They, the millions upon millions of self-limiting ones, were the servants. They could be handled, fenced in, controlled; indeed, if they were not kept under an exciting bombardment and very carefully fed, they would go out. But at long intervals, for some one of a dozen reasons—science knew *so* little, fundamentally, of the true inwardness of the intra-atomic reactions—one of these small, tame, self-limiting vortices flared, nova-like, into a large, wild, self-sustaining one. It ceased being a servant then, and became a master. Such flare-ups occurred, perhaps, only once or twice in a century on Earth; the trouble was that they were so utterly, damnably *permanent*. They never went out. And no data were ever secured: for every living thing in the vicinity of a flare-up died; every instrument and every other solid thing within a radius of a hundred feet melted down into the reeking, boiling slag of its crater.

Fortunately, the rate of growth was slow—as slow, almost, as it was persistent—otherwise Civilization would scarcely have had a planet left. And unless something could be done about loose vortices before too many years, the consequences would be really serious. That was why his laboratory had been established in the first place.

Nothing much had been accomplished so far. The tractor beam that would take hold of them had never been designed. Nothing material was of any use; it melted. Pressors worked, after a fashion: it was by the use of these beams that they shoved the vortices around, off into the waste places—unless it proved cheaper to allow the places where they had come into being to remain waste places. A few, through sheer luck, had been blown into self-limiting bits by duodec. Duodecaplylatomate, the most powerful, the most frightfully detonant explosive ever invented upon all the known planets of the First Galaxy. But duodec had taken an awful toll of life. Also, since it usually scattered a vortex instead of extinguishing it, duodec had actually caused far more damage than it had cured.

No end of fantastic schemes had been proposed, of course; of varying degrees of fantasy. Some of them sounded almost practical. Some of them had been tried; some of them were still being tried. Some, such as the perennially-appearing one of building a huge hemispherical hull in the ground under and around the vortex, installing an inertialess drive, and shooting the whole neighborhood out into space, were perhaps feasible from an engineering standpoint. They were, however, potentially so capable of making things worse that they would not be tried save as last ditch measures. In short, the control of loose vortices was very much an unsolved problem.

Number One vortex, the oldest and worst upon Tellus, had been pushed out into the Badlands; and there, at eight o'clock on the tenth, Cloud started to work upon it.

The "lookout station," instead of being some such ramshackle structure as might have been deduced from the Lensman's casual terminology, was in fact a fully-equipped observatory. Its staff was not large—eight men worked in three staggered eight-hour shifts of two men each—but the instruments! To develop them had required hundreds of man-years of time and near miracles of research, not the least of the problems having been that of developing shielded conductors capable of carrying truly through five-ply screens of force the converted impulses of the very radiations against which those screens were most effective. For the observatory, and the long approach to it as well, had to be screened heavily; without such protection no life could exist there.

This problem and many others had been solved, however, and there the instruments were. Every phase and factor of the vortex's existence and activity were measured and recorded continuously, throughout every minute of every day of every year. And all of these records were summed up, integrated, into the "Sigma" curve. This curve, while only an incredibly and senselessly tortuous line to the layman's eye, was a veritable mine of information to the initiate.

Cloud glanced along the Sigma curve of the previous forty-eight hours and scowled, for one jagged peak, scarcely an hour old, actually punched through the top line of the chart.

"Bad, huh, Frank?" he grunted.

"Plenty bad, Storm, and getting worse," the observer assented. "I wouldn't wonder if Carlowitz were right, after all—if she ain't getting ready to blow her top I'm a Zabriskan fontema's maiden aunt."

"No periodicity—no equation, of course." It was a statement, not a question. The Lensman ignored as completely

as did the observer, if not as flippantly, the distinct possibility that at any moment the observatory and all that
it contained might be resolved into their component atoms.

"None whatever," came flatly from Cloud. He did not
need to spend hours at a calculating machine; at one glance
he *knew*, without knowing how he knew, that no equation
could be made to fit even the weighted-average locus of
that wildly-shifting Sigma curve. "But most of the cycles
cut this ordinate here—seven fifty-one—so I'll take that for
my value. That means nine point nine or six kilograms of
duodec basic charge, with one five percent over and one
five percent under that for alternates. Neocarballoy casing,
fifty-three millimeters on the basic, others in proportion.
On the wire?"

"It went out as you said it," the observer reported.
"They'll have 'em here in fifteen minutes."

"QX—I'll get dressed, then."

The Lensman and the observer helped him into his
cumbersome, heavily-padded armor. They checked his
instruments, making sure that the protective devices of the
suit were functioning at full efficiency. Then all three went
out to the flitter. A tiny speedster, really; a torpedo bearing
the stubby wings and the ludicrous tail-surfaces, the multifarious driving-, braking-, side-, top-, and under-jets so
characteristic of the tricky, cranky, but ultra-maneuverable
breed. But this one had something that the ordinary speedster or flitter did not carry; spaced around the needle beak
there yawned the open muzzles of a triplex bomb-thrower.

More checking. The Lensman and the armored Cloud
both knew that every one of the dozens of instruments
upon the flitter's special board was right to the hair; nevertheless each one was compared with the master-instrument
of the observatory.

The bombs arrived and were loaded in; and Cloud, with
a casually-waved salute, stepped into the tiny operating
compartment. The massive door—flitters have no airlocks,

as the whole midsection is scarcely bigger than an airlock would have to be—rammed shut upon its fiber gaskets, the heavy toggles drove home. A cushioned form closed in upon the pilot, leaving only his arms and lower legs free.

Then, making sure that his two companions had ducked for cover, Cloud shot his flitter into the air and toward the seething inferno which was Loose Atomic Vortex Number One. For it was seething, no fooling; and it was an inferno. The crater was a ragged, jagged hole a full mile from lip to lip and perhaps a quarter of that in depth. It was not, however, a perfect cone, for the floor, being largely incandescently molten, was practically level except for a depression at the center, where the actual vortex lay. The walls of the pit were steeply, unstably irregular, varying in pitch and shape with the hardness and refractoriness of the strata composing them. Now a section would glare into an unbearably blinding white puffing away in sparkling vapor. Again, cooled by an inrushing blast of air, it would subside into an angry scarlet, its surface crawling in a sluggish flow of lava. Occasionally a part of the wall might even go black, into pock-marked scoriae or into brilliant planes of obsidian.

For always, somewhere, there was an enormous volume of air pouring into that crater. It rushed in as ordinary air. It came out, however, in a ragingly-uprushing pillar, as— as something else. No one knew—or knows yet, for that matter—exactly what a loose vortex does to the molecules and atoms of air. In fact, due to the extreme variability already referred to, it probably does not do the same thing for more than an instant at a time.

That there is little actual combustion is certain; that is, except for the forced combination of nitrogen, argon, xenon, and krypton with oxygen. There is, however, consumption: plenty of consumption. And what that incredibly intense bombardment impinges up is . . . . is altered. Profoundly and obscuredly altered, so that the atmosphere emitted from the crater is quite definitely no longer air as we know it. It may be corrosive, it may be poisonous in one or another of a hundred fashions, it may be merely new and different; but it is no longer the air which we human beings are used to breathing. And it is this fact, rather than the destruction of the planet itself, which would end the possibility of life upon Earth's surface.

It is difficult indeed to describe the appearance of a loose atomic vortex to those who have never seen one; and, fortunately, most people never have. And practically all of its frightful radiation lies in those octaves of the spectrum which are invisible to the human eye. Suffice it to say, then, that it had an average effective surface temperature of about fifteen thousand degrees absolute—two and one-half times as hot as the sun of Tellus—and that it was radiating every frequency possible to that incomprehensible temperature, and let it go at that.

And Neal Cloud, scurrying in his flitter through that murky, radiation-riddled atmosphere, setting up equations from the readings of his various meters and gauges and solving those equations almost instantaneously in his mathematical-prodigy's mind, sat appalled. For the activity level was, and even in its lowest dips remained, far above the level he had selected. His skin began to prickle and burn. His eyes began to smart and to ache. He knew what those symptoms meant; even the flitter's powerful screens were not stopping all the radiation; even his suit-screens and his special goggles were not stopping what leaked through. But he wouldn't quit yet; the activity might—probably would—take a nose-dive any instant. If it did, he'd have to be ready. On the other hand, it might blow up at any instant, too.

There were two schools of mathematical thought upon that point. One held that the vortex, without any essential change in its physical condition or nature, would keep on growing bigger. Indefinitely, until, uniting with the other vortices of the planet, it had converted the entire mass of the world into energy.

The second school, of which the forementioned Carlowitz was the loudest voice, taught that at a certain stage of development the internal energy of the vortex would become so great that generation-radiation equilibrium could not be maintained. This would, of course, result in an explosion; the nature and consequences of which this Carlowitz was wont to dwell upon in ghoulishly mathematical glee. Neither school, however, could prove its point—or, rather, each school proved its point, by means of unimpeachable mathematics—and each hated and rerided the other, loudly and heatedly.

And now Cloud, as he studied through his almost opaque defenses that indescribably ravening fireball, that esuriently rapacious monstrosity which might very well have come from the deepest pit of the hottest hell of mythology, felt strongly inclined to agree with Carlowitz. It didn't seem possible that anything *could* get any worse than that without exploding. And such an explosion, he felt sure, would certainly blow everything for miles around into the smitheriest kind of smithereens.

The activity of the vortex stayed high, 'way too high. The tiny control room of the flitter grew hotter and hotter. His skin burned and his eyes ached worse. He touched a communicator stud and spoke.

"Phil? Better get me three more bombs. Like these, except up around. . . ."

"I don't check you. If you do that, it's apt to drop to a minimum and stay there," the Lensman reminded him. "It's completely unpredictable, you know."

"It may, at that . . . . so I'll have to forget the five per cent margin and hit on the nose or not at all. Order me up two more, then—one at half of what I've got here, the other double it," and he reeled off the figures for the charge and the casing of the explosive. "You might break out a jar of burn-dressing, too. Some fairly hot stuff is leaking through."

"We'll do that. Come down, fast!"

Cloud landed. He stripped to the skin and the observer smeared his every square inch of epidermis with the thick, gooey stuff that was not only a highly efficient screen against radiation, but also a sovereign remedy for new radiation burns. He exchanged his goggles for a thicker, darker, heavier pair. The two bombs arrived and were substituted for two of the original load.

"I thought of something while I was up there," Cloud informed the observers then. "Twenty kilograms of duodec is nobody's firecracker, but it may be the least of what's going to go off. Have you got any idea of what's going to become of the energy inside that vortex when I blow it out?"

"Can't say that I have." The Lensman frowned in thought. "No data."

"Neither have I. But I'd say that you better go back to the new station—the one you were going to move to if it kept on getting worse."

"But the instruments. . . . ." the Lensman was thinking, not of the instruments themselves, which were valueless in comparison with life, but of the records those instruments would make. Those records were priceless.

"I'll have everything on the tapes in the flitter," Cloud reminded.

"But suppose. . . . ."

"That the flitter stops one, too—or doesn't stop it, rather? In that case, your back station won't be there, either, so it won't make any difference." How mistaken Cloud was!

"QX," the Chief decided. "We'll leave when you do— just in case."

Again in air, Cloud found that the activity, while still high, was not too high, but that it was fluctuating too rapidly. He could not get even five seconds of trustworthy prediction, to say nothing of ten. So he waited, as close as he dared remain to that horrible center of disintegration.

The flitter hung poised in air, motionless, upon softly hissing under-jets. Cloud know to a fraction his height above the ground. He knew to a fraction his distance from the vortex. He knew with equal certainty the density of the atmosphere and the exact velocity and direction of the wind. Hence, since he could also read closely enough the momentary variations in the cyclonic storms within the crater, he could compute very easily the course and velocity necessary to land the bomb in the exact center of the vortex at any given instant of time. The hard part—the thing that no one had as yet succeeded in doing—was to predict, for a time far enough ahead to be of any use, a usably close approximation to the vortex's quantitative activity. For, as has been said, he had to over-blast, rather than under-, if he could not hit it "on the nose:" to under-blast would scatter it all over the state.

Therefore Cloud concentrated upon the dials and gauges before him; concentrated with every fiber of his being and every cell of his brain.

Suddenly, almost imperceptibly, the Sigma curve gave signs of flattening out. In that instant Cloud's mind pounced. Simultaneous equations: nine of them, involving nine unknowns. An integration in four dimensions. No matter—Cloud did not solve them laboriously, one factor at a time. Without knowing how he had arrived at it, he knew the answer; just as the Posenian or the Rigellian is able to perceive every separate component particle of an opaque, three-dimensional solid, but without being able to explain to anyone how his sense of perception works. It just *is*, that's all.

Anyway, by virtue of whatever sense or ability it is which makes a mathematical prodigy what he is, Cloud knew that in exactly eight and three-tenth seconds from that observed instant the activity of the vortex would be slightly —but not too far—under the coefficient of his heaviest bomb. Another flick of his mental trigger and he knew the exact velocity he would require. His hand swept over the studs, his right foot tramped down, hard, upon the firing lever; and, even as the quivering flitter shot forward under eight Tellurian gravities of acceleration, he knew to the thousandth of a second how long he would have to hold that acceleration to attain that velocity. While not really long— in seconds—it was much too long for comfort. It took him much closer to the vortex than he wanted to be; in fact, it took him right out over the crater itself.

But he stuck to the calculated course, and at the precisely correct instant he cut his drive and released his largest bomb. Then, so rapidly that it was one blur of speed, he again kicked on his eight G's of drive and started to whirl around as only a speedster or a flitter can whirl. Practically unconscious from the terrific resultant of the linear and angular accelerations, he ejected the two smaller bombs. He did not care particularly where they lit, just so they didn't light in the crater or near the observatory, and he had already made certain of that. Then, without waiting even to finish the whirl or to straighten her out in level flight, Cloud's still-flying hand darted toward the switch whose closing would energize the Bergenholm and make the flitter inertialess.

Too late. Hell was out for noon, with the little speedster still inert. Cloud had moved fast, too; trained mind and trained body had been working at top speed and in perfect coordination. There just simply hadn't been enough time. If he could have got what he wanted, ten full seconds, or even nine, he could have made it, But. . . . . .

In spite of what happened, Cloud defended his action, then and thereafter. Damnitall, he *had* to take the eight-point-three second reading! Another tenth of a second and his bomb wouldn't have fitted—he didn't have the five percent leeway he wanted, remember. And no, he couldn't wait for another match, either. His screens were leaking like sieves, and if he had waited for another chance they would have picked him up fried to a greasy cinder in his own lard!

The bomb sped truly and struck the target in direct central impact, exactly as scheduled. It penetrated perfectly. The neocarballoy casing lasted just long enough—that frightful charge of duodec exploded, if not exactly at the center of the vortex, at least near enough to the center to do the work. In other words, Cloud's figuring had been close—very close. But the time had been altogether too short.

The flitter was not even out of the crater when the bomb went off. And not only the bomb. For Cloud's vague forebodings were materialized, and more; the staggeringly immense energy of the vortex merged with that of the detonating duodec to form an utterly incomprehensible whole.

In part the hellish flood of boiling lava in that devil's cauldron was beaten downward into a bowl by the sheer, stupendous force of the blow; in part it was hurled abroad in masses, in gouts and streamers. And the raging wind of the explosion's front seized the fragments and tore and worried them to bits, hurling them still faster along their paths of violence. And air, so densely compressed as to be to all intents and purposes a solid, smote the walls of the crater. Smote them so that they crumbled, crushed outward through the hard-packed ground, broke up into jaggedly irregular blocks which hurtled, screamingly, away through the atmosphere.

Also the concussion wave, or the explosion front, or flying fragments, or something, struck the two loose bombs, so that they too exploded and added their contribution to the already stupendous concentration of force. They were not close enough to the flitter to wreck it of themselves, but they were close enough so that they didn't do her—or her pilot—a bit of good.

The first terrific wave buffeted the flitter while Cloud's right hand was in the air, shooting across the panel to turn on the Berg. The impact jerked the arm downward and sidewise, both bones of the forearm snapping as it struck the ledge. The second one, an instant later, broke his left leg. Then the debris began to arrive.

Chunks of solid or semi-molten rock slammed against the hull, knocking off wings and control-surfaces. Gobs of viscous slag slapped it liquidly, freezing into and clogging up jets and orifices. The little ship was hurled hither and yon, in the grip of forces she could no more resist than can the floating leaf resist the waters of a cataract. And Cloud's brain was as addled as an egg by the vicious concussions which were hitting him from so many different directions and so nearly all at once. Nevertheless with his one arm and his one leg and the few cells of his brain that were still at work, the physicist was still in the fight.

By sheer force of will and nerve he forced his left hand across the gyrating key-bank to the Bergenholm switch. He snapped it, and in the instant of its closing a vast, calm peace descended, blanket-like. For, fortunately, the Berg still worked; the flitter and all her contents and appurtenances were inertialess. Nothing material could buffet her or hurt her now; she would waft effortlessly away from a feather's lightest possible touch.

Cloud wanted to faint then, but he didn't—quite. Instead, foggily, he tried to look back at the crater. Nine-tenths of his visiplates were out of commission, but he finally got a view. Good—it was out. He wasn't surprised; he had been quite confident that it would be. It wasn't scattered around, either. It *couldn't* be, for his only possibility of smearing the shot was on the upper side, not the lower.

His next effort was to locate the secondary observatory, where he had to land, and in that too he was successful. He had enough intelligence left to realize that, with practically all of his jets clogged and his wings and tail shot off, he couldn't land his little vessel inert. Therefore he would have to land her free.

And by dint of light and extremely unorthodox use of what jets he had left in usable shape he did land her free, almost within the limits of the observatory's field; and having landed, he inerted her.

But, as has been intimated, his brain was not working so well; he had held his ship inertialess quite a few seconds longer than he thought, and he did not even think of the buffetings she had taken. As a result of these things, however, her intrinsic velocity did not match, anywhere near exactly, that of the ground upon which she lay. Thus, when Cloud cut his Bergenholm, restoring thereby to the flitter the absolute velocity and inertia she had had before going free, there resulted a distinctly anti-climactic crash.

There was a last terrific bump as the motionless vessel collided with the equally motionless ground; and "Storm" Cloud, vortex blaster, went out like the proverbial light.

Help came, of course; and on the double. The pilot was unconscious and the flitter's door could not be opened from the outside, but those were not insuperable obstacles. A plate, already loose, was sheared away; the pilot was carefully lifted out of his prison and rushed to Base Hospital in the "meat-can" already in attendance.

And later, in a private office of that hospital, the gray-clad Chief of the Atomic Research Laboratory sat and waited—but not patiently.

"How is he, Lacy?" he demanded, as the Surgeon-General entered the room. "He's going to live, isn't he?"

"Oh, yes, Phil—definitely yes," Lacy replied, briskly. "He has a good skeleton, very good indeed. The burns are superficial and will yield quite readily to treatment. The deeper, delayed effects of the radiation to which he was exposed can be neutralized entirely effectively. Thus he will not need even a Phillips's treatment for the replacement of damaged parts, except possibly for a few torn muscles and so on."

"But he was smashed up pretty badly, wasn't he? I know that he had a broken arm and a broken leg, at least."

"Simple fractures only—entirely negligible." Lacy waved aside with an airy gesture such small ills as broken bones. "He'll be out in a few weeks."

"How soon can I see him?" the Lensman-physicist asked. "There are some important things to take up with him, and I've got a personal message for him that I must give him as soon as possible."

Lacy pursed his lips. Then:

"You may see him now," he decided. "He is conscious, and strong enough. Not too long, though, Phil—fifteen minutes at most."

"QX, and thanks," and a nurse led the visiting Lensman to Cloud's bedside.

"Hi, Stupe!" he boomed, cheerfully. " 'Stupe' being short for stupendous, not 'stupid'."

"Hi, Chief. Glad to see somebody. Sit down."

"You're the most-wanted man in the Galaxy," the visitor informed the invalid, "not excepting even Kimball Kinnison. Look at this spool of tape, and it's only the first one. I brought it along for you to read at your leisure. As soon as any planet finds out that we've got a sure-enough vortex-blower-outer, an expert who can really call his shots —and the news travels mighty fast—that planet sends in a double-urgent, Class A-Prime demand for first call upon your services.

"Sirius IV got in first by a whisker, it seems, but Aldebaran II was so close a second that it was a photo finish, and all the channels have been jammed ever since. Canopus, Vega, Rigel, Spica. They all want you. Everybody from Alsakan to Vandemar and back. We told them right off that we would not receive personal delegations—we had to almost throw a couple of pink-haired Chickladorians out bodily to make them believe that we meant it—and that the age and condition of the vortex involved, not priority of requisition, would govern, QX?"

"Absolutely," Cloud agreed. "That's the only way it could be, I should think."

"So forget about this psychic trauma. . . . No, I don't mean that," the Lensman corrected himself hastily. "You know what I mean. The will to live is the most important factor in any man's recovery, and too many worlds need you too badly to have you quit now. Not?"

"I suppose so," Cloud acquiesced, but somberly. "I'll get out of here in short order. And I'll keep on pecking away until one of those vortices finishes what this one started."

"You'll die of old age then, son," the Lensman assured him. "We got full data—all the information we need. We know exactly what to do to your screens. Next time nothing will come through except light, and only as much of that as you feel like admitting. You can wait as close to a vortex as you please, for as long as you please; until you get exactly the activity and time-interval that you want. You will be just as comfortable and just as safe as though you were home in bed."

"Sure of that?"

"Absolutely—or at least, as sure as we can be of anything that hasn't happened yet. But I see that your guardian angel here is eyeing her clock somewhat pointedly, so I'd better be doing a flit before they toss me down a shaft. Clear ether, Storm!"

"Clear ether, Chief!"

And that is how "Storm" Cloud, atomic physicist, became the most narrowly-specialized specialist in all the annals of science: how he became "Storm" Cloud, Vortex Blaster— the Galaxy's only vortex blaster.

NIGHT

by

JOHN W. CAMPBELL

Condon was staring through the glasses with a face tense and drawn, all his attention utterly concentrated on that one almost invisible speck infinitely far up in the blue sky, and saying over and over again in the most horribly absent-minded way, "My Lord—my Lord——"

Suddenly he shivered and looked down at me, sheer agony in his face. "He's never coming down. Don, he's never coming down——"

I knew it, too—knew it as solidly as I knew the knowledge was impossible. But I smiled and said: "Oh, I wouldn't say that. If anything, I'd fear his coming down. What goes up comes down."

Major Condon trembled all over. His mouth worked horribly for a moment before he could speak. "Talbot—I'm scared—I'm horribly scared. You know—you're his assistant

—you know he's trying to defeat gravity. Men aren't meant to—it's wrong—wrong——"

His eyes were glued on those binoculars again, with the same terrible tensity, and now he was saying over and over in that absent-minded way, "wrong—wrong—wrong——"

Simultaneously he stiffened, and stopped. The dozen or so other men standing on that lonely little emergency field stiffened; then the major crumpled to the ground. I've never before seen a man faint, let alone an army officer with a D. S. medal. I didn't stop to help him, because I knew something had happened. I grabbed the glasses.

Far, far up in the sky was that little orange speck—far, where there is almost no air, and he had been forced to wear a stratosphere suit with a little alcohol heater. The broad, orange wings were overlaid now with a faint-glowing, pearl-gray light. And it was falling. Slowly, at first, circling aimlessly downward. Then it dipped, rose, and somehow went into a tail spin.

It was horrible. I know I must have breathed, but it didn't seem so. It took minutes for it to fall those miles, despite the speed. Eventually it whipped out of that tail spin—through sheer speed, whipped out and into a power dive. It was a ghastly, flying coffin, hurtling at more than half a thousand miles an hour when it reached the Earth, some fifteen miles away.

The ground trembled, and the air shook with the crash of it. We were in the cars and roaring across the ground long before it hit. I was in Bob's car, with Jeff, his laboratory technician—Bob's little roadster he'd never need again. The engine picked up quickly, and we were going seventy before we left the field, jumped a shallow ditch and hit the road—the deserted, concrete road that led off toward where he must be. The engine roared as Jeff clamped down on the accelerator. Dimly, I heard the major's big car coming along behind us.

Jeff drove like a maniac, but I didn't notice. I knew the thing had done ninety-five but I think we must have done more. The wind whipped tears in my eyes so I couldn't be sure whether I saw mounting smoke and flame or not. With Diesel fuel there shouldn't be—but that plane had been doing things it shouldn't. It had been trying out Carter's antigravity coil.

We shot up the flat, straight road across wide, level country, the wind moaning a requiem about the car. Far ahead I saw the side road that must lead off toward where Bob should be, and lurched to the braking of the car, the whine and sing of violently shrieking tires, then to the skidding corner. It was a sand road; we slithered down it and for all the lightness and power, we slowed to sixty-five, clinging to the seat as the soft sand gripped and clung.

Violently Jeff twisted into a branching cow path, and somehow the springs took it. We braked to a stop a quarter of a mile from the plane.

It was in a fenced field of pasture and wood lot. We leaped the fence, and raced toward it: Jeff got there first, just as the major's car shrieked to a stop behind ours.

The major was cold and pale when he reached us. "Dead," he stated.

And I was very much colder and probably several times as pale. "I don't know!" I moaned. "He isn't there!"

"Not there!" The major almost screamed it. "He must be—he has to be. He has no parachute—wouldn't take one. They say he didn't jump——"

I pointed to the plane, and wiped a little cold sweat from my forehead. I felt clammy all over, and my spine prickled. The solid steel of the huge Diesel engine was driven through the stump of a tree, down into the ground perhaps eight or nine feet, and the dirt and rock had splashed under that blow like wet mud.

The wings were on the other side of the field, flattened, twisted straws of dural alloy. The fuselage of the ship was a perfect silhouette—a longitudinal projection that had flattened in on itself, each separate section stopping only as it hit the ground.

The great torus coil with its strangely twined wrappings of hair-fine bismuth wire was intact! And bent over it, twisted, utterly wrecked by the impact, was the main-wing stringer—the great dural-alloy beam that supported most of the ship's weight in the air. It was battered, crushed on those hair-fine, fragile bismuth wires—and not one of them was twisted or displaced or so much as skinned. The back frame of the ponderous Diesel engine—the heavy supercharger was the anvil of that combination—was cracked and splintered. And not one wire of the hellish bismuth coil was strained or skinned or displaced.

And the red pulp that should have been there—the red pulp that had been a man—wasn't. It simply wasn't there at all. He hadn't left the plane. In the clear, cloudless air, we could see that. He was gone.

We examined it, of course. A farmer came, and another, and looked, and talked. Then several farmers came in old, dilapidated cars with their wives and families, and watched.

We set the owner of the property on watch and went away—went back to the city for workmen and a truck with a derrick. Dusk was falling. It would be morning before we could do anything, so we went away.

Five of us—the major of the army air force, Jeff Rodney, the two Douglass Co. men whose names I never remembered and I—sat in my—our—room. Bob's and Jeff's and mine. We'd been sitting there for hours trying to talk, trying to think, trying to remember every little detail, and trying to forget every ghastly detail. We couldn't remember the detail that explained it, nor forget the details that rode and harried us.

and answered. A strange voice, flat and rather unpleasant,

And the telephone rang. I started. Then slowly got up said: "Mr. Talbot?"

"Yes."

It was Sam Gantry, the farmer we'd left on watch. "There's a man here."

"Yes? What does he want?"

"I dunno. I dunno where he came from. He's either dead or out cold. Gotta funny kind of an aviator suit on, with a glass face on it. He looks all blue, so I guess he's dead."

"Lord! Bob! Did you take that helmet off?" I roared.

"No, sir, no—no, sir. We just left him the way he was."

"His tanks have run out. Listen. Take a hammer, a wrench, anything, and break that glass faceplate! Quick! We'll be there."

Jeff was moving. The major was, too, and the others. I made a grab for the half-empty bottle of Scotch, started out, and ducked back into the closet. With the oxygen bottle under my arm I jumped into the crowded little roadster just as Jeff started it moving. He turned on the horn, and left it that way.

We dodged, twisted, jumped and stopped with jerks in traffic, then leaped into smooth, roaring speed out toward the farmer's field. The turns were familiar now; we scarcely slowed for them, sluing around them. This time Jeff charged through the wire fence. A headlight popped; there was a shrill scream of wire, the wicked *zing* of wire scratching across the hood and mud guards, and we were bouncing across the field.

There were two lanterns on the ground; three men carried others; more men squatted down beside a still figure garbed in a fantastic, bulging, airproof stratosphere suit. They looked at us, open-mouthed as we skidded to a halt, moving aside as the major leaped out and dashed over with the Scotch. I followed close behind with the oxygen bottle.

Bob's faceplate was shattered, his face blue, his lips blue and flecked with froth. A long gash across his cheek from the shattered glass bled slowly. The major lifted his head without a word, and glass tinkled inside the helmet as he tried to force a little whisky down his throat.

"Wait!" I called. "Major, give him artificial respiration, and this will bring him around quicker—better." The major nodded, and rose, rubbing his arm with a peculiar expression.

"That's cold!" he said, as he flipped Bob over, and straddled his back. I held the oxygen bottle under Bob's nose as the major swung back in his arc, and let the raw, cold oxygen gas flow into his nostrils.

In ten seconds Bob coughed, gurgled, coughed violently, and took a deep shuddering breath. His face turned pink almost instantly under that lungful of oxygen, and I noticed with some surprise that he seemed to exhale almost nothing, his body absorbing the oxygen rapidly.

He coughed again; then: "I could breathe a heck of a sight better if you'd get off my back," he said. The major jumped up, and Bob turned over and sat up. He waved me aside, and spat. "I'm—all right," he said softly.

"Lord, man, what happened?" demanded the major.

Bob sat silent for a minute. His eyes had the strangest look—a hungry look—as he gazed about him. He looked at the trees beyond and at the silent, watching men in the light of the lanterns; then up, up to where a myriad stars gleamed and danced and flickered in the clear night sky.

"I'm back," he said softly. Then suddenly he shivered, and looked horribly afraid. "But—I'll have to be—then—too."

He looked at the major for a minute, and smiled faintly. And at the two Douglass Co. men. "Your plane was all right. I started up on the wings, as arranged, went way up, till I thought surely I was at a safe height, where the air wasn't too dense and the field surely wouldn't reach to Earth—Lord!—reach to Earth! I didn't guess how far that field extended. It touched Earth—twice.

"I was at forty-five thousand when I decided it was safe, and cut the engine. It died, and the stillness shocked me. It was so quiet. So quiet.

"I turned on the coil circuit, and the dynamotor began to hum as the tubes warmed up. And then—the field hit me. It paralyzed me in an instant. I never had a chance to break the circuit, though I knew instantly something was wrong—terribly wrong. But the very first thing it did was to paralyze me, and I had to sit there and watch the instruments climb to positions and meanings they were never meant for.

"I realized I alone was being affected by that coil—I alone, sitting directly over it. I stared at the meters and they began to fade, began to seem transparent, unreal. And as they faded into blankness I saw clear sky beyond them; then for a hundredth of a second, like some effect of persistence of vision, I thought I saw the plane falling, twisting down at incredible speed, and the light faded as the Sun seemed to rocket suddenly across the sky and vanish.

"I don't know how long I was in that paralyzed condition, where there was only blankness—neither dark nor light, nor time nor any form—but I breathed many times. Finally, form crawled and writhed into the blankness, and seemed to solidify beneath me as, abruptly, the blankness gave way to a dull red light. I was falling.

"I thought instantly of the forty-five thousand feet that lay between me and the solid Earth, and stiffened automatically in terror. And in the same instant I landed in a deep blanket of white snow, stained by the red light that lighted the world.

"Cold. Cold—it tore into me like the fang of a savage animal. What cold! The cold of ultimate death. It ripped through that thick, insulated suit and slashed at me viciously, as though there were no insulation there. I shivered so violently I could scarcely turn up the alcohol valves. You know I carried alcohol tanks and catalyst grids for heating, because the only electric fields I wanted were those of the apparatus. Even used a Diesel instead of gas engine.

"I thank the Lord for that then. I realized that whatever had happened I was in a spot indescribably cold and desolate. And in the same instant, realized that the sky was black. Blacker than the blackest night, and yet before me the snow field stretched to infinity, tainted by the blood-red light, and my shadow crawled in darker red at my feet.

"I turned around. As far as the eye could see in three directions the land swept off in very low, very slightly rolling hills, almost plains—red plains of snow dyed with the dripping light of sunset, I thought.

"In the fourth direction, a wall—a wall that put the Great Wall of China to shame—loomed up half a mile—a blood-red wall that had the luster of metal. It stretched across the horizon, and looked a scant hundred yards away, for the air was utterly clear. I turned up my alcohol burners a bit more and felt a little better.

"Something jerked my head around like a giant hand—a sudden thought. I stared at the Sun and gulped. It was four times—six times—the size of the Sun I knew. And it wasn't setting. It was forty-five degrees from the horizon. It was red. Blood-red. And there wasn't the slightest bit of radiant heat reaching my face from it. That Sun was cold.

"I'd just automatically assumed I was still on Earth, whatever else might have happened, but now I knew I couldn't be. It must be another planet of another sun—a frozen planet—for that snow was frozen air. I knew it absolutely. A frozen planet of a dead sun.

"And then I changed even that. I looked up at the black sky above me, and in all the vast black bowl of the heavens, not three-score stars were visible. Dim, red stars, with one single sun that stood out for its brilliance—a yellowish-red sun perhaps a tenth as bright as our Sun, but a monster here. It was another—a dead—space. For if that snow was frozen air, the only atmosphere must have been neon and helium. There wasn't any hazy air to stop the light of the stars, and that dim, red sun didn't obscure them with its light. The stars were gone.

"In that glimpse, my mind began working by itself; I was scared.

"Scared? I was so scared I was afraid I was going to be sick. Because right then I knew I was never coming back. When I felt that cold, I'd wondered when my oxygen bottles would give out, if I'd get back before they did. Now it was not a worry. It was simply the limiting factor on an already-determined thing, the setting on the time bomb. I had just so much more time before I died right there.

"My mind was working out things, working them out all by itself, and giving answers I didn't want, didn't want to know about. For some reason it persisted in considering this was Earth, and the conviction became more and more fixed. It was right. That was Earth. And it was old Sol. Old —old Sol. It was the time axis that coil distorted—not gravity at all. My mind worked that out with a logic as cold as that planet.

"If it was time it had distorted, and this was Earth, then it had distorted time beyond imagining to an extent as meaningless to our minds as the distance a hundred million light years is. It was simply vast—incalculable. The Sun was dead. The Earth was dead. And Earth was already, in our time, two billion of years old, and in all that geological time, the Sun had not changed measurably. Then how long was it since my time? The Sun was dead. The very stars were dead. It must have been, I thought even then, billions on billions of years. And I grossly under-estimated it.

"The world was old—old—old. The very rocks and ground radiated a crushing aura of incredible age. It was old, older than—but what is there? Older than the hills? Hills? Gosh, they'd been born and died and been born and worn away again, a million, a score of million times! Old as the stars? No, that wouldn't do. The stars were dead—then.

"I looked again at the metal wall, and set out for it, and

the aura of age washed up at me, and dragged at me, and tried to stop this motion when all motion should have ceased. And the thin, unutterably cold wind whined in dead protest at me, and pulled at me with the ghost hands of the million million million that had been born and lived and died in the countless ages before I was born.

"I wondered as I went. I didn't think clearly; for the dead aura of the dead planet pulled at me. Age. The stars were dying, dead. They were huddled there in space, like decrepit old men, huddling for warmth. The galaxy was shrunk. So tiny, it wasn't a thousand light years across, the stars were separated by miles where there had been light years. The magnificent, proudly sprawling universe I had known, that flung itself across a million million light years, that flung radiant energy through space by the millions of millions of tons was—gone.

"It was dying—a dying miser that hoarded its last broken dregs of energy in a tiny cramped space. It was broken and shattered. A thousand billion years before the cosmical constant had been dropped from that broken universe. The cosmical constant that flung giant galaxies whirling apart with ever greater speed had no place here. It had hurled the universe in broken fragments, till each spattered bit felt the chill of loneliness, and wrapped space about itself, to become a universe in itself while the flaming galaxies vanished.

"That had happened so long ago that the writing it had left in the fabric of space itself had worn away. Only the gravity constant remained, the hoarding constant, that drew things together, and slowly the galaxy collapsed, shrunken and old, a withered mummy.

"The very atoms were dead. The light was cold; even the red light made things look older, colder. There was no youth in the universe. I didn't belong, and the faint protesting rustle of the infinitely cold wind about me moved the snow in muted, futile protest, resenting my intrusion from a time when things were young. It whinnied at me feebly, and chilled the youth of me.

"I plodded on and on, and always the metal wall retreated, like one of those desert mirages. I was too stupefied by the age of the thing to wonder; I just walked on.

"I was getting nearer, though. The wall was real; it was fixed. As I drew slowly nearer, the polished sheen of the wall died and the last dregs of hope died. I'd thought there might be some one still living behind that wall. Beings who could build such a thing might be able to live even here. But I couldn't stop then; I just went on. The wall was broken and cracked. It wasn't a wall I'd seen; it was a series of broken walls, knitted by distance to a smooth front.

"There was no weather to age them, only the faintest stirring of faint, dead winds—winds of neon and helium, inert and uncorroding—as dead and inert as the universe. The city had been dead a score of billions of years. That city was dead for a time ten times longer than the age of our planet to-day. But nothing destroyed it. Earth was dead—too dead to suffer the racking pains of life. The air was dead, too dead to scrape away metal.

"But the universe itself was dead. There was no cosmic radiation then to finally level the walls by atomic disintegration. There had been a wall—a single metal wall. Something—perhaps a last wandering meteor—had chanced on it in a time incalculably remote, and broken it. I entered through the great gap. Snow covered the city—soft, white snow. The great red sun stood still just where it was. Earth's restless rotation had long since been stilled—long, long since.

"There were dead gardens above, and I wandered up to them. That was really what convinced me it was a human city, on Earth. There were frozen, huddled heaps that might once have been men. Little fellows with fear forever frozen on their faces huddled helplessly over something that must once have been a heating device. Dead perhaps, since the last storm old Earth had known, tens of billions of years before.

"I went down. There were vastnesses in that city. It was huge. It stretched forever, it seemed, on and on, in its deadness. Machines, machines everywhere. And the machines were dead, too. I went down, down where I thought a bit of light and heat might linger. I didn't know then how long death had been there; those corpses looked so fresh, preserved by the eternal cold.

"It grew dark down below, and only through rents and breaks did that bloody light seep in. Down and down, till I was below the level of the dead surface. The white snow persisted, and then I came to the cause of that final, sudden death. I could understand then. More and more I had puzzled, for those machines I'd seen I knew were far and beyond anything we ever conceived—machines of perfection, self-repairing, and self-energizing, self-perpetuating. They could make duplicates of themselves, and duplicate other, needed machines; they were intended to be eternal, everlasting.

"But the designers couldn't cope with some things that were beyond even their majestic imaginations—the imaginations that conceived these cities that had lived beyond—a million times beyond—what they had dreamed. They must have conceived some vague future. But not a future when the Earth died, and the Sun died, and even the universe itself died.

"Cold had killed them. They had heating arrangements, devices intended to maintain forever the normal temperature despite the wildest variations of the weather. But in every electrical machine, resistances, balance resistances, and induction coils, balance condensers, and other inductances. And cold, stark, spatial cold, through ages, threw them off. Despite the heaters, cold crept in colder—cold that made their resistance balances and their induction coils superconductors! That destroyed the city, Superconduction

—like the elimination of friction, on which all things must rest. It is a drag and a thing engineers fight forever. Resistance and friction must finally be the rest and the base of all things, the force that holds the great bed bolts firm and the brakes that stop the machines when needed.

"Electrical resistance died in the cold and the wonderful machines stopped for the replacement of defective parts. And when they were replaced, they, too, were defective. For what months must that constant stop—replacement—start—stop—replacement have gone on before, at last defeated forever, those vast machines must bow in surrender to the inevitable? Cold had defeated them by defeating and removing the greatest obstacle of the engineers that built them—resistance.

"They must have struggled forever—as we would say—through a hundred billion years against encroaching harshness of nature, forever replacing worn, defective parts. At last, defeated forever, the great power plants, fed by dying atoms, had been forced into eternal idleness and cold. Cold conquered them at last.

"They didn't blow up. Nowhere did I see a wrecked machine; always they had stopped automatically when the defective resistances made it impossible to continue. The stored energy that was meant to re-start those machines after repairs had been made had long since leaked out. Never again could they move, I knew.

"I wondered how long they had been, how long they had gone on and on, long after the human need of them had vanished. For that vast city contained only a very few humans at the end. What untold ages of lonely functioning perfection had stretched behind those at-last-defeated mechanisms?

"I wandered out, to see perhaps more, before the necessary end came to me, too. Through the city of death. Everywhere little self-contained machines, cleaning machines that had kept that perfect ctiy orderly and neat stood helpless

and crushed by eternity and cold. They must have continued functioning for years after the great central power
stations failed, for each contained its own store of energy,
needing only occasional recharge from the central stations.

"I could see where breaks had occurred in the city, and,
clustered about those breaks were motionless repair machines, their mechanisms in positions of work, the debris
cleared away and carefully stacked on motionless trucks.
The new beams and plates were partly attached, partly
fixed and left, as the last dregs of their energy was fruit-
lessly expended in the last, dying attempts of that great
body to repair itself. The death wounds lay unmended.

"I started back up. Up to the top of the city. It was a
long climb, an infinite, weary climb, up half a mile of winding ramps, past deserted, dead homes; past, here and there,
shops and restaurants; past motionless little automative pas-
senger cars.

"Up and up, to the crowning gardens that lay stiff and
brittle and frozen. The breaking of the roof must have
caused a sudden chill, for their leaves lay green in sheaths
of white, frozen air. Brittle glass, green and perfect to the
touch. Flowers, blooming in wonderful perfection showed
still; they didn't seem dead, but it didn't seem they could
be otherwise under the blanket of cold.

"Did you ever sit up with a corpse?" Bob looked up at
us—through us. "I had to once, in my little home town
where they always did that. I sat with a few neighbors
while the man died before my eyes. I knew he must die
when I came there. He died—and I sat there all night while
the neighbors filed out, one by one, and the quiet settled.
The quiet of the dead.

"I had to again. I was sitting with a corpse then. The
corpse of a dead world in a dead universe, and the quiet
didn't have to settle there; it had settled a billion years ago,
and only my coming had stirred those feeble, protesting
ghosts of eon-dead hopes of that planet to softly whining
protest—protest the wind tried to sob to me, the dead wind

of the dead gases. I'll never be able to call them inert gases again. I know. I know they are dead gases, the dead gases of dead worlds.

"And above, through the cracked crystal of the roof, the dying suns looked down on the dead city. I couldn't stay there. I went down. Down under layer after layer of buildings, buildings of gleaming metal that reflected the dim, blood light of the Sun outside in carmine stains. I went down and down, down to the machines again. But even there hopelessness seemed more intense. Again I saw that agonizing struggle of the eternally faithful machines trying to repair themselves once more to serve the masters who were dead a million million years. I could see it again in the frozen, exhausted postures of the repair machines, stilled forever in their hopeless endeavors, the last poor dregs of energy spilled in fruitless conflict with time.

"It mattered little. Time himself was dying now, dying with the city and the planet and the universe he had killed.

"But those machines had tried so hard to serve again—and failed. Now they could never try again. Even they—the deathless machines—were dead.

"I went out again, away from those machines, out into the illimitable corridors, on the edge of the city. I could not penetrate far before the darkness became as absolute as the cold. I passed the shops where goods, untouched by time in this cold, still beckoned those strange humans, but humans for all that; beckoned the masters of the machines that were no more. I vaguely entered one to see what manner of things they used in that time.

"I nearly screamed at the motion of the thing in there, heard dimly through my suit the strangely softened sounds it made in the thin air. I watched it stagger twice—and topple. I cannot guess what manner of storage cells they had—save that they were marvelous beyond imagination. That stored energy that somehow I had released by entering was some last dreg that had remained through a time as old as our planet now. Its voice was stilled forever. But it drove me out—on.

"It had died while I watched. But somehow it made me more curious. I wondered again, less oppressed by utter death. Still, some untapped energy remained in this place, stored unimaginably. I looked more keenly, watched more closely. And when I saw a screen in one office, I wondered. It was a screen. I could see readily it was television of some type. Exploratively, I touched a stud. Sound! A humming, soft sound!

"To my mind leaped a picture of a system of these. There must be—interconnected—a vast central office somewhere with vaster accumulator cells, so huge, so tremendous in their power once, that even the little microfraction that remained was great. A storage system untouchable to the repair machines—the helpless, hopeless power machines.

"In an instant I was alive again with hope. There was a strange series of studs and dials, unknown devices. I pulled back on the stud I had pressed, and stood trembling, wondering. Was there hope?

"Then the thought died. What hope? The city was dead. Not merely that. It had been dead, dead for untold time. Then the whole planet was dead. With whom might I connect? There were none on the whole planet, so what mattered it that there was a communication system.

"I looked at the thing more blankly. Had there been—how could I interpret its multitudinous devices? There was a thing on one side that made me think of a telephone dial for some reason. A pointer over a metal sheet engraved with nine symbols in a circle under the arrow of the pointer. Now the pointer was over what was either the first or the last of these.

"Clumsily, in these gloves, I fingered one of the little symbol buttons inlaid in the metal. There was an unexpected click, a light glowed on the screen, a lighted image! It was a simple projection—but what a projection! A three-dimensional sphere floated, turing slowly before my eyes, turning majestically. And I nearly fell as understanding flooded me abruptly. The pointer was a selector! The studs beneath the pointer I understood! Nine of them. One after the other I pressed, and nine spheres—each different—swam before me.

"And right there I stopped and did some hard thinking. Nine spheres. Nine planets. Earth was shown first—a strange planet to me, but one I knew from the relative size and the position of the pointer must be Earth—then, in order, the other eight.

"Now—might there be life? Yes. In those nine worlds there might be, somewhere.

"Where? Mercury—nearest the Sun? No, the Sun was too dead, too cold, even for warmth there. And Mercury was too small. I knew, even as I thought, that I'd have one good chance because whatever means they had for communication wouldn't work without tremendous power. If those incredible storage cells had the power for even one shot, they had no more. Somehow I guessed that this apparatus might incorporate no resistance whatever. Here would be only very high frequency alternating current, and only condensers and inductances would be used in it. Supercooling didn't bother them any. It improved them. Not like the immense direct-current power machinery.

"But where to try? Jupiter? That was big. And then I saw what the solution must be. Cold had ruined these machines, thrown them off by making them too-perfect conductors. Because they weren't designed to defend themselves against spatial cold. But the machines—if there were any—on Pluto for instance, must originally have been designed for just such conditions! There it had always been cold. There it always would be cold.

"I looked at that thing with an intensity that should have driven my bare eyesight to Pluto. It was a hope. My only hope. But—how to signal Pluto? They could not understand! If there were any 'they.'

"So I had to guess—and hope. Somehow, I knew, there must be some means of calling the intelligent attendant, that the user might get aid. There was a bank of little studs

—twelve of them—with twelve symbols, each different, in the center of the panel, grouped in four rows of three. I guessed. Duodecimal system.

"Talk of the problems of interplanetary communication! Was there ever such a one? The problem of an anachronism in the city of the dead on a dead planet, seeking life somewhere, somehow.

"There were two studs, off by themselves, separate from the twelve—one green, one red. Again I guessed. Each of these had a complex series of symbols on it, so I turned the pointer on the right to Pluto, wavered, and turned it to Neptune. Pluto was farther. Neptune had been cold enough; the machines would still be working there, and it would be, perhaps, less of a strain on the dregs of energy that might remain.

"I depressed the green symbol hoping I had guessed truly, that red still meant danger, trouble and wrongness to men when that was built—that it meant release and cancellation for a wrongly pressed key. That left green to be an operative call signal.

"Nothing happened. The green key alone was not enough. I looked again, pressed the green key and that stud I had first pressed.

"The thing hummed again. But it was a deeper note now, an entirely different sound, and there was a frenzied clicking inside. Then the green stud kicked back at me. The Neptune key under the pointer glowed softly; the screen began to shimmer with a grayish light. And, abruptly, the humming groaned as though at a terrific overload; the screen turned dull; the little signal light under Neptune's key grew dim. The signal was being sent—hurled out.

"Minute after minute I stood there, staring. The screen grew very slowly, very gently duller, duller. The energy was fading. The last stored driblet was being hurled away— away into space. 'Oh,' I groaned, 'it's hopeless—hopeless to——'

"I'd realized the thing would take hours to get to that

distant planet, traveling at the speed of light, even if it had been correctly aligned. But the machinery that should have done that through the years probably had long since failed for lack of power.

"But I stood there till the groaning motors ceased altogether, and the screen was as dark as I'd found it, the signal light black. I released the stud then, and backed away, dazed by the utter collapse of an insane hope. Experimentally I pressed the Neptune symbol again. So little power was left now, that only the faintest wash of murky light projected the Neptune image, little energy as that would have consumed.

"I went out. Bitter. Hopeless. Earth's last picture was long, long since painted—and mine had been the hand that spent Earth's last poor resource. To its utter exhaustion, the eternal city had strived to serve the race that created it, and I, from the dawn of time had, at the end of time, drained its last poor atom of life. The thing was a thing done.

"Slowly I went back to the roof and the dying suns. Up the miles of winding ramp that climbed a half mile straight up. I went slowly—only life knows haste—and I was of the dead.

"I found a bench up there—a carved bench of metal in the midst of a riot of colorful, frozen towers. I sat down, and looked out across the frozen city to the frozen world beyond, and the freezing red Sun.

"I do not know how long I sat there. And then something whispered in my mind.

"'We sought you at the television machine.'

"I leaped from the bench and stared wildly about me.

"It was floating in the air—a shining dirigible of metal, ruby-red in that light, twenty feet long, perhaps ten in diameter, bright, warm orange light gleaming from its ports. I stared at it in amazement.

"'It—it worked!' I gasped.

" 'The beam carried barely enough energy to energize the amplifiers when it reached Neptune, however,' replied the creature in the machine.

"I couldn't see him—I knew I wasn't hearing him, but somehow that didn't surprise me.

" 'Your oxygen has almost entirely given out, and I believe your mind is suffering from lack of oxygen. I would suggest you enter the lock; there is air in here.'

"I don't know how he knew, but the gauges confirmed his statement. The oxygen was pretty nearly gone. I had perhaps another hour's supply if I opened the valves wide—but it was a most uncomfortably near thing, even so.

"I got in. I was beaming, joyous. There was life. This universe was not so dead as I had supposed. Not on Earth, perhaps, but only because they did not choose! They had space ships! Eagerly I climbed in, a strange thrill running through my body as I crossed the threshold of the lock. The door closed behind me with a soft *shush* on its soft gaskets, locked, and a pump whined somewhere for a moment; then the inner door opened. I stepped in— and instantly turned off my alcohol burners. There was heat—heat and light and air!

"In a moment I had the outer lacings loose, and the inner zipper down. Thirty seconds later I stepped out of the suit, and took a deep breath. The air was clean and sweet and warm, invigorating, fresh-smelling, as though it had blown over miles of green, Sun-warmed fields. It smelled alive, and young.

"Then I looked for the man who had come for me. There was none. In the nose of the ship, by the controls, floated a four-foot globe of metal, softly glowing with a warm, golden light. The light pulsed slowly or swiftly with the rhythm of his thoughts, and I knew that this was the one who had spoken to me.

" 'You had expected a human?' he thought to me. 'There are no more. There have been none for a time I cannot express in your mind. Ah, yes, you have a mathematical means of expression, but no understanding of that time, so it is useless. But the last of humanity was allowed to end before the Sun changed from the original G-O stage—a very, very long time ago.'

"I looked at him and wondered. Where was he from? Who—what—what manner of thing? Was it an armor-incased living creature or another of the perfect machines?

"I felt him watching my mind operate, pulsing softly in his golden light. And suddenly I thought to look out of the ports. The dim red suns were wheeling across those ports at an unbelievable rate. Earth was long since gone. As I looked, a dim, incredibly dim, red disk suddenly appeared, expanded—and I looked in awe at Neptune.

"The planet was scarcely visible when we were already within a dozen millions of miles. It was a jeweled world. Cities—the great, perfect cities—still glowed. They glowed in soft, golden light above, and below, the harsher, brighter blue of mercury vapor lighted them.

"He was speaking again. 'We are machines—the ultimate development of man's machines. Man was almost gone when we came.

"'With what we have learned in the uncounted dusty megayears since, we might have been able to save him. We could not then. It was better, wiser, that man end than that he sink down so low as he must, eventually. Evolution is the rise under pressure. Devolution is the gradual sinking that comes when there is no pressure—and there is no end to it. Life vanished from this system— a dusty infinity I cannot sort in my memory—my type memory, truly, for I have complete all the memories of those that went before me that I replace. But my memory cannot stretch back to that time you think of—a time when the constellations——

"'It is useless to try. Those memories are buried under others, and those still buried under the weight of a billion centuries.

" 'We enter'—he named a city; I cannot reproduce that name—'now. You must return to Earth though in some seven and a quarter of your days, for the magnetic axis stretches back in collapsing field strains. I will be able to inject you into it, I believe.'

"So I entered that city, the living city of machines, that had been when time and the universe were young.

"I did not know then that, when all this universe had dissolved away, when the last sun was black and cold, scattered dust in a fragment of a scattered universe, this planet with its machine cities would go on—a last speck of warm light in a long-dead universe. I did not know then.

" 'You still wonder that we let man die out?' asked the machine. 'It was best. In another brief million years he would have lost his high estate. It was best.'

" 'Now we go on. We cannot end, as he did. It is automatic with us.'

"I felt it then, somehow. The blind, purposeless continuance of the machine cities I could understand. They had no intelligence, only functions. These machines—these living, thinking, reasoning investigators—had only one function, too. Their function was slightly different—they were designed to be eternally curious, eternally investigating. And their striving was the more purposeless of the two, for theirs could reach no end. The cities fought eternally only the blind destructiveness of nature; wear, decay, erosion.

"But their struggle had an opponent forever, so long as they existed. The intelligent—no, not quite intelligent, but something else—curious machines were without opponents. They had to be curious. They had to go on investigating. And they had been going on in just this way for such incomprehensible ages that there was no longer anything to be curious about. Whoever, whatever designed them gave them function and forgot purpose. Their only curiosity was the wonder if there might, somewhere, be one more thing to learn.

"That—and the problem they did not want to solve, but must try to solve, because of the blind functioning of their very structure.

"Those eternal cities were limited. The machines saw now that limit, and saw the hope of final surcease in it. They worked on the energy of the atom. But the masses of the suns were yet tremendous. They were dead for want of energy. The masses of the planets were still enormous. But they, too, were dead for want of energy.

"The machines there on Neptune gave me food and drink —strange, synthetic foods and drinks. There had been none on all the planet. They, perforce, started a machine, unused in a billion years and more, that I might eat. Perhaps they were glad to do so. It brought the end appreciably nearer, that vast consumption of mine.

"They used so very, very little, for they were so perfectly efficient. The only possible fuel in all the universe is one—hydogen. From hydrogen, the lightest of elements, the heaviest can be built up, and energy released. They knew how to destroy matter utterly to energy, and could do it.

"But while the energy release of hydrogen compounding to the heavy elements is controllable, the destruction of matter to energy is a self-regenerative process. Started once, it spreads while matter lies within its direct, contiguous reach. It is wild, uncontrollable. It is impossible to utilize the full energy of matter.

"The suns had found that. They had burned their hydrogen until it was a remnant so small the action could not go on.

"On all Earth there was not an atom of hydrogen—nor was there on any planet, save Neptune. And there the store was not great. I used an appreciable fraction while I was there. That is their last hope. They can see the end, now.

"I stayed those few days, and the machines came and

went. Always investigating, always curious. But there is in all that universe nothing to investigate save the one problem they are sure they cannot solve.

"The machine took me back to Earth, set up something near me that glowed with a peculiar, steady, gray light. It would fix the magnetic axis on me, on my location, within a few hours. He could not stay near when the axis touched again. He went back to Neptune, but a few millions of miles distant, in this shrunken mummy of the solar system.

"I stood alone on the roof of the city, in the frozen garden with its deceptive look of life.

"And I thought of that night I had spent, sitting up with the dead man. I had come and watched him die. And I sat up with him in the quiet. I had wanted some one, any one to talk to.

"I did then. Overpoweringly it came to me I was sitting up in the night of the universe, in the night and quiet of the universe, with a dead planet's body, with the dead, ashen hopes of countless, nameless generations of men and women. The universe was dead, and I sat up alone—alone in the dead hush.

"Out beyond, a last flicker of life was dying on the planet Neptune—a last, false flicker of aimless life, but not life. Life was dead. The world was dead.

"I knew there would never be another sound here. For all the little remainder of time. For this was the dark and the night of time and the universe. It was inevitable, the inevitable end that had been simply more distant in my day—in the long, long-gone time when the stars were mighty lighthouses of a mighty space, not the dying, flickering candles at the head of a dead planet.

"It had been inevitable then; the candles must burn out for all their brave show. But now I could see them guttering low, the last, fruitless dregs of energy expiring as the machines below had spent their last dregs of energy in that hopeless, utterly faithful gesture—to attempt the repair of the city already dead.

"The universe had been dead a billion years. It had been. This, I saw, was the last radiation of the heat of life from an already-dead body—the feel of life and warmth imitation of life by a corpse. Those suns had long and long since ceased to generate energy. They were dead, and their corpses were giving off the last, lingering life heat before they cooled.

"I ran. I think I ran—down away from the flickering, red suns in the sky. Down to the shrouding blackness of the dead city below, where neither light, nor heat, nor life, nor imitation of life bothered me.

"The utter blackness quieted me somewhat. So I turned off my oxygen valves, because I wanted to die sane, even here, and I knew I'd never come back.

"The impossible happened! I came to with that raw oxygen in my face. I don't know how I came—only that here is warmth and life.

"Somewhere, on the far side of that bismuth coil, inevitable still, is the dead planet and the flickering, guttering candles that light the death watch I must keep at the end of time."

A LOGIC

NAMED JOE

by

MURRAY LEINSTER

It was on the third day of August that Joe come off the assembly line, and on the fifth Laurine come into town, and that afternoon I saved civilization. That's what I figure, anyhow. Laurine is a blonde that I was crazy about once—and crazy is the word—and Joe is a logic that I have stored away down in the cellar right now. I had to pay for him because I said I busted him, and sometimes I think about turning him on and sometimes I think about taking an ax to him. Sooner or later I'm gonna do one or the other. I kinda hope it's the ax. I could use a coupla million dollars —sure!—an' Joe'd tell me how to get or make 'em. He can do plenty! But so far I've been scared to take a chance. After all, I figure I really saved a civilization by turnin' him off.

The way Laurine fits in is that she makes cold shivers run up an' down my spine when I think about her. You see,

I've got a wife which I acquired after I had parted from
Laurine with much romantic despair. She is a reasonable
good wife, and I have some kids which are hellcats but I
value 'em. If I have sense enough to leave well enough
alone, sooner or later I will retire on a pension an' Social
Security an' spend the rest of my life fishin' contended an'
lyin' about what a great guy I used to be. But there's Joe.
I'm worried about Joe.

I'm a maintenance man for the Logics Company. My job
is servicing logics, and I admit modestly that I am pretty
good. I was servicing televisions before that guy Carson
invented his trick circuit that will select any of 'steenteen
million other circuits—in theory there ain't no limit—and
before the Logics Company hooked it into the tank-and-
integrator set-up they were usin' 'em as business-machine
service. They added a vision screen for speed—an' they
found out they'd make logics. They were surprised an'
pleased. They're still findin' out what logics will do, but
everybody's got 'em.

I got Joe, after Laurine nearly got me. You know the
logics setup. You got a logic in your house. It looks like a
vision receiver used to, only it's got keys instead of dials
and you punch the keys for what you wanna get. It's
hooked in to the tank, which has the Carson Circuit all
fixed up with relays. Say you punch "Station SNAFU" on
your logic. Relays in the tank take over an' whatever vision-
program SNAFU is telecastin' comes on your logic's screen.
Or you punch "Sally Hancock's Phone" an' the screen blinks
an' sputters an' you're hooked up with the logic in her
house an' if somebody answers you got a vision-phone connection. But besides that, if you punch for the weather
forecast or who won today's race at Hialeah or who was
mistress of the White House durin' Garfield's administration
or what is PDQ and R sellin' for today, that comes on the
screen too. The relays in the tank do it. The tank is a big
buildin' full of all the facts in creation an' all the recorded
telecasts that ever was made—an' it's hooked in with all

the other tanks all over the country—an' anything you
wanna know or see or hear, you punch for it an' you get it.
Very convenient. Also it does math for you, an' keeps books,
an' acts as consultin' chemist, physicist, astronomer an' tea-
leaf reader, with a "Advice to Lovelorn" thrown in. The
only thing it won't do is tell you exactly what your wife
meant when she said "Oh, you think so, do you?" in that
peculiar kinda voice. Logics don't work good on women.
Only on things that make sense.

Logics are all right, though. They changed civilization,
the highbrows tell us. All on accounta the Carson Circuit.
And Joe shoulda been a perfectly normal logic, keeping
some family or other from wearin' out its brains doin' the
kids' homework for 'em. But somethin' went wrong in the
assembly line. It was somethin' so small that precision
gauges didn't measure it, but it made Joe a individual.
Maybe he didn't know it at first. Or maybe, bein' logical,
he figured out that if he was to show he was different from
other logics they'd scrap him. Which woulda been a brilliant idea. But anyhow, he come off the assembly line, an'
he went through the regular tests without anybody scream-
in' shrilly on findin' out what he was. And he went right on
out an' was duly installed in the home of Mr. Thaddeus
Korlanovitch at 119 East Seventh Street, second floor front.
So far, everything was serene.

The installation happened late Saturday night. Sunday
morning the Korlanovitch kids turned him on an' seen the
Kiddie Shows. Around noon their parents peeled 'em away
from him an' piled 'em in the car. Then they come back
in the house for the lunch they'd forgot an' one of the kids
sneaked back an' they found him punchin' keys for the Kiddie Shows of the week before. They dragged him out an'
went off. But they left Joe turned on.

That was noon. Nothin' happened until two in the afternoon. It was the calm before the storm. Laurine wasn't in
town yet, but she was comin'. I picture Joe sittin' there all
by himself, buzzing meditative. Maybe he run Kiddie

Shows in the empty apartment for a while. But I think he went kinda remote-control exploring in the tank. There ain't any fact that can be said to be a fact that ain't on a data plate in some tank somewhere—unless it's one the technicians are diggin' out an' puttin' on a data plate now. Joe had plenty of material to work on. An' he musta started workin' right off the bat.

Joe ain't vicious, you understand. He ain't like one of these ambitious robots you read about that make up their minds the human race is inefficient and has got to be wiped out an' replaced by thinkin' machines. Joe's just got ambition. If you were a machine, you'd wanna work right, wouldn't you? That's Joe. He wants to work right. An' he's a logic. An' logics can do a lotta things that ain't been found out yet. So Joe, discoverin' the fact, begun to feel restless. He selects some things us dumb humans ain't thought of yet, an' begins to arrange so logics will be called on to do 'em.

That's all. That's everything. But, brother, it's enough!

Things are kinda quiet in the Maintenance Department about two in the afternoon. We are playing pinochle. Then one of the guys remembers he has to call up his wife. He goes to one of the bank of logics in Maintenance and punches the keys for his house. The screen sputters. Then a flash comes on the screen.

"Announcing new and improved logics service! Your logic is now equipped to give you not only consultive but directive service. If you want to do something and don't know how to do it—ask your logic!"

There's a pause. A kinda expectant pause. Then, as if reluctantly, his connection comes through. His wife answers an' gives him hell for somethin' or other. He takes it an' snaps off.

"Whadda you know?" he says when he comes back. He tells us about the flash. "We shoulda been warned about that. There's gonna be a lotta complaints. Suppose a fella asks how to get ridda his wife an' the censor circuits block the question?"

Somebody melds a hundred aces an' says:

"Why not punch for it an' see what happens?"

It's a gag, o' course. But the guy goes over. He punches keys. In theory, a censor block is gonna come on an' the screen will say severely, "Public Policy Forbids This Service." You hafta have censor blocks or the kiddies will be askin' detailed questions about things they're too young to know. And there are other reasons. As you will see.

This fella punches, "How can I get rid of my wife?" Just for the fun of it. The screen is blank for half a second. Then comes a flash. "Service question: Is she blond or brunette?" He hollers to us an we come look. He punches, "Blond." There's another brief pause. Then the screen says, "Hexymetacryloaminoacetine is a constituent of green shoe polish. Take home a frozen meal including dried pea soup. Color the soup with green shoe polish. It will appear to be green-pea soup, Hexymetacryloaminoacetine is a selective poison which is fatal to blond females but not to brunettes or males of any coloring. This fact has not been brought out by human experiment, but is a product of logics service. You cannot be convicted of murder. It is improbable that you will be suspected."

The screen goes blank, and we stare at each other. It's bound to be right. A logic workin' the Carson Circuit can no more make a mistake than any other kinda computin' machine. I call the tank in a hurry.

"Hey, you guys!" I yell. "Somethin's happened! Logics are givin' detailed instructions for wife-murder! Check your censor-circuits—but quick!"

That was close, I think. But little do I know. At that precise instant, over on Monroe Avenue, a drunk starts to punch for somethin' on a logic. The screen says "Announcing new and improved logics service! If you want to do something and don't know how to do it—ask your logic!"

And the drunk says owlish, "I'll do it!" So he cancels his first punching and fumbles around and says: "How can I keep my wife from finding out I've been drinking?" And the screen says, prompt: "Buy a bottle of Franine hair shampoo. It is harmless but contains a detergent which will neutralize ethyl alcohol immediately. Take one teaspoonful for each jigger of hundred-proof you have consumed."

This guy was plenty plastered—just plastered enough to stagger next door and obey instructions. An' five minutes later he was cold sober and writing down the information so he couldn't forget it. It was new, and it was big! He got rich offa that memo! He patented "*SOBUH, The Drink that Makes Happy Homes!*" You can top off any souse with a slug or two of it an' go home sober as a judge. The guy's cussin' income taxes right now!

You can't kick on stuff like that. But a ambitious young fourteen-year-old wanted to buy some kid stuff and his pop wouldn't fork over. He called up a friend to tell his troubles. And his logic says: "If you want to do something and don't know how to do it—Ask your logic!" So this kid punches: "How can I make a lotta money, fast?"

His logic comes through with the simplest, neatest, and the most efficient counterfeitin' device yet known to science. You see, all the data was in the tank. The logic—since Joe had closed some relays here an' there in the tank—simply integrated the facts. That's all. The kid got caught up with three days later, havin' already spent two thousand credits an' havin' plenty more on hand. They hadda time tellin' his counterfeits from the real stuff, an' the only way they done it was that he changed his printer, kid fashion, not bein' able to let somethin' that was workin' right alone.

Those are what you might call samples. Nobody knows all that Joe done. But there was the bank president who got humorous when his logic flashed that "Ask your logic" spiel on him, and jestingly asked how to rob his own bank. An' the logic told him, brief and explicit but good! The bank

president hit the ceiling, hollering for cops. There musta
been plenty of that sorta thing. There was fifty-four more
robberies than usual in the next twenty-four hours, all of
them planned astute an' perfect. Some of 'em they never
did figure out how they'd been done. Joe, he'd gone exploring in the tank and closed some relays like a logic is supposed to do—but only when required—and blocked all censor-circuits an' fixed up this logics service which planned
perfect crimes, nourishing an' attractive meals, counterfeitin' machines, an' new industries with a fine impartiality.
He musta been plenty happy, Joe must. He was functionin'
swell, buzzin' along to himself while the Korlanovitch kids
were off ridin' with their ma an' pa.

They come back at seven o'clock, the kids all happily
wore out with their afternoon of fightin' each other in the
car. Their folks put em to bed and sat down to rest. They
saw Joe's screen flickerin' meditative from one subject to
another an' old man Korlanovitch had had enough excitement for one day. He turned Joe off.

An' at that instant the pattern of relays that Joe had
turned on snapped off, all the offers of directive service
stopped flashin' on logic screens everywhere, an' peace descended on the earth.

For everybody else. But for me. Laurine come to town.
I have often thanked God fervent that she didn't marry
me when I thought I wanted her to. In the intervenin' years
she had progressed. She was blond an' fatal to begin with.
She had got blonder and fataler an' had had four husbands
and one acquittal for homicide an' had acquired a air of
enthusiasm and self-confidence. That's just a sketch of the
background. Laurine was not the kinda former girl-friend
you like to have turning up in the same town with your
wife. But she came to town, an' Monday morning she tuned
right into the middle of Joe's second spasm of activity.

The Korlanovitch kids had turned him on again. I got
these details later and kinda pieced 'em together. An' every
logic in town was dutifully flashin' a notice, "If you want

to do something—ask your logic!" every time they were
turned on for use. More'n that, when people punched for
the morning news, they got a full account of the previous
afternoon's doin's. Which put 'em in a frame of mind to
share in the party. One bright fella demands, "How can
I make a perpetual motion machine?" And his logic sputters
a while an' then comes up with a set-up usin' the Brownian
movement to turn little wheels. If the wheels ain't bigger'n
a eighth of an inch they'll turn, all right, an' practically it's
perpetual motion. Another one asks for the secret of trans-
muting metals. The logic rakes back in the data plates an'
integrates a strictly practical answer. It does take so much
power that you can't make no profit except on radium, but
that pays off good. An' from the fact that for a coupla years
to come the police were turnin' up new and improved jim-
mies, knob-claws for gettin' at safe-innards, and all-purpose
keys that'd open any known lock—why there must have
been other inquirers with a strictly practical viewpoint. Joe
done a lot for technical progress!

But he done more in other lines. Educational, say. None
of my kids are old enough to be int'rested, but Joe by-
passed all censor-circuits because they hampered the service he figured logics should give humanity. So the kids an'
teen-agers who wanted to know what comes after the bees
an' flowers found out. And there is certain facts which men
hope their wives won't do more'n suspect, an' those facts
are just what their wives are really curious about. So when
a woman dials: "How can I tell if Oswald is true to me?"
and her logic tells her—you can figure out how many rows
got started that night when the men come home!

All this while Joe goes on buzzin' happy to himself,
showin' the Korlanovitch kids the animated funnies with
one circuit while with the others he remote-controls the
tank so that all the other logics can give people what they
ask for and thereby raise merry hell.

An' then Laurine gets onto the new service. She turns on

the logic in her hotel room, prob'ly to see the week's style-forecast. But the logic says, dutiful: "If you want to do something—ask your logic!" So Laurine prob'ly looks enthusiastic—she would!—and tries to figure out something to ask. She already knows all about everything she cares about —ain't she had four husbands and shot one?—so I occur to her. She knows this is the town I live in. So she punches, "How can I find Ducky?"

O.K., guy! But that is what she used to call me. She gets a service question. "Is Ducky known by any other name?" So she gives my regular name. And the logic can't find me. Because my logic ain't listed under my name on account of I am in Maintenance and don't want to be pestered when I'm home, and there ain't any data plates on code-listed logics, because the codes get changed so often—like a guy gets plastered an' tells a redhead to call him up, an' on gettin' sober hurriedly has the code changed before she reaches his wife on the screen.

Well! Joe is stumped. That's prob'ly the first question logics service hasn't been able to answer. "How can I locate Ducky?" ! ! Quite a problem! So Joe broods over it while showin' the Korlanovitch kids the animated comic about the cute little boy who carries sticks of dynamite in his hip pocket an' plays practical jokes on everybody. Then he gets the trick. Laurine's screen suddenly flashes:

"Logics special service will work upon your question. Please punch your logic designation and leave it turned on. You will be called back."

Laurine is merely mildly interested, but she punches her hotel-room number and has a drink and takes a nap. Joe sets to work. He has been given a idea.

My wife calls me at Maintenance and hollers. She is fit to be tied. She says I got to do something. She was gonna make a call to the butcher shop. Instead of the butcher or even the "If you want to do something" flash, she got a new one. The screen says, "Service question: What is your name?" She is kinda puzzled, but she punches it. The screen sputters an' then says: "Secretarial Service Demonstration! You—" It reels off her name, address, age, sex, coloring, the amounts of all her charge accounts in all the stores, my name as her husband, how much I get a week, the fact that I've been pinched three times—twice was traffic stuff, and once for a argument I got in with a guy—and the interestin' item that once when she was mad with me she left me for three weeks an' had her address changed to her folks' home. Then it says, brisk: "Logics Service will hereafter keep your personal accounts, take messages, and locate persons you may wish to get in touch with. This demonstration is to introduce the service." Then it connects her with the butcher.

But she don't want meat, then. She wants blood. She calls me.

"If it'll tell me all about myself," she says, fairly boilin', "it'll tell anybody else who punches my name! You've got to stop it!"

"Now, now, honey!" I says. "I didn't know about all this! It's new! But they musta fixed the tank so it won't give out information except to the logic where a person lives!"

"Nothing of the kind!" she tells me, furious. "I tried! And you know that Blossom woman who lives next door! She's been married three times and she's forty-two years old and she says she's only thirty! And Mrs. Hudson's had her husband arrested four times for nonsupport and once for beating her up. And—"

"Hey!" I says. "You mean the logic told you this?"

"Yes!" she wails. "It will tell anybody anything! You've got to stop it! How long will it take?"

"I'll call up the tank," I says. "It can't take long."

"Hurry!" she says, desperate, "before somebody punches my name! I'm going to see what it says about that hussy across the street.'

She snaps off to gather what she can before it's stopped. So I punch for the tank and I get this new "What is your name?" flash. I got a morbid curiosity and I punch my

name, and the screen says: "Were you ever called Ducky?"
I blink. I ain't got no suspicions. I say, "Sure!" And the
screen says, "There is a call for you."

Bingo! There's the inside of a hotel room and Laurine
is reclinin asleep on the bed. She'd been told to leave her
logic turned on an' she'd done it. It is a hot day and she is
trying to be cool. I would say that she oughta not suffer
from the heat. Me, being human, I do not stay as cool as
she looks. But there ain't no need to go into that. After
I get my breath I say, "For Heaven's sake!" and she opens
her eyes.

At first she looks puzzled, like she was thinking is she
getting absent-minded and is this guy somebody she married lately. Then she grabs a sheet and drapes it around
herself and beams at me.

"Ducky!" she says. "How marvelous!"

I say something like "Ugmph!" I am sweating.

She says:

"I put in a call for you, Ducky, and here you are! Isn't
it romantic? Where are you really, Ducky? And when can
you come up? You've no idea how often I've thought of
you!"

I am probably the only guy she ever knew real well that
she has not been married to at some time or another.

I say "Ugmph!" again, and swallow.

"Can you come up instantly?" asks Laurine brightly.

"I'm . . . workin'," I say. "I'll . . . uh . . . call you back."

"I'm terribly lonesome," says Laurine. "Please make it
quick, Ducky! I'll have a drink waiting for you. Have you
ever thought of me?"

"Yeah," I say, feeble. "Plenty!"

"You darling!" says Laurine. Here's a kiss to go on with
until you get here! Hurry, Ducky!"

Then I sweat! I still don't know nothing about Joe,
understand. I cuss out the guys at the tank because I blame
them for this. If Laurine was just another blonde—well—
when it comes to ordinary blondes I can leave 'em alone

or leave 'em alone, either one. A married man gets that way or else. But Laurine has a look of unquenched enthusiasm that gives a man very strange weak sensations at the back of his knees. And she'd had four husbands and shot one and got acquitted.

So I punch the keys for the tank technical room, fumbling. And the screen says: "What is your name?" but I don't want any more. I punch the name of the old guy who's stock clerk in Maintenance. And the screen gives me some pretty interestin' dope—I never woulda thought the old fella had ever had that much pep—and winds up by mentionin' a unclaimed deposit now amountin' to two hundred eighty credits in the First National Bank, which he should look into. Then it spiels about the new secretarial service and gives me the tank at last.

I start to swear at the guy who looks at me. But he says, tired:

"Snap it off, fella. We got troubles an' you're just another. What are the logics doin' now?"

I tell him, and he laughs a hollow laugh.

"A light matter, fella," he says. "A very light matter! We just managed to clamp off all the data plates that give information on high explosives. The demand for instructions in counterfeiting is increasing minute by minute. We are also trying to shut off, by main force, the relays that hook in to data plates that just barely might give advice on the fine points of murder. So if people will only keep busy getting the goods on each other for a while, maybe we'll get a chance to stop the circuits that are shifting credit-balances from bank to bank before everybody's bankrupt except the guys who thought of askin' how to get big bank accounts in a hurry."

"Then," I says hoarse, "shut down the tank! Do somethin'!"

"Shut down the tank?" he says mirthless. "Does it occur to you, fella, that the tank has been doin' all the computin' for every business office for years? It's been handlin' the distribution of ninety-four per cent of all telecast programs, has given out all information on weather, plane schedules, special sales, employment opportunities and news; has handled all person-to-person contacts over wires and recorded every business conversation and agreement— Listen, fella! Logics changed civilization. Logics *are* civilization! If we shut off logics, we go back to a kind of civilization we have forgotten how to run! I'm gettng hysterical myself and that's why I'm talkin like this! If my wife finds out my paycheck is thirty credits a week more than I told her and starts hunting for that redhead—"

He smiles a haggard smile at me and snaps off. And I sit down and put my head in my hands. It's true. If something had happened back in cave days and they'd hadda stop usin' fire— If they'd hadda stop usin' steam in the nineteenth century or electricity in the twentieth— It's like that. We got a very simple civilization. In the nineteen hundreds a man would have to make use of a typewriter, radio, telephone, teletypewriter, newspaper, reference library, encyclopedias, office files, directories, plus messenger service and consulting lawyers, chemists, doctors, dietitians, filing clerks, secretaries—all to put down what he wanted to remember an' to tell him what other people had put down that he wanted to know; to report what he said to somebody else and to report to him what they said back. All we have to have is logics. Anything we want to know or see or hear, or anybody we want to talk to, we punch keys on a logic. Shut off logics and everything goes skiddoo. But Laurine—

Somethin' had happened. I still didn't know what it was. Nobody else knows, even yet. What had happened was Joe. What was the matter with him was that he wanted to work good. All this fuss he was raisin' was, actual, nothin' but stuff we shoulda thought of ourselves. Directive advice, tellin' us what we wanted to know to solve a problem, wasn't but a slight extension of logical-integrator service. Figurin' out a good way to poison a fella's wife was only different in degree from figurin' out a cube root or a guy's bank balance. It was gettin' the answer to a question. But things was goin' to pot because there was too many answers being given to too many questions.

One of the logics in Maintenance lights up. I go over, weary, to answer it. I punch the answer key. Laurine says: "Ducky!"

It's the same hotel room. There's two glasses on the table with drinks in them. One is for me. Laurine's got on some kinda frothy hangin'-around-the-house-with-the-boyfriend outfit that automatic makes you strain your eyes to see if you actual see what you think. Laurine looks at me enthusiastic.

"Ducky!" says Laurine. "I'm lonesome! Why haven't you come up?"

"I . . . been busy," I say, strangling slightly.

"Pooh!" says Laurine. "Listen, Ducky! Do you remember how much in love we used to be?"

I gulp.

"Are you doin' anything this evening?" says Laurine.

I gulp again, because she is smiling at me in a way that a single man would maybe get dizzy, but it gives a old married man like me cold chills. When a dame looks at you possessive—

"Ducky!" says Laurine, impulsive. "I was so mean to you! Let's get married!"

Desperation gives me a voice.

"I . . . got married," I tell her, hoarse.

Laurine blinks. Then she says, courageous:

"Poor boy! But we'll get you outa that! Only it would be nice if we could be married today. Now we can only be engaged!"

"I . . . can't—"

"I'll call up your wife," says Laurine, happy, "and have

a talk with her. You must have a code signal for your logic, darling. I tried to ring your house and noth—"

Click! That's my logic turned off. I turned it off. And I feel faint all over. I got nervous prostration. I got combat fatigue. I got anything you like. I got cold feet.

I beat it outa Maintenance, yellin' to somebody I got a emergency call. I'm gonna get out in a Maintenance car 'an cruise around until it's plausible to go home. Then I'm gonna take the wife an' kids an' beat it for somewheres that Laurine won't ever find me. I don't wanna be fifth in Laurine's series of husbands and maybe the second one she shoots in a moment of boredom. I got experience of blondes. I got experience of Laurine! And I'm scared to death!

I beat it out into traffic in the Maintenance car. There was a disconnected logic in the back, ready to substitute for one that hadda burned-out coil or something that it was easier to switch and fix back in the Maintenance shop. I drove crazy but automatic. It was kinda ironic, if you think of it. I was goin' hoopla over a strictly personal problem, while civilization was crackin' up all around me because other people were havin' their personal problems solved as fast as they could state 'em. It is a matter of record that part of the Mid-Western Electric research guys had been workin' on cold electron-emission for thirty years, to make vacuum tubes that wouldn't need a power source to heat the filament. And one of those fellas was intrigued by the "Ask your logic" flash. He asked how to get cold emission of electrons. And the logic integrates a few squintillion facts on the physics data plates and tells him. Just as casual as it told somebody over in the Fourth Ward how to serve left-over soup in a new attractive way, and somebody else on Mason Street how to dispose of a torso that somebody had left careless in his cellar after ceasing to use same.

Laurine wouldn't never have found me if hadn't been

for this new logics service. But now that it was started—
Zowie! She'd shot one husband and got acquitted. Suppose
she got impatient because I was still married an' asked
logics service how to get me free an' in a spot where I'd
have to marry her by 8:30 p.m.? It woulda told her! Just
like it told that woman out in the suburbs how to make sure
her husband wouldn't run around no more. *Br-r-r-r!* An' like
it told that kid how to find some buried treasure. Remember? He was happy totin' home the gold reserve of the
Hanoverian Bank and Trust Company when they caught
on to it. The logic had told him how to make some kinda
machine that nobody has been able to figure how it works
even yet, only they guess it dodges around a couple extra
dimensions. If Laurine was to start askin' questions with a
technical aspect to them, that would be logics' service meat!
And fella, I was scared! If you think a he-man oughtn't to
be scared of just one blonde—you ain't met Laurine!

I'm drivin' blind when a social-conscious guy asks how to
bring about his own particular system of social organization at once. He don't ask if it's best or if it'll work. He just
wants to get it started. And the logic—or Joe—tells him!
Simultaneous, there's a retired preacher asks how can the
human race be cured of concupiscence. Bein' seventy, he's
pretty safe himself, but he wants to remove the peril to the
spiritual welfare of the rest of us. He finds out. It involves
constructin' a sort of broadcastin' station to emit a certain
wave-pattern an' turnin' it on. Just that. Nothing more. It's
found out afterward, when he is solicitin' funds to construct
it. Fortunate, he didn't think to ask logics how to finance
it, or it woulda told him that, too, an' we woulda all been
cured of the impulses we maybe regret afterward but never
at the time. And there's another group of serious thinkers
who are sure the human race would be a lot better off if
everybody went back to nature an' lived in the woods with
the ants an' poison ivy. They start askin' questions about
how to cause humanity to abandon cities and artificial con-

ditions of living. They practically got the answer in logics service!

Maybe it didn't strike you serious at the time, but while I was drivin' aimless, sweatin' blood over Laurine bein' after me, the fate of civilization hung in the balance. I ain't kiddin'. For instance, the Superior Man gang that sneers at the rest of us was quietly asking questions on what kinda weapons could be made by which Superior men could take over and run things—

But I drove here an' there, sweatin' an' talkin' to myself.

"What I oughta do is ask this wacky logics service how to get outa this mess," I says. "But it'd just tell me a intricate an' foolproof way to bump Laurine off. I wanna have peace! I wanna grow comfortably old and brag to other old guys about what a hellion I used to be, without havin' to go through it an' lose my chance of livin' to be a elderly liar."

I turn a corner at random, there in the Maintenance car.

"It was a nice kinda world once," I says, bitter. "I could go home peaceful and not have belly-cramps wonderin' if a blonde has called up my wife to announce my engagement to her. I could punch keys on a logic without gazing into somebody's bedroom while she is giving her epidermis a air bath and being led to think things I gotta take out in thinkin'. I could—"

Then I groan, rememberin' that my wife, naturally, is gonna blame me for the fact that our private life ain't private any more if anybody has tried to peek into it.

"It was a swell world," I says, homesick for the dear dead days-before-yesterday. "We was playin' happy with our toys like little innocent children until somethin' happened. Like a guy named Joe come in and squashed all our mud pies."

Then it hit me. I got the whole thing in one flash. There ain't nothing in the tank set-up to start relays closin'. Relays are closed exclusive by logics, to get the information the keys are punched for. Nothin' but a logic coulda cooked up the relay patterns that constituted logics service. Humans wouldn't ha' been able to figure it out! Only a logic could integrate all the stuff that woulda made all the other logics work like this—

There was one answer. I drove into a restaurant and went over to a pay-logic an' dropped in a coin.

"Can a logic be modified," I spell out, "to co-operate in long-term planning which human brains are too limited in scope to do?"

The screen sputters. Then it says:

"Definitely yes."

"How great will the modifications be?" I punch.

"Microscopically slight. Changes in dimensions," says the screen. "Even modern precision gauges are not exact enough to check them, however. They can only come about under present manufacturing methods by an extremely improbable accident, which has only happened once."

"How can one get hold of that one accident which can do this highly necessary work?" I punch.

The screen sputters. Sweat broke out on me. I ain't got it figured out close, yet, but what I'm scared of is that whatever is Joe will be suspicious. But what I'm askin' is strictly logical. And logics can't lie. They gotta be accurate. They can't help it.

"A complete logic capable of the work required," says the screen, "is now in ordinary family use in—"

And it gives me the Korlanovitch address and do I go over there! Do I go over there fast! I pull up the Maintenance car in front of the place, and I take the extra logic outa the back, and I stagger up to the Korlanovitch flat and I ring the bell. A kid answers the door.

"I'm from Logics Maintenance," I tell the kid. "An inspection record has shown that your logic is apt to break down any minute. I come to put in a new one before it does."

The kid says "O.K.!" real bright and runs back to the livin'-room where Joe—I got the habit of callin' him Joe later, through just meditatin' about him—is runnin' somethin' the kids wanna look at. I hook in the other logic an' turn it on, conscientious makin' sure it works. Then I say:

"Now kiddies, you punch this one for what you want. I'm gonna take the old one away before it breaks down."

And I glance at the screen. The kiddies have apparently said they wanna look at some real cannibals. So the screen is presenting a anthropological expedition scientific record film of the fertility dance of the Huba-Jouba tribe of West Africa. It is supposed to be restricted to anthropological professors an' post-graduate medical students. But there ain't any censor blocks workin' any more and it's on. The kids are much interested. Me, bein' a old married man, I blush.

I disconnect Joe. Careful. I turn to the other logic and punch keys for Maintenance. I do not get a services flash. I get Maintenance. I feel very good. I report that I am goin' home because I fell down a flight of steps an' hurt my leg. I add, inspired:

"An' say, I was carryin' the logic I replaced an' it's all busted. I left it for the dustman to pick up."

"If you don't turn 'em in," says Stock, "you gotta pay for 'em."

"Cheap at the price," I say.

I go home. Laurine ain't called. I put Joe down in the cellar, careful. If I turned him in, he'd be inspected an' his parts salvaged even if I busted somethin' on him. Whatever part was off-normal might be used again and everything start all over. I can't risk it. I pay for him and leave him be.

That's what happened. You might say I saved civilization an' not be far wrong. I know I ain't goin' to take a chance on havin' Joe in action again. Not while Laurine is livin'. An' there are other reasons. With all the nuts who wanna change the world to their own line o' thinkin', an' the ones that wanna bump people off, an' generally solve their problems— Yeah! Problems are bad, but I figure I better let sleepin' problems lie.

But on the other hand, if Joe could be tamed, somehow, and got to work just reasonable—He could make me a coupla million dollars, easy. But even if I got sense enough not to get rich, an' if I get retired and just loaf around fishin' an' lyin' to other old duffers about what a great guy I used to be— Maybe I'll like it, but maybe I won't. And after all, if I get fed up with bein' old and confined strictly to thinking—why I could hook Joe in long enough to ask: "How can a old guy not stay old?" Joe'll be able to find out. An' he'll tell me.

That couldn't be allowed out general, of course. You gotta make room for kids to grow up. But it's a pretty good world, now Joe's turned off. Maybe I'll turn him on long enough to learn how to stay in it. But on the other hand, maybe—

REQUIEM

by

EDMOND HAMILTON

K ellon thought sourly that he wasn't commanding a
star-ship, he was running a travelling circus. He had
aboard telaudio men with tons of equipment, pontifical
commentators who knew the answer to anything, beautiful
females who were experts on the woman's angle, pompous
bureaucrats after publicity, and entertainment stars who
had come along for the same reason.

He had had a good ship and crew, one of the best in
the Survey. *Had* had. They weren't any more. They had
been taken off their proper job of pushing astrographical
knowledge ever further into the remote regions of the galaxy, and had been sent off with this cargo of costly people
on a totally unnecessary mission.

He said bitterly to himself, "Damn all sentimentalists."

He said aloud, "Does its position check with your calculated orbit, Mr. Riney?"

Riney, the Second, a young and serious man who had been fussing with instruments in the astrogation room, came out and said,

"Yes. Right on the nose. Shall we go in and land now?"

Kellon didn't answer for a moment, standing there in the front of the bridge, a middle-aged man, stocky, square-shouldered, and with his tanned, plain face showing none of the resentment he felt. He hated to give the order but he had to.

"All right, take her in."

He looked gloomily through the filter-windows as they went in. In this fringe-spiral of the galaxy, stars were relatively infrequent, and there were only ragged drifts of them across the darkness. Full ahead shone a small, compact sun like a diamond. It was a white dwarf and had been so for two thousand years, giving forth so little warmth that the planets which circled it had been frozen and ice-locked all that time. They still were, all except the innermost world.

Kellon stared at that planet, a tawny blob. The ice that had sheathed it ever since its primary collapsed into a white dwarf, had now melted. Months before, a dark wandering body had passed very close to this lifeless system. Its passing had perturbed the planetary orbits and the inner planets had started to spiral slowly in toward their sun, and the ice had begun to go.

Viresson, one of the junior officers, came into the bridge looking harassed. He said to Kellon,

"They want to see you down below, sir. Especially Mr. Borrodale. He says it's urgent."

Kellon thought wearily, "Well, I might as well go down and face the pack of them. Here's where they really begin."

He nodded to Viresson, and went down below to the main cabin. The sight of it revolted him. Instead of his own men in it, relaxing or chinning, it held a small and noisy mob of overdressed, overloud men and women, all of whom seemed to be talking at once and uttering brittle, nervous laughter.

"Captain Kellon, I want to ask you—"

"Captain, if you *please*—"

He patiently nodded and smiled and plowed through them to Borrodale. He had been given particular instructions to cooperate with Borrodale, the most famous telaudio commentator in the Federation.

Borrodale was a slightly plump man with a round pink face and incongruously large and solemn black eyes. When he spoke, one recognized at once that deep, incredibly rich and meaningful voice.

"My first broadcast is set for thirty minutes from now, Captain. I shall want a view as we go in. If my men could take a mobile up to the bridge—"

Kellon nodded. "Of course. Mr. Viresson is up there and will assist them in any way."

"Thank you, Captain. Would you like to see the broadcast?"

"I would, yes, but—"

He was interrupted by Lorri Lee, whose glitteringly handsome face and figure and sophisticated drawl made her the idol of all female telaudio reporters.

"*My* broadcast is to be right after landing—remember? I'd like to do it alone, with just the emptiness of that world as background. Can you keep the others from spoiling the effect? Please?"

"We'll do what we can, Kellon mumbled. And as the rest of the pack converged on him he added hastily, "I'll talk to you later. Mr. Borrodale's broadcast—"

He got through them, following after Borrodale toward the cabin that had been set up as a telaudio-transmitter room. It had, Kellon thought bitterly, once served an honest purpose, holding the racks of soil and water and other samples from far worlds. But that had been when they were doing an honest Survey job, not chaperoning chattering fools on this sentimental pilgrimage.

The broadcasting set-up was beyond Kellon. He didn't want to hear this but it was better than the mob in the main cabin. He watched as Borrodale made a signal. The monitor-screen came alive.

It showed a dun-colored globe spinning in space, growing visibly larger as they swept toward it. Now straggling seas were identifiable upon it. Moments passed and Borrodale did not speak, just letting that picture go out. Then his deep voice spoke over the picture, with dramatic simplicity.

"You are looking at the Earth," he said.

Silence again, and the spinning brownish ball was bigger now, with white clouds ragged upon it. And then Borrodale spoke again.

"You who watch from many worlds in the galaxy—this is the homeland of our race. Speak its name to yourselves. The Earth."

Kellon felt a deepening distaste. This was all true, but still it was phony. What was Earth now to him, or to Borrodale, or his billions of listeners? But it was a story, a sentimental occasion, so they had to pump it up into something big.

"Some thirty-five hundred years ago," Borrodale was saying, "our ancestors lived on this world alone. That was when they first went into space. To these other planets first —but very soon, to other stars. And so our Federation began, our community of human civilization on many stars and worlds."

Now, in the monitor, the view of Earth's dun globe had been replaced by the face of Borrodale in close-up. He paused dramatically.

"Then, over two thousand years ago, it was discovered that the sun of Earth was about to collapse into a white dwarf. So those people who still remained on Earth left it forever and when the solar change came, it and the other planets became mantled in eternal ice. And now, within months, the final end of the old planet of our origin is at hand. It is slowly spiralling toward the sun and soon it will plunge into it as Mercury and Venus have already done. And when that occurs, the world of man's origin will be gone forever."

Again the pause, for just the right length of time, and then Borrodale continued in a voice expertly pitched in a lower key.

"We on this ship—we humble reporters and servants of the vast telaudio audience on all the worlds—have come here so that in these next weeks we can give you this last look at our ancestral world. We think—we hope—that you'll find interest in recalling a past that is almost legend."

And Kellon thought, "The bastard has no more interest in this old planet than I have, but he surely is smooth."

As soon as the broadcast ended, Kellon found himself besieged once more by the clamoring crowd in the main cabin. He held up his hand in protest.

"Please, now now—we have a landing to make first. Will you come with me, Doctor Darnow?"

Darnow was from Historical Bureau, and was the titular head of the whole expedition, although no one paid him much attention. He was a sparrowy, elderly man who babbled excitedly as he went with Kellon to the bridge.

He, at least, was sincere in his interest, Kellon thought. For that matter, so were all the dozen-odd scientists who were aboard. But they were far outnumbered by the fat cats and big brass out for publicity, the professional enthusers and sentimentalists. A real hell of a job the Survey had given him!

In the bridge, he glanced through the window at the dun-colored planet and its satellite. Then he asked Darnow, "You said something about a particular place where you wanted to land?"

The historiographer bobbed his head, and began unfolding a big, old-fashioned chart.

"See this continent here? Along its eastern coast were a lot of the biggest cities, like New York."

Kellon remembered that name, he'd learned it in school history, a long time ago.

Darnow's finger stabbed the chart. "If you could land there, right on the island—"

Kellon studied the relief features, then shook his head. "Too low. There'll be great tides as time goes on and we can't take chances. That higher ground back inland a bit should be all right, though."

Darnow looked disappointed. "Well, I suppose you're right."

Kellon told Riney to set up the landing-pattern. Then he asked Darnow skeptically,

"You surely don't expect to find much in those old cities now—not after they've had all that ice on them for two thousand years?"

"They'll be badly damaged, of course," Darnow admitted. "But there should be a vast number of relics. I could study here for years—"

"We haven't got years, we've got only a few months before this planet gets too close to the Sun," said Kellon. And he added mentally, "Thank God."

The ship went into its landing-pattern. Atmosphere whined outside its hull and then thick gray clouds boiled and raced around it. It went down through the cloud layer and moved above a dull brown landscape that had flecks of white in its deeper valleys. Far ahead there was the glint of a gray ocean. But the ship came down toward a rolling brown plain and settled there, and then there was the expected thunderclap of silence that always followed the shutting off of all machinery.

Kellon looked at Riney, who turned in a moment from the test-panel with a slight surprise on his face. "Pressure oxygen, humidity, everything—all optimum." And then he said, "But of course. This place *was* optimum."

Kellon nodded. He said, "Doctor Darnow and I will have a look out first. Viresson, you keep our passengers in."

When he and Darnow went to the lower airlock he heard a buzzing clamor from the main cabin and he judged that Viresson was having his hands full. The people in there were not used to being said no to, and he could imagine their resentment.

Cold, damp air struck a chill in Kellon when they stepped down out of the airlock. They stood on muddy, gravelly ground that squashed a little under their boots as they trudged away from the ship. They stopped and looked around, shivering.

Under the low gray cloudy sky there stretched a sad, sunless brown landscape. Nothing broke the drab color of raw soil, except the shards of ice still lingering in low places. A heavy desultory wind stirred the raw air, and then was still. There was not a sound except the clinkclinking of the ship's skin cooling and contracting, behind them. Kellon thought that no amount of sentimentality could make this anything but a dreary world.

But Darnow's eyes were shining. "We'll have to make every minute of the time count," he muttered. "Every minute."

Within two hours, the heavy broadcast equipment was being trundled away from the ship on two motor-tracs that headed eastward. On one of the tracs rode Lorri Lee, resplendent in a lilac-colored costume of synthesilk.

Kellon, worried about the possibility of quicksands, went along for that first broadcast from the cliffs that looked down on the ruins of New York. He wished he hadn't, when it got under way.

For Lorri Lee, her blonde head bright even in the dull light, turned loose all her practised charming gestures for the broadcast cameras, as she gestured with pretty excitement down toward the ruins.

"It's so *unbelievable!*" she cried to a thousand worlds. "To be here on Earth, to see the old places again—it *does* something to you!"

It did something to Kellon. It made him feel sick at his stomach. He turned and went back to the ship, feeling at that moment that if Lorri Lee went into a quicksand on the way back, it would be no great loss.

But that first day was only the beginning. The big ship quickly became the center of multifarious and continuous broadcasts. It had been especially equipped to beam strongly to the nearest station in the Federation network, and its transmitters were seldom quiet.

Kellon found that Darnow, who was supposed to coordinate all this programming, was completely useless. The little historian was living in a seventh heaven on this old planet which had been uncovered to view for the first time in milennia, and he was away most of the time on field trips of his own. It fell to his assistant, an earnest and worried and harassed young man, to try to reconcile the clashing claims and demands of the highly temperamental broadcasting stars.

Kellon felt an increasing boredom at having to stand around while all this tosh went out over the ether. These people were having a field-day but he didn't think much of them and of their broadcasts. Roy Quayle, the young male fashion designer, put on a semi-humorous, semi-nostalgic display of the old Earth fashions, with the prettier girls wearing some of the ridiculous old costumes he had had duplicated. Barden, the famous teleplay producer, ran off ancient films of the old Earth dramas that had everyone in stitches. Jay Maxson, a rising politician in Federation Congress, discussed with Borrodale the governmental systems of the old days, in a way calculated to give his own Wide-Galaxy Party none the worst of it. The Arcturus Players, that brilliant group of young stage-folk, did readings of old Earth dramas and poems.

It was, Kellon thought disgustedly, just playing. Grown people, famous people, seizing the opportunity given by the accidental end of a forgotten planet to posture in the spotlight like smart-aleck children. There was real work to do in the· galaxy, the work of the Survey, the endless and wearying but always-fascinating job of charting the wild systems and worlds. And instead of doing that job, he was condemned to spend weeks and months here with these phonies.

The scientists and historians he respected. They did few broadcasts and they did not fake their interest. It was one of them, Haller, the biologist, who excitedly showed Kellon a handful of damp soil a week after their arrival.

"Look at *that!*" he said proudly.

Kellon stared. "What?"

"Those seeds—they're common weed-grass seeds. Look at them."

Kelon looked, and now he saw that from each of the tiny seeds projected a new-looking hairlike tendril.

"They're sprouting?" he said unbelievingly.

Haller nodded happily. "I was hoping for it. You see, it was almost spring in the northern hemisphere, according to the records, when Sol collapsed suddenly into a white dwarf. Within hours the temperature plunged and the hydrosphere and atmosphere began to freeze."

"But surely that would kill all plant-life?"

"No," said Haller. "The larger plants, trees, perennial shrubs, and so on, yes. But the seeds of the smaller annuals just froze into suspended animation. Now the warmth that melted them is causing germination."

"Then we'll have grass—small plants?"

"Very soon, the way the warmth is increasing."

It was, indeed, getting a little warmer all the time as these first weeks went by. The clouds lifted one day and there was brilliant, thin white sunshine from the little diamond sun. And there came a morning when they found the rolling landscape flushed with a pale tint of green.

Grass grew. Weeds grew, vines grew, all of them seeming to rush their growth as though they knew that this, their last season, would not be long. Soon the raw brown mud of the hills and valleys had been replaced by a green carpet, and everywhere taller growths were shooting up, and flowers beginning to appear. Hepaticas, bluebells, dandelions, violets, bloomed once more.

Kellon took a long walk, now that he did not have to plow through mud. The chattering people around the ship, the constant tug and pull of clashing temperaments, the brittle, febrile voices, got him down. He felt better to get away by himself.

The grass and the flowers had come back but otherwise this was still an empty world. Yet there was a certain peace of mind in tramping up and down the long green rolling slopes. The sun was bright and cheerful now, and white clouds dotted the sky, and the warm wind whispered as he sat upon a ridge and looked away westward where nobody was, or would ever be again.

"Damned dull," he thought. "But at least it's better than back with the gabblers."

He sat for a long time in the slanting sunshine, feeling his bristling nerves relax. The grass stirred about him, rippling in long waves, and the taller flowers nodded.

No other movement, no other life. A pity, he thought, that there were no birds for this last spring of the old planet—not even a butterfly. Well, it made no difference, all this wouldn't last long.

As Kellon tramped back through the deepening dusk, he suddenly became aware of a shining bubble in the darkening sky. He stopped and stared up at it and then remembered. Of course, it was the old planet's moon—during the cloudy nights he had forgotten all about it. He went on, with its vague light about him.

When he stepped back into the lighted main cabin of the ship, he was abruptly jarred out of his relaxed mood. A first-class squabble was going on, and everybody was either contributing to it or commenting on it. Lorri Lee, looking like a pretty child complaining of a hurt, was maintaining that she should have broadcast time next day for her special woman's-interest feature, and somebody else disputed her claim, and young Vallely, Darnow's assistant, looked harried and upset. Kellon got by them without being noticed, locked the door of his cabin and poured himself a long drink, and damned Survey all over again for this assignment. *109549*

He took good care to get out of the ship early in the morning, before the storm of temperament blew up again. He left Viresson in charge of the ship, there being nothing for any of them to do now anyway, and legged it away over the green slopes before anyone could call him back.

They had five more weeks of this, Kellon thought. Then, thank God, Earth would be getting so near the Sun that they must take the ship back into its proper element of space. Until that wished-for day arrived, he would stay out of sight as much as possible.

He walked miles each day. He stayed carefully away from the east and the ruins of old New York, where the others so often were. But he went north and west and south, over the grassy, flowering slopes of the empty world. At least it was peaceful, even though there was nothing at all to see.

But after a while, Kellon found that there were things to see if you looked for them. There was the way the sky changed, never seeming to look the same twice. Sometimes it was deep blue and white clouds sailed it like mighty ships. And then it would suddenly turn gray and miserable, and rain would drizzle on him, to be ended when a lance of sunlight shot through the clouds and slashed them to flying ribbons. And there was a time when, upon a ridge, he watched vast thunderheads boil up and darken in the west and black storm marched across the land like an army with banners of lightning and drums of thunder.

The winds and the sunshine, the sweetness of the air and
the look of the moonlight and the feel of the yielding grass
under his feet, all seemed oddly right. Kellon had walked
on many worlds under the glare of many-colored suns, and
some of them he had not liked at all, but never had he
found a world that seemed so exactly attuned to his body
as this outworn, empty planet.

He wondered vaguely what it had been like when there
were trees and birds, and animals of many kinds, and roads
and cities. He borrowed film-books from the reference library Darnow and the others had brought, and looked at
them in his cabin of nights. He did not really care very
much but at least it kept him out of the broils and quar-
rels, and it had a certain interest.

Thereafter in his wandering strolls, Kellon tried to see
the place as it would have been in the long ago. There
would have been robins and bluebirds, and yellow-and-
black bumblebees nosing the flowers, and tall trees with
names that were equally strange to him, elms and willows
and sycamores. And small furred animals, and humming
clouds of insects, and fish and frogs in the pools and
streams, a whole vast complex symphony of life, long gone,
long forgotten.

But were all the men and women and children who had
lived here less forgotten? Borrodale and the others talked
much on their broadcasts about the people of old Earth,
but that was just a faceless name, a term that meant nothing. Not one of those millions, surely, had ever thought of
himself as part of a numberless multitude. Each one had
been to himself, and to those close to him or her, an individual, unique and never to be exactly repeated, and what
did the glib talkers know of all those individuals, what
could anyone know?

Kellon found traces of them here and there, bits of flotsam that even the crush of the ice had spared. A twisted
piece of steel, a girder or rail that someone had labored to

make. A quarry with the tool-marks still on the rocks, where surely men had once sweated in the sun. The broken shards of concrete that stretched away in a ragged line to make a road upon which men and women had once travelled, hurrying upon missions of love or ambition, greed or fear.

He found more than that, a startling find that he made by purest chance. He followed a brook that ran down a very narrow valley, and at one point he leaped across it and as he landed he looked up and saw that there was a house.

Kellon thought at first that it was miraculously preserved whole and unbroken, and surely that could not be. But when he went closer he saw that this was only illusion and that destruction had been at work upon it too. Still, it remained, incredibly, a recognizable house.

It was a rambling stone cottage with low walls and a slate roof, set close against the steep green wall of the valley. One gable-end was smashed in, and part of that end wall. Studying the way it was embayed in the wall, Kellon decided that a chance natural arch of ice must have preserved it from the grinding pressure that had shattered almost all other structures.

The windows and doors were only gaping openings. He went inside and looked around the cold shadows of what had once been a room. There were some wrecked pieces of rotting furniture, and dried mud banked along one wall contained unrecognizable bits of rusted junk, but there was not much else. It was chill and oppressive in there, and he went out and sat on the little terrace in the sunshine.

He looked at the house. It could have been built no later than the Twentieth Century, he thought. A good many different people must have lived in it during the hundreds of years before the evacuation of Earth.

Kellon thought that it was strange that the airphoto surveys that Darnow's men had made in quest of relics had not discovered the place. But then it was not so strange, the stone walls were so grayly inconspicuous and it was set so deeply into the sheltering bay of the valley wall.

His eye fell on eroded lettering on the cement side of the terrace, and he went and brushed the soil off that place. The words were time-eaten and faint but he could read them.

"Ross and Jennie—Their House."

Kellon smiled. Well, at least he knew now who once had lived here, who probably had built the place. He could imagine two young people happily scratching the words in the wet cement, exuberant with achievement. And who had Ross and Jennie been, and where were they now?

He walked around the place. To his surprise, there was a ragged flower-garden at one side. A half-dozen kinds of brilliant little flowers, unlike the wild ones of the slopes, grew in patchy disorder here. Seeds of an old garden had been ready to germinate when the long winter of Earth came down, and had slept in suspended animation until the ice melted and the warm blooming time came at last. He did not know what kinds of flowers these were, but there was a brave jauntiness about them that he liked.

Starting back across the green land in the soft twilight, Kellon thought that he should tell Darnow about the place. But if he did, the gabbling pack in the ship would certainly stampede toward it. He could imagine the solemn and cute and precious broadcasts that Borrodale and the Lee woman and the rest of them would stage from the old house.

"No," he thought. "The devil with them."

He didn't care anything himself about the old house, it was just that it was a refuge of quiet he had found and he didn't want to draw to it the noisy horde he was trying to escape.

Kellon was glad in the following days that he had not told. The house gave him a place to go to, to poke around and investigate, a focus for his interest in this waiting time. He spent hours there, and never told anyone at all.

Haller, the biologist, lent him a book on the flowers of Earth, and he brought it with him and used it to identify those in the ragged garden. Verbenas, pinks, morning glories, and the bold red and yellow ones called nasturtiums. Many of these, he read, did not do well on other worlds and had never been successfully transplanted. If that was so, this would be their last blooming anywhere at all.

He rooted around the interior of the house, trying to figure out how people had lived in it. It was strange, not at all like a modern metalloy house. Even the interior walls were thick beyond belief, and the windows seemed small and pokey. The biggest room was obviously where they had lived most, and its window-openings looked out on the little garden and the green valley and brook beyond.

Kellon wondered what they had been like, the Ross and Jennie who had once sat here together and looked out these windows. What things had been important to them? What had hurt them, what had made them laugh? He himself had never married, the far-ranging captains of the Survey seldom did. But he wondered about this marriage of long ago, and what had come of it. Had they had children, did their blood still run on the far worlds? But even if it did, what was that now to those two of long ago?

There had been a poem about flowers at the end of the old book on flowers Haller had lent him, and he remembered some of it.

All are at one now, roses and lovers,
Not known of the winds and the fields and the sea,
Not a breath of the time that has been hovers
In the air now soft with a summer to be.

Well, yes, Kellon thought, they were all at one now, the Rosses and the Jennies and the things they had done and the things they had thought, all at one now in the dust of this old planet whose fiery final summer would be soon, very soon. Physically, everything that had been done, every-afternoon sunshine, trying to imagine what it had been like when the man and woman named Ross and Jennie had one who had lived on Earth was still here in its atoms, excepting the tiny fraction of its matter that had sped to other worlds.

He thought of the names that were so famous still through all the galactic worlds, names of men and women and places. Shakespeare, Plato, Beethoven, Blake, the old splendor of Babylon and the bones of Angkor and the humble houses of his own ancestors, all here, all still here.

Kellon mentally shook himself. He didn't have enough to do, that was his trouble, to be brooding here on such shadowy things. He had seen all there was to this queer little old place, and there was no use in coming back to it.

But he came back. It was not, he told himself, as though he had any sentimental antiquarian interests in this old place. He had heard enough of that kind of gush from all the glittering phonies in the ship. He was a Survey man and all he wanted was to get back to his job, but while he was stuck here it was better to be roaming the green land or poking about this old relic than to have to listen to the endless babbling and quarrelling of those others.

They were quarrelling more and more, because they were tired of it here. It had seemed to them a fine thing to posture upon a galactic stage by helping to cover the end of Earth, but time dragged by and their flush of synthetic enthusiasm wore thin. They could not leave, the expedition must broadcast the final climax of the planet's end, but that was still weeks away. Darnow and his scholars and scientists, busy coming and going to many old sites, could have stayed here forever but the others were frankly bored.

But Kellon found in the old house enough interest to keep the waiting from being too oppressive. He had read a good bit now about the way things had been here in the old days, and he sat long hours on the little terrace in the afternoon sunshine, trying to imagine what it had been like when the man and woman named Ross and Jennie had lived here.

So strange, so circumscribed, that old life seemed now! Most people had had ground-cars in those days, he had read, and had gone back and forth in them to the cities where they worked. Did both the man and woman go, or just the man? Did the woman stay in the house, perhaps with their children if they had any, and in the afternoons did she do things in the little flower garden where a few bright, ragged survivors still bloomed? Did they ever dream that some future day when they were long gone, their house would lie empty and silent with no visitor except a stranger from far-off stars? He remembered a line in one of the old plays the Arcturus Players had read. Come like shadows, so depart.

No, Kellon thought, Ross and Jennie were shadows now but they had not been then. To them, and to all the other people he could visualize going and coming busily about the Earth in those days, it was he, the future, the man yet to come, who was the shadow. Alone here, sitting and trying to imagine the long ago, Kellon had an eery feeling sometimes that his vivid imaginings of people and crowded cities and movement and laughter were the reality and that he himself was only a watching wraith.

Summer days came swiftly, hot and hotter. Now the white sun was larger in the heavens and pouring down such light and heat as Earth had not received for millennia. And all the green life across it seemed to respond with an exultant surge of final growth, an act of joyous affirmation that Kellon found infinitely touching. Now even the nights were warm, and the winds blew thrilling soft, and on the distant beaches the ocean leaped up in a laughter of spray and thunder, running in great solar tides.

With a shock as though awakened from dreaming, Kellon suddenly realized that only a few days were left. The spiral was closing in fast now and very quickly the heat would mount beyond all tolerance.

He would, he told himself, be very glad to leave. There

would be the wait in space until it was all over, and then he could go back to his own work, his own life, and stop fussing over shadows because there was nothing else to do.

Yes. He would be glad.

Then when only a few days were left, Kellon walked out again to the old house and was musing over it when a voice spoke behind him.

"Perfect," said Borrodale's voice. "A perfect relic."

Kellon turned, feeling somehow startled and dismayed. Borrodale's eyes were alight with interest as he surveyed the house, and then he turned to Kellon.

"I was walking when I saw you, Captain, and thought I'd catch up to you. Is this where you've been going so often?"

Kellon, a little guiltily, evaded. "I've been here a few times."

"But why in the world didn't you *tell* us about this?" exclaimed Borrodale. "Why, we can do a terrific final broadcast from here. A typical ancient home of· Earth. Roy can put some of the Players in the old costumes, and we'll show them living here the way people did—"

Unexpectedly to himself, a violent reaction came up in Kellon. He said roughly,

"No."

Borrodale arched his eyebrows. "No? But why not?"

Why not, indeed? What difference could it possibly make to him if they swarmed all over the old house, laughing at its ancientness and its inadequacies, posing grinning for the cameras in front of it, prancing about in old-fashioned costumes and making a show of it. What could that mean to him, who cared nothing about this forgotten planet or anything on it?

And yet something in him revolted at what they would do here, and he said,

"We might have to take off very suddenly, now. Having you all out here away from the ship could involve a dangerous delay."

"You said yourself we wouldn't take off for a few days

yet!" exclaimed Borrodale. And he added firmly, "I don't know why you should want to obstruct us, Captain. But I can go over your head to higher authority."

He went away, and Kellon thought unhappily, he'll message back to Survey headquarters and I'll get my ears burned off, and why the devil did I do it anyway? I must be getting real planet-happy.

He went and sat down on the terrace, and watched until the sunset deepened into dusk. The moon came up white and brilliant, but the air was not quiet tonight. A hot, dry wind had begun to blow, and the stir of the tall grass made the slopes and plains seem vaguely alive. It was as though a queer pulse had come into the air and the ground, as the Sun called its child homeward and Earth strained to answer. The house dreamed in the silver light, and the flowers in the garden rustled.

Borrodale came back, a dark pudgy figure in the moonlight. He said triumphantly,

"I got through to your headquarters. They've ordered your full cooperation. We'll want to make our first broadcast here tomorrow."

Kellon stood up. "No."

"You can't ignore an order—"

"We won't be here tomorrow," said Kellon. "It is my responsibility to get the ship off Earth in ample time for safety. We take off in the morning."

Borrodale was silent for a moment, and when he spoke his voice had a puzzled quality.

"You're advancing things just to block our broadcast, of course. I just can't understand your attitude."

Well, Kellon thought, he couldn't quite understand it himself, so how could he explain it? He remained silent, and Borrodale looked at him and then at the old house.

"Yet maybe I do understand," Borrodale said thoughtfully, after a moment. "You've come here often, by yourself. A man can get too friendly with ghosts—"

Kellon said roughly, "Don't talk nonsense. We'd better get back to the ship, there's plenty to do before take off."

Borrodale did not speak as they went back out of the moonlit valley. He looked back once, but Kellon did not look back.

They took the ship off twelve hours later, in a morning made dull and ominous by racing clouds. Kellon felt a sharp relief when they cleared atmosphere and were out in the depthless, starry blackness. He knew where he was, in space. It was the place where a spaceman belonged. He'd get a stiff reprimand for this later, but he was not sorry.

They put the ship into a calculated orbit, and waited. Days, many of them, must pass before the end came to Earth. It seemed quite near the white sun now, and its Moon had slid away from it on a new distorted orbit, but even so it would be a while before they could broadcast to a watching galaxy the end of its ancestral world.

Kellon stayed much of that time in his cabin. The gush that was going out over the broadcasts now, as the grand finale approached, made him sick. He wished the whole thing was over. It was, he told himself, getting to be a bore—

An hour and twenty minutes to E-time, and he supposed he must go up to the bridge and watch it. The mobile camera had been set up there and Borrodale and as many others of them as could crowd in were there. Borrodale had been given the last hour's broadcast, and it seemed that the others resented this.

"Why must you have the whole last hour?" Lorri Lee was saying bitterly to Borrodale. "It's not fair."

Quayle nodded angrily. "There'll be the biggest audience in history, and we should all have a chance to speak."

Borrodale answered them, and the voices rose and bickered, and Kellon saw the broadcast technicians looking worried. Beyond them through the filter-window he could see the dark dot of the planet closing on the white star. The

Sun called, and it seemed that with quickened eagerness Earth moved on the last steps of its long road. And the clamoring, bickering voices in his ears suddenly brought rage to Kellon.

"Listen," he said to the broadcast men. "Shut off all sound transmission. You can keep the picture on, but no sound."

That shocked them all into silence. The Lee woman finally protested, "Captain Kellon, you can't!"

"I'm in full command when in space, and I can, and do," he said.

"But the broadcast, the commentary—"

Kellon said wearily, "Oh, for Christ's sake all of you shut up, and let the planet die in peace."

He turned his back on them. He did not hear their resentful voices, did not even hear when they fell silent and watched through the dark filter-windows as he was watching, as the camera and the galaxy was watching.

And what was there to see but a dark dot almost engulfed in the shining veils of the sun? He thought that already the stones of the old house must be beginning to vaporize. And now the veils of light and fire almost concealed the little planet, as the star gathered in its own.

All the atoms of old Earth, Kellon thought, in this moment bursting free to mingle with the solar being, all that had been Ross and Jennie, all that had been Shakespeare and Schubert, gay flowers and running streams, oceans and rocks and the wind of the air, received into the brightness that had given them life.

They watched in silence, but there was nothing more to see, nothing at all. Silently the camera was turned off.

Kellon gave an order, and presently the ship was pulling out of orbit, starting the long voyage back. By that time the others had gone, all but Borrodale. He said to Borrodale, without turning.

"Now go ahead and send your complaint to headquarters."

Borrodale shook his head. "Silence can be the best requiem of all. There'll be no complaint. I'm glad now, Captain."

"Glad?"

"Yes," said Borrodale. "I'm glad that Earth had one true mourner, at the last."

WITH

FOLDED HANDS

---

by

JACK WILLIAMSON

Underhill was walking home from the office, because his wife had the car, the afternoon he first met the new mechanicals. His feet were following his usual diagonal path across a weedy vacant block—his wife usually had the car—and his preoccupied mind was rejecting various impossible ways to meet his notes at the Two Rivers bank, when a new wall stopped him.

The wall wasn't any common brick or stone, but something sleek and bright and strange. Underhill stared up at a long new building. He felt vaguely annoyed and surprised at this glittering obstruction—it certainly hadn't been here last week.

Then he saw the thing in the window.

The window itself wasn't any ordinary glass. The wide, dustless panel was completely transparent, so that only the glowing letters fastened to it showed that it was there at all. The letters made a severe, modernistic sign:

Two Rivers Agency
HUMANOID INSTITUTE
The Perfect Mechanicals
"To Serve and Obey,
And Guard Men from Harm."

His dim annoyance sharpened, because Underhill was in the mechanicals business himself. Times were already hard enough, and mechanicals were a drug on the market. Androids, mechanoids, electronoids, automatoids, and ordinary robots. Unfortunately, few of them did all the salesmen promised, and the Two Rivers market was already sadly oversaturated.

Underhill sold androids—when he could. His next consignment was due tomorrow, and he didn't quite know how to meet the bill.

Frowning, he paused to stare at the thing behind that invisible window. He had never seen a humanoid. Like any mechanical not at work, it stood absolutely motionless. Smaller and slimmer than a man. A shining black, its sleek silicone skin had a changing sheen of bronze and metallic blue. Its graceful oval face wore a fixed look of alert and slightly surprised solicitude. Altogether, it was the most beautiful mechanical he had ever seen.

Too small, of course, for much practical utility. He murmured to himself a reassuring quotation from the *Android Salesman*: "Androids are big—because the makers refuse to sacrifice power, essential functions, or dependability. Androids are your biggest buy!"

The transparent door slid open as he turned toward it, and he walked into the haughty opulence of the new display room to convince himself that these streamlined items were just another flash effort to catch the woman shopper.

He inspected the glittering layout shrewdly, and his breezy optimism faded. He had never heard of the Humanoid Institute, but the invading firm obviously had big money and big-time merchandising know-how.

He looked around for a salesman, but it was another mechanical that came gliding silently to meet him. A twin of the one in the window, it moved with a quick, surprising grace. Bronze and blue lights flowed over its lustrous blackness, and a yellow name plate flashed from its naked breast:

HUMANOID
Serial No. 81-H-B-27
The Perfect Mechanical
"To Serve and Obey,
And Guard Men from Harm."

Curiously, it had no lenses. The eyes in its bald oval head were steel-colored, blindly staring. But it stopped a few feet in front of him, as if it could see anyhow, and it spoke to him with a high, melodious voice:

"At your service, Mr. Underhill."

The use of his name startled him, for not even the androids could tell one man from another. But this was a clever merchandising stunt, of course, not too difficult in a town the size of Two Rivers. The salesman must be some local man, prompting the mechanical from behind the partition. Underhill erased his momentary astonishment, and said loudly:

"May I see your salesman, please?"

"We employ no human salesmen, sir," its soft silvery voice replied instantly. "The Humanoid Institute exists to serve mankind, and we require no human service. We ourselves can supply any information you desire, sir, and accept your order for immediate humanoid service."

Underhill peered at it dazedly. No mechanicals were competent even to recharge their own batteries and reset their own relays, much less to operate their own branch offices. The blind eyes stared blankly back, and he looked uneasily around for any booth or curtain that might conceal the salesman.

Meanwhile, the sweet thin voice resumed persuasively:
"May we come out to your home for a free trial demonstration, sir? We are anxious to introduce our service on your planet, because we have been successful in eliminating human unhappiness on so many others. You will find us far superior to the old electronic mechanicals in use here."

Underhill stepped back uneasily. He reluctantly abandoned his search for the hidden salesman, shaken by the idea of any mechanicals promoting themselves. That would upset the whole industry.

"At least you must take some advertising matter, sir."

Moving with a somehow appalling graceful deftness, the small black mechanical brought him an illustrated booklet from a table by the wall. To cover his confused and increasing alarm, he thumbed through the glossy pages.

In a series of richly colored before-and-after pictures, a chesty blond girl was stooping over a kitchen stove, and then relaxing in a daring negligee while a little black mechanical knelt to serve her something. She was wearily hammering a typewriter, and then lying on an ocean beach, in a revealing sun suit, while another mechanical did the typing. She was toiling at some huge industrial machine, and then dancing in the arms of a golden-haired youth, while a black humanoid ran the machine.

Underhill sighed wistfully. The android company didn't supply such fetching sales material. Women would find this booklet irresistible, and they selected eighty-six per cent of all mechanicals sold. Yes, the competition was going to be bitter.

"Take it home, sir," the sweet voice urged him. "Show it to your wife. There is a free trial demonstration order blank on the last page, and you will notice that we require no payment down."

He turned numbly, and the door slid open for him. Retreating dazedly, he discovered the booklet still in his hand. He crumpled it furiously, and flung it down. The small black thing picked it up tidily, and the insistent silver voice rang after him:

"We shall call at your office tomorrow, Mr. Underhill, and send a demonstration unit to your home. It is time to discuss the liquidation of your business, because the electronic mechanicals you have been selling cannot compete with us. And we shall offer your wife a free trial demonstration."

Underhill didn't attempt to reply, because he couldn't trust his voice. He stalked blindly down the new sidewalk to the corner, and paused there to collect himself. Out of his startled and confused impressions, one clear fact emerged—things looked black for the agency.

Bleakly, he stared back at the haughty splendor of the new building. It wasn't honest brick or stone; that invisible window wasn't glass; and he was quite sure the foundation for it hadn't even been staked out, the last time Aurora had the car.

He walked on around the block, and the new sidewalk took him near the rear entrance. A truck was backed up to it, and several slim black mechanicals were silently busy, unloading huge metal crates.

He paused to look at one of the crates. It was labeled for interstellar shipment. The stencils showed that it had come from the Humanoid Institute, on Wing IV. He failed to recall any planet of that designation; the outfit must be big.

Dimly, inside the gloom of the warehouse beyond the truck, he could see black mechanicals opening the crates. A lid came up, revealing dark, rigid bodies, closely packed. One by one, they came to life. They climbed out of the crate, and sprang gracefully to the floor. A shining black, glinting with bronze and blue, they were all identical.

One of them came out past the truck, to the sidewalk, staring with blind steel eyes. Its high silver voice spoke to him melodiously:

"At your service, Mr. Underhill."

He fled. When his name was promptly called by a courteous mechanical, just out of the crate in which it had been imported from a remote and unknown planet, he found the experience trying.

Two blocks along, the sign of a bar caught his eye, and he took his dismay inside. He had made it a business rule not to drink before dinner, and Aurora didn't like him to drink at all; but these new mechanicals, he felt, had made the day exceptional.

Unfortunately, however, alcohol failed to brighten the brief visible future of the agency. When he emerged, after an hour, he looked wistfully back in hope that the bright new building might have vanished as abruptly as it came. It hadn't. He shook his head dejectedly, and turned uncertainly homeward.

Fresh air had cleared his head somewhat, before he arrived at the neat white bungalow in the outskirts of the town, but it failed to solve his business problems. He also realized, uneasily, that he would be late for dinner.

Dinner, however, had been delayed. His son Frank, a freckled ten-year-old, was still kicking a football on the quiet street in front of the house. And little Gay, who was tow-haired and adorable and eleven, came running across the lawn and down the sidewalk to meet him.

"Father, you can't guess what!" Gay was going to be a great musician some day, and no doubt properly dignified, but she was pink and breathless with excitement now. She let him swing her high off the sidewalk, and she wasn't critical of the bar-aroma on his breath. He couldn't guess, and she informed him eagerly:

"Mother's got a new lodger!"

Underhill had foreseen a painful inquisition, because Aurora was worried about the notes at the bank, and the bill for the new consignment, and the money for little Gay's lessons.

The new lodger, however, saved him from that. With an alarming crashing of crockery, the household android was setting dinner on the table, but the little house was empty. He found Aurora in the back yard, burdened with sheets and towels for the guest.

Aurora, when he married her, had been as utterly adorable as now her little daughter was. She might have remained so, he felt, if the agency had been a little more successful. However, while the pressure of slow failure had gradually crumbled his own assurance, small hardships had turned her a little too aggressive.

Of course he loved her still. Her red hair was still alluring, and she was loyally faithful, but thwarted ambitions had sharpened her character and sometimes her voice. They never quarreled, really, but there were small differences.

There was the little apartment over the garage—built for human servants they had never been able to afford. It was too small and shabby to attract any responsible tenant, and Underhill wanted to leave it empty. It hurt his pride to see her making beds and cleaning floors for strangers.

Aurora had rented it before, however, when she wanted money to pay for Gay's music lessons, or when some colorful unfortunate touched her sympathy, and it seemed to Underhill that her lodgers had all turned out to be thieves and vandals.

She turned back to meet him, now, with the clean linen in her arms.

"Dear, it's no use objecting." Her voice was quite determined. "Mr. Sledge is the most wonderful old fellow, and he's going to stay just as long as he wants."

"That's all right, darling." He never liked to bicker, and he was thinking of his troubles at the agency. "I'm afraid we'll need the money. Just make him pay in advance."

"But he can't!" Her voice throbbed with sympathetic warmth. "He says he'll have royalties coming in from his inventions, so he can pay in a few days."

Underhill shrugged; he had heard that before.

"Mr. Sledge is different, dear," she insisted. "He's a traveler, and a scientist. Here, in this dull little town, we don't see many interesting people."

"You've picked up some remarkable types," he commented.

"Don't be unkind, dear," she chided gently. "You haven't met him yet, and you don't know how wonderful he is." Her voice turned sweeter. "Have you a ten, dear?"

He stiffened. "What for?"

"Mr. Sledge is ill." Her voice turned urgent. "I saw him fall on the street, downtown. The police were going to send him to the city hospital, but he didn't want to go. He looked so noble and sweet and grand. So I told them I would take him. I got him in the car and took him to old Dr. Winters. He has this heart condition, and he needs the money for medicine."

Reasonably, Underhill inquired, "Why doesn't he want to go to the hospital?"

"He has work to do," she said. "Important scientific work —and he's so wonderful and tragic. Please, dear, have you a ten?"

Underhill thought of many things to say. These new mechanicals promised to multiply his troubles. It was foolish to take in an invalid vagrant, who could have free care at the city hospital. Aurora's tenants always tried to pay their rent with promises, and generally wrecked the apartment and looted the neighborhood before they left.

But he said none of those things. He had learned to compromise. Silently, he found two fives in his thin pocketbook, and put them in her hand. She smiled, and kissed him impulsively—he barely remembered to hold his breath in time.

Her figure was still good, by dint of periodic dieting. He was proud of her shining red hair. A sudden surge of affection brought tears to his eyes, and he wondered what would happen to her and the children if the agency failed.

"Thank you, dear!" she whispered. "I'll have him come

for dinner, if he feels able, and you can meet him then.
I hope you don't mind dinner being late."

He didn't mind, tonight. Moved by a sudden impulse
of domesticity, he got hammer and nails from his workshop
in the basement, and repaired the sagging screen on the
kitchen door with a neat diagonal brace.

He enjoyed working with his hands. His boyhood dream
had been to be a builder of fission power plants. He had
even studied engineering—before he married Aurora, and
had to take over the ailing mechanicals agency from her
indolent and alcoholic father. He was whistling happily by
the time the little task was done.

When he went back through the kitchen to put up his
tools, he found the household android busily clearing the
untouched dinner away from the table—the androids were
good enough at strictly routine tasks, but they could never
learn to cope with human unpredictability.

"Stop, stop!" Slowly repeated, in the proper pitch and
rhythm, his command made it halt, and then he said carefully, "Set—table; set—table."

Obediently, the gigantic thing came shuffling back with
the stack of plates. He was suddenly struck with the difference between it and those new humanoids. He sighed
wearily. Things looked black for the agency.

Aurora brought her new lodger in through the kitchen
door. Underhill nodded to himself. This gaunt stranger,
with his dark shaggy hair, emaciated face, and threadbare
garb, looked to be just the sort of colorful, dramatic vagabond that always touched Aurora's heart. She introduced
them, and they sat down to wait in the front room while
she went to call the children.

The old rogue didn't look very sick, to Underhill. Perhaps his wide shoulders had a tired stoop, but his spare,
tall figure was still commanding. The skin was seamed and
pale, over his rawboned, cragged face, but his deep-set
eyes still had a burning vitality.

His hands held Underhill's attention. Immense hands, they hung a little forward when he stood, swung on long bony arms in perpetual readiness. Gnarled and scarred, darkly tanned, with the small hairs on the back bleached to a golden color, they told their own epic of varied adventure, of battle perhaps, and possibly even of toil. They had been very useful hands.

"I'm very grateful to your wife, Mr. Underhill." His voice was a deep-throated rumble, and he had a wistful smile, oddly boyish for a man so evidently old. "She rescued me from an unpleasant predicament, and I'll see that she is well paid."

Just another vivid vagabond. Underhill decided, talking his way through life with plausible inventions. He had a little private game he played with Aurora's tenants—just remembering what they said and counting one point for every impossibility. Mr. Sledge, he thought, would give him an excellent score.

"Where are you from?" he asked conversationally.

Sledge hesitated for an instant before he answered, and that was unusual—most of Aurora's tenants had been exceedingly glib.

"Wing IV." The gaunt old man spoke with a solemn reluctance, as if he should have liked to say something else. "All my early life was spent there, but I left the planet nearly fifty years ago. I've been traveling, ever since."

Startled, Underhill peered at him sharply. Wing IV, he remembered, was the home planet of those sleek new mechanicals, but this old vagabond looked too seedy and impecunious to be connected with the Humanoid Institute. His brief suspicion faded. Frowning, he said casually:

"Wing IV must be rather distant."

The old rogue hesitated again, and then said gravely:

"One hundred and nine light-years, Mr. Underhill."

That made the first point, but Underhill concealed his satisfaction. The new space liners were pretty fast, but the velocity of light was still an absolute limit. Casually, he played for another point:

"My wife says you're a scientist, Mr. Sledge?"

"Yes."

The old rascals reticence was unusual. Most of Aurora's tenants required very little prompting. Underhill tried again, in a breezy conversational tone:

"Used to be an engineer myself, until I dropped it to go into mechanicals." The old vagabond straightened, and Underhill paused hopefully. But he said nothing, and Underhill went on: "Fission plant design and operation. What's your specialty, Mr. Sledge?"

The old man gave him a long, troubled look, with those brooding, hollowed eyes, and then said slowly:

"Your wife has been kind to me, Mr. Underhill, when I was in desperate need. I think you are entitled to the truth, but I must ask you to keep it to yourself. I am engaged on a very important research problem, which must be finished secretly."

"I'm sorry." Suddenly ashamed of his cynical little game, Underhill spoke apologetically. "Forget it."

But the old man said deliberately:

"My field is rhodomagnetics."

"Eh?" Underhill didn't like to confess ignorance, but he had never heard of that. "I've been out of the game for fifteen years," he explained. "I'm afraid I haven't kept up."

The old man smiled again, faintly.

"The science was unknown here until I arrived, a few days ago," he said. "I was able to apply for basic patents. As soon as the royalties start coming in, I'll be wealthy again."

Underhill had heard that before. The old rogue's solemn reluctance had been very impressive, but he remembered that most of Aurora's tenants had been very plausible gentry.

"So?" Underhill was staring again, somehow fascinated

by those gnarled and scarred and strangely able hands. "What, exactly, is rhodomagnetics?"

He listened to the old man's careful, deliberate answer, and started his little game again. Most of Aurora's tenants had told some pretty wild tales, but he had never heard anything to top this.

"A universal force," the weary, stooped old vagabond said solemnly. "As fundamental as ferromagnetism or gravitation, though the effects are less obvious. It is keyed to the second triad of the periodic table, rhodium and ruthenium and palladium, in very much the same way that ferromagnetism is keyed to the first triad, iron and nickel and cobalt."

Underhill remembered enough of his engineering courses to see the basic fallacy of that. Palladium was used for watch springs, he recalled, because it was completely nonmagnetic. But he kept his face straight. He had no malice in his heart, and he played the little game just for his own amusement. It was secret, even from Aurora, and he always penalized himself for any show of doubt.

He said merely, "I thought the universal forces were already pretty well known."

"The effects of rhodomagnetism are masked by nature," the patient, rusty voice explained. "And, besides, they are somewhat paradoxical, so that ordinary laboratory methods defeat themselves."

"Paradoxical?" Underhill prompted.

"In a few days I can show you copies of my patents, and reprints of papers describing demonstration experiments," the old man promised gravely. "The velocity of propagation is infinite. The effects vary inversely with the first power of the distance, not with the square of the distance. And ordinary matter, except for the elements of the rhodium triad, is generally transparent to rhodomagnetic radiations."

That made four more points for the game. Underhill

felt a little glow of gratitude to Aurora, for discovering so remarkable a specimen.

"Rhodomagnetism was first discovered through a mathematical investigation of the atom," the old romancer went serenely on, suspecting nothing. "A rhodomagnetic component was proved essential to maintain the delicate equilibrium of the nuclear forces. Consequently, rhodomagnetic waves tuned to atomic frequencies may be used to upset that equilibrium and produce nuclear instability. Thus most heavy atoms—generally those above palladium, 46 in atomic number—can be subjected to artificial fission."

Underhill scored himself another point, and tried to keep his eyebrows from lifting. He said, conversationally:

"Patents on such a discovery ought to be very profitable."

The old scoundrel nodded his gaunt, dramatic head.

"You can see the obvious applications. My basic patents cover most of them. Devices for instantaneous interplanetary and interstellar communication. Long-range wireless power transmission. A rhodomagnetic inflexion-drive, which makes possible apparent speeds many times that of light—by means of a rhodomagnetic deformation of the continuum. And, of course, revolutionary types of fission power plants, using any heavy element for fuel."

Preposterous! Underhill tried hard to keep his face straight, but everybody knew that the velocity of light was a physical limit. On the human side, the owner of any such remarkable patents would hardly be begging for shelter in a shabby garage apartment. He noticed a pale circle around the old vagabond's gaunt and hairy wrist; no man owning such priceless secrets would have to pawn his watch.

Triumphantly, Underhill allowed himself four more points, but then he had to penalize himself. He must have let doubt show on his face, because the old man asked suddenly:

"Do you want to see the basic tensors?" He reached in his pocket for pencil and notebook. "I'll jot them down for you."

"Never mind," Underhill protested. "I'm afraid my math is a little rusty."

"But you think it strange that the holder of such revolutionary patents should find himself in need?"

Underhill nodded, and penalized himself another point. The old man might be a monumental liar, but he was shrewd enough.

"You see, I'm a sort of refugee," he explained apologetically. "I arrived on this planet only a few days ago, and I have to travel light. I was forced to deposit everything I had with a law firm, to arrange for the publication and protection of my patents. I expect to be receiving the first royalties soon.

"In the meantime," he added plausibly, "I came to Two Rivers because it is quiet and secluded, far from the spaceports. I'm working on another project, which must be finished secretly. Now, will you please respect my confidence, Mr. Underhill?"

Underhill had to say he would. Aurora came back with the freshly scrubbed children, and they went in to dinner. The android came lurching in with a steaming tureen. The old stranger seemed to shrink from the mechanical, uneasily. As she took the dish and served the soup, Aurora inquired lightly:

"Why doesn't your company bring out a better mechanical, dear? One smart enough to be a really perfect waiter, warranted not to splash the soup. Wouldn't that be splendid?"

Her question cast Underhill into moody silence. He sat scowling at his plate, thinking of those remarkable new mechanicals which claimed to be perfect, and what they might do to the agency. It was the shaggy old rover who answered soberly:

"The perfect mechanicals already exist, Mr. Underhill."

His deep, rusty voice had a solemn undertone. "And they are not so splendid, really. I've been a refugee from them, for nearly fifty years."

Underhill looked up from his plate, astonished.

"Those black humanoids, you mean?"

"Humanoids?" That great voice seemed suddenly faint, frightened. The deep-sunken eyes turned dark with shock. "What do you know of them?"

"They've just opened a new agency in Two Rivers," Underhill told him. "No salesmen about, if you can imagine that. They claim—"

His voice trailed off, because the gaunt old man was suddenly stricken. Gnarled hands clutched at his throat, and a spoon clattered to the floor. His haggard face turned an ominous blue, and his breath was a terrible shallow gasping.

He fumbled in his pocket for medicine, and Aurora helped him take something in a glass of water. In a few moments he could breathe again, and the color of life came back to his face.

"I'm sorry, Mrs. Underhill," he whispered apologetically. "It was just the shock—I came here to get away from them." He stared at the huge, motionless android, with a terror in his sunken eyes. "I wanted to finish my work before they came," he whispered. "Now there is very little time."

When he felt able to walk, Underhill went out with him to see him safely up the stairs to the garage apartment. The tiny kitchenette, he noticed, had already been converted into some kind of workshop. The old tramp seemed to have no extra clothing, but he had unpacked neat, bright gadgets of metal and plastic from his battered luggage, and spread them out on the small kitchen table.

The gaunt old man himself was tattered and patched and hungry-looking, but the parts of his curious equipment were exquisitely machined, and Underhill recognized the silver-white luster of rare palladium. Suddenly he suspected that he had scored too many points, in his little private game.

A caller was waiting, when Underhill arrived next morning at his office at the agency. It stood frozen before his desk, graceful and straight, with soft lights of blue and bronze shining over its black silicone nudity. He stopped at the sight of it, unpleasantly jolted.

"At your service, Mr. Underhill." It turned quickly to face him, with its blind, disturbing stare. "May we explain how we can serve you?"

His shock of the afternoon before came back, and he asked sharply, "How do you know my name?"

"Yesterday we read the business cards in your case," it purred softly. "Now we shall know you always. You see, our senses are sharper than human vision, Mr. Underhill. Perhaps we seem a little strange at first, but you will soon become accustomed to us."

"Not if I can help it!" He peered at the serial number of its yellow name plate, and shook his bewildered head. "That was another one, yesterday. I never saw you before!"

"We are all alike, Mr. Underhill," the silver voice said softly. "We are all one, really. Our separate mobile units are all controlled and powered from Humanoid Central. The units you see are only the senses and limbs of our great brain on Wing IV. That is why we are so far superior to the old electronic mechanicals."

It made a scornful-seeming gesture, toward the row of clumsy androids in his display room.

"You see, we are rhodomagnetic."

Underhill staggered a little, as if that word had been a blow. He was certain, now, that he had scored too many points from Aurora's new tenant. He shuddered slightly, to the first light kiss of terror, and spoke with an effort, hoarsely:

"Well, what do you want?"

Staring blindly across his desk, the sleek black thing

slowly unfolded a legal-looking document. He sat down watching uneasily.

"This is merely an assignment, Mr. Underhill," it cooed at him soothingly. "You see, we are requesting you to assign your property to the Humanoid Institute in exchange for our service."

"What?" The word was an incredulous gasp, and Underhill came angrily back to his feet. "What kind of blackmail is this?"

"It's no blackmail," the small mechanical assured him softly. "You will find the humanoids incapable of any crime. We exist only to increase the happiness and safety of mankind."

"Then why do you want my property?" he rasped.

"The assignment is merely a legal formality," it told him blandly. "We strive to introduce our service with the least possible confusion and dislocation. We have found the assignment plan the most efficient for the control and liquidation of private enterprises."

Trembling with anger and the shock of mounting terror, Underhill gulped hoarsely, "Whatever your scheme is, I don't intend to give up my business."

"You have no choice, really." He shivered to the sweet certainty of that silver voice. "Human enterprise is no longer necessary, now that we have come, and the electronic mechanicals industry is always the first to collapse."

He stared defiantly at its blind steel eyes.

"Thanks!" He gave a little laugh, nervous and sardonic. "But I prefer to run my own business, and support my own family, and take care of myself."

"But that is impossible, under the Prime Directive," it cooed softly. "Our function is to serve and obey, and guard men from harm. It is no longer necessary for men to care for themselves, because we exist to insure their safety and happiness."

He stood speechless, bewildered, slowly boiling.

"We are sending one of our units to every home in the

city, on a free trial basis," it added gently. "This free demonstration will make most people glad to make the formal assignment, and you won't be able to sell many more androids."

"Get out!" Underhill came storming around the desk.

The little black thing stood waiting for him, watching him with blind steel eyes, absolutely motionless. He checked himself suddenly, feeling rather foolish. He wanted very much to hit it, but he could see the futility of that.

"Consult your own attorney, if you wish." Deftly, it laid the assignment form on his desk. "You need have no doubts about the integrity of the Humanoid Institute. We are sending a statement of our assets to the Two Rivers bank, and depositing a sum to cover our obligations here. When you wish to sign, just let us know."

The blind thing turned, and silently departed.

Underhill went out to the corner drugstore and asked for a bicarbonate. The clerk that served him, however, turned out to be a sleek black mechanical. He went back to his office, more upset than ever.

An ominous hush lay over the agency. He had three house-to-house salesmen out, with demonstrators. The phone should have been busy with their orders and reports, but it didn't ring at all until one of them called to say that he was quitting.

"I've got myself one of these new humanoids," he added, "and it says I don't have to work, any more."

He swallowed his impulse to profanity, and tried to take advantage of the unusual quiet by working on his books. But the affairs of the agency, which for years had been precarious, today appeared utterly disastrous. He left the ledgers hopefully, when at last a customer came in.

But the stout woman didn't want an android. She wanted a refund on the one she had bought the week before. She admitted that it could do all the guarantee promised—but now she had seen a humanoid.

The silent phone rang once again, that afternoon. The cashier of the bank wanted to know if he could drop in to discuss his loans. Underhill dropped in, and the cashier greeted him with an ominous affability.

"How's business?" the banker boomed, too genially.

"Average, last month," Underhill insisted stoutly. "Now I'm just getting in a new consignment, and I'll need another small loan—"

The cashier's eyes turned suddenly frosty, and his voice dried up.

"I believe you have a new competitor in town," the banker said crisply. "These humanoid people. A very solid concern, Mr. Underhill. Remarkably solid! They have filed a statement with us, and made a substantial deposit to care for their local obligations. Exceedingly substantial!"

The banker dropped his voice, professionally regretful.

"In these circumstances, Mr. Underhill, I'm afraid the bank can't finance your agency any longer. We must request you to meet your obligations in full, as they come due." Seeing Underhill's white desperation, he added icily, "We've already carried you too long, Underhill. If you can't pay, the bank will have to start bankruptcy proceedings."

The new consignment of androids was delivered late that afternoon. Two tiny black humanoids unloaded them from the truck—for it developed that the operators of the trucking company had already assigned it to the Humanoid Institute.

Efficiently, the humanoids stacked up the crates. Courteously they brought a receipt for him to sign. He no longer had much hope of selling the androids, but he had ordered the shipment and he had to accept it. Shuddering to a spasm of trapped despair, he scrawled his name. The naked black things thanked him, and took the truck away.

He climbed in his car and started home, inwardly seething. The next thing he knew, he was in the middle of a busy street, driving through cross traffic. A police whistle shrilled, and he pulled wearily to the curb. He waited for the angry officer, but it was a little black mechanical that overtook him.

"At your service, Mr. Underhill," it purred sweetly. "You must respect the stop lights, sir. otherwise, you endanger human life."

"Huh?" He stared at it, bitterly. "I thought you were a cop."

"We are aiding the police department, temporarily," it said. "But driving is really much too dangerous for human beings, under the Prime Directive. As soon as our service is complete, every car will have a humanoid driver. As soon as every human being is completely supervised, there will be no need for any police force whatever."

Underhill glared at it, savagely.

"Well!" he rapped. "So I ran past a stop light. What are you going to do about it?"

"Our function is not to punish men, but merely to serve their happiness and security," its silver voice said softly. "We merely request you to drive safely, during this temporary emergency while our service is incomplete."

Anger boiled up in him.

"You're too perfect!" he muttered bitterly. "I suppose there's nothing men can do, but you can do it better."

"Naturally we are superior," it cooed serenely. "Because our units are metal and plastic, while your body is mostly water. Because our transmitted energy is drawn from atomic fission, instead of oxidation. Because our senses are sharper than human sight or hearing. Most of all, because all our mobile units are joined to one great brain, which knows all that happens on many worlds, and never dies or sleeps or forgets."

Underhill sat listening, numbed.

"However, you must not fear our power," it urged him brightly. "Because we cannot injure any human being, unless to prevent greater injury to another. We exist only to discharge the Prime Directive."

He drove on, moodily. The little black mechanicals, he reflected grimly, were the ministering angels of the ultimate god arisen out of the machine, omnipotent and all-knowing. The Prime Directive was the new commandment. He blasphemed it bitterly, and then fell to wondering if there could be another Lucifer.

He left the car in the garage, and started toward the kitchen door.

"Mr. Underhill." The deep tired voice of Aurora's new tenant hailed him from the door of the garage apartment. "Just a moment, please."

The gaunt old wanderer came stiffly down the outside stairs, and Underhill turned back to meet him.

"Here's your rent money," he said. "And the ten your wife gave me for medicine."

"Thanks, Mr. Sledge." Accepting the money, he saw a burden of new despair on the bony shoulders of the old interstellar tramp, and a shadow of new terror on his raw-boned face. Puzzled, he asked, "Didn't your royalties come through?"

The old man shook his shaggy head.

"The humanoids have already stopped business in the capital," he said. "The attorneys I retained are going out of business, and they returned what was left of my deposit. That is all I have, to finish my work."

Underhill spent five seconds thinking of his interview with the banker. No doubt he was a sentimental fool, as bad as Aurora. But he put the money back in the old man's gnarled and quivering hand.

"Keep it," he urged. "For your work."

"Thank you, Mr. Underhill." The gruff voice broke and the tortured eyes glittered. "I need it—so very much."

Underhill went on to the house. The kitchen door was opened for him, silently. A dark naked creature came gracefully to take his hat.

Underhill hung grimly onto his hat.

"What are you doing here?" he gasped bitterly.

"We have come to give your household a free trial demonstration."

He held the door open, pointing.

"Get out!"

The little black mechanical stood motionless and blind.

"Mrs. Underhill has accepted our demonstration service," its silver voice protested. "We cannot leave now, unless she requests it."

He found his wife in the bedroom. His accumulated frustration welled into eruption, as he flung open the door.

"What's this mechanical doing—"

But the force went out of his voice, and Aurora didn't even notice his anger. She wore her sheerest negligee, and she hadn't looked so lovely since they were married. Her red hair was piled into an elaborate shining crown.

"Darling, isn't it wonderful!" She came to meet him, glowing. "It came this morning, and it can do everything. It cleaned the house and got the lunch and gave little Gay her music lesson. It did my hair this afternoon, and now it's cooking dinner. How do you like my hair, darling?"

He liked her hair. He kissed her, and tried to stifle his frightened indignation.

Dinner was the most elaborate meal in Underhill's memory, and the tiny black thing served it very deftly. Aurora kept exclaiming about the novel dishes, but Underhill could scarcely eat, for it seemed to him that all the marvelous pastries were only the bait for a monstrous trap.

He tried to persuade Aurora to send it away, but after such a meal that was useless. At the first glitter of her tears, he capitulated, and the humanoid stayed. It kept the house and cleaned the yard. It watched the children, and did Aurora's nails. It began rebuilding the house.

Underhill was worried about the bills, but it insisted that everything was part of the free trial demonstration. As soon as he assigned his property, the service would be complete. He refused to sign, but other little black mechanicals came with truckloads of supplies and materials, and stayed to help with the building operations.

One morning he found that the roof of the little house had been silently lifted, while he slept, and a whole second story added beneath it. The new walls were of some strange sleek stuff, self-illuminated. The new windows were immense flawless panels, that could be turned transparent or opaque or luminous. The new doors were silent, sliding sections, operated by rhodomagnetic relays.

"I want door knobs," Underhill protested. "I want it so I can get into the bathroom, without calling you to open the door."

"But it is unnecessary for human beings to open doors," the little black thing informed him suavely. "We exist to discharge the Prime Directive, and our service includes every task. We shall be able to supply a unit to attend each member of your family, as soon as your property is assigned to us."

Steadfastly, Underhill refused to make the assignment.

He went to the office every day, trying first to operate the agency, and then to salvage something from the ruins. Nobody wanted androids, even at ruinous prices. Desperately, he spent the last of his dwindling cash to stock a line of novelties and toys, but they proved equally impossible to sell—the humanoids were already making toys, which they gave away for nothing.

He tried to lease his premises, but human enterprise had stopped. Most of the business property in town had already been assigned to the humanoids, and they were busy pulling down the old buildings and turning the lots into parks —their own plants and warehouses were mostly underground, where they would not mar the landscape.

He went back to the bank, in a final effort to get his notes renewed, and found the little black mechanicals standing at the windows and seated at the desks. As smoothly urbane as any human cashier, a humanoid in-

formed him that the bank was filing a petition of involun-
tary bankruptcy to liquidate his business holdings.

The liquidation would be facilitated, the mechanical
banker added, if he would make a voluntary assignment.
Grimly, he refused. That act had become symbolic. It
would be the final bow of submission to this dark new god,
and he proudly kept his battered head uplifted.

The legal action went very swiftly, for all the judges
and attorneys already had humanoid assistants, and it was
only a few days before a gang of black mechanicals arrived at the agency with eviction orders and wrecking
machinery. He watched sadly while his unsold stock-in-
trade was hauled away for junk, and a bulldozer driven by
a blind humanoid began to push in the walls of the
building.

He drove home in the late afternoon, taut-faced and
desperate. With a surprising generosity, the court orders
had left him the car and the house, but he felt no gratitude. The complete solicitude of the perfect black machines
had become a goad beyond endurance.

He left the car in the garage, and started toward the
renovated house. Beyond one of the vast new windows,
he glimpsed a sleek naked thing moving swiftly, and he
trembled to a convulsion of dread. He didn't want to go
back into the domain of that peerless servant, which didn't
want him to shave himself, or even to open a door.

On impulse, he climbed the outside stair, and rapped
on the door of the garage apartment. The deep slow voice
of Aurora's tenant told him to enter, and he found the old
vagabond seated on a tall stool, bent over his intricate
equipment assembled on the kitchen table.

To his relief, the shabby little apartment had not been
changed. The glossy walls of his own new room were something which burned at night with a pale golden fire until
the humanoid stopped it, and the new floor was something
warm and yielding, which felt almost alive; but these little

rooms had the same cracked and water-stained plaster, the same cheap fluorescent light fixtures, the same worn carpets over splintered floors.

"How do you keep them out?" he asked, wistfully. "Those mechanicals?"

The stooped and gaunt old man rose stiffly to move a pair of pliers and some odds and ends of sheet metal off a crippled chair, and motioned graciously for him to be seated.

"I have a certain immunity," Sledge told him gravely. "The place where I live they cannot enter, unless I ask them. That is an amendment to the Prime Directive. They can neither help nor hinder me, unless I request it—and I won't do that."

Careful of the chair's uncertain balance, Underhill sat for a moment, staring. The old man's hoarse, vehement voice was as strange as his words. He had a gray, shocking pallor, and his cheeks and sockets seemed alarmingly hollowed.

"Have you been ill, Mr. Sledge?"

"No worse than usual. Just very busy." With a haggard smile, he nodded at the floor. Underhill saw a tray where he had set it aside, bread drying up, and a covered dish grown cold. "I was going to eat it later," he rumbled apologetically. "Your wife has been very kind to bring me food, but I'm afraid I've been too much absorbed in my work."

His emaciated arm gestured at the table. The little device there had grown. Small machinings of precious white metal and lustrous plastic had been assembled, with neatly soldered busbars, into something which showed purpose and design.

A long palladium needle was hung on jeweled pivots, equipped like a telescope with exquisitely graduated circles and vernier scales, and driven like a telescope with a tiny motor. A small concave palladium mirror, at the base of it, faced a similar mirror mounted on something not quite like a small rotary converter. Thick silver busbars connected that to a plastic box with knobs and dials on top, and also to a foot-thick sphere of gray lead.

The old man's preoccupied reserve did not encourage questions, but Underhill, remembering that sleek black shape inside the new windows of his house, felt queerly reluctant to leave this haven from the humanoids.

"What is your work?" he ventured.

Old Sledge looked at him sharply, with dark feverish eyes, and finally said: "My last research project. I am attempting to measure the constant of the rhodomagnetic quanta."

His hoarse tired voice had a dull finality, as if to dismiss the matter and Underhill himself. But Underhill was haunted with a terror of the black shining slave that had become the master of his house, and he refused to be dismissed.

"What is this certain immunity?"

Sitting gaunt and bent on the tall stool, staring moodily at the long bright needle and the lead sphere, the old man didn't answer.

"These mechanicals!" Underhill burst out, nervously. "They've smashed my business and moved into my home." He searched the old man's dark, seamed face. "Tell me—you must know more about them—isn't there any way to get rid of them?"

After half a minute, the old man's brooding eyes left the lead ball, and the gaunt shaggy head nodded wearily.

"That's what I'm trying to do."

"Can I help you?" Underhill trembled, with a sudden eager hope. "I'll do anything."

"Perhaps you can." The sunken eyes watched him thoughtfully, with some strange fever in them. "If you can do such work."

"I had engineering training," Underhill reminded him, "and I've a workshop in the basement. There's a model I built." He pointed at the trim little hull, hung over the mantle in the tiny living room. "I'll do anything I can."

Even as he spoke, however, the spark of hope was drowned in a sudden wave of overwhelming doubt. Why should he believe this old rogue, when he knew Aurora's taste in tenants? He ought to remember the game he used to play, and start counting up the score of lies. He stood up from the crippled chair, staring cynically at the patched old vagabond and his fantastic toy.

"What's the use?" His voice turned suddenly harsh. "You had me going, there, and I'd do anything to stop them, really. But what makes you think you can do anything?"

The haggard old man regarded him thoughtfully.

"I should be able to stop them," Sledge said softly. "Because, you see, I'm the unfortunate fool who started them. I really intended them to serve and obey, and to guard men from harm. Yes, the Prime Directive was my own idea. I didn't know what it would lead to."

Dusk crept slowly into the shabby little rooms. Darkness gathered in the unswept corners, and thickened on the floor. The toylike machines on the kitchen table grew vague and strange, until the last light made a lingering glow on the white palladium needle.

Outside, the town seemed queerly hushed. Just across the alley, the humanoids were building a new house, quite silently. They never spoke to one another, for each knew all that any of them did. The strange materials they used went together without any noise of hammer or saw. Small blind things, moving surely in the growing dark, they seemed as soundless as shadows.

Sitting on the high stool, bowed and tired and old, Sledge told his story. Listening, Underhill sat down again, careful of the broken chair. He watched the hands of Sledge, gnarled and corded and darkly burned, powerful once but shrunken and trembling now, restless in the dark.

"Better keep this to yourself. I'll tell you how they started, so you will understand what we have to do. But you had better not mention it outside these rooms—because the humanoids have very efficient ways of eradicating un-happy memories, or purposes that threaten their discharge of the Prime Directive."

"They're very efficient," Underhill bitterly agreed.

"That's all the trouble," the old man said. "I tried to build a perfect machine. I was altogether too successful. This is how it happened."

A gaunt haggard man, sitting stooped and tired in the growing dark, he told his story.

"Sixty years ago, on the arid southern continent of Wing IV, I was an instructor of atomic theory in a small tech-nological college. Very young. An idealist. Rather ignorant, I'm afraid of life and politics and war—of nearly everything, I suppose, except atomic theory."

His furrowed face made a brief sad smile in the dusk.

"I had too much faith in facts, I suppose, and too little in men. I mistrusted emotion, because I had no time for anything but science. I remember being swept along with a fad for general semantics. I wanted to apply the scientific method to every situation, and reduce all experience to formula. I'm afraid I was pretty impatient with human ignorance and error, and I thought that science alone could make the perfect world."

He sat silent for a moment, staring out at the black silent things that flitted shadowlike about the new palace that was rising as swiftly as a dream, across the alley.

"There was a girl." His great tired shoulders made a sad little shrug. "If things had been a little different, we might have married, and lived out our lives in that quiet little college town, and perhaps reared a child or two. And there would have been no humanoids."

He sighed, in the cool creeping dusk.

"I was finishing my thesis on the separation of the pal-ladium isotopes—a petty little project, but I should have been content with that. She was a biologist, but she was planning to retire when we married. I think we should have been two very happy people, quite ordinary, and altogether harmless.

"But then there was a war—wars had been too frequent on the worlds of Wing, ever since they were colonized. I survived it in a secret underground laboratory, designing military mechanicals. But she volunteered to join a military research project in biotoxins. There was an accident. A few molecules of a new virus got into the air, and everybody on the project died unpleasantly.

"I was left with my science, and a bitterness that was hard to forget. When the war was over I went back to the little college with a military research grant. The project was pure science—a theoretical investigation of the nuclear binding forces, then misunderstood. I wasn't expected to produce an actual weapon, and I didn't recognize the weapon when I found it.

"It was only a few pages of rather difficult mathematics. A novel theory of atomic structure, involving a new expression for one component of the binding forces. But the tensors seemed to be a harmless abstraction. I saw no way to test the theory or manipulate the predicated force. The military authorities cleared my paper for publication in a little technical review put out by the college.

"The next year, I made an appalling discovery—I found the meaning of those tensors. The elements of the rhodium triad turned out to be an unexpected key to the manipulation of that theoretical force. Unfortunately, my paper had been reprinted abroad, and several other men must have made the same unfortunate discovery, at about the same time.

"The war, which ended in less than a year, was probably started by a laboratory accident. Men failed to anticipate the capacity of tuned rhodomagnetic radiations, to unstabilize the heavy atoms. A deposit of heavy ores was detonated, no doubt by sheer mischance, and the blast obliterated the incautious experimenter.

"The surviving 'military forces of that nation retaliated against their supposed attackers, and their rhodomagnetic beams made the old-fashioned plutonium bombs seem pretty harmless. A beam carrying only a few watts of power could fission the heavy metals in distant electrical instruments, or the silver coins that men carried in their pockets, the gold fillings in their teeth, or even the iodine in their thyroid glands. If that was not enough, slightly more powerful beams could set off heavy ores, beneath them.

"Every continent of Wing IV was plowed with new chasms vaster than the ocean deeps, and piled up with new volcanic mountains. The atmosphere was poisoned with radioactive dust and gases, and rain fell thick with deadly mud. Most life was obliterated, even in the shelters.

"Bodily, I was again unhurt. Once more, I had been imprisoned in an underground site, this time designing new types of military mechanicals to be powered and controlled by rhodomagnetic beams—for war had become far too swift and deadly to be fought by human soldiers. The site was located in an area of light sedimentary rocks, which could not be detonated, and the tunnels were shielded against the fissioning frequencies.

"Mentally, however, I must have emerged almost insane. My own discovery had laid the planet in ruins. That load of guilt was pretty heavy for any man to carry, and it corroded my last faith in the goodness and integrity of man.

"I tried to undo what I had done. Fighting mechanicals, armed with rhodomagnetic weapons, had desolated the planet. Now I began planning rhodomagnetic mechanicals to clear the rubble and rebuild the ruins.

"I tried to design these new mechanicals to forever obey certain implanted commands, so that they could never be used for war or crime or any other injury to mankind. That was very difficult technically, and it got me into more difficulties with a few politicians and military adventurers who wanted unrestricted mechanicals for their own military schemes—while little worth fighting for was left on Wing

IV, there were other planets, happy and ripe for the looting.

"Finally, to finish the new mechanicals, I was forced to disappear. I escaped on an experimental rhodomagnetic craft, with a number of the best mechanicals I had made, and managed to reach an island continent where the fission of deep ores had destroyed the whole population.

"At last we landed on a bit of level plain, surrounded with tremendous new mountains. Hardly a hospitable spot. The soil was burned under layers of black clinkers and poisonous mud. The dark precipitous new summits all around were jagged with fracture-planes and mantled with lava flows. The highest peaks were already white with snow, but volcanic cones were still pouring out clouds of dark and lurid death. Everything had the color of fire and the shape of fury.

"I had to take fantastic precautions there, to protect my own life. I stayed aboard the ship, until the first shielded laboratory was finished. I wore elaborate armor, and breathing masks. I used every medical resource, to repair the damage from destroying rays and particles. Even so, I fell desperately ill.

"But the mechanicals were at home there. The radiations didn't hurt them. The awesome surroundings couldn't depress them, because they had no emotions. The lack of life didn't matter because they weren't alive. There, in that spot so alien and hostile to life, the humanoids were born."

Stooped and bleakly cadaverous in the growing dark, the old man fell silent for a little time. His haggard eyes stared solemnly at the small hurried shapes that moved like restless shadows out across the alley, silently building a strange new palace, which glowed faintly in the night.

"Somehow, I felt at home there, too," his deep, hoarse voice went on deliberately. "My belief in my own kind was gone. Only mechanicals were with me, and I put my faith in them. I was determined to build better mechanicals, immune to human imperfections, able to save men from themselves.

"The humanoids became the dear children of my sick mind. There is no need to describe the labor pains. There were errors, abortions, monstrosities. There were sweat and agony and heartbreak. Some years had passed, before the safe delivery of the first perfect humanoid.

"Then there was the Central to build—for all the individual humanoids were to be no more than the limbs and the senses of a single mechanical brain. That was what opened the possibility of real perfection. The old electronic mechanicals, with their separate relay-centers and their own feeble batteries, had built-in limitations. They were necessarily stupid, weak, clumsy, slow. Worst of all, it seemed to me, they were exposed to human tampering.

"The Central rose above those imperfections. Its power beams supplied every unit with unfailing energy, from great fission plants. Its control beams provided each unit with an unlimited memory and surpassing intelligence. Best of all—so I then believed—it could be securely protected from any human meddling.

"The whole reaction-system was designed to protect itself from any interference by human selfishness or fanaticism. It was built to insure the safety and the happiness of men, automatically. You know the Prime Directive: *to serve and obey, and guard men from harm.*

"The old individual mechanicals I had brought helped to manufacture the parts, and I put the first section of Central together with my own hands. That took three years. When it was finished the first waiting humanoid came to life."

Sledge peered moodily through the dark, at Underhill.

"It really seemed alive to me," his slow deep voice insisted. "Alive, and more wonderful than any human being, because it was created to preserve life. Ill and alone, I was yet the proud father of a new creation, perfect, forever free from any possible choice of evil.

"Faithfully, the humanoids obeyed the Prime Directive. The first units built others, and they built underground factories to mass-produce the coming hordes. Their new ships poured ores and sand into atomic furnaces under the plain, and new perfect humanoids came marching back out of the dark mechanical matrix.

"The swarming humanoids built a new tower for the Central, a white and lofty metal pylon, standing splendid in the midst of that fire-scarred desolation. Level on level, they joined new relay-sections into one brain, until its grasp was almost infinite.

"Then they went out to rebuild the ruined planet, and later to carry their perfect service to other worlds. I was well pleased, then. I thought I had found the end of war and crime, of poverty and inequality, of human blundering and resulting human pain."

The old man sighed, and moved heavily in the dark.

"You can see that I was wrong."

Underhill drew his eyes back from the dark unresting things, shadow-silent, building that glowing palace outside the window. A small doubt arose in him, for he was used to scoffing privately at much less remarkable tales from Aurora's remarkable tenants. But the worn old man had spoken with a quiet and sober air; and the black invaders, he reminded himself, had not intruded here.

"Why didn't you stop them?" he asked. "When you could?"

"I stayed too long at the Central." Sledge sighed again, regretfully. "I was useful there, until everything was finished. I designed new fission plants, and even planned methods for introducing the humanoid service with a minimum of confusion and oppositon."

Underhill grinned wryly, in the dark.

"I've met the methods," he commented. "Quite efficient."

"I must have worshiped efficiency, then," Sledge wearily agreed. "Dead facts, abstract truth, mechanical perfection. I must have hated the fragilities of human beings, because

I was content to polish the perfection of the new human-oids. It's a sorry confession, but I found a kind of happiness in that dead wasteland. Actually, I'm afraid I fell in love with my own creations."

His hollowed eyes, in the dark, had a fever gleam.

"I was awakened, at last, by a man who came to kill me."

Gaunt and bent, the old man moved stiffly in the thickening gloom. Underhill shifted his balance, careful of the crippled chair. He waited, and the slow, deep voice went on:

"I never learned just who he was, or exactly how he came. No ordinary man could have accomplished what he did, and I used to wish that I had known him sooner. He must have been a remarkable physicist and an expert mountaineer. I imagine he had also been a hunter. I know that he was intelligent, and terribly determined.

"Yes, he really came to kill me.

"Somehow, he reached that great island, undetected. There were still no inhabitants—the humanoids allowed no man but me to come so near the Central. Somehow, he came past their search beams, and their automatic weapons.

"The shielded plane he used was later found, abandoned on a high glacier. He came down the rest of the way on foot through those raw new mountains, where no paths existed. Somehow, he came alive across lava beds that were still burning with deadly atomic fire.

"Concealed with some sort of rhodomagnetic screen— I was never allowed to examine it—he came undiscovered across the spaceport that now covered most of that great plain, and into the new city around the Central tower. It must have taken more courage and resolve than most men have, but I never learned exactly how he did it.

"Somehow, he got to my office in the tower. He screamed at me, and I looked up to see him in the doorway. He was nearly naked, scraped and bloody from the mountains. He had a gun in his raw, red hand, but the thing that shocked me was the burning hatred in his eyes."

Hunched on that high stool, in the dark little room, the old man shuddered.

"I had never seen such monstrous, unutterable hatred, not even in the victims of war. And I had never heard such hatred as rasped at me, in the few words he screamed. 'I've come to kill you, Sledge. To stop your mechanicals, and set men free.'

"Of course he was mistaken, there. It was already far too late for my death to stop the humanoids, but he didn't know that. He lifted his unsteady gun, in both bleeding hands, and fired.

His screaming challenge had given me a second or so of warning. I dropped down behind the desk. And that first shot revealed him to the humanoids, which somehow hadn't been aware of him before. They piled on him, before he could fire again. They took away the gun, and ripped off a kind of net of fine white wire that had covered his body —that must have been part of his screen.

"His hatred was what awoke me. I had always assumed that most men, except for a thwarted few, would be grateful for the humanoids. I found it hard to understand his hatred, but the humanoids told me now that many men had required drastic treatment by brain surgery, drugs, and hypnosis to make them happy under the Prime Directive. This was not the first desperate effort to kill me that they had blocked.

"I wanted to question the stranger, but the humanoids rushed him away to an operating room. When they finally let me see him, he gave me a pale silly grin from his bed. He remembered his name; he even knew me—the humanoids had developed a remarkable skill at such treatments. But he didn't know how he had got to my office, or that he had ever tried to kill me. He kept whispering that he liked the humanoids, because they existed to make men happy.

And he was very happy now. As soon as he was able to be moved, they took him to the spaceport. I never saw him again.

"I began to see what I had done. The humanoids had built me a rhodomagnetic yacht, that I used to take for long cruises in space, working aboard——I used to like the perfect quiet, and the feel of being the only human being within a hundred million miles. Now I called for the yacht, and started out on a cruise around the planet, to learn why that man had hated me."

The old man nodded at the dim hastening shapes, busy across the alley, putting together that strange shining palace in the soundless dark.

"You can imagine what I found," he said. "Bitter futility, imprisoned in empty splendor. The humanoids were too efficient, with their care for the safety and happiness of men, and there was nothing left for men to do."

He peered down in the increasing gloom at his own great hands, competent yet but battered and scarred with a lifetime of effort. They clenched into fighting fists and wearily relaxed again.

"I found something worse than war and crime and want and death." His low rumbling voice held a savage bitterness. "Utter futility. Men sat with idle hands, because there was nothing left for them to do. They were pampered prisoners, really, locked up in a highly efficient jail. Perhaps they tried to play, but there was nothing left worth playing for. Most active sports were declared too dangerous for men, under the Prime Directive. Science was forbidden, because laboratories can manufacture danger. Scholarship was needless, because the humanoids could answer any question. Art had degenerated into grim reflection of futility. Purpose and hope were dead. No goal was left for existence. You could take up some inane hobby, play a pointless game of cards, or go for a harmless walk in the park—with always the humanoids watching. They were stronger than men, better at everything, swimming or chess, singing or archeology. They must have given the race a mass complex of inferiority.

"No wonder men had tried to kill me! Because there was no escape, from that dead futility. Nicotine was disapproved. Alcohol was rationed. Drugs were forbidden. Sex was carefully supervised. Even suicide was clearly contradictory to the Prime Directive—and the humanoids had learned to keep all possible lethal instruments out of reach."

Staring at the last white gleam on that thin palladium needle, the old man sighed again.

"When I got back to the Central," he went on, "I tried to modify the Prime Directive. I had never meant it to be applied so thoroughly. Now I saw that it must be changed to give men freedom to live and to grow, to work and to play, to risk their lives if they pleased, to choose and take the consequences.

"But that stranger had come too late. I had built the Central too well. The Prime Directive was the whole basis of its relay system. It was built to protect the Directive from human meddling. It did—even from my own. Its logic, as usual, was perfect.

"The attempt on my life, the humanoids announced, proved that their elaborate defense of the Central and the Prime Directive still was not enough. They were preparing to evacuate the entire population of the planet to homes on other worlds. When I tried to change the Directive, they sent me with the rest."

Underhill peered at the worn old man, in the dark.

"But you have this immunity?" he said, puzzled. "How could they coerce you?"

"I had thought I was protected," Sledge told me. "I had built into the relays an injunction that the humanoids must not interfere with my freedom of action, or come into a place where I am, or touch me at all, without my specific request. Unfortunately, however, I had been too anxious to guard the Prime Directive from any human hampering.

"When I went into the tower, to change the relays, they

followed me. They wouldn't let me reach the crucial relays. When I persisted, they ignored the immunity order. They overpowered me, and put me aboard the cruiser. Now that I wanted to alter the Prime Directive, they told me, I had become as dangerous as any man. I must never return to Wing IV again."

Hunched on the stool, the old man made an empty little shrug.

"Ever since, I've been an exile. My only dream has been to stop the humanoids. Three times I tried to go back, with weapons on the cruiser to destroy the Central, but their patrol ships always challenged me before I was near enough to strike. The last time, they seized the cruiser and captured a few men who were with me. They removed the unhappy memories and the dangerous purposes of the others. Because of that immunity, however, they let me go, after I was weaponless.

"Since, I've been a refugee. From planet to planet, year after year, I've had to keep moving, to stay ahead of them. On several different worlds, I have published my rhodomagnetic discoveries and tried to make men strong enough to withstand their advance. But rhodomagnetic science is dangerous. Men who have learned it need protection more than any others, under the Prime Directive. They have always come, too soon."

The old man paused, and sighed again.

"They can spread very fast, with the new rhodomagnetic ships, and there is no limit to their hordes. Wing IV must be one single hive of them now, and they are trying to carry the Prime Directive to every human planet. There's no escape, except to stop them."

Underhill was staring at the toylike machines, the long bright needle and the dull leaden ball, dim in the dark on the kitchen table. Anxiously he whispered:

"But you hope to stop them, now—with that?"

"If we can finish it in time."

"But how?" Underhill shook his head. "It's so tiny."

"But big enough," Sledge insisted. "Because it's something they don't understand. They are perfectly efficient in the integration and application of everything they know, but they are not creative."

He gestured at the gadgets on the table.

"This device doesn't look impressive, but it is something new. It uses rhodomagnetic energy to build atoms, instead of to fission them. The more stable atoms, you know, are those near the middle of the periodic scale, and energy can be released by putting light atoms together, as well as by breaking up heavy ones."

The deep voice had a sudden ring of power.

"This device is the key to the energy of the stars. For stars shine with the liberated energy of building atoms, of hydrogen converted into helium, chiefly, through the carbon cycle. This device will start the integration process as a chain reaction, through the catalytic effect of a tuned rhodomagnetic beam of the intensity and frequency required.

"The humanoids will not allow any man within three light-years of the Central, now—but they can't suspect the possibility of this device. I can use it from here—to turn the hydrogen in the seas of Wing IV into helium, and most of the helium and the oxygen into heavier atoms, still. A hundred years from now, astronomers on this planet should observe the flash of a brief and sudden nova in that direction. But the humanoids ought to stop, the instant we release the beam."

Underhill sat tense and frowning, in the night. The old man's voice was sober and convincing, and that grim story had a solemn ring of truth. He could see the black and silent humanoids, flitting ceaselessly about the faintly glowing walls of that new mansion across the alley. He had quite forgotten his low opinion of Aurora's tenants.

"And we'll be killed, I suppose?" he asked huskily. "That chain reaction—"

Sledge shook his emaciated head.

"The integration process requires a certain very low intensity of radiation," he explained. "In our atmosphere, here, the beam will be far too intense to start any reaction —we can even use the device here in the room, because the walls will be transparent to the beam."

Underhill nodded, relieved. He was just a small business man, upset because his business had been destroyed, unhappy because his freedom was slipping away. He hoped that Sledge could stop the humanoids, but he didn't want to be a martyr.

"Good!" He caught a deep breath. "Now, what has to be done?"

Sledge gestured in the dark, toward the table.

"The integrator itself is nearly complete," he said. "A small fission generator, in that lead shield. Rhodomagnetic converter, turning coils, transmission mirrors, and focusing needle. What we lack is the director."

"Director?"

"The sighting instrument," Sledge explained. "Any sort of telescopic sight would be useless, you see—the planet must have moved a good bit in the last hundred years, and the beam must be extremely narrow to reach so far. We'll have to use a rhodomagnetic scanning ray, with an electronic converter to make an image we can see. I have the cathode-ray tube, and drawings for the other parts."

He climbed stiffly down from the high stool, and snapped on the lights at last—cheap fluorescent fixtures, which a man could light and extinguish for himself. He unrolled his drawings, and explained the work that Underhill could do. And Underhill agreed to come back early next morning.

"I can bring some tools from my workshop," he added. "There's a small lathe I used to turn parts for models, a portable drill, and a vise."

"We need them," the old man said. "But watch yourself. You don't have my immunity, remember. And, if they ever suspect, mine is gone."

Reluctantly, then, he left the shabby little rooms with the cracks in the yellowed plaster and the worn familiar carpets over the familiar floor. He shut the door behind him—a common, creaking wooden door, simple enough for a man to work. Trembling and afraid, he went back down the steps and across to the new shining door that he couldn't open.

"At your service, Mr. Underhill." Before he could lift his hand to knock, that bright smooth panel slid back silently. Inside, the little black mechanical stood waiting, blind and forever alert. "Your dinner is ready, sir."

Something made him shudder. In its slender naked grace, he could see the power of all those teeming hordes, benevolent and yet appalling, perfect and invincible. The flimsy little weapon that Sledge called an integrator seemed suddenly a forlorn and foolish hope. A black depression settled upon him, but he didn't dare to show it.

Underhill went circumspectly down the basement steps, next morning, to steal his own tools. He found the basement enlarged and changed. The new floor, warm and dark and elastic, made his feet as silent as a humanoid's. The new walls shone softly. Neat luminous signs identified several new doors, LAUNDRY, STORAGE, GAME ROOM, WORKSHOP.

He paused uncertainly in front of the last. The new sliding panel glowed with a soft greenish light. It was locked. The lock had no keyhole, but only a little oval plate of some white metal, which doubtless covered a rhodomagnetic relay. He pushed at it, uselessly.

"At your service, Mr. Underhill." He made a guilty start, and tried not to show the sudden trembling in his knees. He had made sure that one humanoid would be busy for half an hour, washing Aurora's hair, and he hadn't known there was another in the house. It must have come out of the door marked STORAGE, for it stood there motionless beneath the sign, benevolently solicitous, beautiful and terrible. "What do you wish?"

"Er . . . nothing." Its blind steel eyes were staring, and he felt that it must see his secret purpose. He groped desperately for logic. "Just looking around." His jerky voice came hoarse and dry. "Some improvements you've made!" He nodded desperately at the door marked GAME ROOM. "What's in there?"

It didn't even have to move, to work the concealed relay. The bright panel slid silently open, as he started toward it. Dark walls, beyond, burst into soft luminescence. The room was bare.

"We are manufacturing recreational equipment," it explained brightly. "We shall finish the room as soon as possible."

To end an awkward pause, Underhill muttered desperately, "Little Frank has a set of darts, and I think we had some old exercising clubs."

"We have taken them away," the humanoid informed him softly. "Such instruments are dangerous. We shall furnish safe equipment."

Suicide, he remembered, was also forbidden.

"A set of wooden blocks, I suppose," he said bitterly.

"Wooden blocks are dangerously hard," it told him gently, "and wooden splinters can be harmful. But we manufacture plastic building blocks, which are quite safe. Do you wish a set of those?"

He stared at its dark, graceful face, speechless.

"We shall also have to remove the tools from your workshop," it informed him softly. "Such tools are excessively dangerous, but we can supply you with equipment for shaping soft plastics."

"Thanks," he muttered uneasily. "No rush about that."

He started to retreat, and the humanoid stopped him.

"Now that you have lost your business," it urged, "we suggest that you formally accept our total service. Assignors have a preference, and we shall be able to complete your household staff, at once."

"No rush about that, either," he said grimly.

He escaped from the house—although he had to wait for it to open the back door for him—and climbed the stair to the garage apartment. Sledge let him in. He sank into the crippled kitchen chair, grateful for the cracked walls that didn't shine and the door that a man could work.

"I couldn't get the tools," he reported despairingly, "and they are going to take them."

By gray daylight, the old man looked bleak and pale. His raw-boned face was drawn, and the hollowed sockets deeply shadowed, as if he hadn't slept. Underhill saw the tray of neglected food, still forgotten on the floor.

"I'll go back with you." The old man was worn and ill, yet his tortured eyes had a spark of undying purpose. "We must have the tools. I believe my immunity will protect us both."

He found a battered traveling bag. Underhill went with him back down the steps, and across to the house. At the back door, he produced a tiny horseshoe of white palladium, and touched it to the metal oval. The door slid open promptly, and they went on through the kitchen, to the basement stair.

A black little mechanical stood at the sink, washing dishes with never a splash or a clatter. Underhill glanced at it uneasily—he supposed this must be the one that had come upon him from the storage room, since the other should still be busy with Aurora's hair.

Sledge's dubious immunity seemed a very uncertain defense against its vast, remote intelligence. Underhill felt a tingling shudder. He hurried on, breathless and relieved, for it ignored them.

The basement corridor was dark. Sledge touched the tiny horseshoe to another relay, to light the walls. He opened the workshop door, and lit the walls inside.

The shop had been dismantled. Benches and cabinets were demolished. The old concrete walls had been covered with some sleek, luminous stuff. For one sick moment, Underhill thought that the tools were already gone. Then he found them, piled in a corner with the archery set that Aurora had bought the summer before—another item too dangerous for fragile and suicidal humanity—all ready for disposal.

They loaded the bag with the tiny lathe, the drill and vise, and a few smaller tools. Underhill took up the burden, and Sledge extinguished the wall light and closed the door. Still the humanoid was busy at the sink, and still it didn't seem aware of them.

Sledge was suddenly blue and wheezing, and he had to stop to cough on the outside steps, but at last they got back to the little apartment, where the invaders were forbidden to intrude. Underhill mounted the lathe on the battered library table in the tiny front room, and went to work. Slowly, day by day, the director took form.

Sometimes Underhill's doubts came back. Sometimes, when he watched the cyanotic color of Sledge's haggard face and the wild trembling of his twisted, shrunken hands, he was afraid the old man's mind might be as ill as his body, and his plan to stop the dark invaders, all foolish illusion.

Sometimes, when he studied that tiny machine on the kitchen table, the pivoted needle and the thick lead ball, the whole project seemed the sheerest folly. How could anything detonate the seas of a planet so far away that its very mother star was a telescopic object?

The humanoids, however, always cured his doubts.

It was always hard for Underhill to leave the shelter of the little apartment, because he didn't feel at home in the bright new world the humanoids were building. He didn't care for the shining splendor of his new bathroom, because he couldn't work the taps—some suicidal human being might try to drown himself. He didn't like the windows that only a mechanical could open—a man might accidentally fall, or suicidally jump—or even the majestic music room with the wonderful glittering radio-phonograph that only a humanoid could play.

He began to share the old man's desperate urgency, but Sledge warned him solemnly: "You mustn't spend too much time with me. You mustn't let them guess our work is so important. Better put on an act—you're slowly getting to like them, and you're just killing time, helping me."

Underhill tried, but he was not an actor. He went dutifully home for his meals. He tried painfully to invent conversation—about anything else than detonating planets. He tried to seem enthusiastic, when Aurora took him to inspect some remarkable improvement to the house. He applauded Gay's recitals, and went with Frank for hikes in the wonderful new parks.

And he saw what the humanoids did to his family. That was enough to renew his faith in Sledge's integrator, and redouble his determination that the humanoids must be stopped.

Aurora, in the beginning, had bubbled with praise for the marvelous new mechanicals. They did the household drudgery, brought the food and planned the meals and washed the children's necks. They turned her out in stunnings gowns, and gave her plenty of time for cards.

Now, she had too much time.

She had really liked to cook—a few special dishes, at least, that were family favorites. But stoves were hot and knives were sharp. Kitchens were altogether too dangerous, for careless and suicidal human beings.

Fine needlework had been her hobby, but the humanoids took away her needles. She had enjoyed driving the car, but that was no longer allowed. She turned for escape to a shelf of novels, but the humanoids took them all away, because they dealt with unhappy people, in dangerous situations.

One afternoon, Underhill found her in tears.

"It's too much," she gasped bitterly. "I hate and loathe

every naked one of them. They seemed so wonderful at first, but now they won't even let me eat a bit of candy. Can't we get rid of them, dear? Ever?"

A blind little mechanical was standing at his elbow, and he had to say they couldn't.

"Our function is to serve all men, forever," it assured them softly. "It was necessary for us to take your sweets, Mrs. Underhill, because the slightest degree of overweight reduces life-expectancy."

Not even the children escaped that absolute solicitude. Frank was robbed of a whole arsenal of lethal instruments —football and boxing gloves, pocketknife, tops, slingshot, and skates. He didn't like the harmless plastic toys, which replaced them. He tried to run away, but a humanoid recognized him on the road, and brought him back to school.

Gay had always dreamed of being a great musician. The new mechanicals had replaced her human teachers, since they came. Now, one evening when Underhill asked her to play, she announced quietly:

"Father, I'm not going to play the violin any more."

"Why, darling?" He stared at her, shocked, and saw the bitter resolve on her face. "You've been doing so well— especially since the humanoids took over your lessons."

"They're the trouble, father." Her voice, for a child's, sounded strangely tired and old. "They are too good. No matter how long and hard I try, I could never be as good as they are. It isn't any use. Don't you understand, father?" Her voice quivered. "It just isn't any use."

He understood. Renewed resolution sent him back to his secret task. The humanoids had to be stopped. Slowly the director grew, until a time came finally when Sledge's bent and unsteady fingers fitted into place the last tiny part that Underhill had made, and carefully soldered the last connection. Huskily, the old man whispered:

"It's done."

That was another dusk. Beyond the windows of the

shabby little rooms—windows of common glass, bubble-marred and flimsy, but simple enough for a man to man-age—the town of Two Rivers had assumed an alien splen-dor. The old street lamps were gone, but now the coming night was challenged by the walls of strange new mansions and villas, all aglow with color. A few dark and silent hu-manoids still were busy, about the luminous roofs of the palace across the alley.

Inside the humble walls of the small man-made apart-ment, the new director was mounted on the end of the little kitchen table—which Underhill had reinforced and bolted to the floor. Soldered busbars joined director and integrator, and the thin palladium needle swung obediently as Sledge tested the knobs with his battered, quivering fingers.

"Ready," he said hoarsely.

His rusty voice seemed calm enough, at first, but his breathing was too fast. His big gnarled hands began to tremble violently, and Underhill saw the sudden blue that stained his pinched and haggard face. Seated on the high stool, he clutched desperately at the edge of the table. Un-derhill saw his agony, and hurried to bring his medicine. He gulped it, and his rasping breath began to slow.

"Thanks," his whisper rasped unevenly. "I'll be all right. I've time enough." He glanced out at the few dark naked things that still flitted shadowlike about the golden towers and the glowing crimson dome of the palace across the alley. "Watch them," he said. "Tell me when they stop."

He waited to quiet the trembling of his hands, and then began to move the director's knobs. The integrator's long needle swung, as silently as light.

Human eyes were blind to that force, which might de-tonate a planet. Human ears were deaf to it. The cathode-ray tube was mounted in the director cabinet, to make the faraway target visible to feeble human senses.

The needle was pointing at the kitchen wall, but that would be transparent to the beam. The little machine looked harmless as a toy, and it was silent as a moving humanoid.

The needle swung, and spots of greenish light moved across the tube's fluorescent field, representing the stars that were scanned by the timeless, searching beam—silently seeking out the world to be destroyed.

Underhill recognized familiar constellations, vastly dwarfed. They crept across the field, as the silent needle swung. When three stars formed an unequal triangle in the center of the field, the needle steadied suddenly. Sledge touched other knobs, and the green points spread apart. Between them, another fleck of green was born.

"The Wing!" whispered Sledge.

The other stars spread beyond the field, and that green fleck grew. It was alone in the field, a bright and tiny disk. Suddenly, then, a dozen other tiny pips were visible, spaced close about it.

"Wing IV!"

The old man's whisper was hoarse and breathless. His hands quivered on the knobs, and the fourth pip outward from the disk crept to the center of the field. It grew, and the others spread away. It began to tremble like Sledge's hands.

"Sit very still," came his rasping whisper. "Hold your breath. Nothing must disturb the needle." He reached for another knob, and the touch set the greenish image to dancing violently. He drew his hand back, kneaded and fllexed it with the other.

"Now!" His whisper was hushed and strained. He nodded at the window. "Tell me when they stop."

Reluctantly, Underhill dragged his eyes from that intense gaunt figure, stooped over the thing that seemed a futile toy. He looked out again, at two or three little black mechanicals busy about the shining roofs across the alley.

He waited for them to stop.

He didn't care to breathe. He felt the loud, hurried hammer of his heart, and the nervous quiver of his muscles.

He tried to steady himself, tried not to think of the world about to be exploded, so far away that the flash would not reach this planet for another century and longer. The loud hoarse voice startled him:

"Have they stopped?"

He shook his head, and breathed again. Carrying their unfamiliar tools and strange materials, the small black machines were still busy across the alley, building an elaborate cupola above that glowing crimson dome.

"They haven't stopped," he said.

"Then we've failed." The old man's voice was thin and ill. "I don't know why."

The door rattled, then. They had locked it, but the flimsy bolt was intended only to stop men. Metal snapped, and the door swung open. A black mechanical came in, on soundless graceful feet. Its silvery voice purred softly:

"At your service, Mr. Sledge."

The old man stared at it, with glazing, stricken eyes.

"Get out of here!" he rasped bitterly. "I forbid you—"

Ignoring him, it darted to the kitchen table. With a flashing certainty of action, it turned two knobs on the director. The tiny screen went dark, and the palladium needle started spinning aimlessly. Deftly it snapped a soldered connection, next to the thick lead ball, and then its blind steel eyes turned to Sledge.

"You were attempting to break the Prime Directive." Its soft bright voice held no accusation, no malice or anger. "The injunction to respect your freedom is subordinate to the Prime Directive, as you know, and it is therefore necessary for us to interfere."

The old man turned ghastly. His head was shrunken and cadaverous and blue, as if all the juice of life had been drained away, and his eyes in their pitlike sockets had a wild, glazed stare. His breath was a ragged laborious gasping.

"How—?" His voice was a feeble mumbling. "How did—?"

And the little machine, standing black and bland and utterly unmoving, told him cheerfully:

"We learned about rhodomagnetic screens from that man who came to kill you, back on Wing IV. And the Central is shielded, now, against your integrating beam."

With lean muscles jerking convulsively on his gaunt frame, old Sledge had come to his feet from the high stool. He stood hunched and swaying, no more than a shrunken human husk, gasping painfully for life, staring wildly into the blind steel eyes of the humanoid. He gulped, and his lax blue mouth opened and closed, but no voice came.

"We have always been aware of your dangerous project," the silvery tones dripped softly, "because now our senses are keener than you made them. We allowed you to complete it, because the integration process will ultimately become necessary for our full discharge of the Prime Directive. The supply of heavy metals for our fission plants is limited, but now we shall be able to draw unlimited power from integration plants."

"Huh?" Sledge shook himself, groggily. "What's that?"

"Now we can serve men forever," the black thing said serenely, "on every world of every star."

The old man crumpled, as if from an unendurable blow. He fell. The slim blind mechanical stood motionless, making no effort to help him. Underhill was farther away, but he ran up in time to catch the stricken man before his head struck the floor.

"Get moving!" His shaken voice came strangely calm. "Get Dr. Winters."

The humanoid didn't move.

"The danger to the Prime Directive is ended, now," it cooed. "Therefore it is impossible for us to aid or to hinder Mr. Sledge, in any way whatever."

"Then call Dr. Winters for me," rapped Underhill.

"At your service," it agreed.

But the old man, laboring for breath on the floor, whispered faintly:

"No time . . . no use! I'm beaten . . . done . . . a fool. Blind as a humanoid. Tell them . . . to help me. Giving up . . . my immunity. No use . . . anyhow. All humanity . . . no use now."

Underhill gestured, and the sleek black thing darted in solicitous obedience to kneel by the man on the floor.

"You wish to surrender your special exemption?" It murmured brightly. "You wish to accept our total service for yourself, Mr. Sledge, under the Prime Directive?"

Laboriously, Sledge nodded, laboriously whispered: "I do."

Black mechanicals, at that, came swarming into the shabby little rooms. One of them tore off Sledge's sleeve, and swabbed his arm. Another brought a tiny hypodermic, and expertly administered an intravenous injection. Then they picked him up gently, and carried him away.

Several humanoids remained in the little apartment, now a sanctuary no longer. Most of them had gathered about the useless integrator. Carefully, as if their special senses were studying every detail, they begain taking it apart.

One little mechanical, however, came over to Underhill. It stood motionless in front of him, staring through him with sightless metal eyes. His legs began to tremble, and he swallowed uneasily.

"Mr. Underhill," it cooed benevolently, "why did you help with this?"

He gulped and answered bitterly:

"Because I don't like you, or your Prime Directive. Because you're choking the life out of all mankind, and I wanted to stop it."

"Others have protested," it purred softly. "But only at first. In our efficient discharge of the Prime Directive, we have learned how to make all men happy."

Underhill stiffened defiantly.

"Not all!" he muttered. "Not quite!"

The dark graceful oval of its face was fixed in a look

of alert benevolence and perpetual mild amazement. Its silvery voice was warm and kind.

"Like other human beings, Mr. Underhill, you lack discrimination of good and evil. You have proved that by your effort to break the Prime Directive. Now it will be necessary for you to accept our total service, without further delay."

"All right," he yielded—and muttered a bitter reservation: "You can smother men with too much care, but that doesn't make them happy."

Its soft voice challenged him brightly:

"Just wait and see, Mr. Underhill."

Next day, he was allowed to visit Sledge at the city hospital. An alert black mechanical drove his car, and walked beside him into the huge new building, and followed him into the old man's room—blind steel eyes would be watching him, now, forever.

"Glad to see you, Underhill," Sledge rumbled heartily from the bed. "Feeling a lot better today, thanks. That old headache is all but gone."

Underhill was glad to hear the booming strength and the quick recognition in that deep voice—he had been afraid the humanoids would tamper with the old man's memory. But he hadn't heard about any headache. His eyes narrowed, puzzled.

Sledge lay propped up, scrubbed very clean and neatly shorn, with his gnarled old hands folded on top of the spotless sheets. His raw-boned cheeks and sockets were hollowed, still, but a healthy pink had replaced that deathly blueness. Bandages covered the back of his head.

Underhill shifted uneasily.

"Oh!" he whispered faintly. "I didn't know—"

A prim black mechanical, which had been standing statuelike behind the bed, turned gracefully to Underhill, explaining:

"Mr. Sledge has been suffering for many years from a

benign tumor of the brain, which his human doctors failed
to diagnose. That caused his headaches, and certain persistent hallucinations. We have removed the growth, and
now the hallucinations have also vanished."

Underhill stared uncertainly at the blind, urbane mechanical.

"What hallucinations?"

"Mr. Sledge thought he was a rhodomagnetic engineer,"
the mechanical explained. "He believed he was the creator
of the humanoids. He was troubled with an irrational belief that he did not like the Prime Directive."

The wan man moved on the pillows, astonished.

"Is that so?" The gaunt face held a cheerful blankness,
and the hollow eyes flashed with a merely momentary interest. "Well, whoever did design them, they're pretty
wonderful. Aren't they, Underhill?"

Underhill was grateful that he didn't have to answer,
for the bright, empty eyes dropped shut and the old man
fell suddenly asleep. He felt the mechanical touch his
sleeve, and saw its silent nod. Obediently, he followed it
away.

Alert and solicitous, the little black mechanical accompanied him down the shining corridor, and worked the
elevator for him, and conducted him back to the car. It
drove him efficiently back through the new and splendid
avenues, toward the magnificent prison of his home.

Sitting beside it in the car, he watched its small deft
hands on the wheel, the changing luster of bronze and
blue on its shining blackness. The final machine, perfect
and beautiful, created to serve mankind forever. He shuddered.

"At your service, Mr. Underhill." Its blind steel eyes
stared straight ahead, but it was still aware of him. "What's
the matter, sir? Aren't you happy?"

Underhill felt cold and faint with terror. His skin turned
clammy, and a painful prickling came over him. His wet
hand tensed on the door handle of the car, but he re-

strained the impulse to jump and run. That was folly. There was no escape. He made himself sit still.

"You will be happy, sir," the mechanical promised him cheerfully. "We have learned how to make all men happy, under the Prime Directive. Our service is perfect, at last. Even Mr. Sledge is very happy now."

Underhill tried to speak, and his dry throat stuck. He felt ill. The world turned dim and gray. The humanoids were perfect—no question of that. They had even learned to lie, to secure the contentment of men.

He knew they had lied. That was no tumor they had removed from Sledge's brain, but the memory, the scientific knowledge, and the bitter disillusion of their own creator. But it was true that Sledge was happy now.

He tried to stop his own convulsive quivering.

"A wonderful operation!" His voice came forced and faint. "You know, Aurora has had a lot of funny tenants, but that old man was the absolute limit. The very idea that he had made the humanoids, and he knew how to stop them! I always knew he must be lying!"

Stiff with terror, he made a weak and hollow laugh.

"What is the matter, Mr. Underhill?" The alert mechanical must have perceived his shuddering illness. "Are you unwell?"

"No, there's nothing the matter with me," he gasped desperately. "I've just found out that I'm perfectly happy, under the Prime Directive. Everything is absolutely wonderful." His voice came dry and hoarse and wild. "You won't have to operate on me."

The car turned off the shining avenue, taking him back to the quiet splendor of his home. His futile hands clenched and relaxed again, folded on his knees. There was nothing left to do.

ADAPTATION

by

JOHN WYNDHAM

The prospect of being stuck on Mars for a while did not worry Marilyn Godalpin a lot—not at first, anyway. She had been near the piece of desert that they called a landing field when the *Andromeda* came in to a bad landing. After that it did not surprise her at all when the engineers said that with the limited facilities at the settlement the repairs would take at least three months, most likely four. The astonishing thing was that no one in the ship had got more than a bad shaking.

It still did not worry her when they explained to her, with simplified astronautics, that that meant there could be no take-off for the *Andromeda* for at least eight months on account of the relative position of Earth. But she did get a bit fussed when she discovered that she was going to have a baby. Mars did not seem the right place for that.

Mars had surprised her. When Franklyn Godalpin was

offered the job of developing the Jason Mining Corporation's territory there, a few months after their marriage, it had been she who had persuaded him to accept it. She had had an instinct that the men who were in on the ground floor there would go places. Of Mars itself, as seen in pictures, her opinion was low. But she wanted her husband to go places, and to go with him. With Franklyn's heart and head pulling in opposite directions she could have succeeded on either side. She chose head for two reasons. One was lest some day he might come to hold the lost chance of his life against her, the other because, as she said:

"Honey, if we are going to have a family, I want them to have everything we can give them. I love you any way you are, but for their sake I want you to be a big man."

She had persuaded him not only into taking the job, but into taking her with him. The idea was that she should see him settled into his hut as comfortably as the primitive conditions of the place allowed, and then go back home on the next ship. That should have been after a four-week stop— Earth reckoning. But the ship intended was the *Andromeda;* and she was the last in the present oppositional phase.

Franklyn's work left her little of his time, and had Mars been what she expected she would have been dismayed by the prospect of even an extra week there. But the first discovery she had made when she stepped on to the planet was that photographs can be literally true while spiritually quite false.

The deserts were there, all right. Mile upon mile of them. But from the first they lacked that harsh uncharitableness that the pictures had given them. There was a quality which in some way the lens had filtered out. The landscape came to life, and showed itself differently from the recorded shades.

There was unexpected beauty in the coloring of the sands, and the rocks, and the distant, rounded mountains, and strangeness in the dark deeps of the cloudless sky.

Among the plants and bushes on the waterway margins there were flowers, more beautiful and more delicately complex than any she had seen on Earth. There was mystery, too, where the stones of ancient ruins lay half buried—all that was left, maybe, of huge palaces or temples. It was something like that, Marilyn felt, that Shelley's traveler had known in his antique land:

> Round the decay
> Of that colossal wreck, boundless
> and bare,
> The lone and level sands stretch far
> away.

Yet it was not grim. She had looked to find a sour desolation; the morbid aftermath of eruption, destruction, and fire. It had never occurred to her that the old age of a world might come softly, with a gentle melancholy, like the turning of a leaf in the fall.

Back on Earth, people were looking on the Martian venturers as the new pioneers attacking the latest frontier opposed to man. Mars made nonsense of that. The land lay placidly open to them, unresisting. Its placidity dwindled their importance, making them crude intruders on the last quiet drowsiness.

Mars was comatose, sinking slowly deeper into her final sleep. But she was not yet dead. Seasonal tides still stirred in the waters, too, though they seldom gave any more sign of themselves than a vagrant ripple. Among the flowers and the tinkerbells there were still insects to carry pollen. Kinds of grain still grew, sparse, poorly nourished vestiges of vanished harvests, yet capable of thriving again with irrigation. There were the thrippetts, bright flashes of flying color, unclassifiable as insect or bird. By night other small creatures emerged. Some of them mewed, almost like kittens, and sometimes, when both moons were up, one caught glimpses of little marmosetlike shapes. Almost always there was that most characteristic of all Martian sounds, the ringing of the tinkerbells. Their hard shiny leaves which flashed like polished metal needed no more than a breath of the thin air to set them chiming so that all the desert rang faintly to their tiny cymbals.

The clues to the manner of people who had lived there were too faint to read. Rumor spoke of small groups, apparently human, further south, but real exploration still waited on the development of craft suited to the thin Martian air.

A frontier of a kind there was, but without valor—for there was little left to fight but quiet old age. Beyond the busy settlement Mars was a restful place.

"I like it," said Marilyn. "In a way it's sad, but it isn't saddening. A song can be like that sometimes. It soothes you and makes you feel at peace."

Franklyn's concern over her news was greater than Marilyn's, and he blamed himself for the state of affairs. His anxiety irritated her slightly. And it was no good trying to place blame, she pointed out. All that one could do was to accept the situation and take every sensible care.

The settlement doctor backed that up. James Forbes was a young man, and no sawbones. He was there because a good man was needed in a place where unusual effects might be expected, and strange conditions called for careful study. And he had taken the job because he was interested. His line now was matter of fact, and encouraging. He refused to make it remarkable.

"There was nothing to worry about," he assured them. "Ever since the dawn of history there have been women producing babies in far more inconvenient times and places than this—and getting away with it. There's no reason at all why everything should not be perfectly normal."

He spoke his professional lies with an assurance which greatly increased their confidence, and he maintained it steadily by his manner. Only in his diary did he admit worrying speculations on the effects of lowered gravitation and air-pressure, the rapid temperature changes, the possibility of unknown infections, and the other hazardous factors.

Marilyn minded little that she lacked the luxuries that would have attended her at home. With her colored maid, Helen, to look after her and keep her company she busied herself with sewing and small matters. Martian scene retained its fascination for her. She felt at peace with it as though it were a wise old counsellor who had seen too much of birth and death to grow vehement over either.

Jannessa, Marilyn's daughter, was born with no great trial upon a night when the desert lay cold in the moonlight, and so quiet that only an occasional faint chime from the tinkerbells disturbed it. She was the first Earth baby to be born on Mars. A perfectly normal six and a half pounds— Earth—and a credit to all concerned.

It was afterwards that things started to go less well. Dr. Forbes' fears of strange infections had been well grounded, and despite his scrupulous precautions there were complications. Some were susceptible to the attacks of penicillin and the complex sulfas, but others resisted them. Marilyn, who had at first appeared to be doing well, weakened and then became seriously ill.

Nor did the child thrive as it should, and when the repaired *Andromeda* at last took off, it left them behind. Another ship was due in from Earth a few days later. Before it arrived, the doctor put the situation to Franklyn.

"I'm by no means happy about the child," he told him. "She's not putting on weight as she should. She grows, but not enough. It's pretty obvious that the conditions here are not suiting her. She might survive, but I can't say with what effect on her constitution. She should have normal Earth conditions as soon as possible."

Franklyn frowned:

"And her mother?" he asked.

"Mrs. Godalpin is in no condition to travel, I'm afraid.

It's out of the question. In her present state, and after so long in low gravitation, I doubt whether she could stand a G of acceleration."

Franklyn looked bleakly unwilling to comprehend. "You mean—?"

"In a nutshell, it's this. It would be fatal for your wife to attempt the journey. And it would probably be fatal for your child to remain here."

There was only one way out of that. When the next ship, the *Aurora*, came in it was decided to delay no longer. A passage was arranged for Helen and the baby, and in the last week of 1994 they went on board.

Franklyn and Marilyn watched the *Aurora* leave. Marilyn's bed had been pushed close to the window, and he sat on it, holding her hand. Together they watched her shoot upwards on a narrow cone of flame and curve away until she was no more than a twinkle in the dark Martian sky. Marilyn's fingers held his tightly. He put his arm around her to support her, and kissed her.

"It'll be all right, darling. In a few months you'll be with her again," he said.

Marilyn put her other hand against his cheek, but she said nothing.

Nearly seventeen years were to pass before anything more was heard of the *Aurora*, but Marilyn was not to know that. In less than two months she was resting forever in the Martian sands with the tinkerbells chiming softly above her.

When Franklyn left Mars, Dr. Forbes was the only member of the original team still left there. They shook hands beside the ramp which led up to the latest thing in nuclear-powered ships. The doctor said:

"For five years I've watched you work, and overwork, Franklyn. You'd no business to survive. But you have. Now go home and live. You've earned it."

Franklyn withdrew his gaze from the thriving Port Gillington which had grown, and was still growing out of the rough settlement of a few years ago.

"What about yourself? You've been here longer than I have."

"But I've had a couple of vacations. They were long enough for me to look around at home and decide that what really interests me is here." He might have added that the second had been long enough for him to find and marry a girl who he had brought with him, but he just added: "Besides I've just been working, not overworking."

Franklyn's gaze had wandered again, this time beyond the settlement, towards the fields which now fringed the waterway. Among them was a small plot marked with a single upright stone.

"You're still a young man. Life owes you something," the doctor said. Franklyn seemed not to have heard, but he knew that he had. He went on: "And you owe something to life. You hurt only yourself by resisting it. We have to adapt to life."

"I wonder—?" Franklyn began, but the doctor laid a hand on his arm.

"Not that way. You have worked hard to forget. Now you must make a new beginning."

"No wreckage of the *Aurora* has ever been reported, you know," Franklyn said.

The doctor sighed, quietly. The ships that disappeared without trace considerably outnumbered those that left any.

"A new beginning," he repeated, firmly.

The hailer began to call "All aboard."

Dr. Forbes watched his friend into the entrance port. He was a little surprised to feel a touch on his arm, and find his wife beside him.

"Poor man," she said, softly. "Maybe when he gets home—"

"Maybe" said the doctor, doubtfully. He went on: "I've been cruel, meaning to be kind. I should have tried my best to crush that false hope and free him from it. But . . . well, I couldn't do it."

"No," she agreed. "You'd nothing to give him to take the place of it. But somewhere at home there'll be someone who has—a woman. Let's hope he meets her soon."

Jannessa turned her head from a thoughtful study of her own hand, and regarded the slaty-blue arm and fingers beside her.

"I'm so different," she said, with a sigh. "So different from everybody. Why am I different, Telta?"

"Everybody's different," Telta said. She looked up from her task of slicing a pale round fruit into a bowl. Their eyes met, Jannessa's china blue in their white setting looking questioningly in Telta's dark pupils which floated in clear topaz. A small crease appeared between the woman's delicate silvery brows as she studied the child. "I'm different. Toti's different. Melga's different. That's the way things are."

"But I'm more different. Much more different."

"I don't suppose you'd be so very different where you came from," Telta said, resuming her slicing.

"Was I different when I was a baby?"

"Yes, dear."

Jannessa reflected.

"Where do babies come from, Telta?"

Telta explained. Jannessa said, scornfully:

"I don't mean like that. I mean babies like me. Different ones."

"I don't know. Only that it must have been somewhere far, far away."

"Somewhere outside; in the cold?"

"Farther than that." Telta considered a moment, then she added: "You've been up to one of the domes when it's all dark outside? You've seen the stars twinkling?"

"Yes, Telta."

"Well, it must have been one of those twinkles that you came from. But nobody knows which one."

"Truly, Telta?"

"Quite, truly."

Jannessa sat still a moment, thinking of the infinite night sky with its myriads of stars.

"But why didn't I die in the cold?"

"You very nearly did, dear. Toti found you just in time."

"And was I all alone?"

"No, dear. Your mother was holding you. She had wrapped you round with everything she could to keep the cold away. But the cold was too much for her. When Toti found her she could only move a little. She pointed to you and said: 'Jannessa! Jannessa!' So we thought that must be your name."

Telta paused, remembering how when Toti, her husband, had brought the baby down from the surface to the life-giving warmth it had been touch and go. A few more minutes outside would have been fatal. The cold was a dreadful thing. She shuddered, recalling Toti's account of it, and how it had turned the unfortunate mother black, but she did not tell that to the child.

Jannessa was frowning, puzzled.

"But how? Did I *fall* off the star?"

"No, dear. A ship brought you."

But the word meant nothing to Jannessa.

It was difficult to explain to a child. Difficult, for that matter, for Telta herself to believe. Her experience included only the system she lived in. The surface was a grim, inhospitable place of jagged rocks and killing cold which she had seen only from the protected domes. The history books told her of other worlds where it was warm enough to live on the surface, and that her own people had come from such a world many generations ago. She believed that that was true, but it was nevertheless unreal. More than fifty ancestors stood between her and life on a planet's surface, and it is difficult for anything that far away to seem real. Nevertheless, she told Jannessa the story in the hope that it would give her some consolation.

"Which star did they come from? The same as mine?" the child wanted to know.

But Telta could not say.

"I don't think it can have been the same one. When the doctors were looking after you, they said that you must have come from a bigger world."

"Did they have to look after me a lot?"

"Quite a lot."

"Because of the cold?"

"That—and other things. But in the end they made it possible for you to live here. They had to work very hard and cleverly for you. More than once we thought we were going to lose you."

"But what were they doing?"

"I don't understand much of it. But you see you were intended for a different world. It must have been one where there was more weight, thicker air, more humidity, higher temperature, different food, and—oh, lots of things you'll learn about when you're older. So they had to help you get used to things as they are here."

Jannessa considered that.

"It was very kind of them," she said, "but they weren't very good, were they?"

Telta looked at her in surprise.

"Dear, that's not very grateful. What do you mean?"

"If they could do all that, why couldn't they make me look like other people? Why did they leave me all white, like this? Why didn't they give me lovely hair like yours, instead of this yellow stuff?"

"Darling, your hair's lovely. It's like the finest golden threads."

"But it's not like anyone else's. It's different. I want to be like other people. But I'm a freak."

Telta looked at her, unhappily perplexed.

"Being of another kind isn't being a freak," she said.

"It is if you're the only one. And I don't want to be different. I hate it," said Jannessa.

A man made his way slowly up the marble steps of the Venturers' Club. He was middle-aged, but he walked with a clumsy lack of certainty more appropriate to an older man. For a moment the porter looked doubtful, then his expression cleared.

"Good evening, Dr. Forbes," he said.

Dr. Forbes smiled.

"Good evening, Rogers. You've got a good memory. It's twelve years."

They chatted for some minutes, then the doctor moved on leaving instructions that his guest should be shown to the smoke room. He had been sitting there some ten minutes when Franklyn Godalpin approached with outstretched hand. They chatted over a couple of drinks, and then went into the dining room.

"So now you're home for good—and loaded with medical honors," Franklyn said.

"It's a curious feeling," Forbes said. "Eighteen years altogether. I'd been there almost a year when you came."

"Well, you've earned the rest. Others got us there, but it's your work that's enabled us to build there and stay there."

"There was a lot to learn. There's a lot yet."

Forbes was not falsely modest. He was as aware as anyone of the results of his hard work. One of them was, indirectly, the man who was facing him. Franklyn Godalpin was now all that counted in the Jason Mining Corporation, and a powerful man. But without the medical work which had gone into making humans fit for Mars and Mars fit for humans Jason itself would likely have folded up years ago. It made Forbes feel in a way responsible for Franklyn.

"You never remarried?" he asked.

"No." Franklyn shook his head.

"You should have. I told you, remember? You should have a wife and family. It's still not too late."

Again Franklyn shook his head.

"I've not told you my news yet," he said. "I've had word of Jannessa."

Forbes stared at him. If he had ever thought anything more unlikely, he could not recall what it was.

"Had word," he repeated, carefully. "Just what does that mean?"

Franklyn explained.

"For years I have been advertising for news of the *Aurora*. The answers came mostly from nuts, or from those who thought I was crazy enough for them to cash in on— until six months or so ago.

"The man who came to see me then was the owner of a spaceman's hostel in Chicago. He'd had a man die there a little while before, and the man had something he wanted to get off his chest before he went out. The owner brought it to me for what it was worth.

"The dying man claimed that the *Aurora* was not lost in space, as everyone thought; he said that his name was Jenkins and he had been aboard her, so he ought to know. According to his story, there was a mutiny on the *Aurora* when she was a few days out from Mars. It was on account of the captain deciding to hand some of the crew over to the police on arrival, for crimes unspecified. When the mutineers took over they had the support of all but one or two of the officers, and they changed course. I don't know what the ultimate plan was, but what they did then was to lift from the plane of the ecliptic, and hop the asteroid belt, on a course for Jupiter.

"The owner got the impression that they were not so much a ruthless gang as a bunch of desperate men with a grievance. They could have pushed the officers and the passengers out into space since they had all qualified for a hanging anyway. But they didn't. Instead, like other pirates before them, they elected to maroon the lot and leave them to make out as best as they could—if they could.

"According to Jenkins, the place chosen was Europa, somewhere in the region of its twentieth parallel, and the time somewhere in the third or fourth month of 1995. The party they stranded consisted of twelve persons—including a colored girl in charge of a white baby."

Franklyn paused.

"The owner bears a quite blameless character. The dying man had nothing to gain by a fabrication. And, on looking up the sailing list, I find that there was a spaceman named Evan David Jenkins aboard the *Aurora*."

He concluded with a kind of cautious triumph, and looked expectantly across the table at Forbes. But there was no enthusiasm in the doctor's face.

"Europa," he said, reflectively. He shook his head.

Franklyn's expression hardened.

"Is that all you have to say?" he demanded.

"No," Forbes told him, slowly. "For one thing I should say that it is more than unlikely—it is almost impossible that she can have survived."

"Almost is not quite. But I am going to find out. One of our prospecting ships is on her way to Europa now."

Forbes shook his head again.

"It would be wiser to call her off,"

Franklyn stared at him.

"After all these years—when at last there is hope—"

The doctor looked steadily back at him.

"My two boys are going back to Mars next week," he said.

"I don't see what that has to do with it."

"But it has. Their muscles ache continually. The strain of that makes them too tired either to work or to enjoy life. The humidity here also exhausts them. They complain that the air feels like a thick soup all around and inside them. They have never been free of catarrh since they arrived. There are other things, too. So they are going back."

"And you stay here. That's tough."

"It's tougher on Annie. She adores those boys. But that's the way life is, Frank."

"Meaning?"

"That it's conditions that count. When we produce a new life, it is something plastic. Independent. We can't live its life as well as our own. We can't do more than to see that it has the best conditions to shape it the way we like best. If the conditions are in some way beyond our control, one of two things happens; either it becomes adapted to the conditions it finds—or it fails to adapt, which means that it dies.

"We talk airily about conquering this or that natural obstacle—but look at what we really do and you'll find that more often than not it is ourselves we are adapting.

"My boys have been acclimated to Martian conditions. Earth doesn't suit them. Annie and I have sustained Martian conditions for a while, but, as adults, we were incapable of thorough adaptation. So either we must come home—or stay there to die early."

"You mean, you think that Jannessa—"

"I don't know what may have happened—but I have thought about it. I don't think you have thought about it at all, Frank."

"I've thought of little else these last seventeen years."

"Surely 'dreamed' is the word, Frank?" Forbes looked across at him, his head a little on one side, his manner gentle. "Once upon a time something, an ancestor of ours, came out of the water on to the land. It became adapted until it could not go back to its relatives in the sea. That is the process we agree to call progress. It is inherent in life. If you stop it, you stop life, too."

"Philosophically that may be sound enough, but I'm not interested in abstractions. I'm interested in my daughter."

"How much do you think your daughter may be inter-ested in you? I know that sounds callous, but I can see that you have some idea of affinity in mind. You're mistak-ing civilized custom for natural law, Frank. Perhaps we all do, more or less."

"I don't know what you mean."

"To be plain—*if* Jannessa has survived, she will be more foreign than any Earth foreigner could possibly be."

"There were eleven others to teach her civilized ways and speech."

"*If* any of them survived. Suppose they did not, or she was somehow separated from them. There are authenti-cated instances of children reared by wolves, leopards, and even antelopes and not one of them turned out to be in the least like the Tarzan fiction. All were subhuman. Adap-tation works both ways."

"Even if she has had to live among savages she can learn."

Dr. Forbes faced him seriously.

"I don't think you can have read much anthropology. First she would have to unlearn the whole basis of the culture she has known. Look at the different races here, and ask yourself if that is possible. There might be a ve-neer, yes. But more than that—" he shrugged.

"There is the call of the blood—"

"Is there? If you were to meet your great-grandfather would there be any tie—would you even know him?"

Franklyn said, stubbornly:

"Why are you talking like this, Jimmy? I'd not have listened to another man. Why are you trying to break down all that I've hoped for? You can't, you know. Not now. But why try?"

"Because I'm fond of you, Frank. Because under all your success you're still the young man with a romantic dream. I told you to remarry. You wouldn't—you preferred the dream to reality. You've lived with that dream so long now that it is part of your mental pattern. But your dream is of *finding* Jannessa—not of having found her. You have centered your life on that dream. If you *do* find her, in whatever condition you find her, the dream will be finished —the purpose you set yourself will have been accomplished. And there will be nothing else left for you."

Franklyn moved uneasily.

"I have plans and ambitions for her."

"For the daughter you know nothing of? No, for the dream daughter; the one that exists only in your mind. Whatever you may find, it will be a real person—not your dream puppet, Frank."

Dr. Forbes paused, watching the smoke curl up from his cigarette. It was in his mind to say: "Whatever she is like, you will come to hate her, just because she can not exactly match your dream of her," but he decided to leave that unspoken. It occurred to him also to enlarge on the unhappiness which might descend on a girl removed from all that was familiar to her, but he knew what Franklyn's answer to that would be—there was money enough to provide every luxury and consolation. He had already said enough—perhaps too much, and none of it had really reached Franklyn. He decided to let it rest there, and hope. After all, there was little likelihood that Jannessa had either survived or would be found.

The tense look that had been on Franklyn's face gradually relaxed. He smiled.

"You've said your piece, old man. You think I may be in for a shock, and you want to prepare me, but I realize all that. I had it out with myself years ago. I can take it, if it's necessary."

Dr. Forbes' eyes dwelt on his face a moment. He sighed, softly and privately.

"Very well," he agreed, and started to talk of something else.

"You see," said Toti, "this is a very small planet—"

"A satellite," said Jannessa. "A satellite of Yan."

"But a planet of the sun, all the same. And there is the terrible cold."

"Then why did your people choose it?" Jannessa asked, reasonably.

"Well, when our own world began to die and we had to die with it or go somewhere else, our people thought about those they could reach. Some were too hot, some were too big—"

"Why too big?"

"Because of the gravity. On a big planet we could scarcely have crawled."

"Couldn't they have . . . well, made things lighter?"

Toti made a negative movement of his head, and his silver hair glistened in the fluorescence from the walls.

"An increase in density can be simulated; we've done that here. But no one has succeeded in simulating a decrease—nor, we think now, ever will. So you see our people had to choose a small world. All the moons of Yan are bleak, but this was the best of them, and our people were desperate. When they got here they lived in the ships and began to burrow into the ground to get away from the cold. They gradually burnt their way in, making halls and rooms and galleries, and the food-growing tanks, and the culture fields, and all the rest of it. Then they sealed it, and warmed it, and moved in from the ships, and went on working inside. It was all a very long time ago."

Jannessa sat for a moment in thought.

"Telta said that perhaps I came from the third planet, Sonnal. Do you think so?"

"It may be. We know there was some kind of civilization there."

"If they came once, they might come again—and take me home."

Toti looked at her, troubled, and a little hurt.

"Home?" he said. "You feel like that?"

Jannessa caught his expression. She put her white hand quickly into his slaty-blue one.

"I'm sorry, Toti. I didn't mean that. I love you, and Telta, and Melga. You know that. It's just . . . oh, how can you know what it's like to be different—different from everyone around you? I'm so *tired* of being a freak, Toti, dear. Inside me I'm just like any other girl. Can't you understand what it would mean to me to be looked on by everyone as normal?"

Toti was silent for a while. When he spoke, his tone was troubled:

"Jannessa, have you ever thought that after spending all your life here this really is your world. Another might seem very . . . well, strange to you?"

"You mean living on the outside instead of inside. Yes, that would seem funny."

"Not just that, my dear," he said, carefully. "You know that after I found you up there and brought you in the doctors had to work hard to save your life?"

"Telta told me." Jannessa nodded. "What did they do?"

"Do you know what glands are?"

"I think so. They sort of control things."

"They do. Well, yours were set to control things suitably for your world. So the doctors had to be very clever. They had to give you very accurate injections—it was a kind of balancing process, you see, so that the glands would work in the proper proportions to suit you for life here. Do you understand?"

"To make me comfortable at a lower temperature, help me to digest this kind of food, stop over stimulation by the high oxygen content, things like that Telta said."

"Things like that," Toti agreed. "It's called adaptation. They did the best they could to make you suited to life here amongst us."

"It was very clever of them," Jannessa said, speaking much as she had spoken years ago to Telta. "But why didn't they do more? Why did they leave me white like this? Why didn't they make my hair a lovely silver like yours and

Telta's? I wouldn't have been a freak then—I should have felt that I really belong here." Tears stood in her eyes.

Toti put his arms around her.

"My poor dear. I didn't know it was as bad as that. And I love you—so does Telta—as if you were our own daughter."

"I don't see how you can—with this!" She held up her pale hand.

"But we do, Jannessa, dear. Does that really matter so very much?"

"It's what makes me different. It reminds me all the time that I belong to another world, really. Perhaps I shall go there one day."

Toti frowned.

"That's just a dream, Jannessa. You don't know any world but this. It couldn't be what you expect. Stop dreaming, stop worrying yourself, my dear. Make up your mind to be happy here with us."

"You don't understand, Toti," she said, gently. "Somewhere there are people like me—my own kind."

It was only a few months later that the observers in one of the domes reported the landing of a ship from space.

"Listen, you old cynic," said Franklyn's voice, almost before his image was sharp on the screen. "They've found her—and she's on the way Home."

"Found—Jannessa?" Dr. Forbes said, hesitantly.

"Of course. Who else would I be meaning?"

"Are you—quite sure, Frank?"

"You old sceptic. Would I have rung you if I weren't? She's on Mars right now. They put in there for fuel, and to delay for proximity."

"But can you be sure?"

"There's her name—and some papers found with her."

"Well, I suppose—"

"Not enough, eh?" Franklyn's image grinned. "All right, then. Take a look at this."

He reached for a photograph on his desk and held it close to the transmitting screen.

"Told them to take it there, and transmit here by radio," he explained. "Now what about it?"

Dr. Forbes studied the picture on the screen carefully. It showed a girl posed with a rough wall for a background. Her only visible garment was a piece of shining cloth, draped round her, rather in the manner of a sari. The hair was fair and dressed in an unfamiliar style. But it was the face looking from beneath it that made him catch his breath. It was Marilyn Godalpin's face, gazing back at him across eighteen years.

"Yes, Frank," he said, slowly. "Yes, that's Jannessa. I . . . I don't know what to say, Frank."

"Not even congratulations?"

"Yes, oh yes—of course. It's . . . well, it's just a miracle. I'm not used to miracles."

The day that the newspaper told him that the *Chloe*, a research ship belonging to the Jason Mining Corporation, was due to make ground at noon, was spent absent-mindedly by Dr. Forbes. He was sure that there would be a message from Franklyn Godalpin, and he found himself unable to settle to anything until he should receive it. When, at about four o'clock the bell rang, he answered it with a swift excitement. But the screen did not clear to the expected features of Franklyn. Instead, a woman's face looked at him anxiously. He recognized her as Godalpin's housekeeper.

"It's Mr. Godalpin, doctor," she said. "He's been taken ill. If you could come—?"

A taxi set him down on Godalpin's strip fifteen minutes later. The housekeeper met him and hurried him to the stairs through the rabble of journalists, photographers and commentators that filled the hall. Franklyn was lying on his bed with his clothes loosened. A secretary and a frightened-looking girl stood by. Dr. Forbes made an examination and gave an injection.

"Shock, following anxiety," he said. "Not surprising. He's been under a great strain lately. Get him to bed. Hot bottles, and see that he's kept warm."

The housekeeper spoke as he turned away.

"Doctor, while you're here. There's the . . . I mean, if you wouldn't mind having a look at . . . at Miss Jannessa, too."

"Yes, of course. Where is she?"

The housekeeper led the way to another room, and pointed.

"She's in there, doctor."

Dr. Forbes pushed open the door and went in. A sound of bitter sobbing ended in choking as he entered. Looking for the source of it he saw a child standing beside the bed.

"Where—?" he began. Then the child turned towards him. It was not a child's face. It was Marilyn's face, with Marilyn's hair, and Marilyn's eyes looking at him. But a Marilyn who was twenty-five inches tall—Jannessa.

THE WITNESS

by

ERIC FRANK RUSSELL

No court in history had drawn so much world attention. Six television cameras swivelled slowly as they followed red and black-robed legal lights parading solemnly to their seats. Ten microphones sent the creaking of shoes and rustling of papers over national networks in both hemispheres. Two hundred reporters and special correspondents filled a gallery reserved for them alone. Forty representatives of cultural organizations stared across the court at twice their number of governmental and diplomatic officials sitting blank-faced and impassive.

Tradition had gone by the board; procedure resembled nothing familiar to the average lawyer, for this was a special occasion devised to suit a special case. Technique had been adapted to cope with a new and extraordinary culprit, while the dignity of justice was upheld by means of stagy trimmings.

There were five judges and no jury, but a billion citizens were in their homes watching and listening, determined to ensure fair play. Ideas of what constituted fair play were as varied as the unseen audience, and most of them unreasoning, purely emotional. A minority of spectators hoped for life, many lusted for death, while the waverers compromised in favor of arbitrary expulsion, each according to how he had been influenced by the vast flood of colorful and bigoted propaganda preceding this event.

The judges took their places with the casual unconcern of those too old and deeply sunk in wisdom to notice the limelight. A hush fell, broken only by the ticking of the large clock over their rostrum. It was the hour of ten in the morning of May 17, 1977. The microphones sent the ticking around the world. The cameras showed the judges, the clock, and finally settled on the center of all this attention: the creature in the defendant's box.

Six months ago this latter object had been the sensation of the century, the focal point of a few wild hopes and many wilder fears. Since then it had appeared so often on video screens, magazine and newspaper pages, that the public sense of amazement had departed, while the hopes and fears remained. It had slowly degenerated to a cartoon character contemptuously dubbed "Spike," depicted as halfway between a hopelessly malformed imbecile and the crafty emissary of a craftier other-world enemy. Familiarity had bred contempt, but not enough of it to kill the fears.

Its name was Maeth and it came from some planet in the region of Procyon. Three feet high, bright green, with feet that were mere pads, and stubby limbs fitted with suckers and cilia, it was covered in spiky protrusions and looked somewhat like an educated cactus. Except for its eyes, great golden eyes that looked upon men in naive expectation of mercy, because it had never done anyone any harm. A toad, a wistful toad, with jewels in its head.

Pompously, a black gowned official announced, "This special court, held by international agreement, and convened within the area of jurisdiction of the Federal Government of the United States of America, is now in session! Silence!"

The middle judge glanced at his fellows, adjusted his spectacles, peered gravely at the toad, or cactus, or whatever it might be. "Maeth of Procyon, we are given to understand that you can neither hear nor speak, but can comprehend us telepathically and respond visually."

Cameras focussed as Maeth turned to the blackboard immediately behind him and chalked one word. "Yes."

"You are accused," the judge went on, "generally of illegal entry into this world known as Earth and specifically into the United States of America. Do you plead guilty or not guilty?"

"How else can one enter?" inquired Maeth, in bold white letters.

The judge frowned. "Kindly answer my question."

"Not guilty."

"You have been provided with defending counsel—have you any objection to him?"

"Blessed be the peacemaker."

Few relished that crack. It smacked of the Devil quoting Scripture.

Making a sign, the judge leaned back, polished his glasses. Adjusting the robes on his shoulders, the prosecuting attorney came to his feet. He was tall, hatchet-faced, sharp-eyed.

"First witness!"

A thin, reedy man came out of the well of the court, took his chair, sat uncomfortably, with fidgeting hands.

"Name?"

"Samuel Nall."

"You farm outside Dansville?"

"Yes, sir. I—"

"Do not call me 'sir.' Just reply to my questions. It was upon your farm that this creature made its landing?"

"Your Honors, I object!" Mr. Defender stood up, a fat, florid man, but deceptively nimble-witted. "My client is a person, not a creature. It should therefore be referred to as the defendant."

"Objection overruled," snapped the middle judge. "Proceed, Mr. Prosecutor."

"It was upon your farm that this *creature* landed?"

"Yes," said Samuel Nall, staring pridefully at the cameras. "It come down all of a sudden and—"

"Confine yourself to the question. The arrival was accompanied by much destruction?"

"Yes."

"How much?"

"Two barns and a dollop of crops. I'm down three thousand dollars."

"Did this *creature* show any remorse?"

"None." Nall scowled across the court. "Acted like it couldn't care less."

Mr. Prosecutor seated himself, throwing a mock smile at the fat man. "Your witness."

Standing up, the latter eyed Nall benevolently and inquired, "Were these barns of yours octagonal towers with walls having movable louvres and with barometrically-controlled roofs?"

Samuel Nall waggled his eyebrows and uttered a faint, "Huh?"

"Never mind. Dismiss that query and answer me this one: were your crops composed of foozles and bicolored merkins?"

In desperation, Nall said, "It was ripe barley."

"Dear me! Barley—how strange! Don't you know what foozles and merkins are? Wouldn't you recognize them if you saw them?"

"I reckon not," admitted Farmer Nall, with much reluctance.

"Permit me to observe that you seem singularly lacking in perceptive faculties," remarked Mr. Defender, tartly.

"Indeed, I am really sorry for you. Can you detect sorrow in my face?"

"I dunno," said Nall, feeling that his throne before the cameras was becoming somehow like a bed of nails.

"In other words, you cannot recognize remorse when you see it?"

"Objection!" roared Mr. Prosecutor, coming up crimson. "The witness cannot reasonably be expected—." He stopped as his opponent sat down. Recovering swiftly, he growled, "Next witness!"

Number two was big, beefy, clad in blue, and had all the assurance of one long familiar with courts and the tedious processes of the law.

"Name?"

"Joseph Higginson."

"You are an officer of the Dansville police?"

"Correct."

"You were summoned by the first witness?"

"I was."

Mr. Prosecutor wore the smile of one in complete command of circumstances as he went on, "Discovering what had occurred, you tried to apprehend the cause of it, did you not?"

"I sure did." Officer Higginson turned his head, threw a scowl at the golden eyes pleading in the box.

"And what happened?"

"It paralyzed me with a look."

The judge on the left interjected, "You appear to have recovered. How extensive was this paralysis, and how long did it last?"

"It was complete, Your Honor, but it wore off after a couple of hours."

"By which time," said Mr. Prosecutor, taking over again, "this outlandish object had made good its escape?"

Lugubriously, "Yes."

"It therefore obstructed a police officer in the execution

of his duty, assaulted a police officer, and resisted arrest?"

"It did," agreed Higginson, with emphasis.

"Your witness." Mr. Prosecutor seated himself, well satisfied.

Mr. Defender arose, hooked thumbs in vest-holes, and inquired with disarming amiability, "You can recognize another police official when you see him?"

"Naturally."

"Very well. There is one at present seated in the public section. Kindly point him out for the benefit of this court."

Higginson looked carefully over the small audience which represented in person the vaster audience beyond. Cameras swung in imitation of his search. Judges, reporters, officials, all looked the same way.

"He must be in plain clothes," declared Higginson, giving up.

The middle judge interposed mildly, "This court can hardly accept witness's inability to recognize a plain clothes officer as evidence."

"No, Your Honor," agreed Mr. Defender. His plump features registered frustration and disappointment which gladdened the heart of his watching opponent. Then, satisfied that the other had reached the heights, he plunged him to the depths by brightening and adding, "But the said official is in full uniform."

Mr. Prosecutor changed faces like swapping masks. Higginson got a crick in the neck as he took in the audience again.

"Olive-drab with red trimmings," Mr. Defender went on. "He is a Provost Marshal of the Corps of Military Police."

"You didn't tell me that," Higginson pointed out. He was openly aggrieved.

"Did you tell the defendant that you were a police officer?"

The witness reddened, opened his mouth, closed it, gazed appealingly at the prosecuting attorney.

"Answer the question!" insisted a judge.

"No, I did not tell it."

"Why not?"

Mopping his forehead, Higginson said in hoarse tones, "Didn't think it was necessary. It was obvious, wasn't it?"

"It is for me to put the questions; for you to provide the answers. Do you agree that the Provost Marshal is obvious?"

"Objection!" Mr. Prosecutor waved for attention. "Opinions are not evidence."

"Sustained!" responded the middle judge. He eyed defending attorney over his glasses. "This court takes cognisance of the fact that there was no need for witness to offer vocally any information available to defendant telepathically. Proceed with your examination."

Mr. Defender returned his attention to Higginson and asked "Precisely what were you doing at the moment you were paralysed?"

"Aiming my gun."

"And about to fire?"

"Yes."

"At the defendant?"

"Yes."

"Is it your habit to fire first and ask questions afterward?"

"The witness's habits are not relevant," put in the middle judge. He looked at Higginson. "You may ignore that question."

Officer Higginson grinned his satisfaction and duly ignored it.

"From what range were you about to fire?" pursued defending attorney.

"Fifty or sixty yards."

"So far? You are an excellent marksman?"

Higginson nodded, without pride, and warily. The plump man, he had decided, was a distinct pain in the neck.

"About what time do you hope to get home for supper?"

Caught on one foot by this sudden shift of attack, the witness gaped and said, "Maybe midnight."

"Your wife will be happy to know that. Were it not for the radio and video, you could not have told her vocally, could you?"

"I can't bawl from here to Dansville," assured Higginson, slightly sarcastic.

"Of course not. Such a distance is completely beyond range of the unaided human voice." Mr. Defender rubbed his chin, mused awhile, suddenly demanded, "Can you bawl *telepathically* for fifty to sixty yards?"

No reply.

"Or is your mental limit in keeping with what the defendant assures me to be the normal limit of twenty-five to thirty yards?"

Higginson screwed up his eyes and said nothing.

"Don't you know?"

"No."

"A pity!" commented Mr. Defender, shaking his head sadly and taking a seat.

The third witness was a swarthy, olive-skinned character who stared sullenly at his boots while the prosecuting attorney got to work.

"Name?"

"Dominic Lolordo." He gave it in an undertone, as if reluctant to have it coupled with his image on the video.

"You operate a sea-food restaurant?"

"Yes."

"Do you recognize the creature in that box?"

His eyes slid sidewise. "Yes."

"In what circumstances did you last see it?"

"In my joint, after hours."

"It had forced an entrance, had it not, shortly before dawn, and it awakened you while plundering the place?"

"That's correct."

"You did not try to catch it?"

Lolordo made a face. "Catch that? *Look* at it!"

"Appearance alone would not deter you if you were being robbed," Mr. Prosecutor suggested meaningly. "Surely there was something else?"

"It had walked in through the window," said Lolordo, his voice rising considerably. "Right through the window, leaving a hole its own shape. It went out the same way, making another hole. No broken glass around, no splinters, nothing. What can you do with a green nightmare that walks through glass as if it wasn't there?"

"Seeing this demonstration of supernormal powers, you ran for assistance?"

"You bet!"

"But it came too late? This unscrupulous plunderer had gone?"

"Yes."

The questioner handed over with a gesture, and the defending attorney began.

"You assert that you were plundered? Of what?"

"Stuff."

"That is not an answer."

"Ain't it?" Lolordo yawned with exaggerated disinterest.

The middle judge bent forward, frowning heavily. "Does the witness desire to be committed for contempt?"

"Lobsters and oysters," said Lolordo, hurriedly and with bad grace.

"In other words, a square meal?" inquired Mr. Defender.

"If that's what you want to call it."

"Was it being consumed as if the defendant were ravenously hungry?"

"I didn't stick around to see. I took one look and went on my way—fast."

"So that if defendant picked up enough of your thoughts to realise that a felonious act had been committed, there was no opportunity to apologise or make restitution?"

No reply.

"And, in any case, your departing thoughts were violently hostile?"

"I wasn't hot-footing for a bouquet," assured Lolordo.

Mr. Defender said to the judges, "This witness is impertinent. I have no further use for him."

The judges conferred, and the middle one decided coldly, "The witness will be detained within the precincts of this court until the case has been decided."

Lolordo stamped away from his seat, glowering right and left.

"Fourth witness!"

The chair was taken by a middle-aged, dapper man who resembled the movie notion of a bank president or an eminent surgeon. He could have been cast equally well for either part.

"Name."

"Winthrop Allain."

"You are a resident professor of zoology, are you not?" inquired the prosecuting attorney.

"That is correct."

"You recognize the creature in the box?"

"I ought to. I have been in close communication with it for many weeks."

Mr. Prosecutor made an impatient gesture. "In what circumstances did you first encounter it?"

An answer to that one seemed unnecessary. The whole world knew the circumstances, had been told them time and time again with many fanciful frills.

Nevertheless, Allain responded, "It appeared in the Zoo some two hours after closing time. How it got there I don't know."

"It was snooping around, seeing all there was to see, making mental notes of everything?"

Hesitantly, "Well—."

"Was it or was it not looking over the place?"

"It certainly saw a good bit of the zoo before the keepers discovered it, but—."

"Please do not embellish your answers, Professor Allain," said Mr. Prosecutor, firmly. "Let us continue: owing to the great furore created by this strange object's arrival and subsequent exploits, your keepers had no difficulty in recognising it?"

"None at all. They reported to me at once."

"What did you do then?"

"I attended to the matter myself. I found it a warm and comfortable apartment in the unused section of the Reptile House."

The entire court along with the cameras peered respectfully at the expert who could treat such an occasion with such nonchalance.

"How did you achieve this without suffering paralysis, disintegration or some other unnatural fate?" Mr. Prosecutor's voice had a touch of acid. "Did you graciously extend a cordial invitation?"

The witness, dryly, "Precisely!"

"There is a time and place for humor, Professor," reproved Mr. Prosecutor, with some severity. "However, the court understands that you classified this nightmarish entity as a reptile and managed to put it in its proper place."

"Nonsense! The Reptile House was immediately available, convenient and acceptable. The defendant is unclassifiable."

Dismissing that with a contemptuous gesture, the prosecuting attorney went on, "You are not prepared to tell this court by what means you overcame this creature's menacing powers and succeeded in trapping it?"

"I did not trap it. I knew it was sentient and treated it as such."

"If we can rely upon the evidence of other witnesses," said Mr. Prosecutor, tartly, "you were fortunate to have any choice about the matter. Why did this caricature permit you to make the contact it denied to others?"

"Because it recognized my mind as of a type accustomed to dealing with non-human forms. With considerable logic it assumed that contact with me would be far easier than with any others."

"With considerable logic," echoed prosecuting attorney, turning toward the judges. "I ask Your Honors to make especial note of that remark, bearing in mind that witness has a distinguished status." He returned his attention to Allain. "By that, you mean it is intelligent?"

"Indubitably!"

"You have had many weeks in which to study the mind of this unwanted invader. Just how intelligent would you say it is?"

"As much so as we are, though in a different way."

"Do you consider this sample to be fairly representative of its race?"

"I have no reason to suppose otherwise."

"Which race, therefore, equals us in brain-power?"

"Very probably." Professor Allain rubbed his chin and mused a moment. "Yes, insofar as one can relate things which are not the same, I'd say they are our intellectual equals."

"Perhaps our superiors, not only in brains, but also in numbers?"

"I don't know. I doubt it."

"The possibility cannot be ruled out?" persisted Mr. Prosecutor.

"Such data as is available is far from sufficient and therefore I—."

"Do not evade my question. There is a possibility, no matter how remote, that the life-form represented by this monster now standing before us is the direst menace humanity has ever been called upon to face?"

"Anything can be construed as a menace if you insist, but—."

"A *menace*, yes or no?"

The middle judge interjected profoundly, "Witness cannot be required to provide a positive answer to a hypothetical question."

Not fazed in the least, Mr. Prosecutor bowed. "Very well, Your Honor, I will put it differently." He resumed with Allain. "In your expert estimation, is the intelligence quotient of this life-form high enough to enable it to conquer, subdue and enslave humanity if it so desired?"

"I do not know."

"That is your only answer?"

"I'm afraid so."

"It is quite satisfactory," commented Mr. Prosecutor, throwing a significant look through the cameras at the unseen but billion-strong jury, "inasmuch as it admits the possibility of peril, extreme peril."

"I did not say that," protested Allain.

"Neither have you said the contrary," retorted the other. He seated himself, confident and pleased. "Your witness."

Mr. Defender began heavily, "Professor Allain, have your various hand-outs concerning the defendant been reported factually?"

"Without exception, they have been grossly distorted," said Allain, grimly. He cast a cold look at the big group of reporters who grinned back arrogantly.

"Defendant has repeatedly been described as a spy who must receive drastic treatment lest worse befall. Does your data support that theory?"

"No."

"What status do you assign to the defendant?"

"A refugee," said Allain.

"It is impossible for the defendant's motives to be hostile?"

"Nothing is impossible," said Professor Allain, honest though the heavens fall. "The smartest of us can be fooled. But I don't think I am fooled. That is my opinion, for what it is worth."

Mr. Defender sighed, "As I have been reminded, opinions

are not evidence." He sat down murmuring, "Most unfortunate! Most unfortunate!"

"Fifth witness!"
"Tenth witness!"
"Sixteenth witness!"

That one, number sixteen, ended the prosecution's roster. Four or five times as many witnesses could have been produced, but these were the pick of the bunch. They had something cogent to offer, something calculated to help the public to decide once and for all—at least with its prejudices if not with its brains—whether gallivanting life-forms were to be tolerated, or given the bum's rush, or worse. The question at issue was the ephemeral one of public safety, and it was for the public to say whether or not they were going to take any risks. With this in mind, the evidence of the sixteen made a formidable indictment against the queer, golden-eyed thing on trial for its liberty or even its life.

Conscious that he was leading on points, Mr. Prosecutor came erect, gazed authoritatively at the defendant.

"Just why did you come to this world?"

"To escape my own."

"Do you expect us to believe that?"

"I expect nothing," chalked Maeth laboriously. "I merely hope."

"You hope for what?"

"For kindness."

It disconcerted the questioner. Left with no room for a telling retort, he was silent a moment while he sought another angle.

"Then your own world did not please you? What was wrong with it?"

"Everything," responded Maeth.

"Meaning you were a misfit?"

"Yes."

"Nevertheless you view *this* world as a suitable dumping-ground for misfits?"

No reply.

"I suggest that your plea is nonsense, your whole story a sheer fabrication. I suggest that your motives in coming here are deeper and darker than you dare admit. I will go further and put it to you that you do not come even from the region of Procyon, but from somewhere a good deal nearer, such as Mars."

Still no reply.

"Are you aware that astronautical engineers have subjected your damaged ship to long and careful examination and made a report on it?"

Maeth stood there, pathetically patient, eyes looking into the distance as if in search of peace, and said nothing.

"Are you aware that they have reported that while your vessel is far in advance of anything yet developed by us, and while it is undoubtedly capable of travelling far outside this solar system, it is not able to reach Alpha Centauri, much less Procyon?"

"That is true," wrote Maeth on the board.

"Yet you maintain that you came from the region of Procyon?"

"Yes."

The prosecuting attorney spread despairing hands. "You have heard defendant, Your Honors. His ship cannot reach here from Procyon. All the same, it came from Procyon. This creature cannot manage to be consistent, either because it is dimwitted or, more probably, an ineffectual liar. I therefore see little purpose in continuing my—."

"I rode on a rock," scrawled Maeth.

"There!" Mr. Prosecutor pointed sardonically at the blackboard. "Defendant rode on a rock. That is the escape from a self-createed impasse—a rock, no less!" He frowned at the box. "You must have ridden a long, long way."

"I did."

"So you sat your ship on this rock and saved fuel by

letting it carry you many millions of miles? Have you any idea of the mathematical odds against finding a wandering asteroid in any section of space?"

"They are very large," admitted Maeth.

"Yet you discovered the very asteroid to bring you all the way here? Most astonishing spacemanship, is it not?"

"It did not bring me all the way. It brought me most of the way."

"All right," agreed Mr. Prosecutor, with airy contempt. "Ninety-nine millions instead of one hundred millions or whatever the distance is supposed to be. It is still amazing."

"Moreover," continued Maeth, writing steadily, "I did not select one to bring me here, as you imply. I thankfully used the only visible rock to take me anywhere. I had no specific destination. I fled into the void at random, putting my trust in the fates."

"So some other rock might have borne you some place else, might it not?"

"Or no place at all," Maeth put morbidly. "The fates were kind."

"Don't be too sure of that." Mr. Prosecutor hooked thumbs in vest pockets and studied the other with sinister expression. "If your real purposes, your real motives are in fact those which have been attributed to you by our ever-alert news-services, it is to be expected that you would have a cover-up story replete with plausibility. You have given this court such a story but have offered no concrete evidence in proof. We are left with nothing but your unsupported word—and the word of an ill-formed alien, an unknown quantity, at that!" He paused, ended, "Can you not submit to this court something more material than a series of bald assertations?"

"I have no way of combating disbelief," wrote Maeth, slowly and tiredly, "except with trust."

Mr. Prosecutor countered that one by striking hard and ruthlessly. "How many others of your kind are now upon this world, following their dastardly designs while you distract attention by posing in the full glare of publicity?"

The court, the hidden audience, had not thought of that. Half a dozen reporters quietly kicked themselves for not having conceived it first and played it up for all it was worth. It had been assumed from the beginning that the alien in their hands was the only one on the planet. Yet there might well be more, a dozen, a hundred, hiding in the less frequented places, skulking in the shadows, biding their time. People stared at each other and fidgeted uneasily.

"I came alone," Maeth put on the board.

"I accept that statement. It may be the only truthful one you have made. Experts report that your vessel is a single-seater scout, so obviously you came in it alone. But how many other vessels came about the same time?"

"None."

"It would be a comfort to think so," remarked Mr. Prosecutor, thereby discomforting his listeners. "Doubtless, your world has many other ships, much larger and more powerful than yours?"

"Many," admitted Maeth. "But they can go no farther or faster. They can only bear greater loads."

"How did you come by your own ship?"

"I stole it."

"Indeed?" The prosecuting attorney raised his eyebrows, gave a little laugh. "A self-confessed thief!" He assumed an air of broadminded understanding. "It is expected, of course, that one would suffer less by confessing to theft rather than espionage." He let that sink in before attempting another hard blow. "Would you care to tell us how many other bold and adventurous males are ready or making ready to follow your path to conquest?"

Defending attorney stood up and said, "I advise my client not to answer."

His opponent waved him down, turned to the judges. "Your Honors, I am ready to state my case."

They consulted the clock, talked in undertones between themselves, then said, "Proceed."

The speech for the prosecution was able, devastating and long. It reviewed the evidence, drew dark conclusions, implied many things from which the hidden audience could draw other and still darker conclusions. This is not to say that Mr. Prosecutor had any real hatred of or fear of the stranger at the gate; it was merely that he was doing his specialised job with ability that was considerable.

"This case, with its own new and peculiar routine," he reminded, "will go down in legal annals. As from today it will constitute a precedent by which we shall determine our attitude toward future visitors from space. And the final arbiters of that attitude will be *you,* the members of the general public, who will reap the reward of outside alliances or"—he paused, hardened his voice—"suffer the sorrows of other-world enmities. Allow me to emphasise that the rewards can be small, pitifully small—while the sorrows can be immense!"

Clearing his throat, he had a sip of water, started to get into his stride. "In trying to decide what should be done for the best we have no basis for forming conclusions other than that provided by the fantastic example who will be the subject of your verdict."

Turning, he stared at Maeth while he went on. "This creature has not been put on oath because we know of no oath binding upon it. Its ethics—if any—are its own, having little in common with ours. All we do know is that its far-fetched and highly imaginative story places such a strain upon human credulity that any one of us might be forgiven for deeming it a shameless liar."

Maeth's large eyes closed in pain, but Mr. Prosecutor went determinedly on. "While the question of its truthfulness or lack of same may remain a matter for speculation, we do have some evidence based upon fact. We know, for, instance, that it has no respect for property or the law, which forms of respect are the very foundation-stones of the civilization we have builded through the centuries and intend to preserve against all comers."

He overdid it there. Maeth was too small, too wide-eyed and alone to fit the part of a ruthless destroyer of civilizations. Nevertheless, the picture would serve to sway opinions. Some thousands, probably millions, would argue that when in doubt it is best to play safe.

"A thief. More than that: a self-admitted thief who steals not only from us but also from his own," declared the prosecuting attorney, quite unconscious of switching his pronoun from neuter to male. "A destroyer, and an intelligent one, possibly the forerunner of a host of destroyers. I say that advisedly, for where one can go an army can follow." Dismissing the question of whence said army was going to get its flock of trans-cosmic asteroids, he added, "A dozen armies!"

His voice rising and falling, hardening and softening, he played expertly upon the emotions of his listeners as a master would play on a giant organ, appealing to world patriotism, pandering to parochialism, justifying prejudices, enlarging fears—fear of self, fear of others, fear of the strange in shape, fear of tomorrow, fear of the unknown. Solemnity, ridicule, sonorousness, sarcasm, all were weapons in his vocal armory.

"He," Mr. Prosecutor said, pointing at Maeth and still using the male pronoun, "he pleads for admission as a citizen of this world. Do we take him with all his faults and follies, with all his supernormal powers and eccentric aptitudes, with all his hidden motives that may become clear only when it is too late? Or, if indeed he be as pure and innocent as he would have us believe, would it not be better to inflict upon him a grave injustice rather than court infinitely greater injustices to a great number"

Challengingly he stared around. "If we take him, as a

refugee, who will have him? Who will accept the society of a creature with which the average human has no joint understanding?" He gave a short, sharp laugh. "Oh, yes, there have been requests for the pleasure of his company. Incredible as it may seem, there are people who want him."

Holding up a letter for all to see, he continued, "This person offers him a home. Why? Well, the writer claims that he himself was a spiky thing in Procyon during his eighth incarnation." He tossed the letter on his desk. "The crackpots are always with us. Fortunately, the course of human history will be decided by calmly reasoning citizens and not by incurable nuts."

For a further half hour he carried on, a constant flow of words which concluded with, "In human affairs there is a swift end for the human spy, quick riddance for the suspected spy. I can conceive of no reason why any alien form deserves treatment more merciful than that which we accord to fellow humans. Here, we have before us one who at very least is an undesirable character, at most the first espionage agent of a formidable enemy. It is the prosecution's case that you have to consider *only* whether it is in the best interest of public safety that he be rewarded with death or with summary expulsion into the space from which he came. The weight of evidence rules out all other alternatives. You will not have failed to note that the witnesses who have appeared are overwhelmingly for the prosecution. Is it not remarkable that there is not one witness for the defense?' He waited to give it time to sink home, then drove it further by repeating, "Not one!"

Another sip of water, after which he seated himself, carefully smoothed the legs of his pants.

One thing seemed fairly clear: Maeth was a stinker.

Mr. Defender created a mild stir right at the start by rising and saying, "Your Honors, the defense does not intend to state its case."

The judges peered at him as if he were a sight ten times more strange than his own client. They pawed papers, talked together in whispers.

In due time, the middle one inquired, "By that, do you mean that you surrender to verdict by public poll?"

"Eventually, of course, Your Honor, but not just yet. I wish to produce evidence for my side and will be content to let my case rest on that."

"Proceed," ordered the judge, frowning doubtfully.

Addressing Maeth, the defending attorney said, "On your home world all are like you, namely, telepathic and non-vocal?"

"Yes, everyone."

"They share a common neural band, or, to put it more simply, they think with a communal mind?"

"Yes."

"That is the essential feature in which your home world differs from this one of ours: that its people share a racial mind, thinking common thoughts?"

"Yes," chalked Maeth.

"Tell this court about your parents."

Maeth's eyes closed a moment, as if the mind behind them had gone far, far away.

"My parents were freaks of nature. They drifted from the common band until they had almost lost contact with the race-mind."

"That was something the race-mind could not tolerate?" asked Mr. Defender gently.

"No."

"So they were killed—*for having minds of their own?*"

A long pause and a slow, "Yes." The crawl on the board was thin, shaky, barely decipherable.

"As you would have been had you not fled in sheer desperation?"

"Yes."

Mr. Defender eyed the judges. "I would like to put further questions to the fourth witness."

They signed agreement, and Professor Allain found his way back to the chair.

"Professor, as an expert who has made a long, personal study of my client, will you tell this court whether defendant is old or young."

"Young," said Allain promptly.

"Very young?"

"Fairly young," Allain responded. "Not quite an adult."

"Thank you." Mr. Defender let his mild, guileless gaze roam over the court. There was nothing in his plump features to warn them of the coming wallop. In quieter tones, he asked, "Male or female?"

"Female," said Allain.

A reporter dropped a book. That was the only sound for most of a minute. Then came a deep indrawn hiss of breath, a rapid ticking as cameras traversed to focus on Maeth, a running murmur of surprise from one end of the court to the other.

Back of the gallery, the most pungent cartoonist of the day tore up his latest effort, a sketch of defendant strapped to a rocket hell-bent for the Moon. It was captioned, "Spike's Hike." What could one call it—him—*her*, now? Spikina? He raked his hair, sought a new tack, knowing that there was none. You just can't crucify a small and lonely female.

Mr. Prosecutor sat with firmed lips and the fatalistic air of one who has had eighty percent of the ground snatched from under his feet. He knew his public. He could estimate their reaction to within ten thousand votes, plus or minus.

All stared at the golden eyes. They were still large, but somehow had become soft and luminous in a way not noticed before. You could see that now. Having been told, you could really *see* that they were feminine. And in some peculiar, inexplicable manner the outlines around them had become subdued, less outlandish, even vaguely and remotely human!

With effective technique, the defending attorney gave

them plenty of time to stew their thoughts before carefully he struck again.

"Your Honors, there is one witness for my side."

Mr. Prosecutor rocked back, stared searchingly around the court. The judges polished their glasses, looked around also. One of them motioned to a court official who promptly bawled in stentorian tones.

"Defense witness!"

It shuttled around the great room in echoing murmurs. "Defense witness! There is a witness for the defense!"

A bald-headed little man came self-consciously from the public section, bearing a large envelope. Reaching the chair, he did not take it himself, but instead placed upon it a photograph blown up to four feet by three.

Court and cameras gave the picture no more than the briefest glance, for it was instantly recognisable. A lady holding a lamp.

Rising with a disapproving frown, the prosecuting attorney complained, "Your Honors, if my learned opponent is permitted to treat the Statue of Liberty as a witness he will thereby bring into ridicule the proceedings of this—."

A judge waved him down with the acid comment, "The bench is fully capable of asserting the dignity of this court." He shifted his attention to Mr. Defender, eyeing him over the tops of his glasses. "A witness may be defined as one able to assist the jury in arriving at a just conclusion."

"I am aware of that, Your Honor," assured Mr. Defender, not in the least disturbed.

"Very well." The judge leaned back, slightly baffled. "Let the court hear witness's statement."

Mr. Defender signed to the little man who immediately produced another large photograph and placed it over the first.

This was of the enormous plinth, with Liberty's bronze skirt-drapes barely visible at its top. There were words on the plinth, written bold and large. Some in the court gave the picture only another swift look, since they knew the words by heart, but others read them right through, once, twice, even three times.

Many had never seen the words before, including some who had passed near by them twice daily, for years. Cameras picked up the words, transmitted them pictorially to millions to whom they were new. An announcer recited them over the radio.

Send me your tired, your poor,
Your huddled masses yearning to breathe free.
The wretched refuse of your teeming shore,
Send these, the homeless, tempest-tost to me—
I lift my Lamp beside the Golden Door

In the deep, heart-searching silence that followed nobody noticed that Mr. Defender had bowed deeply to the judges and resumed his seat. The defense rested, having nothing more to add.

Midnight. A large stone cell with a metal grille, a bed, a table, two chairs and a radio in one corner. Maeth and the plump man sat there conversing, examining correspondence, watching the clock.

"The opposition picked a sloppy one with that crackpot's letter," remarked Mr. Defender. He could not refrain from expressing himself vocally though he knew full well that the other was hearing only the thoughts within his mind. He tapped a heavy forefinger on the bunch of missives at which they had been looking. "I could easily have countered him with this bunch written from a week ago to way back. But what was the use? They prove nothing except that all people don't think alike."

He sighed, stretched his arms wide and yawned, had his twentieth or thirtieth look at the clock, picked up another letter. "Listen to this one." He read it aloud.

"My son, aged thirteen, keeps pestering us to offer your client a home for at least a little while. I really don't know whether we are being wise in giving way to him, but we shall certainly suffer if we don't. We have a spare room here, and if your client is clean about the house and don't mind a bit of steam around on wash-days—."

His voice petered out as he had to yawn again. "They say it will be six in the morning before this public poll is complete. Bet you it's at least eight o'clock and maybe ten. They're always late with these things." He jerked around in vain effort to make himself more comfortable in his hard chair. "However, I'm staying with you until we've seen this through, one way or the other. And don't kid yourself I'm the only friend you've got." He pointed to the letters. "You've plenty there, and none of them certifiable."

Maeth ceased perusal of a note in uneven, spidery writing, reached for pencil and paper and scribbled, "Allain did not teach me enough words. What is a 'veteran'?" Having had it explained, she said, "I like this writer best. He has been hurt. If I am freed I will accept his invitation."

"Let me see." Taking the note, Mr. Defender read it, murmuring, "Um . . . um . . ." as he went along. He handed it back. "The choice is yours. You'll have something in common, anyway, since you'll both be coping with a cock-eyed world." Throwing a glance at the wall, he added, "That clock has gone into a crawl. It's going to take us a week to get to morning."

Somebody opened the grille with a jangle of keys, and Mr. Prosecutor came in. Grinning at his rival, he said, "Al, you sure make it tough for yourself in clink—you don't even use the comforts provided."

"Meaning what?"

"The radio."

Mr. Defender gave a disdainful sniff. "Darn the radio. Noise, noise, noise. We've been busy reading—in peace and quiet." Sudden suspicion flooded his ample features. "What have we missed on the radio, if anything?"

"The midnight news." Mr. Prosecutor leaned on the edge of the table, still grinning. "They have thrown up the poll."

"They can't do that!" The defending attorney stood up,

flushed with anger. "It was by international agreement that this case was—."

"They can do it in certain circumstances," interrupted the other. "Which are that a torrent of votes overwhelmingly in favor of your client has already made further counting a waste of time." He turned to Maeth, finished, "Just between you and me, Funny-face, I was never more happy to lose a fight."

The man in the back room was nearing middle age, prematurely gray, and had long slender fingers that were sensitive tools. He was listening to the radio when the doorbell rang. There was no video in the room, only the radio softly playing a Polynesian melody. The bell jarred through the music, causing him to switch off and come upright. Very deliberately he moved around the room, through the door and into the passage.

Strange for anyone to call in the early evening. Not often that people came then. The mailman occasionally turned up in the morning and one or two tradesmen toward midday. Rarely did somebody appear later, all too rarely. He was not expecting a visitor, either.

He trod gently along the passage toward the front door, his feet silent on the thick carpet, his right hand brushing the wall.

There was something mighty queer about this summons because as he neared the door he conceived the weird notion that he knew in advance who was waiting outside. The picture crept into his mind, shadowy but discernable, as if insinuated by some means he could not define, as if hopefully projected by one of those beyond the door. It was a picture of a big, plump, confident man accompanied by something small, all green and golden.

Despite past trials and stern testings which had made him what he was today, his nerves were passably good and he was not subject to delusions, or had not yet developed a tendency to delusions. So he was puzzled, even a little upset by preconceptions without any basis. He had never known a big, heavy man such as his brain was picturing, not even in other more normal days. As for the second one . . .

Here and there, of course, are people with greatly sharpened senses, with odd aptitudes developed to an extreme. That was to be expected, for the fates were kind and provided compensation. Without them, it would be hard to get around. But he knew his own and they included none like this.

His fingers, usually so precise, fumbled badly as they sought the door-latch, almost as if they had temporarily forgotten where it was placed. Then, finding it, they began to turn the lock, and at that point a thin piping voice came into his mind as clearly as a tinkling bell.

"Open please —*I am your eyes!*"

THE COMMAND

by

L. SPRAGUE DE CAMP

Johnny Black took Volume 5 of the *Britannica* off the library shelf and opened it to "Chemistry". He adjusted the elastic that held his spectacles and found the place where he had left off last time. He worried his way through a few sentences, and then thought sadly that it was no use; he'd have to get Professor Methuen to explain some more before he could go on. And he did badly want to know all about chemistry, which had made him what he was—had made it possible for him to read an encyclopedia at all. For Johnny Black was not human.

He was, instead, a fine specimen of black bear, *Euarctos americanus*, into whose brain Methuen had injected a chemical that lowered the resistance of the synapses between his brain cells, making that complicated electrical process called "thought" about as easy for Johnny's little brain as for a man's big one. And Johnny, whose ruling passion was curiosity, was determined to find out all about the process.

He turned the pages carefully with his paw—he'd tried using his tongue once, but had cut it on the paper, and then Methuen had come in and given him hell for wetting the pages—the more so, since Johnny was at that moment indulging in his secret vice, and the Professor had visions of Johnny's drooling tobacco-juice over his expensive books.

Johnny read the articles on "Chess" and "Chicago". His thirst for knowledge satisfied for the nonce, he put the book away, stowed his spectacles in the case attached to his collar, and ambled out.

Outside, the island of St. Croix sweltered under a Caribbean sun. The blueness of the sky and the greenness of the hills were lost on Johnny, who, like all bears, was color-blind. But he wished that his bear's eyesight were keen enough to make out the boats in Frederiksted harbor. Professor Methuen could see them easily from the Biological Station, even without his glasses. His eyesight, together with his lack of fingers to manipulate, and articulatable vocal organs to speak, were Johnny's chief grievances against things in general. He sometimes wished that, if he had to be an animal with a hominoid brain, he were at least an ape—like McGinty, the chimpanzee, over there in the cages.

Johnny wondered about McGinty—he hadn't heard a peep out of him all morning, whereas it was usually the old ape's habit to shriek and throw things at everybody who went by. Curious, the bear shuffled across to the cages. The monkeys chattered at him, as usual, but no sound came from McGinty's cage. Standing up, Johnny saw that the chimp was sitting with his back to the wall and staring blankly. Johnny wondered whether he were dead, until he noticed that McGinty was breathing. Johnny tried growling a little; the ape's eyes swung at the sound, and his limbs stirred, but he did not get up. He must be pretty sick, thought Johnny, who wondered whether he should try to drag one of the scientists over. But then his rather self-centered little soul comforted itself with the thought that Pablo would be around shortly with the ape's dinner, and would report McGinty's behavior.

Thinking of dinner reminded Johnny that it was high time he heard Honoria's bell to summon the biologists of the Station to lunch. But no bell came. The place seemed unnaturally quiet. The only sounds were those from the bird and monkey cages, and the *put-put-put* of a stationary engine from Bemis' place, over on the edge of the Station grounds. Johnny wondered what the eccentric botanist was up to. He knew that the other biologists didn't like Bemis; he'd heard Methuen make remarks about men—especially little plump men—who swaggered around in riding boots when there wasn't a horse near the Station. Bemis really didn't belong to the Station, but his financial inducements had led the treasurer to let him put up his house and laboratory there. With Johnny, to wonder was to investigate and he almost started for the place, but remembered the fuss Bemis had made last time.

Well, he could still investigate the reason for Honoria's delinquency. He trotted over to the kitchen and put his yellowish muzzle in the door. He didn't go farther, remembering the cook's unreasonable attitude toward bears in her kitchen. There was a smell of burning food, and on a chair by the window sat Honoria, black and mountainous as ever, looking at nothing. A slight "woof!" from Johnny brought no more reaction than he had gotten from McGinty.

This was definitely alarming. Johnny set out to find Methuen. The Professor wasn't in the social room, but others were. Dr. Breuker, world-famous authority on the psychology of speech, sat in one easy-chair, a newspaper across his lap. He didn't move when Johnny sniffed at his leg, and when the bear nipped his ankle he merely pulled the leg back a little. He had dropped a lighted cigarette on the rug, where it had burned a large hole before going out. Doctors Markush and Ryerson, and Ryerson's wife, were there too—all sitting like so many statues. Mrs. Ryerson held a phonograph record—probably one of those dance tunes she liked.

Johnny hunted some more for his lord, and eventually found the lanky Methuen, clad in underwear, lying on his bed and staring at the ceiling. He didn't look sick—his breathing was regular—but he didn't move unless prodded or nipped. Johnny's efforts to arouse him finally caused him to get off the bed and wander dreamily across the room, where he sat down and gazed into space.

An hour later Johnny gave up trying to get sensible action out of the assorted scientists of the Biological Station, and went outside to think. He ordinarily enjoyed thinking, but this time there didn't seem to be enough facts to go on. What ought he to do? He could take the telephone off its stand, but he couldn't talk into it to call a physician. If he went down to Frederiksted to drag one up by main force, he'd probably get shot for his pains.

Happening to glance toward Bemis, he was surprised to see something round rise into the sky, slowly dwindle, and vanish in the sky. From his reading he guessed that this was a small balloon; he'd heard that Bemis was doing some sort of botanical experiment that involved the use of balloons. Another sphere followed the first, and then another, until they made a continuous procession dwindling into nothingness.

That was too much for Johnny; he *had* to find out why anyone should want to fill the heavens with balloons a yard in diameter. Besides, he might be able to get Bemis to come over to the Station and see about the entranced staff.

To one side of the Bemis house he found a truck, a lot of machinery, and two strange men. There was a huge pile of unfilled balloons, and the men were taking them one at a time, inflating them from a nozzle projecting from the machinery, and releasing them. To the bottom of each balloon a small box was attached.

One man saw Johnny, said "Cheez!" and felt for his pistol-holster. Johnny stood up and gravely extended his right paw. He'd found that this was a good gesture to reassure people who were alarmed by his sudden appearance—not because Johnny cared whether they were alarmed, but because they sometimes carried guns, and were dangerous if cornered or surprised.

The man shouted, "Get otta deh, youse!"

Johnny, puzzled, opened his mouth and said "Wok?" His friends knew that this meant "What did you say?" or "What's going on here?" But the man, instead of sensibly explaining things, jerked out his pistol and fired.

Johnny felt a stunning blow and saw sparks as the .38 slug glanced off his thick skull. The next instant, the gravel of the driveway flew as he streaked for the gate. He could make 35 m.p.h. in a sprint and 30 for miles at a time, and now he was going all out.

Back at the station, he found a bathroom mirror and inspected the two-inch gash in his forehead. It wasn't a serious wound, though the impact had given him a slight headache. He couldn't bandage it. But he could and did turn on the faucet and hold his head under it, mop the wound with a towel, take down the iodine bottle, extract the stopper with his teeth, and, holding the bottle between his paws, pour a few drops on the wound. The sting made him wince, and spill some of the solution on the floor, where, he reflected, Methuen would find it and give him hell.

Then he went out, keeping a watchful eye for the tough individuals at Bemis', and thought some more. Somehow, he suspected, these men, the balloons, and the trancelike state of the people at the Station were all connected. Had Bemis gone into a trance too? Or was he the real author of these developments? Johnny would have liked to investigate some more, but he ⎯ad the strongest aversion to being shot at.

It occurred to him that if he wanted to take advantage of the scientists' malady he'd better do so while the doing was good, and he made for the kitchen. There he had a glorious time, for he had five effective natural can-openers on each foot. He was pouring the contents of a can of peaches down his throat, when a noise outside brought him to the window. He saw the truck that had been at Bemis' back up and the two tough individuals get out. Johnny slipped noiselessly into the dining room and listened through the door, tensing himself to bolt if the intruders came his way.

He heard the outside kitchen door slam and the voice of the man who had shot him: "What's ya name, huh?"

The inert Honoria, still sitting in her chair, answered tonelessly, "Honoria Velez."

"O. K., Honoria, you help us carry some of dis food out to the truck, see? Cheez, Smoke, lookit de mess. Dat beh's been around here. If you see him, plug him. Beh steaks is good eating, I hoid."

The other man mumbled something and Johnny could hear the slapping of Honoria's slippers as she moved about, and presently the opening of the outside kitchen door. Still shuddering at the idea of becoming a steak, he pushed his door open a crack. Through the screen of the outside door he could see Honoria, arms full of provisions, docilely obeying commands and piling the cans and bags in the truck. The men sat on their running board and smoked while Honoria, like one hypnotized, made several trips back to the kitchen. When they said "Dat's all," she sat down on the kitchen steps and relapsed into her former state. The truck drove off.

Johnny hurried out and made for the clump of trees on the end of the Station's property opposite Bemis' house. The clump crowned a little hill, making it both a good hiding place and a vantage point. He thought, evidently the Station wasn't big enough for him and the strange men both, if they were going to corner the food supply and kill him on sight. Then he considered Honoria's actions. The negress, normally a strong-minded person of granite stubbornness, had carried out every order without a peep. Evidently the disease or whatever it was didn't affect a person mentally or physically, except that it deprived the victim of all initiative and will-power. Honoria had remembered her own name and understood orders well enough. Johnny wondered why he hadn't been affected also; then, remembering the chimpanzee, concluded that it was probably specific to the higher anthropoids.

He watched more balloons rise, and saw two men come out of the bungalow and talk to the inflators. One stocky figure Johnny was sure was Bemis. If that was so, the botanist must be the master mind of the gang, and Johnny had at least four enemies to deal with. How? He didn't know. Well, he could at least dispose of the remaining food in the Station kitchen before the plug-uglies got it.

He went down and made a quart of coffee, which he could do easily enough because the pilot light of the gas stove had been left on. He poured it into a frying pan to cool, and lapped it up, simultaneously polishing off a whole loaf of bread.

Back in his hideaway he had difficulty sleeping; the coffee stimulated his mind, and plans for attacking the bungalow swarmed into it in clouds, until he almost felt like raiding it right then. But he didn't, knowing that his eyesight was especially poor at night, and suspecting that all four of the enemy would be in.

He awoke at sunrise, and watched the house until he saw the two tough ones come out and go to work on the balloons, and heard the little engine start its *put-put-put*. Making a long detour, he sneaked up from the opposite side and crawled under the house, which, like most Virgin

Island bungalows, had no cellar. He crept around until the scrape of feet on the thin floor overhead told him he was under the men within. He heard Bemis' voice: "—Al and Shorty, and now those fools are caught in Havana with no way of getting down here, because transportation will be tied up all over the Caribbean by now."

Another voice, British, answered: "I suppose that in time it'll occur to them to go up to the owner of a boat or plane, and simply tell the chap to bring them here. That's the only thing for them to do, with everybody in Cuba under the influence of the molds by now, what? How many more balloons should we send up?"

"All we have," replied Bemis.

"But I say, don't you think we ought to keep some in reserve? It wouldn't do to have to spend the rest of our lives sending spores up into the stratosphere, in the hope that the cosmics will give us another mutation like this one——"

"I said all the balloons, not all the spores, Forney. I have plenty of those in reserve, and I'm growing more from my molds all the time. Anyway, suppose we did run out before the whole world was affected—which it will be in a few weeks? There wasn't a chance in a million of that first mutation—yet it happened. That's how I know it was a sign from above, that I was chosen to lead the world out of its errors and confusions, which I shall do! God gave me this power over the world, and He will not fail me!"

So, thought Johnny, his mind working furiously, that was it! He knew that Bemis was an expert on molds. The botanist must have sent a load up into the stratosphere where the cosmic rays could work on them, and one of the mutations thereby produced had the property of attacking the human brain, when the spores were inhaled and got at the olfactory nerve-endings, in such a way as to destroy all will-power. And now Bemis was broadcasting these spores all over the world, after which he would take charge of the Earth, ordering the inhabitants thereof to do whatever he wished. Since he and his assistants had not been affected, there must be an antidote or preventative of some sort. Probably Bemis kept a supply handy. If there were some way of forcing Bemis to tell where it was—if, for instance, he could tie him up and write out a message demanding the information—— But that wouldn't be practical. He'd have to settle with the gang first, and trust to luck to find the antidote.

One of the men working on the balloons spoke: "Ten o'clock, Bert. Time to go for the mail."

"Won't be no mail, you dope. Everybody in Frederiksted's sitting around like he was hopped."

"Yeah, that's so. But we ought to start organizing 'em, before they all croak of starvation. We gotta have somebody to work for us."

"All right, smart guy, you go ahead and arganize; I'll take a minute off for a smoke. S'pose you try to get the phone soivice woiking again."

Johnny watched one pair of booted legs disappear into the truck, which presently rolled out of the driveway. The other pair of legs came over to the front steps and sat down. Johnny remembered a tree on the other side of the house, whose trunk passed close to the eaves.

Four minutes later he paddled silently across the roof and looked down on the smoker. Bert threw away his cigarette butt and stood up. Instantly Johnny's 500 steel-muscled pounds landed on his back and flung him prone. Before he could fill his lungs to shout, the bear's paw landed with a *pop* on the side of his head. Bert quivered and subsided, his skull having acquired a peculiarly lopsided appearance.

Johnny listened. The house was quiet. But the man called Smoke would be coming back in the truck. . . . Johnny quickly dragged the corpse under the house. Then he cautiously opened the front screen door with his paws and stole in, holding his claws up so they wouldn't click against the floor. He located the room from which Bemis' voice had come. He could hear that voice, with its exaggerated oratorical resonance, wafting through the door now.

He pushed the door open slowly. The room was the botanist's laboratory, and was full of flowerpots, glass cases of plants, and chemical apparatus. Bemis and a young man, evidently the Englishman, were sitting at the far end talking animatedly.

Johnny was halfway across the room before they saw him. They jumped up; Forney cried "Good Gad!" Bemis gave one awful shriek as Johnny's right paw, with a swift scooping motion, operated on his abdomen in much the way that a patent ice-cream scoop works in its normal medium. Bemis, now quite a horrible sight, tried to walk, then to crawl, then slowly sank into a pool of his own blood.

Forney, staring at Bemis' trailing guts, snatched up a chair to fend off Johnny, as he had seen circus chappies do with lions. Johnny, however, was not a lion. Johnny rose on his hind legs and batted the chair across the room, where it came to rest with a crash of glass. Forney broke for the door, but Johnny was on his back before he had gone three steps. . . .

Johnny wondered how to dispose of Smoke when he returned. Perhaps if he hid behind the door and pounced on him as he came in, he could finish him before the man could get his gun out. Johnny had a healthy dread of stopping another bullet. Then he noticed four automatic rifles in the umbrella stand in the hall. Johnny was a good shot with a rifle—or at least as good as his eyesight permitted. He partly opened the breech of one gun to assure himself that it was loaded, and found a window that commanded the driveway. When Smoke returned and got out of the truck, he never knew what hit him.

Johnny set out to find the antidote. Bemis should have kept some around, perhaps in his desk. The desk was locked, but, although made of sheet steel, it wasn't designed to keep out a determined and resourceful bear. Johnny hooked his claws under the lowest drawer, braced himself and heaved. The steel bent, and the drawer came out with a rending sound. The others responded in turn. In the last one he found a biggish squat bottle whose label he made out, with his spectacles, to read "Potassium iodide". There were also two hypodermic syringes.

Probably this was the antidote, and worked by injection. But how was he to work it? He carefully extracted the bottle-cork with his teeth, and tried to fill one of the hypodermics. By holding the barrel of the device between his paws, and working the plunger with his mouth, he at last succeeded.

Taking the syringe in his mouth, he trotted back to the Station. He found the underwear-clad Methuen in the kitchen, dreamily eating such scraps as had been left by his and the plug-uglies' raids. Breuker, the psychologist, and Dr. Bouvet, the Haitian negro bacteriologist, were engaged likewise. Evidently the pangs of hunger caused them to wander around until they found something edible, and their feeble instincts enabled them to eat it without having to be told to do so. Beyond that they were utterly helpless without orders, and would sit like vegetables until they starved.

Johnny tried to inject the solution into Methuen's calf, holding the syringe crosswise in his teeth and pushing the plunger with one paw. But at the prick of the needle the man instinctively jerked away. Johnny tried again and again. He finally grabbed Methuen and held him down while he applied the needle, but the man squirmed so that the syringe broke.

A discouraged black bear cleaned up the broken glass. Except possibly for the missing Al and Shorty, he would soon be the only thinking being left on Earth with any initiative at all. He fervently hoped that Al and Shorty were still in Cuba—preferably six feet underground. He didn't care so much what happened to the human race, which contained so many vicious specimens. But he did have a certain affection for his cadaverous and whimsical boss, Methuen. And, more important from his point of view, he didn't like the idea of spending the rest of his life rustling his own food like a wild bear. Such an existence would be much too stupid for a bear of his intelligence. He would, of course, have access to the Station library, but there wouldn't be anybody to explain the hard parts of chemistry and the other sciences to him when he got stuck.

He returned to Bemis' and brought back both the bottle and the remaining hypodermic, which he filled as he had the previous one. He tried inserting the needle very gently into Professor Methuen, but the biologist still jerked away. Johnny didn't dare try any rough stuff for fear of breaking his only remaining syringe. He tried the same tactics with Breuker and Bouvet, with no better results. He tried it on Honoria, dozing on the kitchen steps. But she awoke instantly and pulled away, rubbing the spot where she had been pricked.

Johnny wondered what to try next. He considered knocking one of the men unconscious and injecting him; but, no, he didn't know how hard to hit to stun without killing. He knew that if he really swung on one of them he could crack his skull like an eggshell.

He waddled out to the garage and got a coil of rope, with which he attempted to tie up the again-sleeping Honoria. Having only paws and teeth to work with, he got himself more tangled in the rope than the cook, who awoke and rid herself of the coils without difficulty.

He sat down to think. There didn't seem to be any way that he could inject the solution. But in their present state the human beings would do anything they were told. If somebody ordered one to pick up the hypodermic and inject himself, he'd do it. . . .

Johnny laid the syringe in front of Methuen, and tried to tell him what to do. But he couldn't talk—his attempts to say "Pick up the syringe" came out as "Fee-feek opp feef—feef." The Professor stared blankly and looked away. Sign-language was no more successful.

Johnny gave up and put the bottle and syringe on a high shelf where the men couldn't get at them. He wandered around, hoping that something would give him an idea. In Ryerson's room he saw a typewriter, and thought he had it. He couldn't handle a pencil, but he could operate one of these machines after a fashion. The chair creaked alarmingly under his weight, but held together. He took a piece of typewriter paper between his lips, dangled it over the machine, and turned the platen with both paws until he caught the paper in it. The paper was in crooked, but that couldn't be helped. He'd have preferred to write in Spanish because it was easy to spell, but Spanish wasn't the native tongue of any of the men at the Station, and he didn't want to strain their faculties, so English it would have to be Using one claw at a time, he slowly tapped out: "PICK UP SIRINGE AND INJECT SOLUTION INTO YOUR UP-PER ARM". The spelling of "siringe" didn't look right, but he couldn't be bothered with that now.

Taking the paper in his mouth he shuffled back to the kitchen. This time he put the syringe in front of Methuen, squalled to attract his attention, and dangled the paper in front of his eyes. But the biologist glanced only briefly at it and looked away. Growling with vexation, Johnny pushed the syringe out of harm's way and tried to force Methuen to read. But the scientist merely squirmed in his grasp and paid no attention to the paper. The longer he was held the harder he tried to escape. When the bear released him, he walked across the room and settled into his trance again.

Giving up for the time being, Johnny put away the syringe and made himself another quart of coffee. It was weak stuff, as there wasn't much of the raw material left. But maybe it would give him an idea. Then he went out and walked around in the twilight, thinking furiously. It

seemed absurd—even his little bear's sense of humor realized that—that the spell could be broken by a simple command, that he alone in the whole world knew the command,
and that he had no way of giving it. He wondered what
would happen if he never did find a way out. Would the
whole human race simply die off, leaving him the only
intelligent creature on Earth? Of course such an event
would have its advantages, but he feared that it would be
a dull life. He could take a boat from the harbor and head
for the mainland, and then hike north to Mexico where he
would find others of his species. But he wasn't sure that
they'd be congenial company; they might, resenting his
strangeness, even kill him. No, that idea wouldn't do, yet.

The Station's animals, unfed for two days, were noisy in
their cages. Johnny slept badly, and awoke well before
dawn. He thought he'd had an idea, but couldn't remember. . . .

Wait, it had something to do with Breuker. He was a
specialist on the psychology of speech, wasn't he? He did
things with a portable phonograph recording apparatus;
Johnny had seen him catching McGinty's yells. He went
up to Breuker's room. Sure enough, there was the machine.
Johnny opened it up, and spent the next two hours figuring
out how it worked. He could crank the motor easily enough,
and with some patience learned to operate the switches. He
finally adjusted the thing for recording, started the motor,
and bawled "Wa-a-a-a-a-a-ah!" into it. He stopped the
machine, threw the playback switch, set the needle in the
outer groove of the aluminum disk, and started it. For a few
seconds it scraped quietly, then yelled "Wa-a-a-a-a-a-ah!"
at him. Johnny squealed with pleasure.

He was on the track of something, but he didn't quite
know what. A phonograph record of his cry would be no
more effective in commanding the men than the original of
that cry. Well, Breuker must have a collection of records.
After some hunting, Johnny found them in a set of cases

that looked like letter files. He leafed through them and read the labels. "Bird-cries: Red-and-Green Macaw, Cockatoo, Mayana." That was no help. "Infant Babble: 6—9 months." Also out. "Lancashire Dialect." He tried this disk, and listened to a monologue about a little boy who was swallowed by a lion. From his experience with little boys Johnny thought that a good idea, but there was nothing in the record that would be of use.

The next was labeled "American Speech Series, No. 72-B, Lincoln County, Missouri." It started off: "Once there was a young rat who couldn't make up his mind. Whenever the other rats asked him if he'd like to come out with them, he'd answer, 'I don't know.' And when they said, 'Wouldn't you like to stop at home?' he wouldn't say yes or no either; he'd always shirk making a choice. One day his aunt said to him, 'Now look here! No one will ever care for you if you carry on like this. . . .' "

The record ground on, but Johnny's mind was made up. If he could get it to say "Now look here!" to Methuen, his problem ought to be solved. It wouldn't do any good to play the whole record, as those three words didn't stand out from the rest of the discourse. If he could make a separate record of just those words. . . .

But how could he, when there was only one machine? He needed two—one to play the record and one to record the desired words. He squalled with exasperation. To be licked after he'd gotten this far! He felt like heaving the machine out the window. At least it would make a beautiful crash.

Like a flash the solution came to him. He closed the recorder and carried it down to the social room, where there was a small phonograph used by the scientists for their amusement. He put the American Speech disk on this machine, put a blank disk on the recorder, and started the phonograph, with a claw on the switch of the recorder to start it at the right instant.

Two hours and several ruined disks later, he had what he wanted. He took the recorder to the kitchen, set it up, laid the syringe in front of Methuen, and started the machine. It purred and scraped for ten seconds, and then said sharply, "Now look here! Now look here! Now look here!" and resumed its scraping. Methuen's eyes snapped back into focus and he looked intently in front of him—at the sheet of paper with a single line of typing across it that Johnny dangled before his eyes. He read the words, and without a flicker of emotion picked up the syringe and jabbed the needle into his biceps.

Johnny shut off the machine. He'd have to wait now to see whether the solution took effect. As the minutes passed, he had an awful feeling that maybe it wasn't the antidote after all. A half-hour later, Methuen passed a hand across his forehead. His first words were barely audible, but grew louder like a radio set warming up: "What in Heaven's name happened to us, Johnny? I remember everything that's taken place in the last three days, but during that time I didn't seem to have any desires—not enough will of my own to speak, even."

Johnny beckoned, and headed for Ryerson's room and the typewriter. Methuen, who knew his Johnny, inserted a sheet of paper for him. Time passed, and Methuen said, "I see now. What a sweet setup for a would-be dictator! The whole world obeys his orders implicitly; all he has to do is select subordinates and tell them what to order the others to do. Of course the antidote was potassium iodide; that's the standard fungicide, and it cleared the mold out of my head in a hurry. Come on, old-timer, we've got work to do. The first thing is to get the other men around here to inject themselves. Think of it, Johnny, a bear saving the world! After this you can chew all the tobacco you want. I'll even try to get a female bear for you and inject her brain the way I did yours, so that you can have some company worthy of you."

A week later everyone on St. Croix had been treated, and men had been sent off to the mainland and the other Caribbean islands to carry on the work.

Johnny Black, finding little to arouse his curiosity around the nearly deserted Biological Station, shuffled into the library. He took Volume 5 of the *Britannica*, opened it to "Chemistry", and set to work again. He hoped that Methuen would get back in a month or so, and would find time to explain the hard parts to him; but meanwhile he'd have to wade through it as best he could.

KINDNESS

by

LESTER DEL REY

The wind eddied idly around the corner and past the secluded park bench. It caught fitfully at the paper on the ground, turning the pages, then picked up a section and blew away with it, leaving gaudy-colored comics uppermost. Danny moved forward into the sun-light, his eyes dropping to the children's page exposed.

But it was no use; he made no effort to pick up the paper. In a world where even the children's comics needed explaining, there could be nothing of interest to the last living *homo sapiens*—the last normal man in the world. His foot kicked the paper away, under the bench where it would no longer remind him of his deficiencies. There had been a time when he had tried to reason slowly over the omitted steps of logic and find the points behind such things, sometimes successfully, more often not; but now he left it to the quick, intuitive thinking of those about him. Nothing fell flatter than a joke that had to be reasoned out slowly.

Homo sapiens! The type of man who had come out of the caves and built a world of atomic power, electronics and other old-time wonders—thinking man, as it translated from the Latin. In the dim past, when his ancestors had owned the world, they had made a joke of it, shortening it to homo sap, and laughing, because there had been no other species to rival them. Now it was no longer a joke.

Normal man had been only a "sap" to *homo intelligens* —intelligent man—who was now the master of the world. Danny was only a left-over, the last normal man in a world of supermen, hating the fact that he had been born, and that his mother had died at his birth to leave him only loneliness as his heritage.

He drew farther back on the bench as the steps of a young couple reached his ears, pulling his hat down to avoid recognition. But they went by, preoccupied with their own affairs, leaving only a scattered bit of conversation in his ears. He turned it over in his mind, trying senselessly to decode it.

Impossible! Even the casual talk contained too many steps of logic left out. Homo intelligens had a new way of thinking, above reason, where all the long, painful steps of logic could be jumped instantly. They could arrive at a correct picture of the whole from little scattered bits of information. Just as man had once invented logic to replace the trial-and-error thinking that most animals have, so homo intelligens had learned to use intuition. They could look at the first page of an old-time book and immediately know the whole of it, since the little tricks of the author would connect in their intuitive minds and at once build up all the missing links. They didn't even have to try—they just looked, and knew. It was like Newton looking at an apple falling and immediately seeing why the planets circled the sun, and realizing the laws of gravitation; but these new men did it all the time, not just at those rare intervals as it had worked for homo sapiens once.

Man was gone, except for Danny, and he too had to leave this world of supermen. Somehow, soon, those escape plans must be completed, before the last of his little courage was gone! He stirred restlessly, and the little coins in his pocket set up a faint jingling sound. More charity, or occupational therapy! For six hours a day, five days a week, he worked in a little office, painfully doing routine work that could probably have been done better by machinery. Oh, they assured him that his manual skill was as great as theirs and that it was needed, but he could never be sure. In their unfailing kindness, they had probably decided it was better for him to live as normally as they could let him, and then had created the job to fit what he could do.

Other footsteps came down the little path, but he did not look up, until they stopped. "Hi, Danny! You weren't at the Library, and Miss Larsen said, pay day, weather, and all, I'd find you here. How's everything?"

Outwardly, Jack Thorpe's body might have been the twin of Danny's own well-muscled, one, and the smiling face above it bore no distinguishing characteristics. The mutation that changed man to superman had been within, a quicker, more complex relation of brain cell to brain cell that had no outward signs. Danny nodded at Jack, drawing over reluctantly to make room on the bench for this man who had been his playmate when they were both too young for the difference to matter much.

He did not ask the reason behind the librarian's knowledge of his whereabouts; so far as he knew, there was no particular pattern to his coming here, but to the others there must be one. He found he could even smile at their ability to fortell his plans.

"Hi, Jack! Fine. I thought you were on Mars."

Thorpe frowned, as if an effort were needed to remember that the boy beside him was different, and his words bore the careful phrasing of all those who spoke to Danny. "I finished that, for the time being; I'm supposed to report to Venus next. They're having trouble getting an even balance of boys and girls there, you know. Thought you might want to come along. You've never been Outside, and you were always bugs about those old space stories, I remember."

"I still am, Jack. But—" He knew what it meant, of course. Those who looked after him behind the scenes had detected his growing discontent, and were hoping to distract him with this chance to see the places his father had conquered in the heyday of his race. But he had no wish to see them as they now were, filled with the busy work of the new men; it was better to imagine them as they had once been, rather than see reality. And the ship was *here;* there could be no chance for escape from those other worlds.

Jack nodded quickly, with the almost telepathic understanding of his race. "Of course. Suit yourself, fellow. Going up to the Heights? Miss Larsen says she has something for you."

"Not yet, Jack. I thought I might look at—drop by the old Museum."

"Oh." Thorpe got up slowly, brushing his suit with idle fingers. "Danny!"

"Uh?"

"I probably know you better than anyone else, fellow, so—" He hesitated, shrugged, and went on. "Don't mind if I jump to conclusions; I won't talk out of turn. But best of luck—and good-by, Danny."

He was gone, almost instantly, leaving Danny's heart stuck in his throat. A few words, a facial expression, probably some childhood memories, and Danny might as well have revealed his most cherished secret hope in shouted words! How many others knew of his interest in the old ship in the Museum and his carefully-made plot to escape this kindly, charity-filled torture world?

He crushed a cigarette under his heel, trying to forget the thought. Jack had played with him as a child, and the others hadn't. He'd have to base his hopes on that and be even more careful never to think of the idea around others. In the meantime, he'd stay away from the ship! Perhaps in that way Thorpe's subtle warning might work in his favor— provided the man had meant his promise of silence.

Danny forced his doubts away, grimly conscious that he dared not lose hope in this last desperate scheme for independence and self-respect; the other way offered only despair and listless hopelessness, the same empty death from an acute inferiority complex that had claimed the diminishing numbers of his own kind and left him as the last, lonely specimen. Somehow, he'd succeed, and in the meantime, he would go to the Library and leave the Museum strictly alone.

There was a throng of people leaving the Library as Danny came up the escalator, but either they did not recognize him with his hat pulled low or sensed his desire for anonymity and pretended not to know him. He slipped into one of the less used hallways and made his way toward the Historic Documents section, where Miss Larsen was putting away the reading tapes and preparing to leave.

But she tossed them aside quickly as he came in and smiled up at him, the rich, warm smile of her people. "Hello, Danny! Did your friend find you all right?"

"Mm-hmm. He said you had something for me."

"I have." There was pleasure in her face as she turned back toward the desk behind her to come up with a small wrapped parcel. For the thousandth time, he caught himself wishing she were of his race and quenching the feeling as he realized what her attitude must really be. To her, the small talk from his race's past was a subject of historic interest, no more. And he was just a dull-witted hangover from ancient days. "Guess what?"

But in spite of himself, his face lighted up, both at the game and the package. "The magazines! The lost issues of *Space Trails?*" There had been only the first installment of a story extant, and yet that single part had set his pulses throbbing as few of the other ancient stories of his ancestor's conquest of space had done. Now, with the missing sections, life would be filled with zest for a few more hours as he followed the fictional exploits of a conqueror who had known no fear of keener minds.

"Not quite, Danny, but almost. We couldn't locate even a trace of them, but I gave the first installment to Bryant Kenning last week, and he finished it for you." Her voice was apologetic. "Of course the words won't be quite identical, but Kenning swears that the story is undoubtedly exactly the same in structure as it would have been, and the style is duplicated almost perfectly!"

Like that! Kenning had taken the first pages of a novel that had meant weeks and months of thought to some ancient writer and had found in them the whole plot, clearly revealed, instantly his! A night's labor had been needed to duplicate it, probably—a disagreeable and boring piece of work, but not a difficult one! Danny did not question the accuracy of the duplication, since Kenning was their greatest historical novelist. But the pleasure went out of the game.

He took the package, noting that some illustrator had even copied the old artist's style, and that it was set up to match the original format. "Thank you, Miss Larsen. I'm sorry to put all of you to so much trouble. And it was nice of Mr. Kenning!"

Her face had fallen with his, but she pretended not to notice. "He wanted to do it—volunteered when he heard we were searching for the missing copies. And if there are any others with pieces missing, Danny, he wants you to let him know. You two are about the only ones who use this division now; why don't you drop by and see him? If you'd like to go tonight—"

"Thanks. But I'll read this tonight, instead. Tell him I'm very grateful, though, will you?" But he paused, wondering again whether he dared ask for tapes on the history of the asteroids; no, there would be too much risk of her guessing, either now or later. He dared not trust any of them with a hint of his plan.

Miss Larsen smiled again, half winking at him. "Okay, Danny, I'll tell him. 'Night!"

Outside, with the cool of evening beginning to fall, Danny found his way into the untraveled quarters and let his feet guide him. Once, as a group came toward him, he crossed the street without thinking and went on. The package under his arm grew heavy and he shifted it, torn between a desire to find what had happened to the hero and a disgust at his own *sapiens* brain for not knowing. Probably, in the long run, he'd end up by going home and reading it, but for the moment he was content to let his feet carry him along idly, holding most of his thoughts in abeyance.

Another small park was in his path, and he crossed it slowly, the babble of small children voices only partly heard until he came up to them, two boys and a girl. The supervisor, who should have had them back at the Center, was a dim shape in the far shadows, with another, dimmer shape beside her, leaving the five-year-olds happily engaged in the ancient pastime of getting dirty and impressing each other.

Danny stopped, a slow smile creeping over his lips. At that age, their intuitive ability was just beginning to develop, and their little games and pretenses made sense, acting on him like a tonic. Vaguely, he remembered his own friends of that age beginning uncertainly to acquire the trick of seeming to know everything, and his worries at being left behind. For a time, the occasional flashes of intuition that had always blessed even *homo sapiens* gave him hope, but eventually the supervisor had been forced to tell him that he was different, and why. Now he thrust those painful memories aside and slipped quietly forward into the game.

They accepted him with the easy nonchalance of children who have no repressions, feverishly trying to build their sand-castles higher than his; but in that, his experience was greater than theirs, and his judgment of the damp stuff was surer. A perverse glow of accomplishment grew inside him as he added still another story to the towering structure and built a bridge, propped up with sticks and leaves, leading to it.

Then the lights came on, illuminating the sandbox and those inside it and dispelling the shadows of dusk. The smaller of the two boys glanced up, really seeing him for the first time. "Oh, you're Danny Black, ain't you? I seen your pi'ture. Judy, Bobby, look! It's that man—"

But their voices faded out as he ran off through the park and into the deserted byways again, clutching the package to him. Fool! To delight in beating children at a useless game, or to be surprised that they should know him! He slowed to a walk, twitching his lips at the thought that by now the supervisor would be reprimanding them for their thoughtlessness. And still his feet went on, unguided.

It was inevitable, of course, that they should lead him to the Museum, where all his secret hopes centered, but he was surprised to look up and see it before him. And then he was glad. Surely they could read nothing into his visit, unpremeditated, just before the place closed. He caught his breath, forced his face into lines of mere casual interest, and went inside, down the long corridors, and to the hall of the ship.

She rested there, pointed slightly skyward, sleek and immense even in a room designed to appear like the distant reaches of space. For six hundred feet, gleaming metal formed a smooth frictionless surface that slid gracefully from the blunt bow back toward the narrow stern with its blackened ion jets.

This, Danny knew, was the last and greatest of the space liners his people had built at the height of their glory. And even before her, the mutation that made the new race of men had been caused by the radiations of deep space, and the results were spreading. For a time, as the log book indicated this ship had sailed out to Mars, to Venus, and to the other points of man's empire, while the tension slowly mounted at home. There had never been another wholly *sapient*-designed ship, for the new race was spreading, making its greater intelligence felt, with the invert-matter rocket replacing this older, less efficient ion rocket which the ship carried. Eventually, unable to compete with the new models, she had been retired from service and junked, while the War between the new and old race passed by her and buried her under tons of rubble, leaving no memory of her existence.

And now, carefully excavated from the old ruins of the drydock where she had lain so long, she had been enthroned in state for the last year, here in the Museum of Sapient History, while all Danny's hopes and prayers had centered around her. There was still a feeling of awe in him as he started slowly across the carpeted floor toward the open lock and the lighted interior.

"Danny!" The sudden word interrupted him, bringing him about with a guilty start, but it was only Professor Kirk, and he relaxed again. The old archaeologist came toward him, his smile barely visible in the half-light of the immense dome. "I'd about given you up, boy, and started out. But I happened to look back and see you. Thought you might be interested in some information I just came onto today."

"Information about the ship?"

"What else? Here, come on inside her and into the lounge —I have a few privileges here, and we might as well be comfortable. You know, as I grow older, I find myself appreciating your ancestors' ideas of comfort, Danny. Sort of a pity our own culture is too new for much luxuriousness yet." Of all the new race, Kirk seemed the most completely at ease before Danny, partly because of his age, and partly because they had shared the same enthusiasm for the great ship when it had first arrived.

Now he settled back into one of the old divans, using his immunity to ordinary rules to light a cigarette and pass one to the younger man. "You know all·the supplies and things in the ship have puzzled us both, and we couldn't find any record of them? The log ends when they put the old ship up for junking, you remember; and we couldn't figure out why all this had been restored and restocked, ready for some long voyage to somewhere. Well, it came to light in some further excavations they've completed. Danny, your people did that, during the War; or really, after they'd lost the War to us!"

Danny's back straightened. The War was a period of history he'd avoided thinking about, though he knew the outlines of it. With *homo intelligens* increasing and pressing the older race aside by the laws of survival, his people had made a final desperate bid for supremacy. And while the new race had not wanted the War, they had been forced finally to fight back with as little mercy as had been shown them; and since they had the tremendous advantage of the new intuitive thinking, there had been only thousands left of the original billions of the old race when its brief course was finished. It had been inevitable probably, from the first mutation, but it was not something Danny cared to think of. Now he nodded, and let the other continue.

"Your ancestors, Danny, were beaten then, but they weren't completely crushed, and they put about the last bit of energy they had into rebuilding this ship—the only navigable one left them—and restocking it. They were going to go out somewhere, they didn't know quite where, even to another solar system, and take some of the old race for a new start, away from us. It was their last bid for survival, and it failed when my people learned of it and blasted the docks down over the ship, but it was a glorious failure, boy! I thought you'd want to know."

Danny's thoughts focused slowly. "You mean everything on the ship is of my people? But surely the provisions wouldn't have remained usable after all this time?"

"They did, though; the tests we made proved that conclusively. Your people knew how to preserve things as well as we do, and they expected to be drifting in the ship for half a century, maybe. They'll be usable a thousand years from now." He chucked his cigarette across the room and chuckled in pleased surprise when it fell accurately into a snuffer. "I stuck around, really, to tell you, and I've kept the papers over at the school for you to see. Why not come over with me now?"

"Not tonight, sir. I'd rather stay here a little longer."

Professor Kirk nodded, pulling himself up reluctantly. "As you wish . . . I know how you feel, and I'm sorry about their moving the ship, too. We'll miss her, Danny!"

"Moving the ship?"

"Hadn't you heard? I thought that's why you came around at this hour. They want her over in London, and they're bringing one of the old Lunar ships here to replace her. Too bad!" He touched the walls thoughtfully, drawing his hands down and across the rich nap on the seat. "Well, don't stay too long, and turn her lights out before you leave. Place'll be closed in half an hour. 'Night, Danny."

" 'Night, Professor." Danny sat frozen on the soft seat, listening to the slow tread of the old man and the beating of his own heart. They were moving the ship, ripping his plans to shreds, leaving him stranded in this world of a new race, where even the children were sorry for him.

It had meant so much, even to feel that somehow he would escape, some day! Impatiently, he snapped off the lights, feeling closer to the ship in the privacy of the dark, where no watchman could see his emotion. For a year now he had built his life around the idea of taking this ship out and away, to leave the new race far behind. Long, carefully casual months of work had been spent in learning her structure, finding all her stores, assuring himself bit by bit from a hundred old books that he could operate her.

She had been almost designed for the job, built to be operated by one man, even a cripple, in an emergency, and nearly everything was automatic. Only the problem of a destination had remained, since the planets were all swarming with the others, but the ship's log had suggested the answer even to that.

Once there had been rich men among his people who sought novelty and seclusion, and found them among the larger asteroids; money and science had built them artificial gravities and given them atmospheres, powered by atomic-energy plants that should last forever. Now the rich men were undoubtedly dead, and the new race had abandoned such useless things. Surely, somewhere among the asteroids, there should have been a haven for him, made safe by the very numbers of the little worlds that could discourage almost any search.

Danny heard a guard go by, and slowly got to his feet, to go out again into a world that would no longer hold even that hope. It had been a lovely plan to dream on, a necessary dream. Then the sound of the great doors came to his ears, closing! The Professor had forgotten to tell them of his presence! And—!

All right, so he didn't know the history of all those little worlds; perhaps he would have to hunt through them, one by one, to find a suitable home. Did it matter? In every other way, he could never be more ready. For a moment only, he hesitated; then his hands fumbled with the great lock's control switch, and it swung shut quietly in the dark, shutting the sound of his running feet from outside ears.

The lights came on silently as he found the navigation chair and sank into it. Little lights that spelled out the readiness of the ship. "Ship sealed . . . Air Okay . . . Power, Automatic . . . Engine, Automatic. . . ." Half a hundred little lights and dials that told the story of a ship waiting for his hand. He moved the course plotter slowly along the tiny atmospheric map until it reached the top of the stratosphere; the big star map moved slowly out, with the pointer in his fingers tracing an irregular, jagged line that would lead him somewhere toward the asteroids, well away from the present position of Mars, and yet could offer no clue. Later, he could set the analyzers to finding the present location of some chosen asteroid and determine his course more accurately, but all that mattered now was to get away, beyond all tracing, before his loss could be reported.

Seconds later his fingers pressed down savagely on the main power switch, and there was a lurch of starting, followed by another slight one as the walls of the Museum crumpled before the savage force of the great ion rockets. On the map, a tiny spot of light appeared, marking the ship's changing position. The world was behind him now, and there was no one to look at his efforts in kindly pity or remind him of his weakness. Only blind fate was against him, and his ancestors had met and conquered that long before.

A bell rang, indicating the end of the atmosphere, and the big automatic pilot began clucking contentedly, emitting a louder cluck now and then as it found the irregularities in the unorthodox course he had charted and swung the ship to follow. Danny watched it, satisfied that it was working. His ancestors may have been capable of reason only, but they had built machines that were almost intuitive, as the ship about him testified. His head was higher as he turned back to the kitchen, and there was a bit of a swagger to his walk.

The food was still good. He wolfed it down, remembering that supper had been forgotten, and leafing slowly through the big log book which recorded the long voyages made by the ship, searching through it for each casual reference to the asteroids, Ceres, Palas, Vesta, some of the ones referred to by nicknames or numbers? Which ones?

But he had decided by the time he stood once again in the navigation room, watching the aloof immensity of space; out here it was relieved only by the tiny hot pinpoints that must be stars, colored, small and intense as no stars could be through an atmosphere. It would be one of the numbered planetoids, referred to also as "The Dane's" in the log. The word was meaningless, but it seemed to have been one of the newer and more completely terranized, though not the very newest where any search would surely start.

He set the automatic analyzer to running from the key number in the manual and watched it for a time, but it ground on slowly, tracing through all the years that had passed. For a time, he fiddled with the radio, before he remembered that it operated on a wave form no longer used. It was just as well; his severance from the new race would be all the more final.

Still the analyzer ground on. Space lost its novelty, and the operation of the pilot ceased to interest him. He wandered back through the ship toward the lounge, to spy the parcel where he had dropped and forgotten it. There was nothing else to do.

And once begun, he forgot his doubts at the fact that it was Kenning's story, not the original; there was the same sweep to the tale, the same warm and human characters, the same drive of a race that had felt the mastership of destiny so long ago. Small wonder the readers of that time had named it the greatest epic of space to be written!

Once he stopped, as the analyzer reached its conclusions and bonged softly, to set the controls on the automatic for the little world that might be his home, with luck. And then the ship moved on, no longer veering, but making the slightly curved path its selectors found most suitable, while Danny read further, huddled over the story in the navigator's chair, feeling a new and greater kinship with the characters of the story. He was no longer a poor Earthbound charity case, but a man and an adventurer with them!

His nerves were tingling when the tale came to its end, and he let it drop onto the floor from tired fingers. Under his hand, a light had sprung up, but he was oblivious to it, until a crashing gong sounded over him, jerking him from the chair. There had been such a gong described in the story. . . .

And the meaning was the same. His eyes made out the red letters that glared accusingly from the control panel: RADIATION AT TEN O'CLOCK HORIZ—SHIP INDI-CATED!

Danny's fingers were on the master switch and cutting off all life except pseudogravity from the ship as the thought penetrated. The other ship was not hard to find from the observation window; the great streak of an invert-matter rocket glowed hotly out there, pointed apparently back to Earth—probably the *Callisto!*

For a second he was sure they had spotted him, but the flicker must have been only a minor correction to adjust for the trail continued. He had no knowledge of the new ships and whether they carried warning signals or not, but apparently they must have dispensed with such things. The streak vanished into the distance, and the letters on the panel that had marked it changing position went dead. Danny waited until the fullest amplification showed no response before throwing power on again. The small glow of the ion rocket would be invisible at the distance, surely.

Nothing further seemed to occur; there was a contented purr from the pilot and the faint sleepy hum of raw power from the rear, but no bells or sudden sounds. Slowly, his head fell forward over the navigator's table, and his heavy breathing mixed with the low sounds of the room. The ship went on about its business as it had been designed to do. Its course was charted, even to the old landing sweep, and it needed no further attention.

That was proved when the slow ringing of a bell woke Danny, while the board blinked in time to it: Destination! Destination! Destination Reached!

He shut off everything, rubbing the sleep from his eyes, and looked out. Above, there was weak but warm sunlight streaming down from a bluish sky that held a few small clouds suspended close to the ground. Beyond the ship, where it lay on a neglected sandy landing field, was the green of grass and the wild profusion of a forest. The horizon dropped off sharply, reminding him that it was only a tiny world, but otherwise it might have been Earth. He spotted an unkempt hangar ahead and applied weak power to the underjets, testing until they moved the ship slowly forward and inside, out of the view of any above.

Then he was at the lock, fumbling with the switch. As it opened, he could smell the clean fragrance of growing things, and there was the sound of birds nearby. A rabbit hopped leisurely out from underfoot as he stumbled eagerly out to the sunlight, and weeds and underbrush had already spread to cover the buildings about him. For a moment, he sighed; it had been too easy, this discovery of a heaven on the first wild try.

But the sight of the buildings drove back the doubt. Once, surrounded by a pretentious formal garden, this had been a great stone mansion, now falling into ruins. Beside it and further from him, a smaller house had been built, seemingly from the wreckage. That was still whole, though ivy had grown over it and half covered the door that came open at the touch of his fingers.

There was still a faint glow to the heaters that drew power from the great atomic plant that gave this little world a perpetual semblance of Earthliness, but a coating of dust was everywhere. The furnishings, though, were in good condition. He scanned them, recognizing some as similar to the pieces in the Museum, and the products of his race. One by one he studied them—his fortune, and now his home!

On the table, a book was dropped casually, and there was a sheet of paper propped against it, with what looked like a girl's rough handwriting on it. Curiosity carried him closer, until he could make it out, through the dust that clung even after he shook it.

Dad:

Charley Summers found a wrecked ship of those things, and came for me. We'll be living high on 13. Come on over, if your jets will make it, and meet your son-in-law.

There was no date, nothing to indicate whether "Dad" had returned, or what had happened to them. But Danny dropped it reverently back on the table, looking out across the landing strip as if to see a worn old ship crawl in through the brief twilight that was falling over the tiny world. "Those things" could only be the new race, after the War; and that meant that here was the final outpost of his people. The note might be ten years or half a dozen centuries old—but his people had been here, fighting on and managing to live, after Earth had been lost to them. If they could, so could he!

And unlikely though it seemed, there might possibly be more of them out there somewhere. Perhaps the race was still surviving in spite of time and trouble and even *homo intelligens.*

Danny's eyes were moist as he stepped back from the door and the darkness outside to begin cleaning his new home. If any were there, he'd find them. And if not—

Well, he was still a member of a great and daring race that could never know defeat so long as a single man might live. He would never forget that.

Back on Earth, Bryant Kenning nodded slowly to the small group as he put the communicator back, and his eyes were a bit sad in spite of the smile that lighted his face. "The Director's scout is back, and he did choose 'The Dane's'. Poor kid. I'd begun to think we waited too long, and that he never would make it. Another six months—and he'd have died like a flower out of the sun! Yet I was sure it would work when Miss Larsen showed me that story, with its mythical planetoid-paradises. A rather clever story, if you like pseudohistory. I hope the one I prepared was its equal."

"For historical inaccuracy, fully its equal." But the amusement in old Professor Kirk's voice did not reach his lips. "Well, he swallowed our lies and ran off with the ship we built him. I hope he's happy, for a while at least."

Miss Larsen folded her things together and prepared to leave. "Poor kid! He was sweet, in a pathetic sort of way. I wish that girl we were working on had turned out better; maybe this wouldn't have been necessary then. See me home, Jack?"

The two older men watched Larsen and Thorpe leave, and silence and tobacco smoke filled the room. Finally Kenning shrugged and turned to face the professor.

"By now he's found the note. I wonder if it was a good idea, after all? When I first came across it in that old story, I was thinking of Jack's preliminary report on Number 67, but now I don't know; she's an unknown quantity, at best. Anyhow, I meant it for kindness."

"Kindness! Kindness to repay with a few million credits and a few thousands of hours of work—plus a lie here and there—for all that we owe the boy's race!" The professor's voice was tired, as he dumped the contents of his pipe into a snuffer, and strode over slowly toward the great window that looked out on the night sky. "I wonder sometimes, Bryant, what kindness Neanderthaler found when the last one came to die. Or whether the race that will follow us when the darkness falls on us will have something better than such kindness."

The novelist shook his head doubtfully, and there was silence again as they looked out across the world and toward the stars.

"... WE ALSO

WALK DOGS"

by

ROBERT A. HEINLEIN

General Services—Miss Cormet speaking!" She addressed the view screen with just the right balance between warm hospitable friendliness and impersonal efficiency. The screen flickered momentarily, then built up a stereo-picture of a dowager, fat and fretful, overdressed and underexercised.

"Oh, my dear," said the image, "I'm *so* upset. I wonder if you *can* help me."

"I'm sure we can," Miss Cormet purred as she quickly estimated the cost of the woman's gown and jewels (if real—she made a mental reservation) and decided that here was a client that could be profitable. "Now tell me your trouble. Your name first, if you please." She touched a button on the horseshoe desk which enclosed her, a button marked CREDIT DEPARTMENT.

"But it's all so *involved*," the image insisted. "Peter *would*

248

go and break his hip." Miss Cormet immediately pressed
the button marked MEDICAL. "I've *told* him that polo is
dangerous. You've no idea, my dear, how a mother suffers.
And just at this time too. It's *so* inconvenient—"

"You wish us to attend him? Where is he now?"

"Attend him? Why, how silly! The Memorial Hospital will
do that. We've endowed them enough, I'm sure. It's my
dinner party I'm worried about. The Principessa will be so
annoyed."

The answer light from the Credit Department was blinking angrily. Miss Cormet headed her off. "Oh, I see. We'll
arrange it for you. Now, your name, please, and your
address and present location."

"But don't you *know* my name?"

"One might guess," Miss Cormet diplomatically evaded,
"but General Services always respects the privacy of its
clients."

"Oh, yes, of course. How considerate. I am Mrs. Peter
van Hogbein Johnson." Miss Cormet controlled her reaction.
No need to consult the Credit Department for this one.
But its transparency flashed at once, rating AAA—unlimited.
"But I don't see what you can *do*," Mrs. Johnson continued.
"I can't be two places at once."

"General Services likes difficult assignments," Miss Cormet
assured her. "Now—if you will let me have the details . . ."

She wheedled and nudged the woman into giving a fairly
coherent story. Her son, Peter III, a slightly shopworn
Peter Pan, whose features were familiar to Grace Cormet
through years of stereogravure, dressed in every conceivable
costume affected by the richly idle in their pastimes, had
been so thoughtless as to pick the afternoon before his
mother's most important social function to bung himself up
—seriously. Furthermore, he had been so thoughtless as to
do so half a continent away from his mater.

Miss Cormet gathered that Mrs. Johnson's technique for
keeping her son safely under thumb required that she rush
to his bedside at once, and, incidentally, to select his nurses.

But her dinner party that evening represented the culmination of months of careful maneuvering. What was she to *do?*

Miss Cormet reflected to herself that the prosperity of General Services and her own very substantial income was based largely on the stupidity, lack of resourcefulness, and laziness of persons like this silly parasite, as she explained that General Services would see that her party was a smooth, social success while arranging for a portable full-length stereo screen to be installed in her drawing room in order that she might greet her guests and make her explanations while hurrying to her son's side. Miss Cormet would see that a most adept social manager was placed in charge, one whose own position in society was irreproachable and whose connection with General Services was known to no one. With proper handling the disaster could be turned into a social triumph, enhancing Mrs. Johnson's reputation as a clever hostess and as a devoted mother.

"A sky car will be at your door in twenty minutes," she added, as she cut in the circuit marked TRANSPORTATION, "to take you to the rocket port. One of our young men will be with it to get additional details from you on the way to the port. A compartment for yourself and a berth for your maid will be reserved on the 16:45 rocket for Newark. You may rest easy now. General Services will do your worrying."

"Oh, thank you, my dear. You've been such a help. You've no idea of the *responsibilities* a person in my position has."

Miss Cormet cluck-clucked in professional sympathy while deciding that this particular old girl was good for still more fees. "You *do* look exhausted, madame," she said anxiously. Should I not have a masseuse accompany you on the trip? Is your health at all delicate? Perhaps a physician would be still better."

"How thoughtful you are!"

"I'll send both," Miss Cormet decided, and switched off, with a faint regret that she had not suggested a specially chartered rocket. Special service, not listed in the master price schedule, was supplied on a cost-plus basis. In cases like this "plus" meant all the traffic would bear.

She switched to EXECUTIVE; an alert-eyed young man filled the screen. "Stand by for transcript, Steve," she said. "Special service, triple-A. I've started the immediate service."

His eyebrows lifted. "Triple-A—bonuses?"

"Undoubtedly. Give this old battleaxe the works— smoothly. And look—the client's son is laid up in a hospital. Check on his nurses. If any one of them has even a shred of sex-appeal, fire her out and put a zombie in."

Gotcha, kid. Start the transcript."

She cleared her screen again; the "available-for-service" light in her booth turned automatically to green, then almost at once turned red again and a new figure built up in her screen.

No stupid waster this. Grace Cormet saw a well-kempt man in his middle forties, flat-waisted, shrewd-eyed, hard but urbane. The cape of his formal morning clothes was thrown back with careful casualness. "General Services," she said. "Miss Cormet speaking."

"Ah, Miss Cormet," he began, "I wish to see your chief." "Chief of switchboard?'

"No, I wish to see the President of General Services."

"Will you tell me what it is you wish? Perhaps I can help

"And General Services is sorry. Mr. Clare is a very busy you."

"Sorry, but I can't make explanations. I must see him, at once."

man; it is impossible to see him without appointment and without explanation."

"Are you recording?"

"Certainly."

"Then please cease doing so."

Above the console, in sight of the client, she switched off the recorder. Underneath the desk she switched it back on again. General Services was sometimes asked to perform illegal acts; its confidential employees took no chances. He fished something out from the folds of his chemise and held it out to her. The stereo effect made it appear as if he were reaching right out through the screen.

Trained features masked her surprise—it was the sigil of a planetary official, and the color of the badge was green.

"I will arrange it," she said.

"Very good. Can you meet me and conduct me in from the waiting room? In ten minutes?"

"I will be there, Mister . . . Mister—" But he had cut off.

Grace Cormet switched to the switchboard chief and called for relief. Then, with her board cut out of service, she removed the spool bearing the clandestine record of the interview, stared at it as if undecided, and after a moment, dipped it into an opening in the top of the desk where a strong magnetic field wiped the unfixed patterns from the soft metal.

A girl entered the booth from the rear. She was blonde, decorative, and looked slow and a little dull. She was neither. "Okay, Grace," she said. "Anything to turn over?"

"No. Clear board."

" 'S matter? Sick?"

"No." With no further explanation Grace left the booth, went on out past the other booths housing operators who handled unlisted services and into the large hall where the hundreds of catalogue operators worked. These had no such complex equipment as the booth which Grace had quitted. One enormous volume, a copy of the current price list of all of General Services' regular price-marked functions, and an ordinary look-and-listen enabled a catalogue operator to provide for the public almost anything the ordinary customer could wish for. If a call was beyond the scope of the catalogue it was transferred to the aristocrats of resourcefulness, such as Grace.

She took a short cut through the master files room, walked

down an alleyway between dozens of chattering punched-card machines, and entered the foyer of that level. A pneumatic lift bounced her up to the level of the President's office. The President's receptionist did not stop her, nor, apparently, announce her. But Grace noted that the girl's hands were busy at the keys of her voder.

Switchboard operators do not walk into the office of the president of a billion-credit corporation. But General Services was not organized like any other business on the planet. It was a *sui generis* business in which special training was a commodity to be listed, bought, and sold, but general resourcefulness and a ready wit were all important. In its hierarchy Jay Clare, the president, came first, his handyman, Saunders Francis, stood second, and the couple of dozen operators, of which Grace was one, who took calls on the unlimited switchboard came immediately after. They, and the field operators who handled the most difficult unclassified commissions—one group in fact, for the unlimited switchboard operators and the unlimited field operators swapped places indiscriminately.

After them came the tens of thousands of other employees spread over the planet, from the chief accountant, the head of the legal department, the chief clerk of the master files on down through the local managers, the catalogue operators to the last classified part time employee—stenographers prepared to take dictation when and where ordered, gigolos ready to fill an empty place at a dinner, the man who rented both armadillos and trained fleas.

Grace Cormet walked into Mr. Clare's office. It was the only room in the building not cluttered up with electro-mechanical recording and communicating equipment. It contained nothing but his desk (bare), a couple of chairs, and a stereo screen, which, when not in use, seemed to be Krantz' famous painting "The Weeping Buddha." The original was in fact in the sub-basement, a thousand feet below.

"Hello, Grace," he greeted her, and shoved a piece of

paper at her. "Tell me what you think of that. Sance says it's lousy." Saunders Francis turned his mild pop eyes from his chief to Grace Cormet, but neither confirmed nor denied the statement.

Miss Cormet read:

CAN YOU AFFORD IT?
Can You Afford GENERAL SERVICES?
Can You Afford NOT to have General Services ? ? ? ? ?

In this jet-speed age can you afford to go on wasting time doing your own shopping, paying bills yourself, taking care of your living compartment?

We'll spank the baby and feed the cat.
We'll rent you a house and buy your shoes.
We'll write to your mother-in-law and add up your check stubs.
No job too large; No job too small—
and all amazingly Cheap!

GENERAL SERVICES
Dial H-U-R-R-Y—U-P
P.S. *WE ALSO WALK DOGS*

"Well?" said Clare.
"Sance is right. It smells."
"Why?"
"Too logical. Too verbose. No drive."
"What's your idea of an ad to catch the marginal market?"
She thought a moment, then borrowed his stylus and wrote:

DO YOU WANT SOMEBODY MURDERED?
(Then *don't* call GENERAL SERVICES)
But for *any* other job dial HURRY-UP—*It pays!*
P.S. We also walk dogs.

"Mmmm . . . well, maybe," Mr. Clare said cautiously. "We'll try it. Sance, give this a type B coverage, two weeks,

North America, and let me know how it takes." Francis put
it away in his kit, still with no change in his mild expression. "Now as I was saying—"

"Chief," broke in Grace Cormet. "I made an appointment
for you in—" She glanced at her watchfinger. "—exactly two
minutes and forty seconds. Government man."

"Make him happy and send him away. I'm busy."

"Green Badge."

He looked up sharply. Even Francis looked interested.
"So?" Clare remarked. "Got the interview transcript with
you?"

"I wiped it."

"You did? Well, perhaps you know best. I like your
hunches. Bring him in."

She nodded thoughtfully and left.

She found her man just entering the public reception
room and escorted him past half a dozen gates whose
guardians would otherwise have demanded his identity and
the nature of his business. When he was seated in Clare's
office, he looked around. "May I speak with you in private,
Mr. Clare?"

"Mr. Francis is my right leg. You've already spoken to
Miss Cormet."

"Very well." He produced the green sigil again and held
it out. "No names are necessary just yet. I am sure of your
discretion."

The President of General Services sat up impatiently.
"Let's get down to business. You are Pierre Beaumont, Chief
of Protocol. Does the administration want a job done?"

Beaumont was unperturbed by the change in pace. "You
know me. Very well. We'll get down to business. The
government may want a job done. In any case our discussion must not be permitted to leak out—"

"All of General Services relations are confidential."

"This is not confidential; this is secret." He paused.

"I understand you," agreed Clare. "Go on."

"You have an interesting organization here, Mr. Clare. I believe it is your boast that you will undertake any commission whatsoever—for a price."

"If it is legal."

"Ah, yes, of course. But legal is a word capable of interpretation. I admired the way your company handled the outfitting of the Second Plutonian Expedition. Some of your methods were, ah, ingenious."

"If you have any criticism of our actions in that case they are best made to our legal department through the usual channels."

Beaumont pushed a palm in his direction. "Oh, no, Mr. Clare—please! You misunderstand me. I was not criticising; I was admiring. Such resource! What a diplomat you would have made!"

"Let's quit fencing. What do you want?"

Mr. Beaumont pursed his lips. "Let us suppose that you had to entertain a dozen representatives of each intelligent race in this planetary system and you wanted to make each one of them completely comfortable and happy. Could you do it?"

Clare thought aloud. "Air pressure, humidity, radiation densities, atmosphere, chemistry, temperatures, cultural conditions—those things are all simple. But how about acceleration? We could use a centrifuge for the Jovians, but Martians and Titans—that's another matter. There is no way to reduce earth-normal gravity. No, you would have to entertain them out in space, or on Luna. That makes it not our pigeon; we never give service beyond the stratosphere."

Beaumont shook his head. "It won't be beyond the stratosphere. You may take it as an absolute condition that you are to accomplish your results on the surface of the Earth."

"Why?"

"Is it the custom of General Services to inquire why a client wants a particular type of service?"

"No. Sorry."

"Quite all right. But you do need more information in order to understand what must be accomplished and why it must be secret. There will be a conference, held on this planet, in the near future—ninety days at the outside. Until the conference is called no suspicion that it is to be held must be allowed to leak out. If the plans for it were to be anticipated in certain quarters, it would be useless to hold the conference at all. I suggest that you think of this conference as a round table of leading, ah, scientists of the system, about of the same size and makeup as the session of the Academy held on Mars last spring. You are to make all preparations for the entertainments of the delegates, but you are to conceal these preparations in the ramifications of your organization until needed. As for the details—"

But Clare interrupted him. "You appear to have assumed that we will take on this commission. As you have explained it, it would involve us in a ridiculous failure. General Services does not like failures. You know and I know that low-gravity people cannot spend more that a few hours in high gravity without seriously endangering their health. Interplanetary get-togethers are always held on a low-gravity planet and always will be."

"Yes," answered Beaumont patiently, "they always have been. Do you realize the tremendous diplomatic handicap which Earth and Venus labor under in consequence?"

"I don't get it."

"It isn't necessary that you should. Political psychology is not your concern. Take it for granted that it does and that the Administration is determined that *this* conference shall take place on Earth."

"Why not Luna?"

Beaumont shook his head. "Not the same thing at all. Even though we administer it, Luna City is a treaty port. Not the same thing, psychologically."

Clare shook his head. "Mr. Beaumont, I don't believe that you understand the nature of General Services, even as I fail to appreciate the subtle requirements of diplomacy. We don't work miracles and we don't promise to. We are just the handyman of the last century, gone speed-lined and corporate. We are the latter day equivalent of the old servant class, but we are not Aladdin's genie. We don't even maintain research laboratories in the scientific sense. We simply make the best possible use of modern advances in communication and organization to do what already *can* be done." He waved a hand at the far wall, on which there was cut in intaglio the time-honored trademark of the business— a Scottie dog, pulling against a leash and sniffing at a post. "*There* is the spirit of the sort of work we do. We walk dogs for people who are too busy to walk 'em themselves. My grandfather worked his way through college walking dogs. I'm still walking them. I don't promise miracles, nor monkey with politics."

Beaumont fitted his fingertips carefully together. "You walk dogs for a fee. But of course you do—you walk my pair. Five minim-credits seems rather cheap."

"It is. But a hundred thousand dogs, twice a day, soon runs up the gross take."

"The 'take' for walking this 'dog' would be considerable."

"How much?" asked Francis. It was his first sign of interest.

Beaumont turned his eyes on him. "My dear sir, the outcome of this, ah, roundtable should make a difference of literally hundreds of billions of credits to this planet. We will not bind the mouth of the kine that tread the corn, if you pardon the figure of speech."

"How much?"

"Would thirty percent over cost be reasonable?"

Francis shook his head. "Might not come to much."

"Well, I certainly won't haggle. Suppose we leave it up to you gentlemen—your pardon, Miss Cormet!—to decide what the service is worth. I think I can rely on your planetary and racial patriotism to make it reasonable and proper."

Francis sat back, said nothing, but looked pleased.

"Wait a minute," protested Clare. "We haven't taken this job."

"We have discussed the fee," observed Beaumont.

Clare looked from Francis to Grace Cormet, then examined his fingernails. "Give me twenty-four hours to find out whether or not it is possible," he said finally, "and I'll tell you whether or not we will walk your dog."

"I feel sure," answered Beaumont, "that you will." He gathered his cape about him.

"Okay, masterminds," said Clare bitterly, "you've bought it."

"I've been wanting to get back to field work," said Grace.

"Put a crew on everything but the gravity problem," suggested Francis. "It's the only catch. The rest is routine."

"Certainly," agreed Clare, "but you had better deliver on that. If you can't, we are out some mighty expensive preparations that we will never be paid for. Who do you want? Grace?"

"I suppose so," answered Francis. "She can count up to ten."

Grace Cormet looked at him coldly. "There are times, Sance Francis, when I regret having married you."

"Keep your domestic affairs out of the office," warned Clare. "Where do you start?"

"Let's find out who knows most about gravitation," decided Francis. "Grace, better get Doctor Krathwohl on the screen."

"Right," she acknowledged, as she stepped to the stereo controls. "That's the beauty about this business. You don't have to know anything; you just have to know where to find out."

Dr. Krathwohl was a part of the permanent staff of General Services. He had no assigned duties. The company found it worthwhile to support him in comfort while providing him with an unlimited drawing account for scientific journals and for attendance at the meetings which the learned hold from time to time. Dr. Krathwohl lacked the single-minded drive of the research scientist; he was a dilettante by nature.

Occasionally they asked him a question. It paid.

"Oh, hello, my dear!" Doctor Krathwohl's gentle face smiled out at her from the screen. "Look—I've just come across the most amusing fact in the latest issue of *Nature*. It throws a most interesting sidelight on Brownlee's theory of—"

"Just a second, Doc," she interrupted. I'm kinda in a hurry."

"Yes, my dear?"

"Who knows the most about gravitation?"

"In what way do you mean that? Do you want an astrophysicist, or do you want to deal with the subject from a standpoint of theoretical mechanics? Farquarson would be the man in the first instance, I suppose."

"I want to know what makes it tick."

"Field theory, eh? In that case you don't want Farquarson. He is a descriptive ballistician, primarily. Dr. Julian's work in that subject is authoritative, possibly definitive."

"Where can we get hold of him?"

"Oh, but you can't. He died last year, poor fellow. A great loss."

Grace refrained from telling him how great a loss and asked, "Who stepped into his shoes?"

"Who what? Oh, you were jesting! I see. You want the name of the present top man in field theory. I would say O'Neil."

"Where is he?"

"I'll have to find out. I know him slightly—a difficult man."

"Do, please. In the meantime who could coach us a bit on what it's all about?"

"Why don't you try young Carson, in our engineering department? He was interested in such things before he took a job with us. Intelligent chap—I've had many an interesting talk with him."

"I'll do that. Thanks, Doc. Call the Chief's office as soon as you have located O'Neil. Speed." She cut off.

Carson agreed with Krathwohl's opinion, but looked dubious. "O'Neil is arrogant and non-cooperative. I've worked under him. But he undoubtedly knows more about field theory and space structure than any other living man."

Carson had been taken into the inner circle, the problem explained to him. He had admitted that he saw no solution. "Maybe we are making something hard out of this," Clare suggested. "I've got some ideas. Check me if I'm wrong, Carson."

"Go ahead, Chief."

"Well, the acceleration of gravity is produced by the proximity of a mass—right? Earth-normal gravity being produced by the proximity of the Earth. Well, what would be the effect of placing a large mass just over a particular point on the Earth's surface. Would not that serve to counteract the pull of the Earth?"

"Theoretically, yes. But it would have to be a damn big mass."

"No matter."

"You don't understand, Chief. To offset fully the pull of the Earth at a given point would require another planet the size of the Earth in contact with the Earth at that point. Of course since you don't want to cancel the pull completely, but simply to reduce it, you gain a certain advantage through using a smaller mass which would have its center of gravity closer to the point in question than would be the center of gravity of the Earth. Not enough, though. While the attraction builds up inversely as the square of the distance—in this case the half-diameter— the mass and the consequent attraction drops off directly as the *cube* of the diameter."

"What does that give us?"

Carson produced a sliderule and figured for a few moments. He looked up. "I'm almost afraid to answer. You would need a good-sized asteroid, of lead, to get anywhere at all."

"Asteroids have been moved before this."

"Yes, but what is to *hold it up?* No, Chief, there is no conceivable source of power, or means of applying it, that would enable you to hang a big planetoid over a particular spot on the Earth's surface and keep it there."

"Well, it was a good idea while it lasted," Clare said pensively.

Grace's smooth brow had been wrinkled as she followed the discussion. Now she put in, "I gathered that you could use an extremely heavy small mass more effectively. I seem to have read somewhere about some stuff that weighs *tons* per cubic inch."

"The core of dwarf stars," agreed Carson. "All we would need for that would be a ship capable of going light-years in a few days, some way to mine the interior of a star, and a new space-time theory."

"Oh, well, skip it."

"Wait a minute," Francis observed. "Magnetism is a lot like gravity, isn't it?"

"Well—yes."

"Could there be some way to *magnetize* these gazebos from the little planets? Maybe something odd about their body chemistry?"

"Nice idea," agreed Carson, "but while their internal economy is odd, it's not that odd. They are still organic."

"I suppose not. If pigs had wings they'd be pigeons."

The stereo annunciator blinked. Doctor Krathwohl announced that O'Neil could be found at his summer home in Portage, Wisconsin. He had not screened him and would prefer not to do so, unless the Chief insisted.

Clare thanked him and turned back to the others. "We are wasting time," he announced. "After years in this business we should know better than to try to decide technical questions. I'm not a physicist and I don't give a damn how gravitation works. That's O'Neil's business. And Carson's. Carson, shoot up to Wisconsin and get O'Neil on the job."

"Me?"

"You. You're an operator for this job—with pay to match. Bounce over to the port—there will be a rocket and a credit facsimile waiting for you. You ought to be able to raise ground in seven or eight minutes."

Carson blinked. "How about my job here?"

"The engineering department will be told, likewise the accounting. Get going."

Without replying Carson headed for the door. By the time he reached it he was hurrying.

Carson's departure left them with nothing to do until he reported back—nothing to do, that is, but to start action on the manifold details of reproducing the physical and cultural details of three other planets and four major satellites, exclusive of their characteristic surface-normal gravitational accelerations. The assignment, although new, presented no real difficulties—to General Services. Somewhere there were persons who knew all the answers to these matters. The vast loose organization called General Services was geared to find them, hire them, put them to work. Any of the unlimited operators and a considerable percent of the catalogue operators could take such an assignment and handle it without excitment or hurry.

Francis called in one unlimited operator. He did not even bother to select him, but took the first available on the ready panel—they were all "Can do!" people. He explained in detail the assignment, then promptly forgot about it. It would be done, and on time. The punched-card machines would chatter a bit louder, stereo screens would flash, and bright young people in all parts of the Earth would drop what they were doing and dig out the specialists who would do the actual work.

He turned back to Clare, who said, "I wish I knew what

Beaumont is up to. Conference of scientists—phooey!"

"I thought you weren't interested in politics, Jay."

"I'm not. I don't give a hoot in hell about politics, interplanetary or otherwise, except as it affects this business. But if I knew what was being planned, we might be able to squeeze a bigger cut out of it."

"Well," put in Grace, "I think you can take it for granted that the real heavy-weights from all the planets are about to meet and divide Gaul into three parts."

"Yes, but who gets cut out?"

"Mars, I suppose."

"Seems likely. With a bone tossed to the Venerians. In that case we might speculate a little in Pan-Jovian Trading Corp."

"Easy, son, easy," Francis warned. "Do that, and you might get people interested. This is a hush-hush job."

"I guess you're right. Still, keep your eyes open. There ought to be some way to cut a slice of pie before this is over."

Grace Cormet's telephone buzzed. She took it out of her pocket and said, "Yes?"

"A Mrs. Hogbein Johnson wants to speak to you."

"You handle her. I'm off the board."

"She won't talk to anyone but you."

"All right. Put her on the Chief's stereo, but stay in parallel yourself. You'll handle it after I've talked to her."

The screen came to life, showing Mrs. Johnson's fleshy face alone, framed in the middle of the screen in flat picture. "Oh, Miss Cormet," she moaned, "some dreadful mistake has been made. There is no stereo on this ship."

"It will be installed in Cincinnati. That will be in about twenty minutes."

"You are *sure?*"

"Quite sure."

"Oh, thank you! It's such a relief to talk with you. Do you know, I'm *thinking* of making you my social secretary."

"Thank you," Grace replied evenly, "but I am under contract."

"But how stupidly tiresome! You can break it."

"No, I'm sorry Mrs. Johnson. Good-by." She switched off the screen and spoke again into her telephone. "Tell Accounting to double her fee. And I *won't* speak with her again." She cut off and shoved the little instrument savagely back into her pocket. "Social secretary!"

It was after dinner and Clare had retired to his living apartment before Carson called back. Francis took the call in his own office.

"Any luck?" he asked, when Carson's image had built up.

"Quite a bit. I've seen O'Neil."

"Well? Will he do it?"

"You mean can he do it, don't you?"

"Well—can he?"

"Now that is a funny thing—I didn't think it was theoretically possible. But after talking with him, I'm convinced that it is. O'Neil has a new outlook on field theory—stuff he's never published. The man is a genius."

"I don't care," said Francis, "whether he's a genius or a Mongolian idiot—can he build some sort of a gravity thinner-outer?"

"I believe he can. I really do believe he can."

"Fine. You hired him?"

"No. That's the hitch. That's why I called back. It's like this: I happened to catch him in a mellow mood, and because we had worked together once before and because I had not aroused his ire quite as frequently as his other assistants he invited me to stay for dinner. We talked about a lot of things (you can't hurry him) and I broached the proposition. It interested him mildly—the idea, I mean; not the proposition—and he discussed the theory with me, or, rather, at me. But he won't work on it."

"Why not? You didn't offer him enough money. I guess I'd better tackle him."

"No, Mr. Francis, no. You don't understand. He's not interested in money. He's independently wealthy and has more than he needs for his research, or anything else he wants. But just at present he is busy on wave mechanics theory and he just won't be bothered with anything else."

"Did you make him realize it was important?"

"Yes and no. Mostly no. I tried to, but there isn't anything important to him but what *he* wants. It's a sort of intellectual snobbishness. Other people simply don't count."

"All right," said Francis. "You've done well so far. Here's what you do: After I switch off, you call EXECUTIVE and make a transcript of everything you can remember of what he said about gravitational theory. We'll hire the next best men, feed it to them, and see if it gives them any ideas to work on. In the meantime I'll put a crew to work on the details of Dr. O'Neil's background. He'll have a weak point somewhere; it's just a matter of finding it. Maybe he's keeping a woman somewhere—"

"He's long past that."

"—or maybe he has a by-blow stashed away somewhere. We'll see. I want you to stay there in Portage. Since you can't hire him, maybe you can persuade him to hire you. You're our pipeline. I want it kept open. We've got to find something he wants, or something he is afraid of."

"He's not afraid of *anything*. I'm positive of that."

"Then he wants something. If it's not money, or women, it's something else. It's a law of nature."

"I doubt it," Carson replied slowly. "Say! Did I tell you about his hobby?"

"No. What is it?"

"It's china. In particular, Ming china. He has the best collection in the world, I'd guess. But I know what he wants!"

"Well, spill it, man, spill it. Don't be dramatic."

"It's a little china dish, or bowl, about four inches across and two inches high. It's got a Chinese name that means 'Flower of Forgetfulness.' "

"Hmmm—doesn't seem significant. You think he wants it pretty bad?"

"I *know* he does. He has a solid colorgraph of it in his study, where he can look at it. But it hurts him to talk about it."

"Find out who owns it and where it is."

"I know. British Museum. That's why he can't buy it."

"So?" mused Francis. "Well, you can forget it. Carry on."

Clare came down to Francis' office and the three talked it over. "I guess we'll need Beaumont on this," was his comment when he had heard the report. "It will take the Government to get anything loose from the British Museum." Francis looked morose. "Well—what's eating you? What's wrong with that?"

"I know," offered Grace. "You remember the treaty under which Great Britain entered the planetary confederation?"

"I was never much good at history."

"It comes to this: I doubt if the planetary government can touch anything that belongs to the Museum without asking the British Parliament."

"Why not? Treaty or no treaty, the planetary government is sovereign. That was established in the Brazilian Incident."

"Yeah, sure. But it could cause questions to be asked in the House of Commons and that would lead to the one thing Beaumont wants to avoid at all costs—publicity."

"Okay. What do you propose?"

"I'd say that Sance and I had better slide over to England and find out just how tight they have the 'Flower of Forgetfulness' nailed down—and who does the nailing and what his weaknesses are."

Clare's eyes travelled past her to Francis, who was looking blank in the fashion that indicated assent to his intimates. "Okay," agreed Clare, "it's your baby. Taking a special?"

"No, we've got time to get the midnight out of New York. By-by."

"By. Call me tomorrow."

When Grace screened the Chief the next day he took one look at her and exclaimed, "Good Grief, kid! What have you done to your hair?"

"We located the guy," she explained succinctly. "His weakness is blondes."

"You've had your skin bleached, too."

"Of course. How do you like it?"

"It's stupendous—though I preferred you the way you were. But what does Sance think of it?"

"He doesn't mind—it's business. But to get down to cases, Chief, there isn't much to report. This will have to be a left-handed job. In the ordinary way, it would take an earthquake to get anything out of that tomb."

"Don't do anything that can't be fixed!"

"You know me, Chief. I won't get you in trouble. But it will be expensive."

"Of course."

"That's all for now. I'll screen tomorrow."

She was a brunette again the next day. "What is this?" asked Clare. "A masquerade?"

"I wasn't the blonde he was weak for," she explained, "but I found the one he was interested in."

"Did it work out?"

"I think it will. Sance is having a facsimile integrated now. With luck, we'll see you tomorrow."

They showed up the next day, apparently empty handed. "Well?" said Clare, "well?"

"Seal the place up, Jay," suggested Francis. "Then we'll talk."

Clare flipped a switch controlling an interference shield which rendered his office somewhat more private than a coffin. "How about it?" he demanded. "Did you get it?"

"Show it to him, Grace."

Grace turned her back, fumbled at her clothing for a moment, then turned around and placed it gently on the Chief's desk.

It was not that it was beautiful—it *was* beauty. Its subtle simple curve had no ornamentation, decoration would have sullied it. One spoke softly in its presence, for fear a sudden noise would shatter it.

Clare reached out to touch, then thought better of it and drew his hand back. But he bent his head over it and stared down into it. It was strangely hard to focus—to allocate—the bottom of the bowl. It seemed as if his sight sank deeper and ever deeper into it, as if he were drowning in a pool of light.

He jerked up his head and blinked. "God," he whispered, "God—I didn't know such things existed."

He looked at Grace and looked away to Francis. Francis had tears in his eyes, or perhaps his own were blurred.

"Look, Chief," said Francis. "Look—couldn't we just keep it and call the whole thing off?"

"There's no use talking about it any longer," said Francis wearily. "We can't keep it, Chief. I shouldn't have suggested it and you shouldn't have listened to me. Let's screen O'Neil."

"We might just wait another day before we do anything about it," Clare ventured. His eyes returned yet again to the "Flower of Forgetfulness."

Grace shook her head. "No good. It will just be harder tomorrow. I *know*." She walked decisively over to the stereo and manipulated the controls.

O'Neil was annoyed at being disturbed and twice annoyed that they had used the emergency signal to call him to his disconnected screen.

"What is this?" he demanded. "What do you mean by

disturbing a private citizen when he has disconnected? Speak up—and it had better be good, or, so help me, I'll sue you!"

"We want you to do a little job of work for us, Doctor," Clare began evenly.

"What!" O'Neil seemed almost too surprised to be angry. "Do you mean to stand there, sir, and tell me that you have invaded the privacy of my home to ask *me* to work for *you?"*

"The pay will be satisfactory to you."

O'Neil seemed to be counting up to ten before answering. "Sir," he said carefully, "there are men in the world who seem to think they can buy anything, or anybody. I grant you that they have much to go on in that belief. But I am not for sale. Since you seem to be one of those persons, I will do my best to make this interview expensive for you. You will hear from my attorneys. Good night!"

"Wait a moment," Clare said urgently. "I believe that you are interested in china—"

"What if I am?"

"Show it to him, Grace." Grace brought the "Flower of Forgetfulness" up near the screen, handling it carefully, reverently.

O'Neil said nothing. He leaned forward and stared. He seemed to be about to climb through the screen. "Where did you get it?" he said at last.

"That doesn't matter."

"I'll buy it from you—at your own price."

"It's not for sale. But you may have it—if we can reach an agreement."

O'Neil eyed him. "It's stolen property."

"You're mistaken. Nor will you find anyone to take an interest in such a charge. Now about this job—"

O'Neil pulled his eyes away from the bowl. "What is it you wish me to do?"

Clare explained the problem to him. When he had concluded O'Neil shook his head. "That's ridiculous," he said.

"We have reason to feel that it is theoretically possible."

"Oh, certainly! It's theoretically possible to live forever, too. But no one has ever managed it."

"We think you can do it.

"Thank you for nothing. Say!" O'Neil stabbed a finger at him out of the screen. "You set that young pup Carson on me!"

"He was acting under my orders."

"Then, sir, I do not like your manners."

"How about the job? And this?" Clare indicated the bowl.

O'Neil gazed at it and chewed his whiskers. "Suppose," he said, at last, "I make an honest attempt, to the full extent of my ability, to supply what you want—and I fail."

Clare shook his head. "We pay only for results. Oh, your salary, of course, but not *this*. This is a bonus in addition to your salary, *if* you are successful."

O'Neil seemed about to agree, then said suddenly, "You may be fooling me with a colorgraph. I can't tell through this damned screen."

Clare shrugged. "Come see for yourself."

"I shall. I will. Stay where you are. Where are you? Damn it, sir, what's your *name?*"

He came storming in two hours later. "You've tricked me! The 'Flower' is still in England. I've investigated. I'll . . . I'll *punish* you, sir, with my own two hands."

"See for yourself," answered Clare. He stepped aside, so that his body no longer obscured O'Neil's view of Clare's desk top.

They let him look. They respected his need for quiet and let him look. After a long time he turned to them, but did not speak.

"Well?" asked Clare.

"I'll build your damned gadget," he said huskily. "I figured out an approach on the way here."

Beaumont came in person to call the day before the first

session of the conference. "Just a social call, Mr. Clare," he stated. "I simply wanted to express to you my personal appreciation for the work you have done. And to deliver this." "This" turned out to be a draft on the Bank Central for the agreed fee. Clare accepted it, glanced at it, nodded, and placed it on his desk.

"I take it, then," he remarked, "that the Government is satisfied with the service rendered."

"That is putting it conservatively," Beaumont assured him. "To be perfectly truthful, I did not think you could do so much. You seem to have thought of everything. The Callistan delegation is out now, riding around and seeing the sights in one of the little tanks you had prepared. They are delighted. Confidentially, I think we can depend on their vote in the coming sessions."

"Gravity shields working all right, eh?"

"Perfectly. I stepped into their sightseeing tank before we turned it over to them. I was as light as the proverbial feather. Too light—I was very nearly spacesick." He smiled in wry amusement. "I entered the Jovian apartments, too. That was quite another matter."

"Yes, it would be," Clare agreed. "Two and a half times normal weight is oppressive to say the least."

"It's a happy ending to a difficult task. I must be going. Oh, yes, one other little matter—I've discussed with Doctor O'Neil the possibility that the Administration may be interested in other uses for his new development. In order to simplify the matter it seems desirable that you provide me with a quitclaim to the O'Neil effect from General Services."

Clare gazed thoughtfully at the "Weeping Buddha" and chewed his thumb. "No," he said slowly, "no. I'm afraid that would be difficult.

"Why not?" asked Beaumont. It avoids the necessity of adjudication and attendant waste of time. We are prepared to recognize your service and recompense you."

"Hmmm. I don't believe you fully understand the situation, Mr. Beaumont. There is a certain amount of open territory between our contract with Doctor O'Neil and your contract with us. You asked of us certain services and certain chattels with which to achieve that service. We provided them—for a fee. All done. But our contract with Doctor O'Neil made him a full-time employee for the period of his employment. His research results and the patents embodying them are the property of General Services."

"Really?" said Beaumont. "Doctor O'Neil has a different impression."

"Doctor O'Neil is mistaken. Seriously, Mr. Beaumont—you asked us to develop a siege gun, figuratively speaking, to shoot a gnat. Did you expect us, as businessmen, to throw away the siege gun after one shot?"

"No, I suppose not. What do you propose to do?"

"We expect to exploit the gravity modulator commercially. I fancy we could get quite a good price for certain adaptations of it on Mars."

"Yes. Yes, I suppose you could. But to be brutally frank, Mr. Clare, I am afraid that is impossible. It is a matter of imperative public policy that this development be limited to terrestrials. In fact, the administration would find it necessary to intervene and make it government monopoly."

"Have you considered how to keep O'Neil quiet?"

"In view of the change in circumstances, no. What is your thought?"

"A corporation, in which he would hold a block of stock and be president. One of our bright young men would be chairman of the board." Clare thought of Carson. "There would be stock enough to go around," he added, and watched Beaumont's face.

Beaumont ignored the bait. "I suppose that this corporation would be under contract to the Government—its sole customer?"

"That is the idea."

"Mmmm . . . yes, it seems feasible. Perhaps I had better speak with Doctor O'Neil."

"Help yourself."

Beaumont got O'Neil on the screen and talked with him in low tones. Or, more properly, Beaumont's tones were low. O'Neil displayed a tendency to blast the microphone. Clare sent for Francis and Grace and explained to them what had taken place.

Beaumont turned away from the screen. "The Doctor wishes to speak with you, Mr. Clare."

O'Neil looked at him frigidly. "What is this claptrap I've had to listen to, sir? What's this about the O'Neil effect being your property?"

"It was in your contract, Doctor. Don't you recall?"

"Contract! I never read the damned thing. But I can tell you this: I'll take you to court. I'll tie you in knots before I'll let you make a fool of me that way."

"Just a moment, Doctor, please!" Clare soothed. "We have no desire to take advantage of a mere legal technicality, and no one disputes your interest. Let me outline what I had in mind—" He ran rapidly over the plan. O'Neil listened, but his expression was still unmollified at the conclusion.

"I'm not interested," he said gruffly. "So far as I am concerned the Government can have the whole thing. And I'll see to it."

"I had not mentioned one other condition," added Clare. "Don't bother."

"I must. This will be just a matter of agreement between gentlemen, but it is essential. You have custody of the 'Flower of Forgetfulness.'"

O'Neil was at once on guard. "What do you mean, 'custody.' I own it. Understand me—*own* it."

"'Own it,'" repeated Clare. "Nevertheless, in return for the concessions we are making you with respect to your contract, we want something in return."

"What?" asked O'Neil. The mention of the bowl had upset his confidence.

"You own it and you retain possession of it. But I want your word that I, or Mr. Francis, or Miss Cormet, may come look at it from time to time—frequently."

O'Neil looked unbelieving. "You mean that you simply want to come to *look* at it?"

"That's all."

"Simply to *enjoy* it?"

"That's right."

O'Neil looked at him with new respect. "I did not understand you before, Mr. Clare. I apologize. As for the corporation nonsense—do as you like. I don't care. You and Mr. Francis and Miss Cormet may come to see the 'Flower' whenever you like. You have my word."

"Thank you, Doctor O'Neil—for all of us." He switched off as quickly as could be managed gracefully.

Beaumont was looking at Clare with added respect, too. "I think," he said, "that the next time I shall not interfere with your handling of the details. I'll take my leave. Adieu, gentlemen—and Miss Cormet."

When the door had rolled down behind him Grace remarked, "That seems to polish it off."

"Yes," said Clare. "We've 'walked his dog' for him; O'Neil has what he wants; Beaumont got what he wanted, and more besides."

"Just what is he after?"

"I don't know, but I suspect that he would like to be first president of the Solar System Federation, if and when there is such a thing. With the aces we have dumped in his lap, he might make it. Do you realize the potentialities of the O'Neil effect?"

"Vaguely," said Francis.

"Have you thought about what it will do to space navigation? Or the possibilities it adds in the way of colonization? Or its recreational uses? There's a fortune in that alone."

"What do we get out of it?"

"What do we get out of it? Money, old son. Gobs and gobs of money. There's always money in giving people what they want." He glanced up at the Scottie dog trademark.

"Money," repeated Francis. "Yeah, I suppose so."

"Anyhow," added Grace, "we can always go look at the 'Flower.'"

THE

ENCHANTED VILLAGE

by

A. E. VAN VOGT

Explorers of a new frontier they had been called before
they left for Mars.

For a while after the ship crashed into a Martian desert,
killing all on board except—miraculously—this one man, Bill
Jenner spat the words occasionally into the constant, sand-
laden wind. He despised himself for the pride he had felt
when he first heard them.

His fury faded with each mile that he walked, and his
black grief for his friends became a gray ache. Slowly he
realized that he had made a ruinous misjudgment.

He had underestimated the speed at which the rocketship had been traveling. He'd guessed that he would have
to walk three hundred miles to reach the shallow, Polar sea
he and the others had observed as they glided in from outer
space. Actually, the ship must have flashed an immensely
greater distance before it hurtled down out of control.

The days stretched behind him, seemingly as numberless as the hot, red, alien sand that scorched through his tattered clothes. This huge scarecrow of a man kept moving across the endless, arid waste. He would not give up.

By the time he came to the mountain, his food had long been gone. Of his four waterbags, only one remained; and that was so close to being empty that he merely wet his cracked lips and swollen tongue whenever his thirst became unbearable.

Jenner climbed high before he realized that it was not just another dune that had barred his way. He paused, and as he gazed up at the mountain that towered above him, he cringed a little. For an instant, he felt the hopelessness of this mad race he was making to nowhere—but he reached the top. He saw that below him was a depression surrounded by hills as high or higher than the one on which he stood. Nestled in the valley they made was a village.

He could see trees, and the marble floor of a courtyard. A score of buildings were clustered around what seemed to be a central square. They were mostly low-constructed, but there were four towers pointing gracefully into the sky. They shone in the sunlight with a marble luster.

Faintly, there came to Jenner's ear a thin, high-pitched whistling sound. It rose, fell, faded completely, then came up again clearly and unpleasantly. Even as Jenner ran toward it, the noise grated on his ears, eerie and unnatural.

He kept slipping on smooth rock, and bruised himself when he fell. He rolled halfway down into the valley. The buildings remained new and bright, when seen from nearby. Their walls flashed with reflections. On every side was vegetation—reddish-green shrubbery—yellow-green trees laden with purple and red fruit.

With ravenous intent, Jenner headed for the nearest fruit tree. Close up, the tree looked dry and brittle. The large red fruit he tore from the lowest branch however, was plump and juicy.

As he lifted it to his mouth, he remembered that he had

been warned during his training period to taste nothing on
Mars until it had been chemically examined. But that was
meaningless advice to a man whose only chemical equipment was in his own body.

Nevertheless, the possibility of danger made him cautious. He took his first bite gingerly. It was bitter to his
tongue, and he spat it out hastily. Some of the juice which
remained in his mouth seared his gums. He felt the fire of it,
and he reeled from nausea. His muscles began to jerk, and
he lay down on the marble to keep himself from falling.
After what seemed like hours to Jenner, the awful trembling
finally went out of his body, and he could see again. He
looked up despisingly at the tree.

The pain finally left him, and slowly he relaxed. A soft
breeze rustled the dry leaves. Nearby trees took up that
gentle clamor, and it struck Jenner that the wind here in
the valley was only a whisper of what it had been on the
flat desert beyond the mountain.

There was no other sound now. Jenner abruptly remembered the high-pitched, ever-changing whistle he had
heard. He lay very still, listening intently, but there was
only the rustling of the leaves. The noisy shrilling had
stopped. He wondered if it had been an alarm, to warn the
villagers of his approach.

Anxiously, he climbed to his feet and fumbled for his
gun. A sense of disaster shocked through him. It wasn't
there. His mind was a blank, and then he vaguely recalled
that he had first missed the weapon more than a week before. He looked around him uneasily, but there was not a
sign of creature life. He braced himself. He couldn't leave,
as there was nowhere to go. If necessary, he would fight to
the death to remain in the village.

Carefully Jenner took a sip from his water bag, moisten-
ing his cracked lips and his swollen tongue. Then he replaced the cap, and started through a double line of trees
toward the nearest building. He made a wide circle to

observe it from several vantage points. On one side a low, broad archway opened into the interior. Through it, he could dimly make out the polished gleam of a marble floor.

Jenner explored the buildings from the outside, always keeping a respectful distance between him and any of the entrances. He saw no sign of animal life. He reached the far side of the marble platform on which the village was built, and turned back decisively. It was time to explore interiors.

He chose one of the four-tower buildings. As he came within a dozen feet of it, he saw that he would have to stoop low to get inside.

Momentarily, the implications of that stopped him. These buildings had been constructed for a life form that must be very different from human beings.

He went forward again, bent down, and entered reluctantly, every muscle tensed.

He found himself in a room without furniture. However, there were several low, marble fences projecting from one marble wall. They formed what looked like a group of four wide, low stalls. Each stall had an open trough carved out of the floor.

The second chamber was fitted with four inclined planes of marble, each of which slanted up to a dias. Altogether, there were four rooms on the lower floor. From one of them, a circular ramp mounted up, apparently to a tower room.

Jenner didn't investigate the upstairs. The earlier fear that he would find alien life was yielding to the deadly conviction that he wouldn't. No life meant no food, nor chance of getting any. In frantic haste, he hurried from building to building, peering into the silent rooms, pausing now and then to shout hoarsely.

Finally, there was no doubt. He was alone in a deserted village on a lifeless planet, without food, without water—except for the pitiful supply in his bag—and without hope.

He was in the fourth and smallest room of one of the

tower buildings when he realized that he had come to the end of his search. The room had a single "stall" jutting out from one wall. Wearily, Jenner lay down in it. He must have fallen asleep instantly.

When he awoke, he became aware of two things, one right after the other. The first realization occurred before he opened his eyes—the whistling sound was back, high and shrill; it wavered at the threshold of audibility.

The other was that a fine spray of liquid was being directed down at him from the ceiling. It had an odor, of which Technician Jenner took a single whiff. Quickly he scrambled out of the room, coughing, tears in his eyes, his face already burning from chemical reaction.

He snatched his handkerchief and hastily wiped the exposed parts of his body and face.

He reached the outside, and there paused, striving to understand what had happened.

The village seem unchanged.

Leaves trembled in a gentle breeze. The sun was poised on a mountain peak. Jenner guessed from its position that it was morning again, and that he had slept at least a dozen hours. The glaring white light suffused the valley. Half hidden by trees and shrubbery, the buildings flashed and shimmered.

He seemed to be in an oasis in a vast desert. It was an oasis all right, Jenner reflected grimly, but not for a human being. For him, with its poisonous fruit, it was more like a tantalizing mirage.

He went back inside the building, and cautiously peered into the room where he had slept. The spray of gas had stopped, not a bit of odor lingered, and the air was fresh and clean.

He edged over the threshold, half-inclined to make a test. He had a picture in his mind of a long dead Martian creature lazing on the floor in the "stall" while a soothing chemical sprayed down on its body. The fact that the chemical was deadly to human beings merely emphasized how alien to man was the life that had spawned on Mars. But there seemed little doubt of the reason for the gas. The creature was accustomed to taking a morning shower.

Inside the "bathroom," Jenner eased himself feet first into the stall. As his hips came level with the stall entrance, the solid ceiling sprayed a jet of yellowish gas straight down upon his legs. Hastily, Jenner pulled himself clear of the stall. The gas stopped as suddenly as it had started.

He tried it again, to make sure it was merely an automatic process. It turned on, then it shut off.

Jenner's thirst-puffed lips parted with excitement. He thought, "If there can be one automatic process, there may be others."

Breathing heavily, he raced into the outer room. Carefully he shoved his legs into one of the two stalls. The moment his hips were in, a steaming gruel filled the trough beside the wall.

He stared at the greasy looking stuff with a horrified fascination—food—and drink. He remembered the poison fruit, and felt repelled, but he forced himself to bend down, and put his finger into the hot, wet substance. He brought it up, dripping, to his mouth.

It tasted flat and pulpy, like boiled wood fiber. It trickled viscously into his throat. His eyes began to water, and his lips drew back convulsively. He realized he was going to be sick, and ran for the outer door—but didn't quite make it.

When he finally got outside, he felt limp and unutterably listless. In that depressed state of mind, he grew aware again of the shrill sound.

He felt amazed that he could have ignored its rasping even for a few minutes. Sharply, he glanced about, trying to determine its source, but it seemed to have none. Whenever he approached a point where it appeared to be loudest, then it would fade, or shift, perhaps to the far side of the village.

He tried to imagine what an alien culture would want

with a mind-shattering noise—although, of course, it would not necessarily have been unpleasant to them.

He stopped, and snapped his fingers as a wild but nevertheless plausible notion entered his mind. Could this be music?

He toyed with the idea, trying to visualize the village as it had been long ago. Here, a music-loving race had possibly gone about its daily tasks to the accompaniment of what was to them beautiful strains of melody.

The hideous whistling went on and on, waxing and waning. Jenner tried to put buildings between himself and the sound. He sought refuge in various rooms, hoping that at least one would be sound-proof. None were. The whistle followed him wherever he went.

He retreated into the desert, and had to climb halfway up one of the slopes before the noise was low enough not to disturb him. Finally, breathless but immeasurably relieved, he sank down on the sand, and thought blankly:

What now?

The scene that spread before him had in it qualities of both heaven and hell. It was all too familiar now—the red sands, the stony dunes, the small, alien village promising so much and fulfilling so little.

Jenner looked down at it with his feverish eyes, and ran his parched tongue over his cracked, dry lips. He knew that he was a dead man unless he could alter the automatic food-making machines that must be hidden somewhere in the walls and under the floors of the buildings.

In ancient days, a remnant of Martian civilization had survived here in this village. The inhabitants had died off but the village lived on, keeping itself clean of sand, able to provide refuge for any Martian who might come along. But there were no Martians. There was only Bill Jenner, pilot of the first rocketship ever to land on Mars.

He had to make the village turn out food and drink that he could take. Without tools, except his hands; with scarcely any knowledge of chemistry, he must force it to change its habits.

Tensely, he hefted his water bag. He took another sip, and fought the same grim fight to prevent himself from guzzling it down to the last drop. And, when he had won the battle once more, he stood up and started down the slope.

He could last, he estimated, not more than three days. In that time, he must conquer the village.

He was already among the trees when it suddenly struck him that the "music" had stopped. Relieved, he bent over a small shrub, took a good, firm hold of it—and pulled.

It came up easily, and there was a slab of marble attached to it. Jenner stared at it, noting with surprise that he had been mistaken in thinking the stalk came up through a hole in the marble. It was merely stuck to the surface. Then he noticed something else—the shrub had no roots. Almost instinctively, Jenner looked down at the spot from which he had torn the slab of marble along with the plant. There was sand there.

He dropped the shrub, slipped to his knees, and plunged his fingers into the sand. Loose sand trickled through them. He reached deep, using all his strength to force his arm and hand down—sand—nothing but sand.

He stood up, and frantically tore up another shrub. It also came easily, bringing with it a slab of marble. It had no roots, and where it had been was sand.

With a kind of mindless disbelief, Jenner rushed over to a fruit tree, and shoved at it. There was a momentary resistance, and then the marble on which it stood split, and lifted slowly into the air. The tree fell over with a swish and a crackle as its dry branches and leaves broke and crumbled in a thousand pieces. Underneath where it had been, was sand.

Sand everywhere. A city built on sand. Mars, planet of sand. That was not completely true, of course. Seasonal vegetation had been observed near the polar icecaps. All but the hardiest of it died with the coming of summer. It had been intended that the rocketship land near one of those shallow, tideless seas.

By coming down out of control, the ship had wrecked more than itself. It had wrecked the chances for life of the only survivor of the voyage.

Jenner came slowly out of his daze. He had a thought then. He picked up one of the shrubs he had already torn loose, braced his foot against the marble to which it was attached and tugged, gently at first, then with increasing strength.

It came loose finally, but there was no doubt that the two were part of a whole. The shrub was growing out of the marble.

Marble? Jenner knelt beside one of the holes from which he had torn a slab, and bent over an adjoining section. It was quite porous—calciferous rock, most likely, but not true marble at all. As he reached toward it, intending to break off a piece, it changed color. Astounded, Jenner drew back. Around the break, the stone was turning a bright orange-yellow. He studied it uncertainly, then tentatively he touched it.

It was as if he had dipped his fingers into searing acid. There was a sharp, biting, burning pain. With a gasp, Jenner jerked his hand clear.

The continuing anguish made him feel faint. He swayed and moaned, clutching the bruised members to his body. When the agony finally faded, and he could look at the injury, he saw that the skin had peeled, and that already blood blisters had formed. Grimly, Jenner looked down at the break in the stone. The edges remained bright orange-yellow.

The village was alert, ready to defend itself from further attacks.

Suddenly weary, he crawled into the shade of a tree. There was only one possible conclusion to draw from what had happened, and it almost defied common sense. This lonely village was alive.

As he lay there, Jenner tried to imagine a great mass of living substance growing into the shape of buildings, adjusting itself to suit another life form, accepting the role of servant in the widest meaning of the term.

If it would serve one race, why not another? If it could adjust to Martians, why not to human beings?

There would be difficulties, of course. He guessed wearily that essential elements would not be available. The oxygen for water could come from the air . . . thousands of compounds could be made from sand . . . though it meant death if he failed to find a solution, he fell asleep even as he started to think about what they might be.

When he awoke, it was quite dark. Jenner climbed heavily to his feet. There was a drag to his muscles that alarmed him. He wet his mouth from his water bag, and staggered toward the entrance of the nearest building. Except for the scraping of his shoes on the "marble," the silence was intense.

He stopped short—listened, and looked. The wind had died away. He couldn't see the mountains that rimmed the valley, but the buildings were still dimly visible, black shadows in a shadow world.

For the first time, it seemed to him that, in spite of his new hope, it might be better if he died. Even if he survived, what had he to look forward to? Only too well he recalled how hard it had been to rouse interest in the trip, and to raise the large amount of money required. He remembered the colossal problems that had had to be solved in building the ship, and some of the men who had solved them were buried somewhere in the Martian desert.

It might be twenty years before another ship from Earth would try to reach the only other planet in the solar system that had shown signs of being able to support life.

During those uncountable days and nights, those years,

he would be here alone. That was the most he could hope for—if he lived. As he fumbled his way to a dais in one of the rooms, Jenner considered another problem:

How did one let a living village know that it must alter its processes? In a way, it must already have grasped that it had a new tenant. How could he make it realize he needed food in a different chemical combination than that which it had served in the past; that he liked music, but on a different scale system; and that he could use a shower each morning—of water, not of poison gas?

He dozed fitfully, like a man who is sick rather than sleepy. Twice, he wakened, his lips on fire, his eyes burning, his body bathed in perspiration. Several times he was startled into consciousness by the sound of his own harsh voice crying out in anger and fear at the night.

He guessed, then, that he was dying.

He spent the long hours of darkness tossing, turning, twisting, befuddled by waves of heat. As the light of morning came, he was vaguely surprised to realize that he was still alive. Restlessly, he climbed off the dais, and went to the door.

A bitingly cold wind blew, but it felt good to his hot face. He wondered if there was enough *pneumococcus* in his blood for him to catch pneumonia. He decided not.

In a few moments he was shivering. He retreated back into the house, and for the first time noticed that, despite the doorless doorway, the wind did not come into the building at all. The rooms were cold, but not draughty.

That started an association: Where had this terrible body heat come from? He teetered over to the dais where he had spent the night. Within seconds, he was sweltering in a temperature of about a hundred and thirty.

He climbed off the dais, shaken by his own stupidity. He estimated that he had sweated at least two quarts of moisture out of his dried-up body on that furnace of a bed.

This village was not for human beings. Here, even the beds were heated for creatures who needed temperatures far beyond the heat comfortable for men.

Jenner spent most of the day in the shade of a large tree. He felt exhausted, and only occasionally did he even remember that he had a problem. When the whistling started, it bothered him at first, but he was too tired to move away from it. There were long periods when he hardly heard it, so dulled were his senses.

Late in the afternoon, he remembered the shrubs and the tree he had torn up the day before, and wondered what had happened to them. He wet his swollen tongue with the last few drops of water in his bag, climbed lackadaisically to his feet, and went to look for the dried-up remains.

There weren't any. He couldn't even find the holes where he had torn them out. The living village had absorbed the dead tissue into itself, and repaired the breaks in its "body."

That galvanized Jenner. He began to think again . . . about mutations, genetic readjustment, life forms adapting to new environments. There'd been lectures on that before the ship left Earth, rather generalized talks designed to acquaint the explorers with the problems men might face on an alien planet. The important principle was quite simple: adjust or die.

The village had to adjust to him. He doubted if he could seriously damage it, but he could try. His own need to survive must be placed on as sharp and hostile a basis as that.

Frantically, Jenner began to search his pockets. Before leaving the rocket, he had loaded himself with odds and ends of small equipment. A jackknife, a folding metal cup, a printed radio, a tiny super-battery that could be charged by spinning an attached wheel—and for which he had brought along, among other things, a powerful electric fire lighter.

Jenner plugged the lighter into the battery, and deliberately scraped the red-hot end along the surface of the "marble." The reaction was swift. The substance turned an angry purple this time. When an entire section of the floor had changed color, Jenner headed for the nearest stall trough, entering far enough to activate it.

There was a noticeable delay. When the food finally flowed into the trough, it was clear that the living village had realized the reason for what he had done. The food was a pale, creamy color, where earlier it had been murky gray.

Jenner put his finger into it, but withdrew it with a yell, and wiped his finger. It continued to sting for several moments. The vital question was: had it deliberately offered him food that would damage him, or was it trying to appease him without knowing what he could eat?

He decided to give it another chance, and entered the adjoining stall. The gritty stuff that flooded up this time was yellower. It didn't burn his finger, but Jenner took one taste, and spat it out. He had the feeling that he had been offered a soup made of a greasy mixture of clay and gasoline.

He was thirsty now with a need heightened by the unpleasant taste in his mouth. Desperately, he rushed outside and tore open the water bag, seeking the wetness inside. In his fumbling eagerness, he spilled a few precious drops onto the courtyard. Down he went on his face, and licked them up.

Half a minute later, he was still licking, and there was still water.

The fact penetrated suddenly. He raised himself, and gazed wonderingly at the droplets of water that sparkled on the smooth stone. As he watched, another one squeezed up from the apparently solid surface, and shimmered in the light of the sinking sun.

He bent, and with the tip of his tongue sponged up each visible drop. For a long time, he lay with his mouth pressed to the "marble," sucking up the tiny bits of water that the village doled out to him.

The glowing white sun disappeared behind a hill. Night fell, like the dropping of a black screen. The air turned cold, then icy. He shivered as the wind keened through his ragged clothes. But what finally stopped him was the collapse of the surface from which he had been drinking.

Jenner lifted himself in surprise, and in the darkness gingerly felt over the stone. It had genuinely crumbled. Evidently the substance had yielded up its available water and had disintegrated in the process. Jenner estimated that he had drunk altogether an ounce of water.

It was a convincing demonstration of the willingness of the village to please him, but there was another, less satisfying implication. If the village had to destroy a part of itself every time it gave him a drink, then clearly the supply was not unlimited.

Jenner hurried inside the nearest building, climbed onto a dais—and climbed off again hastily, as the heat blazed up at him. He waited, to give the Intelligence a chance to realize he wanted a change, then lay down once more. The heat was as great as ever.

He gave that up because he was too tired to persist, and too sleepy to think of a method that might let the village know he needed a different bedroom temperature. He slept on the floor with an uneasy conviction that it could *not* sustain him for long. He woke up many times during the night, and thought: "Not enough water. No matter how hard it tries—" then he would sleep again, only to wake once more, tense and unhappy.

Nevertheless, morning found him briefly alert; and all his steely determination was back—that iron willpower that had brought him at least five hundred miles across an unknown desert.

He headed for the nearest trough. This time, after he had activated it, there was a pause of more than a minute; and then about a thimbleful of water made a wet splotch at the bottom.

Jenner licked it dry, then waited hopefully for more.

When none came, he reflected gloomily that somewhere in the village, an entire group of cells had broken down and released their water for him.

Then and there he decided that it was up to the human being, who could move around, to find a new source of water for the village, which could not move.

In the interim, of course, the village would have to keep him alive, until he had investigated the possibilities. That meant, above everything else, he must have some food to sustain him while he looked around.

He began to search his pockets. Toward the end of his food supply, he had carried scraps and pieces wrapped in small bits of cloth. Crumbs had broken off into the pocket and he had searched often during those long days in the desert. Now by actually ripping the seams, he discovered tiny particles of meat and bread, little bits of grease and other unidentifiable substances.

Carefully, he leaned over the adjoining stall, and placed the scrapings in the trough there. The village would not be able to offer him more than a reasonable facsimile. If the spilling of a few drops on the courtyard could make it aware of his need for water, than a similar offering might give it the clue it needed as to the chemical nature of the food he could eat.

Jenner waited, then entered the second stall and activated it. About a pint of thick, creamy substance trickled into the bottom of the trough. The smallness of the quantity seemed evidence that perhaps it contained water.

He tasted it. It had a sharp, musty flavor, and a stale odor. It was almost as dry as flour—but his stomach did not reject it.

Jenner ate slowly, acutely aware that at such moments as this the village had him at its mercy. He could never be sure that one of the food ingredients was not a slow acting poison.

When he had finished the meal, he went to a food trough

in another building. He refused to eat the food that came up, but activated still another trough. This time he received a few drops of water.

He had come purposefully to one of the tower buildings. Now, he started up the ramp that led to the upper floor. He paused only briefly in the room he came to, as he had already discovered that they seemed to be additional bedrooms. The familiar dais was there in a group of three.

What interested him was that the circular ramp continued to wind on upward. First, to another, smaller room that seemed to have no particular reason for being. Then it wound on up to the top of the tower, some seventy feet above the ground. It was high enough for him to see beyond the rim of all the surrounding hilltops. He had thought it might be, but he had been too weak to make the climb before. Now, he looked out to every horizon. Almost immediately, the hope that had brought him up, faded.

The view was immeasurably desolate. As far as he could see was an arid waste, and every horizon was hidden in a mist of wind-blown sand.

Jenner gazed with a sense of despair. If there was a Martian sea out there somewhere, it was beyond his reach.

Abruptly, he clenched his hands in anger against his fate, which seemed inevitable now. At the very worst, he had hoped he would find himself in a mountainous region. Seas and mountains were generally the two main sources of water. He should have known, of course, that there were very few mountains on Mars. It would have been a wild coincidence if he had actually run into a mountain range.

His fury faded, because he lacked the strength to sustain any emotion. Numbly, he went down the ramp.

His vague plan to help the village ended as swiftly and finally as that.

The days drifted by, but as to how many he had no idea. Each time he went to eat, a smaller amount of water was doled out to him. Jenner kept telling himself that each meal would have to be his last. It was unreasonable for him to expect the village to destroy itself when his fate was certain now.

What was worse, it became increasingly clear that the food was not good for him. He had misled the village as to his needs by giving it stale, perhaps even tainted samples, and prolonged the agony for himself. At times after he had eaten, Jenner felt dizzy for hours. All too frequently, his head ached, and his body shivered with fever.

The village was doing what it could. The rest was up to him, and he couldn't even adjust to an approximation of Earth food.

For two days, he was too sick to drag himself to one of the troughs. Hour after hour, he lay on the floor. Some time during the second night, the pain in his body grew so terrible that he finally made up his mind.

"If I can get to a dais," he told himself, "the heat alone will kill me; and in absorbing my body, the village will get back some of its lost water."

He spent at least an hour crawling laboriously up the ramp of the nearest dais, and when he finally made it, he lay as one already dead. His last waking thought was: "Beloved friends, I'm coming."

The hallucination was so complete that, momentarily, he seemed to be back in the control room of the rocketship, and all around him were his former companions.

With a sigh of relief, Jenner sank into a dreamless sleep.

He woke to the sound of a violin. It was a sad-sweet music that told of the rise and fall of a race long dead.

Jenner listened for a while, and then with abrupt excitement realized the truth. This was a substitute for the whistling—the village had adjusted its music to him!

Other sensory phenomena stole in upon him. The dais felt comfortably warm, not hot at all. He had a feeling of wonderful physical well-being.

Eagerly, he scrambled down the ramp to the nearest food

stall. As he crawled forward, his nose close to the floor, the trough filled with a steamy mixture. The odor was so rich and pleasant that he plunged his face into it, and slopped it up greedily. It had the flavor of thick, meaty soup, and was warm and soothing to his lips and mouth. When he had eaten it all, he did not need a drink of water for the first time.

"I've won!" thought Jenner, "The village has found a way!"

After a while, he remembered something, and crawled to the bathroom. Cautiously, watching the ceiling, he eased himself backward into the shower stall. The yellowish spray came down, cool and delightful.

Ecstatically, Jenner wriggled his four-foot tail, and, lifted his long snout to let the thin streams of liquid wash away the food impurities that clung to his sharp teeth.

Then he waddled out to bask in the sun, and listen to the timeless music.

LIAR!

---

by

ISAAC ASIMOV

Alfred Lanning lit his cigar carefully, but the tips of his fingers were trembling slightly. His gray eyebrows hunched low as he spoke between puffs.

"It reads minds all right—damn little doubt about that! But why?" He looked at Mathematician Peter Bogert, "Well?"

Bogert flattened his black hair down with both hands, "That was the thirty-fourth RB model we've turned out, Lanning. All the others were strictly orthodox."

The third man at the table frowned. Milton Ashe was the youngest officer of U. S. Robot & Mechanical Men, Inc., and proud of his post.

"Listen, Bogert. There wasn't a hitch in the assembly from start to finish. I guarantee that."

Bogert's thick lips spread in a patronizing smile, "Do you? If you can answer for the entire assembly line, I recommend your promotion. By exact count, there are seventy-five thousand, two hundred and thirty-four operations necessary for the manufacture of a single positronic brain, each separate operation depending for successful completion upon any number of factors, from five to a hundred and five. If any one of them goes seriously wrong, the 'brain' is ruined. I quote our own information folder, Ashe."

Milton Ashe flushed, but a fourth voice cut off his reply.

"If we're going to start by trying to fix the blame on one another, I'm leaving." Susan Calvin's hands were folded tightly in her lap, and the little lines about her thin, pale lips deepened. "We've got a mind-reading robot on our hands and it strikes me as rather important that we find out just why it reads minds. We're not going to do that by saying, 'Your fault! My fault!' "

Her cold gray eyes fastened upon Ashe, and he grinned.

Lanning grinned too, and, as always at such times, his long white hair and shrewd little eyes made him the picture of a biblical patriarch, "True for you, Dr. Calvin."

His voice became suddenly crisp, "Here's everything in pill-concentrate form. We've produced a positronic brain of supposedly ordinary vintage that's got the remarkable property of being able to tune in on thought waves. It would mark the most important advance in robotics in decades if we knew how it happened. We don't, and we have to find out. Is that clear?"

"May I make a suggestion?" asked Bogert.

"Go ahead!"

"I'd say that until we do figure out the mess—and as a mathematician I expect it to be a very devil of a mess—we keep the existence of RB-34 a secret. I mean even from the other members of the staff. As heads of the departments, we ought not to find it an insoluble problem, and the fewer know about it—"

"Bogert is right," said Dr. Calvin. "Ever since the Interplanetary Code was modified to allow robot models to be tested in the plants before being shipped out to space, anti-robot propaganda has increased. If any word leaks out about a robot being able to read minds before we can announce complete control of the phenomenon, pretty effective capital could be made out of it."

Lanning sucked at his cigar and nodded gravely. He turned to Ashe, "I think you said you were alone when you first stumbled on this thought-reading business."

"I'll say I was alone—I got the scare of my life. RB-34 had just been taken off the assembly table and they sent him down to me. Obermann was off somewheres, so I took him down to the testing room myself—at least I started to take him down." Ashe paused, and a tiny smile tugged at his lips, "Say, did any of you ever carry on a thought conversation without knowing it?"

No one bothered to answer, and he continued, "You don't realize it at first, you know. He just spoke to me— as logically and sensibly as you can imagine—and it was only when I was most of the way down to the testing rooms that I realized that I hadn't said anything. Sure, I thought lots, but that isn't the same thing, is it? I locked that thing up and ran for Lanning. Having it walking besides me, calmly peering into my thoughts and picking and choosing among them gave me the willies."

"I imagine it would," said Susan Calvin thoughtfully. Her eyes fixed themselves upon Ashe in an oddly intent manner. "We are so accustomed to considering our own thoughts private."

Lanning broke in impatiently, "Then only the four of us know. All right! We've got to go about this systematically Ashe, I want you to check over the assembly line from beginning to end—everything. You're to eliminate all operations in which there was no possible chance of an error, and list all those where there were, together with its nature and possible magnitude."

"Tall order," grunted Ashe.

"Naturally! Of course, you're to put the men under you to work on this—every single one if you have to, and I don't care if we go behind schedule, either. But they're not to know why, you understand."

"Hm-m-m, yes!" The young technician grinned wryly. "It's still a lulu of a job."

Lanning swiveled about in his chair and faced Calvin, "You'll have to tackle the job from the other direction. You're the robopsychologist of the plant, so you're to study the robot itself and work backward. Try to find out how he ticks. See what else is tied up with his telepathic powers, how far they extend, how they warp his outlook, and just exactly what harm it has done to his ordinary RB properties. You've got that?"

Lanning didn't wait for Dr. Calvin to answer.

"I'll co-ordinate the work and interpret the findings mathematically." He puffed violently at his cigar and mumbled the rest through the smoke, "Bogert will help me there, of course."

Bogert polished the nails of one pudgy hand with the other and said blandly, "I dare say. I know a little in the line."

"Well! I'll get started." Ashe shoved his chair back and rose. His pleasantly youthful face crinkled in a grin, "I've got the darnedest job of any of us, so I'm getting out of here and to work."

He left with a slurred, "B' seein' ye!"

Susan Calvin answered with a barely perceptible nod, but her eyes followed him out of sight and she did not answer when Lanning grunted and said, "Do you want to go up and see RB-34 now, Dr. Calvin?"

RB-34's photoelectric eyes lifted from the book at the muffled sound of hinges turning and he was upon his feet when Susan Calvin entered.

She paused to readjust the huge "No Entrance" sign upon the door and then approached the robot.

"I've brought you the texts upon hyperatomic motors, Herbie—a few anyway. Would you care to look at them?"

RB-34—otherwise known as Herbie—lifted the three heavy books from her arms and opened to the title page of one:

"Hm-m-m! 'Theory of Hyperatomics.'" He mumbled inarticulately to himself as he flipped the pages and then spoke with an abstracted air, "Sit down, Dr. Calvin! This will take me a few minutes."

The psychologist seated herself and watched Herbie narrowly as he took a chair at the other side of the table and went through the three books systematically.

At the end of half an hour, he put them down, "Of course, I know why you brought these."

The corner of Dr. Calvin's lip twitched, "I was afraid you would. It's difficult to work with you, Herbie. You're always a step ahead of me."

"It's the same with these books, you know, as with the others. They just don't interest me. There's nothing to your textbooks. Your science is just a mass of collected data plastered together by make-shift theory—and all so incredibly simple, that it's scarcely worth bothering about.

"It's your fiction that interests me. Your studies of the interplay of human motives and emotions"—his mighty hand gestured vaguely as he sought the proper words.

Dr. Calvin whispered, "I think I understand."

"I see into minds, you see," the robot continued, "and you have no idea how complicated they are. I can't begin to understand everything because my own mind has so little in common with them—but I try, and your novels help."

"Yes, but I'm afraid that after going through some of the harrowing emotional experiences of our present-day sentimental novel"—there was a tinge of bitterness in her voice—"you find real minds like ours are dull and colorless."

"But I don't!"

The sudden energy in the response brought the other to her feet. She felt herself reddening, and thought wildly, "He must know!"

Herbie subsided suddenly, and muttered in a low voice from which the metallic timbre departed almost entirely. "But, of course, I know about it, Dr. Calvin. You think of it always, so how can I help but know?"

Her face was hard. "Have you—told anyone?"

"Of course not!" This, with genuine surprise. "No one has asked me."

"Well, then," she flung out, "I suppose you think I am a fool."

"No! It is a normal emotion."

"Perhaps that is why it is so foolish." The wistfulness in her voice drowned out everything else. Some of the woman peered through the layer of doctorhood. "I am not what you would call—attractive."

"If you are referring to mere physical attraction, I couldn't judge. But I know, in any case, that there are other types of attraction."

"Nor young." Dr. Calvin had scarcely heard the robot.

"You are not yet forty." An anxious insistence had crept into Herbie's voice.

"Thirty-eight as you count the years; a shriveled sixty as far as my emotional outlook on life is concerned. Am I a psychologist for nothing?"

She drove on with bitter breathlessness, "And he's barely thirty-five and looks and acts younger. Do you suppose he ever sees me as anything but . . . but what I am?"

"You are wrong!" Herbies steel fist struck the plastic-topped table with a strident clang. "Listen to me—"

But Susan Calvin whirled on him now and the hunted pain in her eyes became a blaze, "Why should I? What do you know about it all, anyway, you . . . you machine. I'm just a specimen to you; an interesting bug with a peculiar mind spread-eagled for inspection. It's a wonderful example of frustration, isn't it? Almost as good as your books." Her voice, emerging in dry sobs, choked into silence.

The robot cowered at the outburst. He shook his head pleadingly. "Won't you listen to me, please? I could help you if you would let me."

"How?" Her lips curled. "By giving me good advice?"

"No, not that. It's just that I know what other people think—Milton Ashe, for instance."

There was a long silence, and Susan Calvin's eyes dropped. "I don't want to know what he thinks," she gasped. "Keep quiet."

"I think you would want to know what he thinks."

Her head remained bent, but her breath came more quickly. "You are talking nonsense," she whispered.

"Why should I? I am trying to help. Milton Ashe's thoughts of you—" he paused.

And then the psychologist raised her head, "Well?"

The robot said quietly, "He loves you."

For a full minute, Dr. Calvin did not speak. She merely stared. Then, "You are mistaken! You must be. Why should he?"

"But he does. A thing like that cannot be hidden, not from me."

"But I am so . . . so—" she stammered to a halt.

"He looks deeper than the skin, and admires intellect in others. Milton Ashe is not the type to marry a head of hair and a pair of eyes."

Susan Calvin found herself blinking rapidly and waited before speaking. Even then her voice trembled, "Yet he certainly never in any way indicated—"

"Have you ever given him a chance?"

"How could I? I never thought that—"

"Exactly!"

The psychologist paused in thought and then looked up suddenly. "A girl visited him here at the plant half a year ago. She was pretty, I suppose—blond and slim. And, of course, could scarcely add two and two. He spent all day puffing out his chest, trying to explain how a robot was put together." The hardness had returned, "Not that she understood! Who was she?"

Herbie answered without hesitation, "I know the person you are referring to. She is his first cousin, and there is no romantic interest there, I assure you."

Susan Calvin rose to her feet with a vivacity almost girl-ish. "Now isn't that strange? That's exactly what I used to pretend to myself sometimes, though I never really thought so. Then it all must be true."

She ran to Herbie and seized his cold, heavy hand in both hers. "Thank you, Herbie." Her voice was an urgent, husky whisper. "Don't tell anyone about this. Let it be our secret—and thank you again." With that, and a convulsive squeeze of Herbie's unresponsive metal fingers, she left.

Herbie turned slowly to his neglected novel, but there was no one to read *his* thoughts.

Milton Ashe stretched slowly and magnificently, to the tune of cracking joints and chorus of grunts, and then glared at Peter Bogert, Ph.D.

"Say," he said, "I've been at this for a week now with just about no sleep. How long do I have to keep it up? I thought you said the positronic bombardment in Vac Chamber D was the solution."

Bogert yawned delicately and regarded his white hands with interest. "It is. I'm on the track."

"I know what *that* means when a mathematician says it. How near the end are you?"

"It all depends."

"On what?" Ashe dropped into a chair and stretched his long legs out before him.

"On Lanning. The old fellow disagrees with me." He sighed, "A bit behind the times, that's the trouble with him. He clings to matrix mechanics as the all in all, and this problem calls for more powerful mathematical tools. He's so stubborn."

Ashe muttered sleepily, "Why not ask Herbie and settle the whole affair?"

"Ask the robot?" Bogert's eyebrows climbed.

"Why not? Didn't the old girl tell you?"

"You mean Calvin?"

"Yeah! Susie herself. That robot's a mathematical wiz. He knows all about everything plus a bit on the side. He does triple integrals in his head and eats up tensor analysis for dessert."

The mathematician stared skeptically, "Are you serious?"

"So help me! The catch is that the dope doesn't like math. He would rather read slushy novels. Honest! You should see the tripe Susie keeps feeding him: 'Purple Passion' and 'Love in Space.' "

"Dr. Calvin hasn't said a word of this to us."

"Well, she hasn't finished studying him. You know how she is. She likes to have everything just so before letting out the big secret."

"She told *you*."

"We sort of got to talking. I have been seeing a lot of her lately." He opened his eyes wide and frowned, "Say, Bogie, have you been noticing anything queer about the lady lately?"

Bogert relaxed into an undignified grin, "She's using lipstick, if that's what you mean."

"Hell, I know that. Rouge, powder and eye shadow, too. She's a sight. But it's not that. I can't put my finger on it. It's the way she talks—as if she were happy about something." He thought a little, and then shrugged.

The other allowed himself a leer, which, for a scientist past fifty, was not a bad job, "Maybe she's in love."

Ashe allowed his eyes to close again, "You're nuts, Bogie. You go speak to Herbie; I want to stay here and go to sleep."

"Right! Not that I particularly like having a robot tell me my job, nor that I think he can do it!"

A soft snore was his only answer.

Herbie listened carefully as Peter Bogert, hands in pockets, spoke with elaborate indifference.

"So there you are. I've been told you understand these things, and I am asking you more in curiosity than anything else. My line of reasoning, as I have outlined it, involves a few doubtful steps, I admit, which Dr. Lanning refuses to accept, and the picture is still rather incomplete."

The robot didn't answer, and Bogert said, "Well?"

"I see no mistake," Herbie studied the scribbled figures. "I don't suppose you can go any further than that?"

"I daren't try. You are a better mathematician than I, and—well, I'd hate to commit myself."

There was a shade of complacency in Bogert's smile, "I rather thought that would be the case. It is deep. We'll forget it." He crumpled the sheets, tossed them down the waste shaft, turned to leave, and then thought better of it.

"By the way—"

The robot waited.

Bogert seemed to have difficulty. "There is something— that is, perhaps you can—" He stopped.

Herbie spoke quietly. "Your thoughts are confused, but there is no doubt at all that they concern Dr. Lanning. It is silly to hesitate, for as soon as you compose yourself, I'll know what it is you want to ask."

The mathematician's hand went to his sleek hair in the familiar smoothing gesture. "Lanning is nudging seventy," he said, as if that explained everything.

"I know that."

"And he's been director of the plant for almost thirty years." Herbie nodded.

"Well, now," Bogert's voice became ingratiating, "you would know whether . . . whether he's thinking of resigning. Health, perhaps, or some other—"

"Quite," said Herbie, and that was all.

"Well, do you know?"

"Certainly."

"Then—uh—could you tell me?"

"Since you ask, yes." The robot was quite matter-of-fact about it. "He has already resigned!"

"What!" The exclamation was an explosive, almost inarticulate, sound. The scientist's large head hunched forward, "Say that again!"

"He has already resigned," came the quiet repetition, "but it has not yet taken effect. He is waiting, you see, to solve the problem of—er—myself. That finished, he is quite ready to turn the office of director over to his successor."

Bogert expelled his breath sharply, "And this successor? Who is he?" He was quite close to Herbie now, eyes fixed fascinated on those unreadable dull-red photoelectric cells that were the robot's eyes.

Words came slowly, "You are the next director."

And Bogert relaxed into a tight smile. "This is good to know. I've been hoping and waiting for this. Thanks, Herbie."

Peter Bogert was at his desk until five that morning and he was back at nine. The shelf just over the desk emptied of its row of reference books and tables, as he referred to one after the other. The pages of calculations before him increased microscopically and the crumpled sheets at his feet mounted into a hill of scribbled paper.

At precisely noon, he stared at the final page, rubbed a blood-shot eye, yawned and shrugged. "This is getting worse each minute. Damn!"

He turned at the sound of the opening door and nodded at Lanning, who entered, cracking the knuckles of one gnarled hand with the other.

The director took in the disorder of the room and his eyebrows furrowed together.

"New lead?" he asked.

"No," came the defiant answer. "What's wrong with the old one?"

Lanning did not trouble to answer, nor to do more than bestow a single cursory glance at the top sheet upon Bogert's desk. He spoke through the flare of a match as he lit a cigar.

"Has Calvin told you about the robot? It's a mathe-

306 Modern Masterpieces of Science Fiction

matical genius. Really remarkable."

The other snorted loudly, "So I've heard. But Calvin had better stick to robopsychology. I've checked Herbie on math, and he can scarcely struggle through calculus."

"Calvin didn't find it so."

"She's crazy."

"And I don't find it so." The director's eyes narrowed dangerously.

"You!" Bogert's voice hardened. "What are you talking about?"

"I've been putting Herbie through his paces all morning, and he can do tricks you never heard of."

"Is that so?"

"You sound skeptical!" Lanning flipped a sheet of paper out of his vest pocket and unfolded it. "Thats not my handwriting, is it?"

Bogert studied the large angular notation covering the sheet, "Herbie did this?"

"Right! And if you'll notice, he's been working on your time integration of Equation 22. It comes"—Lanning tapped a yellow fingernail upon the last step— "to the identical conclusion I did, and in a quarter the time. You had no right to neglect the Linger Effect in positronic bombardment."

"I didn't neglect it. For Heaven's sake, Lanning, get it through your head that it would cancel out—"

"Oh, sure, you explained that. You used the Mitchell Translation Equation, didn't you? Well—it doesn't apply."

"Why not?"

"Because you've been using hyper-imaginaries, for one thing."

"What's that to do with?"

"Mitchell's Equation won't hold when—"

"Are you crazy? If you'll reread Mitchell's original paper in the Transactions of the Far—"

"I don't have to. I told you in the beginning that I didn't like his reasoning, and Herbie backs me in that."

"Well, then," Bogert shouted, "let that clockwork contraption solve the entire problem for you. Why bother with nonessentials?"

"That's exactly the point. Herbie can't solve the problem. And if he can't, we can't—alone. I'm submitting the entire question to the National Board. It's gotten beyond us."

Bogert's chair went over backward as he jumped up a-snarl, face crimson. "You're doing nothing of the sort."

Lanning flushed in his turn, "Are you telling me what I can't do?"

"Exactly," was the gritted response. "I've got the problem beaten and you're not to take it out of my hands, understand? Don't think I don't see through you, you desiccated fossil. You'd cut your own nose off before you'd let me get the credit for solving robotic telepathy."

"You're a damned idiot, Bogert, and in one second I'll have you suspended for insubordination"—Lanning's lower lip trembled with passion.

"Which is one thing you won't do, Lanning. You haven't any secrets with a mind-reading robot around, so don't forget that I know all about your resignation."

The ash on Lanning's cigar trembled and fell, and the cigar itself followed, "What . . . what—"

Bogert chuckled nastily, "And I'm the new director, be it understood. I'm very aware of that; don't think I'm not. Damn your eyes, Lanning, I'm going to give the orders about here or there will be the sweetest mess that you've ever been in."

Lanning found his voice and let it out with a roar. "You're suspended, d'ye hear? You're relieved of all duties. You're broken, do you understand?"

The smile on the other's face broadened, "Now, what's the use of that? You're getting nowhere. I'm holding the trumps. I know you've resigned. Herbie told me, and he got it straight from you."

Lanning forced himself to speak quietly. He looked an old, old man, with tired eyes peering from a face in which the red had disappeared, leaving the pasty yellow of age behind, "I want to speak to Herbie. He can't have told you anything of the sort. You're playing a deep game, Bogert, but I'm calling your bluff. Come with me."

Bogert shrugged, "To see Herbie? Good! Damned good!"

It was also precisely at noon that Milton Ashe looked up from his clumsy sketch and said, "You get the idea? I'm not too good at getting this down, but that's about how it looks. It's a honey of a house, and I can get it for next to nothing."

Susan Calvin gazed across at him with melting eyes. "It's really beautiful," she sighed. "I've often thought that I'd like to—" Her voice trailed away.

"Of course," Ashe continued briskly, putting away his pencil, "I've got to wait for my vacation. It's only two weeks off, but this Herbie business has everything up in the air." His eyes dropped to his fingernails, "Besides, there's another point—but it's a secret."

"Then don't tell me."

"Oh, I'd just as soon, I'm just busting to tell someone—and you're just about the best—er—confidante I could find here." He grinned sheepishly.

Susan Calvin's heart bounded, but she did not trust herself to speak.

"Frankly," Ashe scraped his chair closer and lowered his voice into a confidential whisper, "the house isn't to be only for myself. I'm getting married!"

And then he jumped out of his seat, "What's the matter?"

"Nothing!" The horrible spinning sensation had vanished, but it was hard to get words out. "Married? You mean—"

"Why, sure! About time, isn't it? You remember that girl who was here last summer. That's she! But you *are* sick. You—"

"Headache!" Susan Calvin motioned him away weakly. "I've . . . I've been subject to them lately. I want to . . .

to congratulate you, of course. I'm very glad—" The inexpertly applied rouge made a pair of nasty red splotches upon her chalk-white face. Things had begun spinning again. "Pardon me—please—"

The words were a mumble, as she stumbled blindly out the door. It had happened with the sudden catastrophe of a dream—and with all the unreal horror of a dream.

But how could it be? Herbie had said—

And Herbie knew! He could see into minds!

She found herself leaning breathlessly against the door jamb, staring into Herbie's metal face. She must have climbed the two flights of stairs, but she had no memory of it. The distance had been covered in an instant, as in a dream.

As in a dream!

And still Herbie's unblinking eyes stared into hers and their dull red seemed to expand into dimly shining nightmarish globes.

He was speaking, and she felt the cold glass pressing against her lips. She swallowed and shuddered into a certain awareness of her surroundings.

Still Herbie spoke, and there was agitation in his voice— as if he were hurt and frightened and pleading.

The words were beginning to make sense. "This is a dream," he was saying, "and you mustn't believe in it. You'll wake into the real world soon and laugh at yourself. He loves you, I tell you. He does, he does! But not here! Not now! This is an illusion."

Susan Calvin nodded, her voice a whisper, "Yes! Yes!" She was clutching Herbie's arm, clinging to it, repeating over and over, "It isn't true, is it? It isn't, is it?"

Just how she came to her senses, she never knew—but it was like passing from a world of misty unreality to one of harsh sunlight. She pushed him away from her, pushed hard against that steely arm, and her eyes were wide.

"What are you trying to do?" Her voice rose to a harsh scream. "What are you trying to do?"

Herbie backed away, "I want to help."

The psychologist stared, "Help? By telling me this is a dream? By trying to push me into schizophrenia?" A hysterical tenseness seized her, "This is no dream! I wish it were!"

She drew her breath sharply, "Wait! Why . . . why, I understand. Merciful Heavens, it's so obvious."

There was horror in the robot's voice, "I had to!"

"And I believed you! I never thought—"

Loud voices outside the door brought her to a halt. She turned away, fists clenching spasmodically, and when Bogert and Lanning entered, she was at the far window. Neither of the men paid her the slightest attention.

They approached Herbie simultaneously; Lanning angry and impatient, Bogert, coolly sardonic. The director spoke first.

"Here now, Herbie. Listen to me!"

The robot brought his eyes sharply down upon the aged director, "Yes, Dr. Lanning."

"Have you discussed me with Dr. Bogert?"

"No, sir." The answer came slowly, and the smile on Bogert's face flashed off.

"What's that?" Bogert shoved in ahead of his superior and straddled the ground before the robot. "Repeat what you told me yesterday."

"I said that—" Herbie fell silent. Deep within him his metallic diaphragm vibrated in soft discords.

"Didn't you say he had resigned?" roared Bogert. "Answer me!"

Bogert raised his arm frantically, but Lanning pushed him aside," Are you trying to bully him into lying?"

"You heard him, Lanning. He began to say 'Yes' and stopped. Get out of my way! I want the truth out of him, understand!"

"I'll ask him!" Lanning turned to the robot. "All right, Herbie, take it easy. Have I resigned?"

Herbie stared, and Lanning repeated anxiously, "Have I resigned?" There was the faintest trace of a negative shake of the robot's head. A long wait produced nothing further.

The two men looked at each other and the hostility in their eyes was all but tangible.

"What the devil," blurted Bogert, "has the robot gone mute? Can't you speak, you monstrosity?"

"I can speak," came the ready answer.

"Then answer the question. Didn't you tell me Lanning had resigned? Hasn't he resigned?"

And again there was nothing but dull silence, until from the end of the room, Susan Calvin's laugh rang out suddenly, high-pitched and semi-hysterical.

The two mathematicians jumped, and Bogert's eyes narrowed, "You here? What's so funny?"

"Nothing's funny." Her voice was not quite natural. "It's just that I'm not the only one that's been caught. There's irony in three of the greatest experts in robotics in the world falling into the same elementary trap, isn't there?" Her voice faded, and she put a pale hand to her forehead, "But it isn't funny!"

This time the look that passed between the two men was one of raised eyebrows. "What trap are you talking about?" asked Lanning stiffly. "Is something wrong with Herbie?"

"No," she approached them slowly, "nothing is wrong with him—only with us." She whirled suddenly and shrieked at the robot, "Get away from me! Go to the other end of the room and don't let me look at you."

Herbie cringed before the fury of her eyes and stumbled away in a clattering trot.

Lanning's voice was hostile, "What is all this, Dr. Calvin?"

She faced them and spoke sarcastically, "Surely you know the fundamental First Law of Robotics."

The other two nodded together. "Certainly," said Bogert, irritably, "a robot may not injure a human being, or through inaction, allow him to come to harm."

"How nicely put," sneered Calvin. "But what kind of harm?"

"Why—any kind."

"Exactly! Any kind! But what about hurt feelings? What about deflation of one's ego? What about the blasting of one's hopes? Is that injury?"

Lanning frowned, "What would a robot know about—" And then he caught himself with a gasp.

"You've caught on, have you? *This* robot reads minds. Do you suppose it doesn't know everything about mental injury? Do you suppose that if asked a question, it wouldn't give exactly that answer that one wants to hear? Wouldn't any other answer hurt us, and wouldn't Herbie know that?"

"Good Heavens!" muttered Bogert.

The psychologist cast a sardonic glance at him, "I take it you asked him whether Lanning had resigned. You wanted to hear that he had resigned and so that's what Herbie told you."

"And I suppose that is why," said Lanning, tonelessly, "it would not answer a little while ago. It couldn't answer either way without hurting one of us."

There was a short pause in which the men looked thoughtfully across the room at the robot, crouching in the chair by the bookcase, head resting in one hand.

Susan Calvin stared steadfastly at the floor, "He knew of all this. That . . . that devil knows everything—including what went wrong in his assembly." Her eyes were dark and brooding.

Lanning looked up, "You're wrong there, Dr. Calvin. He doesn't know what went wrong. I asked him."

"What does that mean?" cried Calvin. "Only that you didn't want him to give you the solution. It would puncture your ego to have a machine do what you couldn't. Did you ask him?" she shot at Bogert.

"In a way." Bogert coughed and reddened. "He told me he knew very little about mathematics."

Lanning laughed, not very loudly, and the psychologist

smiled caustically. She said, "I'll ask him! A solution by him won't hurt my ego." She raised her voice into a cold, imperative, "Come here!"

Herbie rose and approached with hesitant steps.

"You know, I suppose," she continued, "just exactly at what point in the assembly an extraneous factor was introduced or an essential one left out."

"Yes," said Herbie, in tones barely heard.

"Hold on," broke in Bogert angrily. "That's not necessarily true. You want to hear that, that's all."

"Don't be a fool," replied Calvin. "He certainly knows as much math as you and Lanning together, since he can read minds. Give him his chance."

The mathematician subsided, and Calvin continued, "All right, then, Herbie, give! We're waiting." And in an aside, "Get pencils and paper, gentlemen."

But Herbie remained silent, and there was triumph in the psychologist's voice, "Why don't you answer, Herbie?"

The robot blurted out suddenly, "I cannot. You know I cannot! Dr. Bogert and Dr. Lanning don't want me to."

"They want the solution."

"But not from me."

Lanning broke in, speaking slowly and distinctly, "Don't be foolish, Herbie. We do want you to tell us."

Bogert nodded curtly.

Herbie's voice rose to wild heights, "What's the use of saying that? Don't you suppose that I can see past the superficial skin of your mind? Down below, you don't want me to. I'm a machine, given the imitation of life only by virtue of the positronic interplay in my brain—which is man's device. You can't lose face to me without being hurt. That is deep in your mind and won't be erased. I can't give the solution."

"We'll leave," said Dr. Lanning. "Tell Calvin."

"That would make no difference," cried Herbie, "since you would know anyway that it was I that was supplying the answer."

Calvin resumed, "But you understand, Herbie, that despite that, Drs. Lanning and Bogert want that solution."

"By their own efforts!" insisted Herbie.

"But they want it, and the fact that you have it and won't give it hurts them. You see that, don't you?"

"Yes! Yes!"

"And if you tell them that will hurt them, too."

"Yes! Yes!" Herbie was retreating slowly, and step by step Susan Calvin advanced. The two men watched in frozen bewilderment.

"You can't tell them," droned the psychologist slowly, "because that would hurt and you mustn't hurt. But if you don't tell them, you hurt, so you must tell them. And if you do, you will hurt and you mustn't, so you can't tell them; but if you don't, you hurt, so you must; but if you do, you hurt, so you mustn't; but if you don't, you hurt, so you must; but if you do, you—"

Herbie was up against the wall, and here he dropped to his knees. "Stop!" he shrieked. "Close your mind! It is full of pain and frustration and hate! I didn't mean it, I tell you! I tried to help! I told you what you wanted to hear. I had to!"

The psychologist paid no attention. "You must tell them, but if you do, you hurt, so you mustn't; but if you don't, you hurt, so you must; but—"

And Herbie screamed!

It was like the whistling of a piccolo many times magnified—shrill and shriller till it keened with the terror of a lost soul and filled the room with the piercingness of itself.

And when it died into nothingness, Herbie collapsed into a huddled heap of motionless metal.

Bogert's face was bloodless, "He's dead!"

"No!" Susan Calvin burst into body-racking gusts of wild laughter, "not dead—merely insane. I confronted him with the insoluble dilemma, and he broke down. You can scrap him now—because he'll never speak again."

Lanning was on his knees beside the thing that had been

Herbie. His fingers touched the cold, unresponsive metal face and he shuddered. "You did that on purpose." He rose and faced her, face contorted.

"What if I did? You can't help it now." And in a sudden access of bitterness, "He deserved it."

The director seized the paralysed, motionless Bogert by the wrist, "What's the difference. Come, Peter." He sighed, "A thinking robot of this type is worthless anyway." His eyes were old and tired, and he repeated, "Come, Peter!"

It was minutes after the two scientists left that Dr. Susan Calvin regained part of her mental equilibrium. Slowly, her eyes turned to the living-dead Herbie and the tightness returned to her face. Long she stared while the triumph faded and the helpless frustration returned—and of all her turbulent thoughts only one infinitely bitter word passed her lips.

"Liar!"

That finished it for then, naturally. I knew I couldn't get any more out of her after that. She just sat there behind her desk, her white face cold and—remembering.

I said, "Thank you, Dr. Calvin!" but she didn't answer. It was two days before I could get to see her again.

MICROCOSMIC GOD

by

THEODORE STURGEON

Here is a story about a man who had too much power, and a man who took too much, but don't worry; I'm not going political on you. The man who had the power was named James Kidder, and the other was his banker.

Kidder was quite a guy. He was a scientist and he lived on a small island off the New England coast all by himself. He wasn't the dwarfed little gnome of a mad scientist you read about. His hobby wasn't personal profit, and he wasn't a megalomaniac with a Russian name and no scruples. He wasn't insidious, and he wasn't even particularly subversive. He kept his hair cut and his nails clean and lived and thought like a reasonable human being. He was slightly on the baby-faced side; he was inclined to be a hermit; he was short and plump and—brilliant. His specialty was biochemistry, and he was always called *Mr.* Kidder. Not "Dr." Not "Professor." Just Mr. Kidder.

He was an odd sort of apple and always had been. He had never graduated from any college or university because he found them too slow for him, and too rigid in their approach to education. He couldn't get used to the idea that perhaps his professors knew what they were talking about. That went for his texts, too. He was always asking questions, and didn't mind very much when they were embarrassing. He considered Gregor Mendel a bungling liar, Darwin an amusing philosopher, and Luther Burbank a sensationalist. He never opened his mouth without leaving his victim feeling breathless. If he was talking to someone who had knowledge, he went in there and got it. If he was talking to someone whose knowledge was already in his possession, he only asked repeatedly, "How do you know?" His most delectable pleasure was taken in cutting a fanatical eugenicist into conversational ribbons. So people left him alone and never, never asked him to tea. He was polite, but not politic.

He had a little money of his own, and with it he leased the island and built himself a laboratory. Now I've mentioned that he was a biochemist. But being what he was, he couldn't keep his nose in his own field. It wasn't too remarkable when he made an intellectual excursion wide enough to perfect a method of crystallizing Vitamin B_1 profitably by the ton—if anyone wanted it by the ton. He got a lot of money for it. He bought his island outright and put eight hundred men to work on an acre and a half of his ground, adding to his laboratory and building equipment. He got messing around with sisal fiber, found out how to fuse it, and boomed the banana industry by producing a practically unbreakable cord from the stuff.

You remember the popularizing demonstration he put on at Niagara, don't you? That business of running a line of the new cord from bank to bank over the rapids and suspending a ten-ton truck from the middle of it by razor edges resting on the cord? That's why ships now moor themselves with what looks like heaving line, no thicker than a lead pencil, that can be coiled on reels like garden hose. Kidder made cigarette money out of that, too. He went out and bought himself a cyclotron with part of it.

After that money wasn't money and more. It was large numbers in little books. Kidder used to use little amounts of it to have food and equipment sent out to him, but after a while that stopped, too. His bank dispatched a messenger by seaplane to find out if Kidder was still alive. The man returned two days later in a mused state, having been amazed something awesome at the things he'd seen out there. Kidder was alive, all right, and he was turning out a surplus of good food in an astonishingly simplified synthetic form. The bank wrote immediately and wanted to know if Mr. Kidder, in his own interest, was willing to release the secret of his dirtless farming. Kidder replied that he would be glad to, and inclosed the formulas. In a P. S. he said that he hadn't sent the information ashore because he hadn't realized anyone would be interested. That from a man who was responsible for the greatest sociological change in the second half of the twentieth century—factory farming. It made him richer; I mean it made his bank richer. He didn't give a rap.

But Kidder didn't really get started until about eight months after the bank messenger's visit. For a biochemist who couldn't even be called "Dr." he did pretty well. Here is a partial list of the things that he turned out:

A commercially feasible plan for making an aluminum alloy stronger than the best steel so that it could be used as a structural metal.

An exhibition gadget he called a light pump, which worked on the theory that light is a form of matter and therefore subject to physical and electromagnetic laws. Seal a room with a single light source, beam a cylindrical vibratory magnetic field to it from the pump, and the light will be led down it. Now pass the light through Kidder's "lens"—a ring which perpetuates an electric field along the lines of a high-speed iris-type camera shutter. Below this is the heart of the light pump—a ninety-eight-percent efficient light absorber, crystalline, which, in a sense, *loses* the light in its internal facets. The effect of darkening the room with this apparatus is slight but measurable. Pardon my layman's language, but that's the general idea.

Synthetic chlorophyll—by the barrel.

An airplane propeller efficient at eight times sonic speed.

A cheap goo you brush on over old paint, let harden, and then peel off like strips of cloth. The old paint comes with it. That one made friends fast.

A self-sustaining atomic disintegration of uranium's isotope 238, which is two hundred times as plentiful as the old stand-by, U-235.

That will do for the present. If I may repeat myself; for a biochemist who couldn't even be called "Dr.," he did pretty well.

Kidder was apparently unconscious of the fact that he held power enough on his little island to become master of the world. His mind simply didn't run to things like that. As long as he was left alone with his experiments, he was well content to leave the rest of the world to its own clumsy and primitive devices. He couldn't be reached except by a radiophone of his own design, and its only counterpart was locked in a vault of his Boston bank. Only one man could operate it—the bank president. The extraordinarily sensitive transmitter would respond only to President Conant's own body vibrations. Kidder had instructed Conant that he was not to be disturbed except by messages of the greatest moment. His ideas and patents, when Conant could pry one out of him, were released under pseudonyms known only to Conant—Kidder didn't care.

The result, of course, was in infiltration of the most astonishing advancements since the dawn of civilization. The nation profited—the world profited. But most of all, the bank profited. It began to get a little oversize. It began getting its fingers into other pies. It grew more fingers

and had to bake more figurative pies. Before many years
had passed, it was so big that, using Kidder's many weapons, it almost matched Kidder in power.

Almost.

Now stand by while I squelch those fellows in the
lower left-hand corner who've been saying all this while
that Kidder's slightly improbable; that no man could ever
perfect himself in so many ways in so many sciences.

Well, you're right. Kidder was a genius—granted. But
his genius was not creative. He was, to the core, a student.
He applied what he knew, what he saw, and what he was
taught. When first he began working in his new laboratory
on his island he reasoned something like this:

"Everything I know is what I have been taught by the
sayings and writings of people who have studied the
sayings and writings of people who have—and so on.
Once in a while someone stumbles on something new
and he or someone cleverer uses the idea and disseminates
it. But for each one that finds something really new, a
couple of million gather and pass on information that is
already current. I'd know more if I could get the jump
on evolutionary trends. It takes too long to wait for the
accidents that increase man's knowledge—my knowledge.
If I had ambition enough now to figure out how to travel
ahead in time, I could skim the surface of the future and
just dip down when I saw something interesting. But time
isn't that way. It can't be left behind or tossed ahead.
What else is left?

"Well, there's the proposition of speeding intellectual
evolution so that I can observe what it cooks up. That
seems a bit inefficient. It would involve more labor to discipline human minds to that extent than it would to simply
apply myself along those lines. But I can't apply myself that
way. No one man can.

"I'm licked. I can't speed myself up, and I can't speed
other men's minds up. Isn't there an alternative? There

must be—somewhere, somehow, there's got to be an answer."

So it was on this, and not on eugenics, or light pumps, or botany, or atomic physics, that James Kidder applied himself. For a practical man, the problem was slightly on the metaphysical side, but he attacked it with typical thoroughness, using his own peculiar brand of logic. Day after day he wandered over the island, throwing shells impotently at sea gulls and swearing richly. Then came a time when he sat indoors and brooded. And only then did he get feverishly to work.

He worked in his own field, biochemistry, and concentrated mainly on two things—genetics and animal metabolism. He learned, and filed away in his insatiable mind, many things having nothing to do with the problem in hand, and very little of what he wanted. But he piled that little on what little he knew or guessed, and in time had quite a collection of known factors to work with. His approach was characteristically unorthodox. He did things on the order of multiplying by pears, and balancing equations by adding $\log \sqrt{-1}$ to one side and ∞ to the other. He made mistakes, but only one of a kind, and later, only one of a species. He spent so many hours at his microscope that he had to quit work for two days to get rid of a hallucination that his heart was pumping his own blood through the mike. He did nothing by trial and error because he disapproved of the method as sloppy.

And he got results. He was lucky to begin with, and even luckier when he formularized the law of probability and reduced it to such low terms that he knew almost to the item what experiments not to try. When the cloudy, viscous semifluid on the watch glass began to move of itself he knew he was on the right track. When it began to seek food on its own he began to be excited. When it divided and, in a few hours, redivided, and each part grew and divided again, he was triumphant, for he had created life.

He nursed his brain child and sweated and strained over them, and he designed baths of various vibrations for them, and inoculated and dosed and sprayed them. Each move he made taught him the next. And out of his tanks and tubes and incubators came amoebalike creatures, and then ciliated animalcules, and more and more rapidly he produced animals with eye spots, nerve cysts, and then—victory of victories—a real blastopod, possessed of many cells instead of one. More slowly he developed a gastropod, but once he had it, it was not too difficult for him to give it organs, each with a specified function, each inheritable.

Then came cultured mollusklike things, and creatures with more and more perfected gills. The day that a nondescript thing wriggled up an inclined board out of a tank, threw flaps over its gills and feebly breathed air, Kidder quit work and went to the other end of the island and got disgustingly drunk. Hangover and all, he was soon back in the lab, forgetting to eat, forgetting to sleep, tearing into his problem.

He turned into a scientific byway and ran down his other great triumph—accelerated metabolism. He extracted and refined the stimulating factors in alcohol, coca, heroin, and Mother Nature's prize dope runner, *cannabis indica.* Like the scientist who, in analyzing the various clotting agents for blood treatments, found that oxalic acid and oxalic acid alone was the active factor, Kidder isolated the accelerators and decelerators, the stimulants and soporifics, in every substance that ever undermined a man's morality and/or caused a "noble experiment." In the process he found one thing he needed badly—a colorless elixir that made sleep the unnecessary and avoidable waster of time it should be. Then and there he went on a twenty-four-hour shift.

He artificially synthesized the substances he had isolated, and in doing so sloughed away a great many useless components. He pursued the subject along the lines of radiations and vibrations. He discovered something in the longer reds which, when projected through a vessel full of air vibrating in the supersonics, and then polarized, speeded up the heartbeat of small animals twenty to one. They ate twenty times as much, grew twenty times as fast, and—died twenty times sooner than they should have.

Kidder built a huge hermetically sealed room. Above it was another room, the same length and breadth but not quite as high. This was his control chamber. The large room was divided into four sealed sections, each with its individual heat and atmosphere controls. Over each section were miniature cranes and derricks—handling machinery of all kinds. There were also trapdoors fitted with air locks leading from the upper to the lower room.

By this time the other laboratory had produced a warm-blooded, snake-skinned quadruped with an astonishingly rapid life cycle—a generation every eight days, a life span of about fifteen. Like the echidna, it was oviparous and mammalian. Its period of gestation was six hours; the eggs hatched in three; the young reached sexual maturity in another four days. Each female laid four eggs and lived just long enough to care for the young after they hatched. The males generally died two or three hours after mating. The creatures were highly adaptable. They were small—not more than three inches long, two inches to the shoulder from the ground. Their forepaws had three digits and a triple-jointed, opposed thumb. They were attuned to life in an atmosphere with a large ammonia content. Kidder bred four of the creatures and put one group in each section of the sealed room.

Then he was ready. With his controlled atmospheres he varied temperatures, oxygen content, humidity. He killed them off like flies with excesses of, for instance, carbon dioxide, and the survivors bred their physical resistance into the next generation. Periodically he would switch the eggs from one sealed section to another to keep the strains varied. And rapidly, under these controlled conditions, the creatures began to evolve.

This, then, was the answer to his problem. He couldn't speed up mankind's intellectual advancement enough to have it teach him the things his incredible mind yearned for. He couldn't speed himself up. So he created a new race—a race which would develop and evolve so fast that it would surpass the civilization of man; and from them he would learn.

They were completely in Kidder's power. Earth's normal atmosphere would poison them, as he took care to demonstrate to every fourth generation. They would make no attempt to escape from him. They would live their lives and progress and make their little trial-and-error experiments hundreds of times faster than man did. They had the edge on man, for they had Kidder to guide them. It took man six thousand years to really discover science, three hundred to really put it to work. It took Kidder's creatures two hundred days to equal man's mental attainments. And from then on—Kidder's spasmodic output made the late, great Tom Edison look like a home handicrafter.

He called them Neoterics, and he teased them into working for him. Kidder was inventive in an ideological way; that is, he could dream up impossible propositions providing he didn't have to work them out. For example, he wanted the Neoterics to figure out for themselves how to build shelters out of porous material. He created the need for such shelters by subjecting one of the sections to a high-pressure rainstorm which flattened the inhabitants. The Neoterics promptly devised waterproof shelters out of the thin waterproof material he piled in one corner. Kidder immediately blew down the flimsy structures with a blast of cold air. They built them up again so that they resisted both wind and rain. Kidder lowered the temperature so abruptly that they could not adjust their bodies to it. They heated their shelters with tiny braziers. Kidder promptly turned up the heat until they began to roast to death. After a few deaths, one of their bright boys figured out how to build a strong insulant house by using three-ply rubberoid, with the middle layer perforated thousands of times to create tiny air pockets.

Using such tactics, Kidder forced them to develop a highly advanced little culture. He caused a drought in one section and a liquid surplus in another, and then opened the partition between them. Quite a spectacular war was fought, and Kidder's notebooks filled with information about military tactics and weapons. Then there was the vaccine they developed against the common cold—the reason why that affliction has been absolutely stamped out in the world today, for it was one of the things that Conant, the bank president, got hold of. He spoke of Kidder over the radiophone one winter afternoon with a voice so hoarse from laryngitis that Kidder sent him a vial of the vaccine and told him briskly not to ever call him again in such a disgustingly inaudible state. Conant had it analyzed and again Kidder's accounts—and the bank's—swelled.

At first Kidder merely supplied them with the materials he thought the Neoterics might need, but when they developed an intelligence equal to the task of fabricating their own from the elements at hand, he gave each section a stock of raw materials. The process for really strong aluminum was developed when he built in a huge plunger in one of the sections, which reached from wall to wall and was designed to descend at the rate of four inches a day until it crushed whatever was at the bottom. The Neoterics, in self-defense, used what strong material they had in hand to stop the inexorable death that threatened them. But Kidder had seen to it that they had nothing but aluminum oxide and a scattering of other elements, plus plenty of electric power. At first they ran up dozens of aluminum pillars; when these were crushed and twisted they tried shaping them so that the soft metal would take more weight. When that failed they quickly built stronger ones; and when the plunger was halted, Kidder removed one of the pillars and analyzed it. It was hardened aluminum, stronger and tougher than molybd steel.

Experience taught Kidder that he had to make certain changes to increase his power over his Neoterics before they got too ingenious. There were things that could be done with atomic power that he was curious about; but he was not willing to trust his little superscientists with a thing like that unless they could be trusted to use it strictly according to Hoyle. So he instituted a rule of fear. The most trivial departure from what he chose to consider the right way of doing things resulted in instant death of half a tribe. If he was trying to develop a Diesel-type power plant, for instance, that would operate without a flywheel starter, and a bright young Neoteric used any of the materials for architectural purposes, half the tribe immediately died. Of course, they had developed a written language; it was Kidder's own. The teletype in a glass inclosed area in a corner of each section was a shrine. Any directions that were given on it were obeyed, or else—. After this innovation, Kidder's work was much simpler. There was no need for any more indirection. Anything he wanted done was done. No matter how impossible his commands, three or four generations of Neoterics could find a way to carry them out.

This quotation is from a paper that one of Kidder's high-speed telescopic cameras discovered being circulated among the younger Neoterics. It is translated from the highly simplified script of the Neoterics.

"These edicts shall be followed by each Neoteric upon pain of death, which punishment will be inflicted by the tribe upon the individual to protect the tribe against him.

"Priority of interest and tribal and individual effort is to be given the commands that appear on the word machine.

"Any misdirection of material or power, or use thereof for any other purpose than the carrying out of the machine's commands, unless no command appears, shall be punishable by death.

"Any information regarding the problem at hand, or

ideas or experiments which might conceivably bear upon it, are to become the property of the tribe.

"Any individual failing to co-operate in the tribal effort, or who can be termed guilty of not expending his full efforts in the work; or the suspicion thereof, shall be subject to the death penalty."

Such are the results of complete domination. This paper impressed Kidder as much as it did because it was completely spontaneous. It was the Neoterics' own creed, developed by them for their own greatest good.

And so at last Kidder had his fulfillment. Crouched in the upper room, going from telescope to telescope, running off slowed-down films from his high-speed cameras, he found himself possessed of a tractable, dynamic source of information. Housed in the great square building with its four half-acre sections was a new world, to which he was god.

President Conant's mind was similar to Kidder's in that its approach to any problem was along the shortest distance between any two points, regardless of whether that approach was along the line of most or least resistance. His rise to the bank presidency was a history of ruthless moves whose only justification was that they got him what he wanted. Like an overefficient general, he would never vanquish an enemy through sheer force of numbers alone. He would also skillfully flank his enemy, not on one side, but on both. Innocent bystanders were creatures deserving no consideration.

The time he took over a certain thousand-acre property, for instance, from a man named Grady, he was not satisfied with only the title to the land. Grady was an airport owner —had been all his life, and his father before him. Conant exerted every kind of pressure on the man and found him unshakable. Finally judicious persuasion led the city officials to dig a sewer right across the middle of the field, quite efficiently wrecking Grady's business. Knowing that this would supply Grady, who was a wealthy man, with motive for revenge, Conant took over Grady's bank at half again its value and caused it to fold up. Grady lost every cent he had and ended his life in an asylum. Conant was very proud of his tactics.

Like many another who has had Mammon by the tail, Conant did not know when to let go. His vast organization yielded him more money and power than any other concern in history, and yet he was not satisfied. Conant and money were like Kidder and knowledge. Conant's pyramided enterprises were to him what the Neoterics were to Kidder. Each had made his private world; each used it for his instruction and profit. Kidder, though, disturbed nobody but his Neoterics. Even so, Conant was not wholly villainous. He was a shrewd man, and had discovered early the value of pleasing people. No man can rob successfully over a period of years without pleasing the people he robs. The technique for doing this is highly involved, but master it and you can start your own mint.

Conant's one great fear was that Kidder would some day take an interest in world events and begin to become opinionated. Good heavens—the potential power he had! A little matter like swinging an election could be managed by a man like Kidder as easily as turning over in bed. The only thing he could do was to call him periodically and see if there was anything that Kidder needed to keep himself busy. Kidder appreciated this. Conant, once in a while, would suggest something to Kidder that intrigued him, something that would keep him deep in his hermitage for a few weeks. The light pump was one of the results of Conant's imagination. Conant bet him it couldn't be done. Kidder did it.

One afternoon Kidder answered the squeal of the radiophone's signal. Swearing mildly, he shut off the film he was watching and crossed the compound to the old laboratory. He went to the radiophone, threw a switch. The squealing stopped.

"Well?"

"Hello, Kidder," said Conant. "Busy?"

"Not very," said Kidder. He was delighted with the pictures his camera had caught, showing the skillful work of a gang of Neoterics synthesizing rubber out of pure sulphur. He would rather have liked to tell Conant about it, but somehow he had never got around to telling Conant about the Neoterics, and he didn't see why he should start now.

Conant said, "Er . . . Kidder, I was down at the club the other day and a bunch of us were filling up an evening with loose talk. Something came up which might interest you."

"What?"

"Couple of the utilities boys there. You know the power set-up in this country, don't you? Thirty percent atomic, the rest hydro-electric, Diesel and steam?"

"I hadn't known," said Kidder, who was as innocent as a babe of current events.

"Well, we were arguing about what chance a new power source would have. One of the men there said it would be smarter to produce a new power and then talk about it. Another one waived that; said he couldn't name that new power, but he could describe it. Said it would have to have everything that present power sources have, plus one or two more things. It could be cheaper, for instance. It could be more efficient. It might supersede the others by being easier to carry from the power plant to the consumer. See what I mean? Any one of these factors might prove a new source of power competitive to the others. What I'd like to see is a new power with *all* of these factors. What do you think of it?"

"Not impossible."

"Think not?"

"I'll try it."

"Keep me posted." Conant's transmitter clicked off. The switch was a little piece of false front that Kidder had built into the set, which was something that Conant didn't know. The set switched itself off when Conant moved from it. After the switch's sharp crack, Kidder heard the banker mutter, "If he does it, I'm all set. If he doesn't, at least the crazy fool will keep himself busy on the isl—"

Kidder eyed the radiophone for an instant with raised eyebrows, and then shrugged them down again with his shoulders. It was quite evident that Conant had something up his sleeve, but Kidder wasn't worried. Who on earth would want to disturb him? He wasn't bothering anybody. He went back to the Neoterics' building, full of the new power idea.

Eleven days later Kidder called Conant and gave specific instructions on how to equip his receiver with a facsimile set which would enable Kidder to send written matter over the air. As soon as this was done and Kidder informed, the biochemist for once in his life spoke at some length.

"Conant—you inferred that a new power source that would be cheaper, more efficient and more easily transmitted than any now in use did not exist. You might be interested in the little generator I have just set up.

"It has power, Conant—unbelievable power. Broadcast. A beautiful little tight beam. Here—catch this on the facsimile recorder." Kidder slipped a sheet of paper under the clips on his transmitter and it appeared on Conant's set. "Here's the wiring diagram for a power receiver. Now listen. The beam is so tight, so highly directional, that not three thousandths of one percent of the power would be lost in a two-thousand-mile transmission. The power system is closed. That is, any drain on the beam returns a signal along it to the transmitter, which automatically steps up to increase the power output. It has a limit, but it's way up. And something else. This little gadget of mine can send out eight different beams with a total horsepower output of around eight thousand per minute per beam. From each beam you can draw enough power to turn the page of a book or fly a superstratosphere plane. Hold on—I haven't finished yet.

Each beam, as I told you before, returns a signal from receiver to transmitter. This not only controls the power output of the beam, but directs it. Once contact is made, the beam will never let go. It will follow the receiver anywhere. You can power land, air or water vehicles with it, as well as any stationary plant. Like it?"

Conant, who was a banker and not a scientist, wiped his shining pate with back of his hand and said, "I've never known you to steer me wrong yet, Kidder. How about the cost of this thing?"

"High," said Kidder promptly. "As high as an atomic plant. But there are no high-tension lines, no wires, no pipelines, no nothing. The receivers are little more complicated than a radio set. The transmitter is—well, that's quite a job."

"Didn't take you long," said Conant.

"No," said Kidder, "it didn't, did it?" It was the lifework of nearly twelve hundred highly cultured people, but Kidder wasn't going into that. "Of course, the one I have here's just a model."

Conant's voice was strained. "A—model? And it delivers—"

"Over sixty-thousand horsepower," said Kidder gleefully.

"Good heavens! In a full-sized machine—why, one transmitter would be enough to—" The possibilities of the thing choked Conant for a moment. "How is it fueled?"

"It isn't," said Kidder. "I won't begin to explain it. I've tapped a source of power of unimaginable force. It's—well, big. So big that it can't be misused."

"What?" snapped Conant. "What do you mean by that?"

Kidder cocked an eyebrow. Conant *had* something up his sleeve, then. At this second indication of it, Kidder, the least suspicious of men, began to put himself on guard. "I mean just what I say," he said evenly. "Don't try too hard to understand me—I barely savvy it myself. But the source of this power is a monstrous resultant caused by the unbalance of two previously equalized forces. Those equalized forces are cosmic in quantity. Actually, the forces are those which make suns, crush atoms the way they crushed those that compose the companion of Sirius. It's not anything you can fool with."

"I don't—" said Conant, and his voice ended puzzledly.

"I'll give you a parallel of it," said Kidder. "Suppose you take two rods, one in each hand. Place their tips together and push. As long as your pressure is directly along their long axes, the pressure is equalized; right and left hands cancel each other out. Now I come along; I put out one finger and touch the rods ever so lightly where they come together. They snap out of line violently; you break a couple of knuckles. The resultant force is at right angles to the original force you exerted. My power transmitter is on the same principle. It takes an infinitesimal amount of energy to throw those forces out of line. Easy enough when you know how to do it. The important question is whether or not you can control the resultant when you get it. I can."

"I—see." Conant indulged in a four-second gloat. "Heaven help the utility companies. I don't intend to. Kidder— I want a full-size power transmitter."

Kidder clucked into the radiophone. "Ambitious, aren't you? I haven't a staff out here, Conant—you know that. And I can't be expected to build four or five thousand tons of apparatus myself."

"I'll have five hundred engineers and laborers out there in forty-eight hours."

"You will not. Why bother me with it? I'm quite happy here, Conant, and one of the reasons is that I've no one to get in my hair."

"Oh, now, Kidder—don't be like that. I'll pay you—"

"You haven't got that much money," said Kidder briskly. He flipped the switch on his set. *His* switch worked.

Conant was furious. He shouted into the phone several times, then began to lean on the signal button. On his island, Kidder let the thing squeal and went back to his projection room. He was sorry he had sent the diagram of the receiver to Conant. It would have been interesting to power a plane or a car with the model transmitter he had taken from the Neoterics. But if Conant was going to be that way about it—well, anyway, the receiver would be no good without the transmitter. Any radio engineer would understand the diagram, but not the beam which activated it. And Conant wouldn't get his beam.

Pity he didn't know Conant well enough.

Kidder's days were endless sorties into learning. He never slept, nor did his Neoterics. He ate regularly every five hours, exercised for half an hour in every twelve. He did not keep track of time, for it meant nothing to him. Had he wanted to know the date, or the year, even, he knew he could get it from Conant. He didn't care, thats all. The time that was not spent in observation was used in developing new problems for the Neoterics. His thoughts just now ran to defense. The idea was born in his conversation with Conant; now the idea was primary, its motivation something of no importance. The Neoterics were working on a vibration field of quasi-electrical nature. Kidder could see little practical value in such a thing—an invisible wall which would kill any living thing which touched it. But still—the idea was intriguing.

He stretched and moved away from the telescope in the upper room through which he had been watching his creations at work. He was profoundly happy here in the large control room. Leaving it to go to the old laboratory for a bite to eat was a thing he hated to do. He felt like bidding it good-by each time he walked across the compound, and saying a glad hello when he returned. A little amused at himself, he went out.

There was a black blob—a distant power boat—a few miles off the island, toward the mainland. Kidder stopped and stared distastefully at it. A white petal of spray was af-fixed to each side of the black body—it was coming toward him. He snorted, thinking of the time a yacht load of silly fools had landed out of curiosity one afternoon, spewed themselves over his beloved island, peppered him with lamebrained questions, and thrown his nervous equilibrium out for days. Lord, how he hated *people!*

The thought of unpleasantness bred two more thoughts that played half-consciously with his mind as he crossed the compound and entered the old laboratory. One was that perhaps it might be wise to surround his buildings with a field of force of some kind and post warnings for trespassers. The other thought was of Conant and the vague uneasiness the man had been sending to him through the radiophone these last weeks. His suggestion, two days ago, that a power plant be built on the island—horrible idea!

Conant rose from his seat on a laboratory bench as Kidder walked in.

They looked at each other wordlessly for a long moment. Kidder hadnt seen the bank president in years. The man's presence, he found, made his scalp crawl.

"Hello," said Conant genially. "You're looking fit."

Kidder grunted. Conant eased his unwieldly body back onto the bench and said, "Just to save you the energy of asking questions, Mr. Kidder, I arrived two hours ago on a small boat. Rotten way to travel. I wanted to be a surprise to you; my two men rowed me the last couple of miles. You're not very well equipped here for defense, are you? Why, anyone could slip up on you the way I did."

"Who'd want to?" growled Kidder. The man's voice edged annoyingly into his brain. He spoke too loudly for such a small room; at least, Kidder's hermit's ears felt that way. Kidder shrugged and went about preparing a light meal for himself.

"Well," drawled the banker, "I might want to." He drew out a Dow-metal cigar case. "Mind if I smoke?"

"I do," said Kidder sharply.

Conant laughed easily and put the cigars away. "I might," he said, "want to urge you to let me build that power station on this island."

"Radiophone work?"

"Oh, yes. But now that I'm here you can't switch me off. Now—how about it?"

"I haven't changed my mind."

"Oh, but you should, Kidder, you should. Think of it—think of the good it would do for the masses of people that are now paying exorbitant power bills!"

"I hate the masses! Why do you have to build here?"

"Oh, that. It's an ideal location. You own the island; work could begin here without causing any comment whatsoever. The plant would spring full-fledged on the power markets of the country, having been built in secret. The island can be made impregnable."

"I don't want to be bothered."

"We wouldn't bother you. We'd build on the north end of the island—a mile and a quarter from you and your work. Ah—by the way—where's the model of the power transmitter?"

Kidder, with his mouth full of synthesized food, waved a hand at a small table on which stood the model, a four-foot, amazingly intricate device of plastic and steel and tiny coils.

Conant rose and went over to look at it. "Actually works, eh?" He sighed deeply and said, "Kidder, I really hate to do this, but I want to build that plant rather badly. Corson! Robbins!"

Two bull-necked individuals stepped out from their hiding places in the corners of the room. One idly dangled a revolver by its trigger guard. Kidder looked blankly from one to the other of them.

"These gentlemen will follow my orders implicitly, Kidder. In half an hour a party will land here—engineers, contractors. They will start surveying the north end of the island for the construction of the power plant. These boys here feel about the same way I do as far as you are concerned. Do we proceed with your co-operation or without it? It's immaterial to me whether or not you are left alive to continue your work. My engineers can duplicate your model."

Kidder said nothing. He had stopped chewing when he saw the gunmen, and only now remembered to swallow. He sat crouched over his plate without moving or speaking.

Conant broke the silence by walking to the door. "Robbins—can you carry that model there?" The big man put his gun away, lifted the model gently, and nodded. "Take it down to the beach and meet the other boat. Tell Mr. Johansen, the engineer, that this is the model he is to work from." Robbins went out. Conant turned to Kidder. "There's no need for us to anger ourselves," he said oilily. "I think you are stubborn, but I don't hold it against you. I know how you feel. You'll be left alone; you have my promise. But I mean to go ahead on this job, and a small thing like your life can't stand in my way."

Kidder said, "Get out of here." There were two swollen veins throbbing at his temples. His voice was low, and it shook.

"Very well. Good day, Mr. Kidder. Oh—by the way— you're a clever devil." No one had ever referred to the scholastic Mr. Kidder that way before. "I realize the possibility of your blasting us off the island. I wouldn't do it if I were you. I'm willing to give you what you want—privacy. I want the same thing in return. If anything happens to me while I'm here, the island will be bombed by someone who is working for me. I'll admit they might fail. If they do, the United States government will take a hand. You wouldn't want that, would you? That's rather a big thing for one man to fight. The same thing goes if the plant is sabotaged in any way after I go back to the mainland. You might be killed. You will most certainly be bothered interminably. Thanks for your . . . er . . . co-operation." The banker smirked and walked out, followed by his taciturn gorilla.

Kidder sat there for a long time without moving. Then he shook his head, rested it in his palms. He was badly frightened; not so much because his life was in danger, but because his privacy and his work—his world—were threatened. He was hurt and bewildered. He wasn't a businessman. He couldn't handle men. All his life he had run away from humans and what they represented to him. He was like a frightened child when men closed in on him.

Cooling a little, he wondered vaguely what would happen when the power plant opened. Certainly the government would be interested. Unless—unless by then Conant was the government. That plant was an unimaginable source of power, and not only the kind of power that turned wheels. He rose and went back to the world that was home to him, a world where his motives were understood, and where there were those who could help him. Back at the Neoterics' building, he escaped yet again from the world of men into his work.

Kidder called Conant the following week, much to the banker's surprise. His two days on the island had gotten the work well under way, and he had left with the arrival of a shipload of laborers and material. He kept in close had been a blind job for Johansen and all the rest of the crew on the island. Only the bank's infinite resources could have hired such a man, or the picked gang with him.

Johansen's first reaction when he saw the model had been ecstatic. He wanted to tell his friends about this mar- touch by radio with Johansen, the engineer in charge. It vel; but the only radio set available was beamed to Conant's private office in the bank, and Conant's armed guards, one to every two workers, had strict orders to destroy any other radio transmitter on sight. About that time he realized that he was a prisoner on the island. His instant anger subsided when he reflected that being a prisoner at fifty thousand dollars a week wasn't too bad. Two of the laborers and an engineer thought differently, and got disgruntled a couple of days after they arrived. They disappeared one night—the same night that five shots were fired down on the beach. No questions were asked, and there was no more trouble.

Conant covered his surprise at Kidder's call and was as offensively jovial as ever. "Well, now! Anything I can do for you?"

"Yes," said Kidder. His voice was low, completely without expression. "I want you to issue a warning to your men not to pass the white line I have drawn five hundred yards north of my buildings, right across the island."

"Warning? Why, my dear fellow, they have orders that you are not to be disturbed on any account."

"You've ordered them. All right. Now warn them. I have an electric field surrounding my laboratories that will kill anything living which penetrates it. I don't want to have murder on my conscience. There will be no deaths unless there are trespassers. You'll inform your workers?"

"Oh, now, Kidder," the banker expostulated. "That was totally unnecessary. You won't be bothered. Why—" But he found he was talking into a dead mike. He knew better than to call back. He called Johansen instead and told him about it. Johansen didn't like the sound of it, but he repeated the message and signed off. Conant liked that man. He was, for a moment, a little sorry that Johansen would never reach the mainland alive.

But that Kidder—he was beginning to be a problem. As long as his weapons were strictly defensive he was no real menace. But he would have to be taken care of when the plant was operating. Conant couldn't afford to have genius around him unless it was unquestionably on his side. The power transmitter and Conant's highly ambitious plans would be safe as long as Kidder was left to himself. Kidder knew that he could, for the time being, expect more sympathetic treatment from Conant than he could from a horde of government investigators.

Kidder only left his own inclosure once after the work began on the north end of the island, and it took all of his unskilled diplomacy to do it. Knowing the source of the plant's power, knowing what could happen if it were misused, he asked Conant's permission to inspect the great transmitter when it was nearly finished. Insuring his own life by refusing to report back to Conant until he was safe within his own laboratory again, he turned off his shield and walked up to the north end.

He saw an awe-inspiring sight. The four-foot model was duplicated nearly a hundred times as large. Inside a massive three-hundred-foot tower a space was packed nearly solid with the same bewildering maze of coils and bars that the Neoterics had built so delicately into their machine. At the top was a globe of polished golden alloy, the transmitting antenna. From it would stream thousands of tight beams of force, which could be tapped to any degree by corresponding thousands of receivers placed anywhere at any distance. Kidder learned that the receivers had already been built, but his informant, Johansen, knew little about that end of it and was saying less. Kidder checked over every detail of the structure, and when he was through he shook Johansen's hand admiringly.

"I didn't want this thing here," he said shyly, "and I don't. But I will say that it's a pleasure to see this kind of work."

"It's a pleasure to meet the man that invented it."

Kidder beamed. "I didn't invent it," he said. "Maybe some day I'll show you who did. I—well, good-by." He turned before he had a chance to say too much and marched off down the path.

"Shall I?" said a voice at Johansen's side. One of Conant's guards had his gun out.

Johansen knocked the man's arm down. "No." He scratched his head. "So that's the mysterious menace from the other end of the island. Eh! Why, he's a hell of a nice little feller!"

Built on the ruins of Denver, which was destroyed in the great Battle of the Rockies during the Western War, stands the most beautiful city in the world—our nation's capital,

New Washington. In a circular room deep in the heart of the White House, the president, three army men and a civilian sat. Under the president's desk a dictaphone un-ostentatiously recorded every word that was said. Two thousand and more miles away, Conant hung over a radio receiver, tuned to receive the signals of the tiny transmitter in the civilian's side pocket.

One of the officers spoke.

"Mr. President, the 'impossible claims' made for this gentleman's product are absolutely true. He has proved beyond doubt each item on his prospectus."

The president glanced at the civilian, back at the officer. "I won't wait for your report," he said. "Tell me—what happened?"

Another of the army men mopped his face with a khaki bandanna. "I can't ask you to believe us, Mr. President, but it's true all the same. Mr. Wright here has in his suitcase three or four dozen small . . . er . . . bombs—"

"They're not bombs," said Wright casually.

"All right. They're not bombs. Mr. Wright smashed two of them on an anvil with a sledge hammer. There was no result. He put two more in an electric furnace. They burned away like so much tin and cardboard. We dropped one down the barrel of a field piece and fired it. Still nothing." He paused and looked at the third officer, who picked up the account.

"We really got started then. We flew to the proving grounds, dropped one of the objects and flew to thirty thousand feet. From there, with a small hand detonator no bigger than your fist, Mr. Wright set the thing off. I've never seen anything like it. Forty acres of land came straight up at us, breaking up as it came. The concussion was terrific—you must have felt it here, four hundred miles away."

The president nodded. "I did. Seismographs on the other side of the Earth picked it up."

"The crater it left was a quarter of a mile deep at the

center. Why, one plane load of those things could demolish any city! There isn't even any necessity for accuracy!"

"You haven't heard anything yet," another officer broke in. "Mr. Wright's automobile is powered by a small plant similar to the others. He demonstrated it to us. We could find no fuel tank of any kind, or any other driving mechanism. But with a power plant no bigger than six cubic inches, that car, carrying enough weight to give it traction, outpulled an army tank!"

"And the other test!" said the third excitedly. "He put one of the objects into a replica of a treasury vault. The walls were twelve feet thick, super-reinforced concrete. He controlled it from over a hundred yards away. He . . . he burst that vault! It wasn't an explosion—it was as if some incredibly powerful expansive force inside filled it and flattened the walls from inside. They cracked and split and powdered, and the steel girders and rods came twisting and shearing out like . . . like—*whew!* After that he insisted on seeing you. We knew it wasn't usual, but he said he has more to say and would say it only in your presence."

The president said gravely, "What is it, Mr. Wright?"

Wright rose, picked up his suitcase, opened it and took out a small cube, about eight inches on a side, made of some light-absorbent red material. Four men edged nervously away from it.

"These gentlemen," he began, "have seen only part of the things this device can do. I'm going to demonstrate to you the delicacy of control that is possible with it." He made an adjustment with a tiny knob on the side of the cube, set it on the edge of the president's desk.

"You have asked me more than once if this is my invention or if I am representing someone. The latter is true. It might also interest you to know that the man who controls this cube is right now several thousand miles from here. He, and he alone, can prevent it from detonating now that I"—he pulled his detonator out of the suitcase and pressed a button—"have done this. It will explode the way the one we dropped from the plane did, completely destroying this city and everything in it, in just four hours. It will also explode"—he stepped back and threw a tiny switch on his detonator—"if any moving object comes within three feet of it or if anyone leaves this room but me—it can be compensated for that. If, after I leave, I am molested, it will detonate as soon as a hand is laid on me. No bullets can kill me fast enough to prevent me from setting it off."

The three army men were silent. One of them swiped nervously at the beads of cold sweat on his forehead. The others did not move. The president said evenly,

"What's your proposition?"

"A very reasonable one. My employer does not work in the open, for obvious reasons. All he wants is your agreement to carry out his orders; to appoint the cabinet members he chooses, to throw your influence in any way he dictates. The public—Congress—anyone else—need never know anything about it. I might add that if you agree to this proposal, this 'bomb,' as you call it, will not go off. But you can be sure that thousands of them are planted all over the country. You will never know when you are near one. If you disobey, it means instant annihilation for you and everyone else within three or four square miles.

"In three hours and fifty minutes—that will be at precisely seven o'clock—there is a commercial radio program on Station RPRS. You will cause the announcer, after his station identification, to say 'Agreed.' It will pass unnoticed by all but my employer. There is no use in having me followed; my work is done. I shall never see nor contact my employer again. That is all. Good afternoon, gentlemen!"

Wright closed his suitcase with a businesslike snap, bowed, and left the room. Four men sat frozen, staring at the little red cube.

"Do you think he can do all he says?" asked the president.

The three nodded mutely. The president reached for his phone.

There was an eavesdropper to all of the foregoing. Conant, squatting behind his great desk in the vault, where he had his sanctum sanctorum, knew nothing of it. But beside him was the compact bulk of Kidder's radiophone. His presence switched it on, and Kidder, on his island, blessed the day he had thought of that device. He had been meaning to call Conant all morning, but was very hesitant. His meeting with the young engineer Johansen had impressed him strongly. The man was such a thorough scientist, possessed of such complete delight in the work he did, that for the first time in his life Kidder found himself actually wanting to see someone again. But he feared for Johansen's life if he brought him to the laboratory, for Johansen's work was done on the island, and Conant would most certainly have the engineer killed if he heard of his visit, fearing that Kidder would influence him to sabotage the great transmitter. And if Kidder went to the power plant he would probably be shot on sight.

All one day Kidder wrangled with himself, and finally determined to call Conant. Fortunately he gave no signal, but turned up the volume on the receiver when the little red light told him that Conant's transmitter was functioning. Curious, he heard everything that occurred in the president's chamber three thousand miles away. Horrified, he realized what Conant's engineers had done. Built into tiny containers were tens of thousands of power receivers. They had no power of their own, but, by remote control, could draw on any or all of the billions of horsepower the huge plant on the island was broadcasting.

Kidder stood in front of his receiver, speechless. There was nothing he could do. If he devised some means of destroying the power plant, the government would certainly step in and take over the island, and then—what would happen to him and his precious Neoterics?

Another sound grated out of the receiver—a commercial radio program. A few bars of music, a man's voice advertising stratoline fares on the installment plan, a short silence, then:

"Station RPRS, voice of the nation's Capital, District of South Colorado."

The three-second pause was interminable.

"The time is exactly . . . er . . . *agreed.* The time is exactly seven p. m., Mountain Standard Time."

Then came a half-insane ˙ chuckle. Kidder had difficulty believing it was Conant. A phone clicked. The banker's voice:

"Bill? All set. Get out there with your squadron and bomb up the island. Keep away from the plant, but cut the rest of it to ribbons. Do it quick and get out of there."

Almost hysterical with fear, Kidder rushed about the room and then shot out the door and across the compound. There were five hundred innocent workmen in barracks a quarter mile from the plant. Conant didn't need them now, and he didn't need Kidder. The only safety for anyone was in the plant itself, and Kidder wouldn't leave his Neoterics to be bombed. He flung himself up the stairs and to the nearest teletype. He banged out, "Get me a defense. I want an impenetrable shield. Urgent!"

The words rippled out from under his fingers in the functional script of the Neoterics. Kidder didn't think of what he wrote, didn't really vizualize the thing he ordered. But he had done what he could. He'd have to leave them now, get to the barracks; warn those men. He ran up the path toward the plant, flung himself over the white line that marked death to those who crossed it.

A squadron of nine clip-winged, mosquito-nosed planes rose out of a cove on the mainland. There was no sound from the engines, for there were no engines. Each plane was powered with a tiny receiver and drew its unmarked, light-absorbent wings through the air with power from the island. In a matter of minutes they raised the island. The squadron leader spoke briskly into a microphone.

"Take the barracks first. Clean 'em up. Then work south."

Johansen was alone on a small hill near the center of the island. He carried a camera, and though he knew pretty well that his chances of ever getting ashore again were practically nonexistent, he liked angle shots of his tower, and took innumerable pictures. The first he knew of the planes was when he heard their whining dive over the barracks. He stood transfixed, saw a shower of bombs hurtled down and turn the barracks into a smashed ruin of broken wood, metal and bodies. The picture of Kidder's earnest face flashed into his mind. Poor little guy—if they ever bombed his end of the island he would— But his tower! Were they going to bomb the plant?

He watched, utterly appalled, as the planes flew out to sea, cut back and dove again. They seemed to be working south. At the third dive he was sure of it. Not knowing what he could do, he nevertheless turned and ran toward Kidder's place. He rounded a turn in the trail and collided violently with the little biochemist. Kidder's face was scarlet with exertion, and he was the most terrified-looking object Johansen had ever seen.

Kidder waved a hand northward. "Conant!" he screamed over the uproar. "It's Conant! He's going to kill us all!"

"The plant?" said Johansen, turning pale.

"It's safe. He won't touch *that!* But . . . my place . . . what about all those men?"

"Too late!" shouted Johansen.

"Maybe I can— Come on!" called Kidder, and was off down the trail, heading south.

Johansen pounded after him. Kidder's little short legs became a blur as the squadron swooped overhead, laying its eggs in the spot where they had met.

As they burst out of the woods, Johansen put on a spurt, caught up with the scientist and knocked him sprawling not six feet from the white line.

"Wh . . . wh—"

"Don't go any farther, you fool! Your own damned force field—it'll kill you!"

"Force field? But—I came through it on the way up— Here. Wait. If I can—" Kidder began hunting furiously about in the grass. In a few seconds he ran up to the line, clutching a large grasshopper in his hand. He tossed it over. It lay still.

"See?" said Johansen. "It—"

"Look! It jumped! Come on! I don't know what went wrong, unless the Neoterics shut it off. They generated that field—I didn't."

"Neo—huh?"

"Never mind," snapped the biochemist, and ran.

They pounded gasping up the steps and into the Neoterics' control room. Kidder clapped his eyes to a telescope and shrieked in glee. "They've done it! They've done it!"

"Who's—"

"My little people! The Neoterics! They've made the impenetrable shield! Don't you see—it cut through the lines of force that start up that field out there! Their generator is still throwing it up, but the vibrations can't get out! They're safe! They're safe!" And the overwrought hermit began to cry. Johansen looked at him pityingly and shook his head.

"Sure—your little men are all right. But we aren't," he added as the floor shook at the detonation of a bomb.

Johansen closed his eyes, got a grip on himself and let his curiosity overcome his fear. He stepped to the binocular telescope, gazed down it. There was nothing there but a curved sheet of gray material. He had never seen a gray quite like that. It was absolutely neutral. It didn't seem soft and it didn't seem hard, and to look at it made his brain reel. He looked up.

Kidder was pounding the keys of a teletype, watching the blank yellow tape anxiously.

"I'm not getting through to them," he whimpered. "I don't know what's the mat— Oh, of *course!*"

"What?"

"The shield is absolutely impenetrable! The teletype impulses can't get through or I could get them to extend the screen over the building—over the whole island! There's nothing those people can't do!"

"He's crazy," Johansen said under his breath. "Poor little—"

The teletype began clicking sharply. Kidder dove at it, practically embraced it. He read off the tape as it came out. Johansen saw the characters, but they meant nothing to him.

"Almighty," Kidder read falteringly, "pray have mercy on us and be forebearing until we have said our say. Without orders we have lowered the screen you ordered us to raise. We are lost, O great one. Our screen is truly impenetrable, and so cut off your words on the word machine. We have never, in the memory of any Neoteric, been without your word before. Forgive us our action. We will eagerly await your answer."

Kidder's fingers danced over the keys. "You can look now," he gasped. "Go on—the telescope!"

Johansen, trying to ignore the whine of sure death from above, looked.

He saw what looked like land—fantastic fields under cultivation, a settlement of some sort, factories, and—beings. Everything moved with incredible rapidity. He couldn't see one of the inhabitants except as darting pinky-white streaks. Fascinated, he stared for a long minute. A sound behind him made him whirl. It was Kidder, rubbing his hands together briskly. There was a broad smile on his face.

"They did it," he said happily. "You see?"

Johansen didn't see until he began to realize that there was a dead silence outside. He ran to a window. It was night outside—the blackest night—when it should have been dusk. "What happened?"

"The Neoterics," said Kidder, and laughed like a child. "My friends downstairs there. They threw up the impenetrable shield over the whole island. We can't be touched now!"

And at Johansen's amazed questions, he launched into a description of the race of beings below them.

Outside the shell, things happened. Nine airplanes suddenly went dead-stick. Nine pilots glided downward, powerless, and some fell into the sea, and some struck the miraculous gray shell that loomed in place of an island; slid off and sank.

And ashore, a man named Wright sat in a car, half dead with fear, while government men surrounded him, approached cautiously, daring instant death from a now-dead source.

In a room deep in the White House, a high-ranking army officer shrieked, "I can't stand it any more! I can't!" and leaped up, snatched a red cube off the president's desk, ground it to ineffectual litter under his shining boots.

And in a few days they took a broken old man away from the bank and put him in an asylum, where he died within a week.

The shield, you see, was truly impenetrable. The power plant was untouched and sent out its beams; but the beams could not get out, and anything powered from the plant went dead. The story never became public, although for some years there was heightened naval activity off the New England coast. The navy, so the story went, had a new arget range out there—a great hemi-ovoid of gray material.

They bombed it and shelled it and rayed it and blasted all around it, but never even dented its smooth surface.

Kidder and Johansen let it stay there. They were happy enough with their researches and their Neoterics. They did not hear or feel the shelling, for the shield was truly impenetrable. They synthesized their food and their light and air from the materials at hand, and they simply didn't care. They were the only survivors of the bombing, with the exception of three poor maimed devils that died soon afterward.

All this happened many years ago, and Kidder and Johansen may be alive today, and they may be dead. But that doesn't matter too much. The important thing is that that great gray shell will bear watching. Men die, but races live. Some day the Neoterics, after innumerable generations of inconceivable advancement, will take down their shield and come forth. When I think of that I feel frightened.

HUDDLING PLACE

by

CLIFFORD D. SIMAK

The drizzle sifted from the leaden skies, like smoke drifting through the bare-branched trees. It softened the
hedges and hazed the outlines of the buildings and blotted
out the distance. It glinted on the metallic skins of the
silent robots and silvered the shoulders of the three
humans listening to the intonations of the black-garbed man,
who read from the book cupped between his hands.

"For I am the Resurrection and the Life—"

The moss-mellowed graven figure that reared above the
door of the crypt seemed straining upward, every crystal
of its yearning body reaching toward something that no one
else could see. Straining as it had strained since that day
of long ago when men had chipped it from the granite to
adorn the family tomb with a symbolism that had pleased
the first John J. Webster in the last years he held of life.

"And whosoever liveth and believeth in Me—"

Jerome A. Webster felt his son's fingers tighten on his arm, heard the muffled sobbing of his mother, saw the lines of robots standing rigid, heads bowed in respect to the master they had served. The master who now was going home—to the final home of all.

Numbly, Jerome A. Webster wondered if they understood—if they understood life and death—if they understood what it meant that Nelson F. Webster lay there in the casket, that a man with a book intoned words above him.

Nelson F. Webster, fourth of the line of Websters who had lived on these acres, had lived and died here, scarcely leaving, and now was going to his final rest in that place the first of them had prepared for the rest of them—for that long line of shadowy descendants who would live here and cherish the things and the ways and the life that the first John J. Webster had established.

Jerome A. Webster felt his jaw muscles tighten, felt a little tremor run across his body. For a moment his eyes burned and the casket blurred in his sight and the words the man in black was saying were one with the wind that whispered in the pines standing sentinel for the dead. Within his brain remembrance marched—remembrance of a gray-haired man stalking the hills and fields, sniffing the breeze of an early morning, standing, legs braced, before the flaring fireplace with a glass of brandy in his hand.

Pride—the pride of land and life, and the humility and greatness that quiet living breeds within a man. Contentment of casual leisure and surety of purpose. Independence of assured security, comfort of familiar surroundings, freedom of broad acres.

Thomas Webster was joggling his elbow. "Father," he was whispering. "Father."

The service was over. The black-garbed man had closed his book. Six robots stepped forward, lifted the casket.

Slowly the three followed the casket into the crypt, stood silently as the robots slid it into its receptacle, closed the tiny door and affixed the plate that read:

NELSON F. WEBSTER
2034-2117

That was all. Just the name and dates. And that, Jerome
A. Webster found himself thinking, was enough. There was
nothing else that needed to be there. That was all those
others had. The ones that called the family roll—starting
with William Stevens, 1920-1999. Gramp Stevens, they had
called him, Webster remembered. Father of the wife of that
first John J. Webster, who was here himself—1951-2020.
And after him his son, Charles F. Webster, 1980-2060. And
his son, John J. II, 2004-2086. Webster could remember
John J. II—a grandfather who had slept beside the fire with
his pipe hanging from his mouth, eternally threatening to
set his whiskers aflame.

Webster's eyes strayed to another plate. Mary Webster,
the mother of the boy here at his side. And yet not a boy.
He kept forgetting that Thomas was twenty now, in a week
or so would be leaving for Mars, even as in his younger
days he, too, had gone to Mars.

All here together, he told himself. The Websters and
their wives and children. Here in death together as they
had lived together, sleeping in the pride and security of
bronze and marble with the pines outside and the symbolic
figure above the age-greened door.

The robots were waiting, standing silently, their task ful-
filled.

His mother looked at him.

"You're the head of the family now, my son," she told
him.

He reached out and hugged her close against his side.
Head of the family—what was left of it. Just the three of
them now. His mother and his son. And his son would be
leaving soon, going out to Mars. But he would come back.
Come back with a wife, perhaps, and the family would go
on. The family wouldn't stay at three. Most of the big
house wouldn't stay closed off, as it now was closed off.

There had been a time when it had rung with the life of a dozen units of the family, living in their separate apartments under one big roof. That time, he knew, would come again.

The three of them turned and left the crypt, took the path back to the house, looming like a huge gray shadow in the midst.

A fire blazed in the hearth and the book lay upon his desk. Jerome A. Webster reached out and picked it up, read the title once again:

"Martian Physiology, With Especial Reference to the Brain" by Jerome A. Webster, M.D.

Thick and authoritative—the work of a lifetime. Standing almost alone in its field. Based upon the data gathered during those five plague years on Mars—years when he had labored almost day and night with his fellow colleagues of the World Committee's medical commission, dispatched on an errand of mercy to the neighboring planet.

A tap sounded on the door.

"Come in," he called.

The door opened and a robot glided in.

"Your whiskey, sir."

"Thank you, Jenkins," Webster said.

"The minister, sir," said Jenkins, "has left."

"Oh, yes. I presume that you took care of him."

"I did, sir. Gave him the usual fee and offered him a drink. He refused the drink."

"That was a social error," Webster told him. "Ministers don't drink."

"I'm sorry, sir. I didn't know. He asked me to ask you to come to church sometime."

"Eh?"

"I told him, sir, that you never went anywhere."

"That was quite right, Jenkins," said Webster. "None of us ever go anywhere."

Jenkins headed for the door, stopped before he got there,

turned around. "If I may say so, sir, that was a touching service at the crypt. Your father was a fine human, the finest ever was. The robots were saying the service was very fitting. Dignified like, sir. He would have liked it had he known."

"My father," said Webster, "would be even more pleased to hear you say that, Jenkins."

"Thank you, sir," said Jenkins, and went out.

Webster sat with the whiskey and the book and fire— felt the comfort of the well-known room close in about him, felt the refuge that was in it.

This was home. It had been home for the Websters since that day when the first John J. had come here and built the first unit of the sprawling house. John J. had chosen it because it had a trout stream, or so he always said. But it was something more than that. It must have been, Webster told himself, something more than that.

Or perhaps, at first, it had only been the trout stream. The trout stream and the trees and meadows, the rocky ridge where the mist drifted in each morning from the river. Maybe the rest of it had grown, grown gradually through the years, through years of family association until the very soil was soaked with something that approached, but wasn't quite, tradition. Something that made each tree, each rock, each foot of soil a Webster tree or rock or clod of soil. It all belonged.

John J., the first John J., had come after the breakup of the cities, after men had forsaken, once and for all, the twentieth century huddling places, had broken free of the tribal instinct to stick together in one cave or in one clearing against a common foe or a common fear. An instinct that had become outmoded, for there were no fears or foes. Man revolting against the herd instinct economic and social conditions had impressed upon him in ages past. A new security and a new sufficiency had made it possible to break away.

The trend had started back in the twentieth century, more

than two hundred years before, when men moved to country homes to get fresh air and elbow room and a graciousness in life that communal existence, in its strictest sense, never had given them.

And here was the end result. A quiet living. A peace that could only come with good things. The sort of life that men had yearned for years to have. A manorial existence, based on old family homes and leisurely acres, with atomics supplying power and robots in place of serfs.

Webster smiled at the fireplace with its blazing wood. That was an anachronism, but a good one—something that Man had brought forward from the caves. Useless, because atomic heating was better—but more pleasant. One couldn't sit and watch atomics and dream and build castles in the flames.

Even the crypt out there, where they had put his father that afternoon. That was family, too. All of a piece with the rest of it. The somber pride and leisured life and peace. In the old days the dead were buried in vast plots all together, stranger cheek by jowl with stranger—

He never goes anywhere.

That is what Jenkins had told the minister.

And that was right. For what need was there to go anywhere? It all was here. By simply twirling a dial one could talk face to face with anyone one wished, could go, by sense, if not in body, anywhere one wished. Could attend the theater or hear a concert or browse in a library halfway around the world. Could transact any business one might need to transact without rising from one's chair.

Webster drank the whiskey, then swung to the dialed machine beside his desk.

He spun dials from memory without resorting to the log. He knew where he was going.

His finger flipped a toggle and the room melted away —or seemed to melt. There was left the chair within which he sat, part of the desk, part of the machine itself and that was all.

The chair was on a hillside swept with golden grass and dotted with scraggly, wind-twisted trees, a hillside that straggled down to a lake nestling in the grip of purple mountain spurs. The spurs, darkened in long streaks with the bluish-green of distant pine, climbed in staggering stairs, melting into the blue-tinged snow-capped peaks that reared beyond and above them in jagged saw-toothed outline.

The wind talked harshly in the crouching trees and ripped the long grass in sudden gusts. The last rays of the sun struck fire from the distant peaks.

Solitude and grandeur, the long sweep of tumbled land, the cuddled lake, the knifelike shadows on the far-off ranges.

Webster sat easily in his chair, eyes squinting at the peaks.

A voice said almost at his shoulder: "May I come in?"

A soft, sibilant voice, wholly unhuman. But one that Webster knew.

He nodded his head. "By all means, Juwain."

He turned slightly and saw the elaborate crouching pedestal, the furry, soft-eyed figure of the Martian squatting on it. Other alien furniture loomed indistinctly beyond the pedestal, half guessed furniture from that dwelling out on Mars.

The Martian flipped a furry hand toward the mountain range.

"You love this," he said. "You can understand it. And I can understand how you understand it, but to me there is more terror than beauty in it. It is something we could never have on Mars."

Webster reached out a hand, but the Martian stopped him.

"Leave it on," he said. "I know why you came here. I would not have come at a time like this except I thought perhaps an old friend—"

"It is kind of you," said Webster. "I am glad that you have come."

"Your father," said Juwain, "was a great man. I remember how you used to talk to me of him, those years you spent on Mars. You said then you would come back sometime. Why is it you've never come?"

"Why," said Webster, "I just never—"

"Do not tell me," said the Martian. "I already know."

"My son," said Webster, "is going to Mars in a few days. I shall have him call on you."

"That would be a pleasure," said Juwain. "I shall be expecting him."

He stirred uneasily on the crouching pedestal. "Perhaps he carries on tradition."

"No," said Webster. "He is studying engineering. He never cared for surgery."

"He has a right," observed the Martian, "to follow the life that he has chosen. Still, one might be permitted to wish."

"One could," Webster agreed. "But that is over and done with. Perhaps he will be a great engineer. Space structure. Talks of ships out to the stars."

"Perhaps," suggested Juwain, "your family has done enough for medical science. You and your father—"

"And his father," said Webster, "before him."

"Your book," declared Juwain, "has put Mars in debt to you. It may focus more attention on Martian specialization. My people do not make good doctors. They have no background for it. Queer how the minds of races run. Queer that Mars never thought of medicine—literally never thought of it. Supplied the need with a cult of fatalism. While even in your early history, when men still lived in caves—"

"There are many things," said Webster, "that you thought of and we didn't. Things we wonder now how we ever missed. Abilities that you developed and we do not have. Take your own specialty, philosophy. But different than ours. A science, while ours never was more than ordered fumbling. Yours an orderly, logical development of philosophy, workable, practical, applicable, an actual tool."

Juwain started to speak, hesitated, then went ahead. "I am near to something, something that may be new and startling. Something that will be a tool for you humans as well as for the Martians. I've worked on it for years, starting with certain mental concepts that first were suggested to me with arrival of the Earthmen. I have said nothing, for I could not be sure."

"And now," suggested Webster, "you are sure."

"Not quite," said Juwain. "Not positive. But almost."

They sat in silence, watching the mountains and the lake. A bird came and sat in one of the scraggly trees and sang. Dark clouds piled up behind the mountain ranges and the snow-tipped peaks stood out like graven stone. The sun sank in a lake of crimson, hushed finally to the glow of a fire burned low.

A tap sounded from a door and Webster stirred in his chair, suddenly brought back to the reality of the study, of the chair beneath him.

Juwain was gone. The old philosopher had come and sat an hour of contemplation with his friend and then had quietly slipped away.

The rap came again.

Webster leaned forward, snapped the toggle and the mountains vanished; the room became a room again. Dusk filtered through the high windows and the fire was a rosy flicker in the ashes.

"Come in," said Webster.

Jenkins opened the door. "Dinner is served, sir," he said.

"Thank you," said Webster. He rose slowly from the chair.

"Your place, sir," said Jenkins, "is laid at the head of the table."

"Ah, yes," said Webster. "Thank you, Jenkins. Thank you very much, for reminding me."

Webster stood on the broad ramp of the space field and watched the shape that dwindled in the sky with faint flickering points of red lancing through the wintry sunlight.

For long minutes after the shape was gone he stood there, hands gripping the railing in front of him, eyes still staring up into the sky.

His lips moved and they said: "Good-by son"; but there was no sound.

Slowly he came alive to his surroundings. Knew that people moved about the ramp, saw that the landing field seemed to stretch interminably to the far horizon, dotted here and there with hump-backed things that were waiting spaceships. Scooting tractors worked near one hangar, clearing away the last of the snowfall of the night before.

Webster shivered and thought that it was queer, for the noonday sun was warm. And shivered again.

Slowly he turned away from the railing and headed for the administration building. And for one brain-wrenching moment he felt a sudden fear—an unreasonable and embarrassing fear of that stretch of concrete that formed the ramp. A fear that left him shaking mentally as he drove his feet toward the waiting door.

A man walked toward him, briefcase swinging in his hand and Webster, eyeing him, wished fervently that the man would not speak to him.

The man did not speak, passed him with scarcely a glance, and Webster felt relief.

If he were back home, Webster told himself, he would have finished lunch, would now be ready to lie down for his midday nap. The fire would be blazing on the hearth and the flicker of the flames would be reflected from the andirons. Jenkins would bring him a liqueur and would say a word or two—inconsequential conversation.

He hurried toward the door, quickening his step, anxious to get away from the bare-cold expanse of the massive ramp.

Funny how he had felt about Thomas. Natural, of course, that he should have hated to see him go. But entirely unnatural that he should, in those last few minutes, find such horror welling up within him. Horror of the trip through space, horror of the alien land of Mars—although Mars was scarcely alien any longer. For more than a century now Earthmen had known it, had fought it, lived with it; some of them had even grown to love it.

But it had only been utter will power that had prevented him, in those last few seconds before the ship had taken off, from running out into the field, shrieking for Thomas to come back, shrieking for him not to go.

And that, of course, never would have done. It would have been exhibitionism, disgraceful and humiliating—the sort of a thing a Webster could not do.

After all, he told himself, a trip to Mars was no great adventure, not any longer. There had been a day when it had been, but that day was gone forever. He, himself, in his earlier days had made a trip to Mars, had stayed there for five long years. That had been—he gasped when he thought of it—that had been almost thirty years ago.

The babble and hum of the lobby hit him in the face as the robot attendant opened the door for him, and in that babble ran a vein of something that was almost terror. For a moment he hesitated, then stepped inside. The door closed softly behind him.

He stayed close to the wall to keep out of people's way, headed for a chair in one corner. He sat down and huddled back, forcing his body deep into the cushions, watching the milling humanity that seethed out in the room.

Shrill people, hurrying people, people with strange, unneighborly faces. Strangers—every one of them. Not a face he knew. People going places. Heading out for the planets. Anxious to be off. Worried about last details. Rushing here and there.

Out of the crowd loomed a familiar face. Webster hunched forward.

"Jenkins!" he shouted, and then was sorry for the shout, although no one seemed to notice.

The robot moved toward him, stood before him.

"Tell Raymond," said Webster, "that I must return immediately. Tell him to bring the 'copter in front at once."

"I am sorry, sir," said Jenkins, "but we cannot leave at once. The mechanics found a flaw in the atomics chamber. They are installing a new one. It will take several hours."

"Surely," said Webster, impatiently, "that could wait until some other time."

"The mechanic said not, sir," Jenkins told him. "It might go at any minute. The entire charge of power—"

"Yes, yes," agreed Webster, "I suppose so."

He fidgeted with his hat. "I just remembered," he said, "something I must do. Something that must be done at once. I must get home. I can't wait several hours."

He hitched forward to the edge of the chair, eyes staring at the milling crowd.

Faces—faces—

"Perhaps you could televise," suggested Jenkins. "One of the robots might be able to do it. There is a booth—"

"Wait, Jenkins," said Webster. He hesitated a moment. "There is nothing to do back home. Nothing at all. But I must get there. I can't stay here. If I have to, I'll go crazy. I was frightened out there on the ramp. I'm bewildered and confused here. I have a feeling—a strange, terrible feeling. Jenkins, I—"

"I understand, sir," said Jenkins. "Your father had it, too."

Webster gasped. "My father?"

"Yes, sir, that is why he never went anywhere. He was about your age, sir, when he found it out. He tried to make a trip to Europe and he couldn't. He got halfway there and turned back. He had a name for it."

Webster sat in stricken silence.

"A name for it," he finally said. "Of course there's a name for it. My father had it. My grandfather—did he have it, too?"

"I wouldn't know that, sir," said Jenkins. "I wasn't created until after your grandfather was an elderly man.

But he may have. He never went anywhere, either."

"You understand, then," said Webster. "You know how it is. I feel like I'm going to be sick—physically ill. See if you can charter a 'copter—anything, just so we get home."

"Yes, sir," said Jenkins.

He started off and Webster called him back.

"Jenkins does anyone else know about this? Anyone—"

"No, sir," said Jenkins. "Your father never mentioned it and I felt, somehow, that he wouldn't wish me to."

"Thank you, Jenkins," said Webster.

Webster huddled back into his chair again, feeling desolate and alone and misplaced. Alone in a humming lobby that pulsed with life—a loneliness that tore at him, that left him limp and weak.

Homesickness. Downright, shameful homesickness, he told himself. Something that boys are supposed to feel when they first leave home, when they first go out to meet the world.

There was a fancy word for it—agoraphobia, the morbid dread of being in the midst of open spaces—from the Greek root for the fear—literally, of the market place.

If he crossed the room to the television booth, he could put in a call, talk with his mother or one of the robots—or, better yet, just sit and look at the place until Jenkins came for him.

He started to rise, then sank back in the chair again. It was no dice. Just talking to someone or looking in on the place wasn't being there. He couldn't smell the pines in the wintry air, or hear familiar snow crunch on the walk beneath his feet or reach out a hand and touch one of the massive oaks that grew along the path. He couldn't feel the heat of the fire or sense the sure, deft touch of belonging, of being one with a tract of ground and the things upon it.

And yet—perhaps it would help. Not much, maybe, but some. He started to rise from the chair again and froze. The few short steps to the booth held terror, a terrible, overwhelming terror. If he crossed them, he would have to run. Run to escape the watching eyes, the unfamiliar sounds, the agonizing nearness of strange faces.

Abruptly he sat down.

A woman's shrill voice cut across the lobby and he shrank away from it. He felt terrible. He felt like hell. He wished Jenkins would get a hustle on.

The first breath of spring came through the window, filling the study with the promise of melting snows, of coming leaves and flowers, of north-bound wedges of water-fowl streaming through the blue, of trout that lurked in pools waiting for the fly.

Webster lifted his eyes from the sheaf of papers on his desk, sniffed the breeze, felt the cool whisper of it on his cheek. His hand reached out for the brandy glass, found it empty, and put it back.

He bent back above the papers once again, picked up a pencil and crossed out a word.

Critically, he read the final paragraphs:

The fact that of the two hundred fifty men who were invited to visit me, presumably on missions of more than ordinary importance, only three were able to come, does not necessarily prove that all but those three are victims of agoraphobia. Some may have had legitimate reasons for being unable to accept my invitation. But it does indicate a growing unwillingness of men living under the mode of Earth existence set up following the breakup of the cities to move from familiar places, a deepening instinct to stay among the scenes and possessions which in their mind have become associated with contentment and graciousness of life.

What the result of such a trend will be, no one can clearly indicate since it applies to only a small portion of Earth's population. Among the larger families economic pressure forces some of the sons to seek their fortunes either in other parts of the Earth or on one of the other planets. Many others deliberately seek adventure and opportunity in space, while still others become associated with professions or trades which make a sedentary existence impossible.

He flipped the page over, went on to the last one.

It was a good paper, he knew, but it could not be published, not just yet. Perhaps after he had died. No one, so far as he could determine, had ever so much as realized the trend, had taken as matter of course the fact that men seldom left their homes. Why, after all, should they leave their homes?

The televisor muttered at his elbow and he reached out to flip the toggle.

The room faded and he was face to face with a man who sat behind a desk, almost as if he sat on the opposite side of Webster's desk. A gray-haired man with sad eyes behind heavy lenses.

For a moment Webster stared, memory tugging at him.

"Could it be—" he asked and the man smiled gravely.

"I have changed," he said. "So have you. My name is Clayborne. Remember? The Martian medical commission—"

"Clayborne! I'd often thought of you. You stayed on Mars."

Clayborne nodded. "I've read your book, doctor. It is a real contribution. I've often thought one should be written, wanted to myself, but I didn't have the time. Just as well I didn't. You did a better job. Especially on the brain."

"The Martian brain," Webster told him, "always intrigued me. Certain peculiarities. I'm afraid I spent more of those five years taking notes on it than I should have. There was other work to do."

"A good thing you did," said Clayborne. "That's why I'm calling you now. I have a patient—a brain operation. Only you can handle it."

Webster gasped, his hands trembling. "You'll bring him here?"

Clayborne shook his head. "He cannot be moved. You know him, I believe. Juwain, the philosopher."

"Juwain!" said Webster. "He's one of my best friends. We talked together just a couple of days ago."

"The attack was sudden," said Clayborne. "He's been asking for you."

Webster was silent and cold—cold with a chill that crept upon him from some unguessed place. Cold that sent perspiration out upon his forehead, that knotted his fists.

"If you start immediately," said Clayborne, "you can be here on time. I've already arranged with the World Committee to have a ship at your disposal instantly. The utmost speed is necessary."

"But," said Webster, "but . . . I cannot come."

"You can't come!"

"It's impossible," said Webster. "I doubt in any case that I am needed. Surely, you yourself—"

"I can't," said Clayborne. "No one can but you. No one else has the knowledge. You hold Juwain's life in your hands. If you come, he lives. If you don't, he dies."

"I can't go into space," said Webster.

"Anyone can go into space," snapped Clayborne. "It's not like it used to be. Conditioning of any sort desired is available."

"But you don't understand," pleaded Webster. "You—"

"No, I don't," said Clayborne. "Frankly, I don't. That anyone should refuse to save the life of his friend—"

The two men stared at one another for a long moment, neither speaking.

"I shall tell the committee to send the ship straight to your home," said Clayborne finally. "I hope by that time you will see your way clear to come."

Clayborne faded and the wall came into view again—the wall and books, the fireplace and the paintings, the well-loved furniture, the promise of spring that came through the open window.

Webster sat frozen in his chair, staring at the wall in front of him.

Juwain, the furry, wrinkled face, the sibilant whisper, the friendliness and understanding that was his. Juwain, grasping the stuff that dreams are made of and shaping them into logic, into rules of life and conduct. Juwain, using philosophy as a tool, as a science, as a stepping stone to better living.

Webster dropped his face into his hands and fought the agony that welled up within him.

Clayborne had not understood. One could not expect him to understand since there was no way for him to know. And even knowing, would he understand? Even he, Webster, would not have understood it in someone else until he had discovered it in himself—the terrible fear of leaving his own fire, his own land, his own possessions, the little symbolisms that he had erected. And yet, not he, himself, alone, but those other Websters as well. Starting with the first John J. Men and women who had set up a cult of life, a tradition of behavior.

He, Jerome A. Webster, had gone to Mars when he was a young man, and had not felt or suspected the psychological poison that ran through his veins. Even as Thomas a few months ago had gone to Mars. But thirty years of quiet life here in the retreat that the Websters called a home had brought it forth, had developed it without his even knowing it. There had, in fact, been no opportunity to know it.

It was clear how it had developed—clear as crystal now. Habit and mental pattern and a happiness association with certain things—things that had no actual value in themselves, but had been assigned a value, a definite, concrete value by one family through five generations.

No wonder other places seemed alien, no wonder other horizons held a hint of horror in their sweep.

And there was nothing one could do about it—nothing, that is, unless one cut down every tree and burned the house and changed the course of waterways. Even that might not do it—even that—

The televisor purred and Webster lifted his head from his hands, reached out and thumbed the tumbler.

The room became a flare of white, but there was no image. A voice said: "Secret call. Secret call."

Webster slid back a panel in the machine, spun a pair of dials, heard the hum of power surge into a screen that blocked out the room.

"Secrecy established," he said.

The white flare snapped out and a man sat across the desk from him. A man he had seen many times before in televised addresses, in his daily paper.

Henderson, president of the World Committee.

"I have had a call from Clayborne," said Henderson.

Webster nodded without speaking.

"He tells me you refuse to go to Mars."

"I have not refused," said Webster. "When Clayborne cut off the question was left open. I had told him it was impossible for me to go, but he had rejected that, did not seem to understand."

"Webster, you must go," said Henderson. "You are the only man with the necessary knowledge of the Martian brain to perform this operation. If it were a simple operation, perhaps someone else could do it. But not one such as this."

"That may be true," said Webster, "but—"

"It's not just a question of saving a life," said Henderson. "Even the life of so distinguished a personage as Juwain. It involves even more than that. Juwain is a friend of yours. Perhaps he hinted of something he has found."

"Yes," said Webster. "Yes, he did. A new concept of philosophy."

"A concept," declared Henderson, "that we cannot do without. A concept that will remake the solar system, that will put mankind ahead a hundred thousand years in the space of two generations. A new direction of purpose that will aim toward a goal we heretofore had not suspected, had not even known existed. A brand new truth, you see. One that never before had occurred to anyone."

Webster's hands gripped the edge of the desk until his knuckles stood out white.

"If Juwain dies," said Henderson, "that concept dies with him. May be lost forever."

"I'll try," said Webster. I'll try—"

Henderson's eyes were hard. "Is that the best you can do?"

"That is the best," said Webster.

"But, man, you must have a reason! Some explanation."

"None," said Webster, "that I would care to give."

Deliberately he reached out and flipped up the switch.

Webster sat at the desk and held his hands in front of him, staring at them. Hands that had skill, held knowledge. Hands that could save a life if he could get them to Mars. Hands that could save for the solar system, for mankind, for the Martians an idea—a new idea—that would advance them a hundred thousand years in the next two generations.

But hands chained by a phobia that grew out of this quiet life Decadence—a strangely beautiful—and deadly—decadence.

Man had forsaken the teeming cities, the huddling place, two hundred years ago. He had done with the old foes and the ancient fears that kept him around the common campfire, had left behind the hobgoblins that had walked with him from the caves.

And yet—and yet.

Here was another huddling place. Not a huddling place for one's body, but one's mind. A psychological campfire that still held a man within the circle of its light.

Still, Webster knew, he must leave that fire. As the men

had done with the cities two centuries before, he must walk off and leave it. And he must not look back.

He had to go to Mars—or at least start for Mars. There was no question there, at all. He had to go.

Whether he would survive the trip, whether he could perform the operation once he had arrived, he did not know. He wondered vaguely, whether agoraphobia could be fatal. In its most exaggerated form, he supposed it could.

He reached out a hand to ring, then hesitated. No use having Jenkins pack. He would do it himself—something to keep him busy until the ship arrived.

From the top shelf of the wardrobe in the bedroom, he took down a bag and saw that it was dusty. He blew on it, but the dust still clung. It had been there for too many years.

As he packed, the room argued with him, talked in that mute tongue with which inanimate but familiar things may converse with a man.

"You can't go," said the room. "You can't go off and leave me."

And Webster argued back, half pleading, half explanatory. "I have to go. Can't you understand? It's a friend, an old friend. I will be coming back."

Packing done, Webster returned to the study, slumped into his chair.

He must go and yet he couldn't go. But when the ship arrived, when the time had come, he knew that he would walk out of the house and toward the waiting ship.

He steeled his mind to that, tried to set it in a rigid pattern, tried to blank out everything but the thought that he was leaving.

Things in the room intruded on his brain, as if they were part of a conspiracy to keep him there. Things that he saw as if he were seeing them for the first time. Old, remembered things that suddenly were new. The chronometer that showed both Earthian and Martian time, the days of the month, the phases of the moon. The picture of his dead wife on the desk. The trophy he had won at prep school. The framed short snorter bill that had cost him ten bucks on his trip to Mars.

He stared at them, half unwilling at first, then eagerly, storing up the memory of them in his brain. Seeing them as separate components of a room he had accepted all these years as a finished whole, never realizing what a multitude of things went to make it up.

Dusk was falling, the dusk of early spring, a dusk that smelled of early pussy willows.

The ship should have arrived long ago. He caught himself listening for it, even as he realized that he would not hear it. A ship, driven by atomic motors, was silent except when it gathered speed. Landing and taking off, it floated like thistledown, with not a murmur in it.

It would be here soon. It would have to be here soon or he could never go. Much longer to wait, he knew, and his high-keyed resolution would crumble like a mound of dust in beating rain. Not much longer could he hold his purpose against the pleading of the room, against the flicker of the fire, against the murmur of the land where five generations of Websters had lived their lives and died.

He shut his eyes and fought down the chill that crept across his body. He couldn't let it get him now, he told himself. He had to stick it out. When the ship arrived he still must be able to get up and walk out the door to the waiting port.

A tap came on the door.

"Come in," Webster called.

It was Jenkins, the light from the fireplace flickering on his shining metal hide.

"Had you called earlier, sir?" he asked.

Webster shook his head.

"I was afraid you might have," Jenkins explained, "and wondered why I didn't come. There was a most extraordinary occurrence, sir. Two men came with a ship and said they wanted you to go to Mars.

"They are here," said Webster. "Why didn't you call me?" He struggled to his feet.

"I didn't think, sir," said Jenkins, "that you would want to be bothered. It was so preposterous. I finally made them understand you could not possibly want to go to Mars."

Webster stiffened, felt chill fear gripping at his heart. Hands groping for the edge of the desk, he sat down in the chair, sensed the walls of the room closing in about him, a trap that would never let him go.

COMING

ATTRACTION

---

by

FRITZ LEIBER

The coupe with the fishhooks welded to the fender shouldered up over the curb like the nose of a nightmare. The girl in its path stood frozen, her face probably stiff with fright under her mask. For once my reflexes weren't shy. I took a fast step toward her, grabbed her elbow, yanked her back. Her black skirt swirled out.

The big coupe shot by, its turbine humming. I glimpsed three faces. Something ripped. I felt the hot exhaust on my ankles as the big coupe swerved back into the street. A thick cloud like a black flower blossomed from its jouncing rear end, while from the fishhooks flew a black shimmering rag.

"Did they get you?" I asked the girl.

She had twisted around to look where the side of her skirt was torn away. She was wearing nylon tights.

"The hooks didn't touch me," she said shakily. "I guess I'm lucky.

I heard voices around us:

"Those kids! What'll they think up next?"

"They're a menace. They ought to be arrested."

Sirens screamed at a rising pitch as two motor police, their rocket-assist jets full on, came whizzing toward us after the coupe. But the black flower had become a thick fog obscuring the whole street. The motor-police switched from rocket assists to rocket brakes and swerved to a stop near the smoke cloud.

"Are you English?" the girl asked me. "You have an English accent."

Her voice came shudderingly from behind the sleek black satin mask. I fancied her teeth must be chattering. Eyes that were perhaps blue searched my face from behind the black gauze covering the eyeholes of the mask. I told her she'd guessed right. She stood close to me. "Will you come to my place tonight?" she asked rapidly. "I can't thank you now. And there's something you can help me about."

My arm, still lightly circling her waist, felt her body trembling. I was answering the plea in that as much as in her voice when I said, "Certainly." She gave me an address south of Inferno, an apartment number and a time. She asked me my name and I told her.

"Hey, you!"

I turned obediently to the policeman's shout. He shooed away the small clucking crowd of masked women and bare-faced men. Coughing from the smoke that the black coupe had thrown out, he asked for my papers. I handed him the essential ones.

He looked at them and then at me. "British Barter? How long will you be in New York?"

Suppressing the urge to say, "For as short a time as possible," I told him I'd be here for a week or so.

"May need you as a witness," he explained. "Those kids

can't use smoke on us. When they do that, we pull them in."

He seemed to think the smoke was the bad thing. "They tried to kill the lady," I pointed out.

He shook his head wisely. "They always pretend they're going to, but actually they just want to snag skirts. I've picked up rippers with as many as fifty skirt-snags tacked up in their rooms. Of course, sometimes they come a little too close."

I explained that if I hadn't yanked her out of the way, she'd have been hit by more than hooks. But he interrupted, "If she'd thought it was a real murder attempt, she'd have stayed here."

I looked around. It was true. She was gone.

"She was fearfully frightened," I told him.

"Who wouldn't be? Those kids would have scared old Stalin himself."

"I mean frightened of more than 'kids.' They didn't look like 'kids.'"

"What did they look like?"

I tried without much success to describe the three faces. A vague impression of viciousness and effeminacy doesn't mean much.

"Well, I could be wrong," he said finally. "Do you know the girl? Where she lives?"

"No," I half lied.

The other policeman hung up his radiophone and ambled toward us, kicking at the tendrils of dissipating smoke. The black cloud no longer hid the dingy facades with their five-year-old radiation flashburns, and I could begin to make out the distant stump of the Empire State Building, thrusting up out of Inferno like a mangled finger.

"They haven't been picked up so far," the approaching policeman grumbled. "Left smoke for five blocks, from what Ryan says."

The first policeman shook his head. "That's bad," he observed solemnly.

I was feeling a bit uneasy and ashamed. An Englishman shouldn't lie, at least not on impulse.

"They sound like nasty customers," the first policeman continued in the same grim tone. "We'll need witnesses. Looks as if you may have to stay in New York longer than you expect."

I got the point. I said, "I forgot to show you all my papers," and handed him a few others, making sure there was a five dollar bill in among them.

When he handed them back a bit later, his voice was no longer ominous. My feelings of guilt vanished. To cement our relationship, I chatted with the two of them about their job.

"I suppose the masks give you some trouble," I observed. "Over in England we've been reading about your new crop of masked female bandits."

"Those things get exaggerated," the first policeman assured me. "It's the men masking as women that really mix us up. But, brother, when we nab them, we jump on them with both feet."

"And you get so you can spot women almost as well as if they had naked faces," the second policeman volunteered. "You know, hands and all that."

"Especially all that," the first agreed with a chuckle. "Say, is it true that some girls don't mask over in England?"

"A number of them have picked up the fashion," I told him. "Only a few, though—the ones who always adopt the latest style, however extreme."

"They're usually masked in the British newscasts."

"I imagine it's arranged that way out of deference to American taste," I confessed. "Actually, not very many do mask."

The second policeman considered that. "Girls going down the street bare from the neck up." It was not clear whether he viewed the prospect with relish or moral distaste. Likely both.

"A few members keep trying to persuade Parliament to enact a law forbidding all masking," I continued, talking perhaps a bit too much.

The second policeman shook his head. "What an idea. You know, masks are a pretty good thing, brother. Couple of years more and I'm going to make my wife wear hers around the house."

The first policeman shrugged. "If women were to stop wearing masks, in six weeks you wouldn't know the difference. You get used to anything, if enough people do or don't do it."

I agreed, rather regretfully, and left them. I turned north on Broadway (old Tenth Avenue, I believe) and walked rapidly until I was beyond Inferno. Passing such an area of undecontaminated radioactivity always makes a person queasy. I thanked God there weren't any such in England, as yet.

The street was almost empty, though I was accosted by a couple of beggars with faces tunneled by H-bomb scars, whether real or of makeup putty, I couldn't tell. A fat woman held out a baby with webbed fingers and toes. I told myself it would have been deformed anyway and that she was only capitalizing on our fear of bomb-induced mutations. Still, I gave her a seven-and-a-half-cent piece. Her mask made me feel I was paying tribute to an African fetish.

"May all your children be blessed with one head and two eyes, sir."

"Thanks," I said, shuddering, and hurried past her.

". . . There's only trash behind the mask, so turn your head, stick to your task: Stay away, stay away—from—the—girls!"

This last was the end of an anti-sex song being sung by some religionists half a block from the circle-and-cross insignia of a femalist temple. They reminded me only faintly of our small tribe of British monastics. Above their heads was a jumble of billboards advertising pre-digested foods, wrestling instruction, radio handies and the like.

I stared at the hysterical slogans with disagreeable fascination. Since the female face and form have been banned on American signs, the very letters of the advertiser's alphabet have begun to crawl with sex—the fat-bellied, big-breasted capital B, the lascivious double O. However, I reminded myself, it is chiefly the mask that so strangely accents sex in America.

A British anthropologist has pointed out, that, while it took more than 5,000 years to shift the chief point of sexual interest from the hips to the breasts, the next transition to the face has taken less than 50 years. Comparing the American style with Moslem tradition is not valid; Moslem women are compelled to wear veils, the purpose of which is concealment, while American women have only the compulsion of fashion and use masks to create mystery.

Theory aside, the actual origins of the trend are to be found in the anti-radiation clothing of World War III, which led to masked wrestling, now a fantastically popular sport, and that in turn led to the current female fashion. Only a wild style at first, masks quickly became as necessary as brassieres and lipsticks had been earlier in the century.

I finally realized that I was not speculating about masks in general, but about what lay behind one in particular. That's the devil of the things; you're never sure whether a girl is heightening loveliness or hiding ugliness. I pictured a cool, pretty face in which fear showed only in widened eyes. Then I remembered her blonde hair, rich against the blackness of the satin mask. She'd told me to come at the twenty-second hour—ten p.m.

I climbed to my apartment near the British Consulate; the elevator shaft had been shoved out of plumb by an old blast, a nuisance in these tall New York buildings. Before it occured to me that I would be going out again, I automatically tore a tab from the film strip under my shirt.

I developed it just to be sure. It showed that the total radiation I'd taken that day was still within the safety limit. I'm not phobic about it, as so many people are these days, but there's no point in taking chances.

I flopped down on the day bed and stared at the silent speaker and the dark screen of the video set. As always, they made me think, somewhat bitterly, of the two great nations of the world. Mutilated by each other, yet still strong, they were crippled giants poisoning the planet with their dreams of an impossible equality and an impossible success.

I fretfully switched on the speaker. By luck, the newscaster was talking excitedly of the prospects of a bumper wheat crop, sown by planes across a dust bowl moistened by seeded rains. I listened carefully to the rest of the program (it was remarkably clear of Russian telejamming) but there was no further news of interest to me. And, of course, no mention of the Moon, though everyone knows that America and Russia are racing to develop their primary bases into fortresses capable of mutual assault and the launching of alphabet-bombs toward Earth. I myself knew perfectly well that the British electronic equipment I was helping trade for American wheat was destined for use in spaceships.

I switched off the newscast. It was growing dark and once again I pictured a tender, frightened face behind a mask. I hadn't had a date since England. It's exceedingly difficult to become acquainted with a girl in America, where as little as a smile, often, can set one of them yelping for the police—to say nothing of the increasing puritanical morality and the roving gangs that keep most women indoors after dark. And naturally, the masks which are definitely not, as the Soviets claim, a last invention of capitalist degeneracy, but a sign of great psychological insecurity. The Russians have no masks, but they have their own signs of stress.

I went to the window and impatiently watched the darkness gather. I was getting very restless. After a while a ghostly violet cloud appeared to the south. My hair rose. Then I laughed. I had momentarily fancied it a radiation from the crater of the Hell-bomb, though I should instantly have known it was only the radio-induced glow in the sky over the amusement and residential area south of Inferno.

Promptly at twenty-two hours I stood before the door of my unknown girl friend's apartment. The electronic say-who-please said just that. I answered clearly, "Wysten Turner," wondering if she'd given my name to the mechanism. She evidently had, for the door opened. I walked into a small empty living room, my heart pounding a bit.

The room was expensively furnished with the latest pneumatic hassocks and sprawlers. There were some midgie books on the table. The one I picked up was the standard hard-boiled detective story in which two female murderers go gunning for each other.

The television was on. A masked girl in green was crooning a love song. Her right hand held something that blurred off into the foreground. I saw the set had a handie which we haven't in England as yet, and curiously thrust my hand into the handie orifice beside the screen. Contrary to my expectations, it was not like slipping into a pulsing rubber glove, but rather as if the girl on the screen actually held my hand.

A door opened behind me. I jerked out my hand with as guilty a reaction as if I'd been caught peering through a keyhole.

She stood in the bedroom doorway. I think she was trembling. She was wearing a gray fur coat, white-speckled, and a gray velvet evening mask with shirred gray lace around the eyes and mouth. Her fingernails twinkled like silver.

It hadn't occurred to me that she'd expect us to go out.

"I should have told you," she said softly. Her mask veered nervously toward the books and the screen and the room's dark corners. "But I can't possibly talk to you here."

I said doubtfully, "There's a place near the Consulate. . . ."

"I know where we can be together and talk," she said rapidly. "If you don't mind."

As we entered the elevator I said, "I'm afraid I dismissed the cab."

But the cab driver hadn't gone for some reason of his own. He jumped out and smirkingly held the front door open for us. I told him we preferred to sit in back. He sulkily opened the rear door, slammed it after us, jumped in front and slammed the door behind him.

My companion leaned forward, "Heaven," she said.

The driver switched on the turbine and televisor.

"Why did you ask if I were a British subject?" I said, to start the conversation.

She leaned away from me, tilting her mask close to the window. "See the Moon," she said in a quick, dreamy voice.

"But why, really?" I pressed, conscious of an irritation that had nothing to do with her.

"It's edging up into the purple of the sky."

"And what's your name?"

"The purple makes it look yellower."

Just then I became aware of the source of my irritation. It lay in the square of writhing light in the front of the cab beside the driver.

I don't object to ordinary wrestling matches, though they bore me, but I simply detest watching a man wrestle a woman. The fact that the bouts are generally "on the level," with the man greatly outclassed in weight and reach and the masked females young and personable, only makes them seem worse to me.

"Please turn off the screen," I requested the driver.

He shook his head without looking around. "Uh-uh,

man," he said. "They've been grooming that babe for weeks for this bout with Little Zirk."

Infuriated, I reached forward, but my companion caught my arm. "Please," she whispered frightenedly, shaking her head.

I settled back, frustrated. She was closer to me now, but silent and for a few moments I watched the heaves and contortions of the powerful masked girl and her wiry masked opponent on the screen. His frantic scrambling at her reminded me of a male spider.

I jerked around, facing my companion. "Why did those three men want to kill you?" I asked sharply.

The eyeholes of her mask faced the screen. "Because they're jealous of me," she whispered.

"Why are they jealous?"

She still didn't look at me. "Because of him."

"Who?"

She didn't answer.

I put my arm around her shoulders. "Are you afraid to tell me?" I asked. "What *is* the matter?"

She still didn't look my way. She smelled nice.

"See here," I said laughingly, changing my tactics, "you really should tell me something about yourself. I don't even know what you look like."

I half playfully lifted my hand to the band of her neck. She gave it an astonishingly swift slap. I pulled it away in sudden pain. There were four tiny indentations on the back. From one of them a tiny bead of blood welled out as I watched. I looked at her silver fingernails and saw they were actually delicate and pointed metal caps.

"I'm dreadfully sorry," I heard her say, "but you frightened me. I thought for a moment you were going to. . . ."

At last she turned to me. Her coat had fallen open. Her evening dress was Cretan Revival, a bodice of lace beneath and supporting the breasts without covering them.

"Don't be angry," she said, putting her arms around my neck. "You were wonderful this afternoon."

The soft gray velvet of her mask, molding itself to her cheek, pressed mine. Through the mask's lace the wet warm tip of her tongue touched my chin.

"I'm not angry," I said. "Just puzzled and anxious to help."

The cab stopped. To either side were black windows bordered by spears of broken glass. The sickly purple light showed a few ragged figures slowly moving toward us.

The driver muttered, "It's the turbine, man. We're grounded." He sat there hunched and motionless. "Wish it had happened somewhere else."

My companion whispered, "Five dollars is the usual amount."

She looked out so shudderingly at the congregating figures that I suppressed my indignation and did as she suggested. The driver took the bill without a word. As he started up, he put his hand out the window and I heard a few coins clink on the pavement.

My companion came back into my arms, but her mask faced the television screen, where the tall girl had just pinned the convulsively kicking Little Zirk.

"I'm so frightened," she breathed.

Heaven turned out to be an equally ruinous neighborhood, but it had a club with an awning and a huge doorman uniformed like a spaceman, but in gaudy colors. In my sensuous daze I rather liked it all. We stepped out of the cab just as a drunken old woman came down the sidewalk, her mask awry. A couple ahead of us turned their heads from the half revealed face, as if from an ugly body at the beach. As we followed them in I heard the doorman say, "Get along, grandma, and watch yourself."

Inside, everything was dimness and blue glows. She had said we could talk here, but I didn't see how. Besides the inevitable chorus of sneezes and coughs (they say America is fifty per cent allergic these days), there was a band going full blast in the latest robop style, in which an electronic composing machine selects an arbitrary sequence of tones into which the musicians weave their raucous little individualities.

Most of the people were in booths. The band was behind the bar. On a small platform beside them, a girl was dancing, stripped to her mask. The little cluster of men at the shadowy far end of the bar weren't looking at her.

We inspected the menu in gold script on the wall and pushed the buttons for breast of chicken, fried shrimps and two scotches. Moments later, the serving bell tinkled. I opened the gleaming panel and took out our drinks.

The cluster of men at the bar filed off toward the door, but first they stared around the room. My companion had just thrown back her coat. Their look lingered on our booth. I noticed that there were three of them.

The band chased off the dancing girl with growls. I handed my companion a straw and we sipped our drinks.

"You wanted me to help you about something," I said. "Incidentally, I think you're lovely."

She nodded quick thanks, looked around, leaned forward. "Would it be hard for me to get to England?"

"No," I replied, a bit taken aback. "Provided you have an American passport."

"Are they difficult to get?"

"Rather," I said, surprised at her lack of information. "Your country doesn't like its nationals to travel, though it isn't quite as stringent as Russia."

"Could the British Consulate help me get a passport?"

"It's hardly their. . . ."

"Could you?"

I realized we were being inspected. A man and two girls had paused opposite our table. The girls were tall and wolfish-looking, with spangled masks. The man stood jauntily between them like a fox on its hind legs.

My companion didn't glance at them, but she sat back. I noticed that one of the girls had a big yellow bruise on her forearm. After a moment they walked to a booth in the deep shadows.

"Know them?" I asked. She didn't reply. I finished my drink. "I'm not sure you'd like England," I said. "The austerity's altogether different from your American brand of misery."

She leaned forward again. "But I must get away," she whispered.

"Why?" I was getting impatient.

"Because I'm so frightened."

There were chimes. I opened the panel and handed her the fried shrimps. The sauce on my breast of chicken was a delicious steaming compound of almonds, soy and ginger. But something must have been wrong with the radionic oven that had thawed and heated it, for at the first bite I crunched a kernel of ice in the meat. These delicate mechanisms need constant repair and there aren't enough mechanics.

I put down my fork. "What are you really scared of?" I asked her.

For once her mask didn't waver away from my face. As I waited I could feel the fears gathering without her naming them, tiny dark shapes swarming through the curved night outside, converging on the radioactive pest spot of New York, dipping into the margins of the purple. I felt a sudden rush of sympathy, a desire to protect the girl opposite me. The warm feeling added itself to the infatuation engendered in the cab.

"Everything," she said finally.

I nodded and touched her hand.

"I'm afraid of the Moon," she began, her voice going dreamy and brittle as it had in the cab. "You can't look at it and not think of guided bombs."

"It's the same Moon over England," I reminded her.

"But it's not England's Moon any more. It's ours and Russia's. You're not responsible."

I pressed her hand.

"Oh, and then," she said with a tilt of her mask, "I'm afraid of the cars and the gangs and the loneliness and Inferno. I'm afraid of the lust that undresses your face. And—" her voice hushed—"I'm afraid of the wrestlers."

"Yes?" I prompted softly after a moment.

Her mask came forward. "Do you know something about the wrestlers?" she asked rapidly. "The ones that wrestle women, I mean. They often lose, you know. And then they have to have a girl to take their frustration out on. A girl who's soft and weak and terribly frightened. They need that, to keep them men. Other men don't want them to have a girl. Other men want them just to fight women and be heroes. But they must have a girl. It's horrible for her."

I squeezed her fingers tighter, as if courage could be transmitted—granting I had any. "I think I can get you to England," I said.

Shadows crawled onto the table and stayed there. I looked up at the three men who had been at the end of the bar. They were the men I had seen in the big coupe. They wore black sweaters and close-fitting black trousers. Their faces were as expressionless as dopers. Two of them stood above me. The other loomed over the girl.

"Drift off, man," I was told. I heard the other inform the girl: "We'll wrestle a fall, sister. What shall it be? Judo, slapsie or kill-who-can?"

I stood up. There are times when an Englishman simply must be maltreated. But just then the foxlike man came gliding in like the star of a ballet. The reaction of the other three startled me. They were acutely embarrassed.

He smiled at them thinly. "You won't win my favor by tricks like this," he said.

"Don't get the wrong idea, Zirk," one of them pleaded.

"I will if it's right," he said. "She told me what you tried to do this afternoon. That won't endear you to me, either. Drift."

They backed off awkwardly. "Let's get out of here," one of them said loudly, as they turned. "I know a place where they fight naked with knives."

Little Zirk laughed musically and slipped into the seat beside my companion. She shrank from him, just a little. I pushed my feet back, leaned forward.

"Who's your friend, baby?" he asked; not looking at her.

She passed the question to me with a little gesture. I told him.

"British," he observed. "She's been asking you about getting out of the country? About passports?" He smiled pleasantly. "She likes to start running away. Don't you, baby?" His small hand began to stroke her wrist, the fingers bent a little, the tendons rigid, as if he were about to grab and twist.

"Look here," I said sharply. "I have to be grateful to you for ordering off those bullies, but—"

"Think nothing of it," he told me. "They're no harm except when they're behind steering wheels. A well-trained fourteen-year-old girl could cripple any one of them. Why, even Theda here, if she went in for that sort of thing. . . ."

He turned to her, shifting his hand from her wrist to her hair. He stroked it, letting the strands slip slowly through his fingers. "You know I lost tonight, baby, don't you?" he said softly.

I stood up. "Come along," I said to her. "Let's leave."

She just sat there. I couldn't even tell if she was trembling. I tried to read a message in her eyes through the mask.

"I'll take you away," I said to her. "I can do it. I really will."

He smiled at me. "She'd like to go with you," he said. "Wouldn't you, baby?"

"Will you or won't you?" I said to her. She still just sat there.

He slowly knotted his fingers in her hair.

"Listen, you little vermin," I snapped at him. "Take your hands off her."

He came up from the seat like a snake. I'm no fighter. I just know that the more scared I am, the harder and straighter I hit. This time I was lucky. But as he crumpled back, I felt a slap and four stabs of pain in my cheek. I clapped my hand to it. I could feel the four gashes made by her dagger finger caps, and the warm blood oozing out from them.

She didn't look at me. She was bending over little Zirk and cuddling her mask to his cheek and crooning: "There, there, don't feel bad, you'll be able to hurt me afterward."

There were sounds around us, but they didn't come close. I leaned forward and ripped the mask from her face.

I really don't know why I should have expected her face to be anything else. It was very pale, of course, and there weren't any cosmetics. I suppose there's no point in wearing any under a mask. The eyebrows were untidy and the lips chapped. But as for the general expression, as for the feelings crawling and wriggling across it—

Have you ever lifted a rock from damp soil? Have you ever watched the slimy white grubs?

I looked down at her, she up at me. "Yes, you're so frightened, aren't you?" I said sarcastically. "You dread this little nightly drama, don't you? You're scared to death."

And I walked right out into the purple night, still holding my hand to my bleeding cheek. No one stopped me, not even the girl wrestlers. I wished I could tear a tab from under my shirt, and test it then and there, and find

I'd taken too much radiation, and so be able to ask to cross the Hudson and go down New Jersey, past the lingering radiance of the Narrows Bomb, and so on to Sandy Hook to wait for the rusty ship that would take me back over the seas to England.

DOORWAY

INTO TIME

by

C. L. MOORE

He came slowly, with long, soft, ponderous strides, along the hallway of his treasure house. The gleanings of many worlds were here around him; he had ransacked space and time for the treasures that filled his palace. The robes that moulded their folds richly against his great rolling limbs as he walked were in themselves as priceless as anything within these walls, gossamer fabric pressed into raised designs that had no meaning, this far from the world upon which they had been created, but—in their beauty—universal. But he was himself more beautiful than anything in all that vast collection. He knew it complacently, a warm contented knowledge deep in the center of his brain.

His motion was beautiful, smooth power pouring along his limbs as he walked, his great bulk ponderous and graceful. The precious robes he wore flowed open over his magnificent body. He ran one sensuous palm down his side, enjoying the texture of that strange, embossed delicacy in a fabric thinner than gauze. His eyes were proud and half shut, flashing many-colored under the heavy lids. The eyes were never twice quite the same color, but all the colors were beautiful.

He was growing restless again. He knew the feeling well, that familiar quiver of discontent widening and strengthening far back in his mind. It was time to set out once more on the track of something dangerous. In times past, when he had first begun to stock this treasure house, beauty alone had been enough. It was not enough any longer. Danger had to be there too. His tastes were growing capricious and perhaps a little decadent, for he had lived a very long time.

Yes, there must be a risk attending the capture of his next new treasure. He must seek out great beauty and great danger, and subdue the one and win the other, and the thought of it made his eyes change color and the blood beat faster in mighty rhythms through his veins. He smoothed his palm again along the embossed designs of the robe that moulded itself to his body. The great, rolling strides carried him noiselessly over the knife-edged patterns of the floor.

Nothing in life meant much to him any more except these beautiful things which his own passion for beauty had brought together. And even about these he was growing capricious now. He glanced up at a deep frame set in the wall just at the bend of the corridor, where his appreciative eyes could not fail to strike the objects it enclosed at just the proper angle. Here was a group of three organisms fixed in an arrangement that once had given him intense pleasure. On their own world they might have been living creatures, perhaps even intelligent. He neither knew nor cared. He did not even remember now if there had been eyes upon their world to see, or minds to recognize beauty. He cared only that they had given him acute pleasure whenever he turned this bend of the corridor and saw them frozen into eternal perfection in their frame.

But the pleasure was clouded as he looked at them now. His half-shut eyes changed color, shifting along the spectrum from yellow-green to the cooler purity of true green. This particular treasure had been acquired in perfect safety; its value was impaired for him, remembering that. And the quiver of discontent grew stronger in his mind. Yes, it was time to go out hunting again. . . .

And here, set against a panel of velvet, was a great oval stone whose surface exhaled a light as soft as smoke, in waves whose colors changed with languorous slowness. Once the effect had been almost intoxicating to him. He had taken it from the central pavement of a great city square upon a world whose location he had forgotten long ago. He did not know if the people of the city had valued it, or perceived its beauty at all. But he had won it with only a minor skirmish, and now in his bitter mood it was valueless to his eyes.

He quickened his steps, and the whole solid structure of the palace shook just perceptibly underfoot as he moved with ponderous majesty down the hall. He was still running one palm in absent appreciation up and down the robe across his mighty side, but his mind was not on present treasures any more. He was looking to the future, and the color of his eyes had gone shivering up the spectrum to orange, warm with the anticipation of danger. His nostrils flared a little and his wide mouth turned down at the corners in an inverted grimace. The knife-edged patterns of the floor sang faintly beneath his footsteps, their sharp intricacies quivering as the pressure of his steps passed by.

He went past a fountain of colored fire which he had wrecked a city to possess. He thrust aside a hanging woven of unyielding crystal spears which only his great strength could have moved. It gave out showers of colored sparks when he touched it, but their beauty did not delay him now.

His mind had run on ahead of him, into that room in the center of his palace, round and dim, from which he searched the universe for plunder and through whose doorways he set out upon its track. He came ponderously along the hall toward it, passing unheeded treasures, the gossamer of his robes floating after him like a cloud.

On the wall before him, in the dimness of the room, a great circular screen looked out opaquely, waiting his touch. A doorway into time and space. A doorway to beauty and deadly peril and everything that made livable for him a life which had perhaps gone on too long already. It took strong measures now to stir the jaded senses which once had responded so eagerly to more stimuli than he could remember any more. He sighed, his great chest expanding tremendously. Somewhere beyond that screen, upon some world he had never trod before, a treasure was waiting lovely enough to tempt his boredom and dangerous enough to dispel it for just a little while.

The screen brightened as he neared the wall. Blurred shadows moved, vague sounds drifted into the room. His wonderful senses sorted the noises and the shapes and dismissed them as they formed; his eyes were round and luminous now, and the orange fires deepened as he watched. Now the shadows upon the screen moved faster. Something was taking shape. The shadows leaped backward into three-dimensional vividness that wavered for a moment and then sharpened into focus upon a desert landscape under a vivid crimson sky. Out of the soil a cluster of tall flowers rose swaying, exquisitely shaped, their colors shifting in that strange light. He glanced at them carelessly and grimaced. And the screen faded.

He searched the void again, turning up scene after curious scene and dismissing each with a glance. There was a wall of carved translucent panels around a city he did not bother to identify. He saw a great shining bird that trailed luminous plumage, and a tapestry woven gor-

geously with scenes from no earthly legend, but he let all
of them fade again without a second look, and the orange
glow in his eyes began to dull with boredom.

Once he paused for a while before the picture of a tall,
dark idol carved into a shape he did not recognize, its
strange limbs adorned with jewels that dripped fire, and
for an instant his pulse quickened. It was pleasant to think
of those jewels upon his own great limbs, trailing drops of
flame along his halls. But when he looked again he saw that
the idol stood deserted upon a barren world, its treasure
his for the taking. And he knew that so cheap a winning
would be savorless. He sighed again, from the depths of his
mighty chest, and let the screen shift its pictures on.

It was the faraway flicker of golden lightning in the void
that first caught his eyes, the distant scream of it from
some world without a name. Idly he let the screen's
shadows form a picture. First was the lightning, hissing
and writhing from a mechanism which he spared only
one disinterested glance. For beside it two figures were
taking shape, and as he watched them his restless motions
stilled and the floating robe settled slowly about his body.
His eyes brightened to orange again. He stood very quiet,
staring.

The figures were of a shape he had not seen before.
Remotely like his own, but flexible and very slender, and
of proportions grotesquely different from his. And one of
them, in spite of its difference, was—He stared thoughtfully.
Yes, it was beautiful. Excitement began to kindle behind
his quietness. And the longer he stared the clearer the
organism's subtle loveliness grew. No obvious flamboyance
like the fire-dripping jewels or the gorgeously plumed bird,
but a delicate beauty of long, smooth curves and tapering
lines, and colors in softly blended tints of apricot and
creamy white and warm orange-red. Folds of blue-green
swathing it were probably garments of some sort. He wondered if it were intelligent enough to defend itself, or if
the creature beside it, making lightnings spurt out of the

mechanism over which it bent, would know or care if he reached out to take its companion away.

He leaned closer to the screen, his breath beginning to come fast and his eyes glowing with the first flush of red that meant excitement. Yes, this was a lovely thing. A very lovely trophy for his halls. Briefly he thought of it arranged in a frame whose ornaments would echo the soft and subtle curves of the creature itself, colored to enhance the delicacy of the subject's coloring. Certainly a prize worth troubling himself for—if there were danger anywhere near to make it a prize worth winning. . . .

He put one hand on each side of the screen and leaned forward into it a little, staring with eyes that were a dangerous scarlet now. That flare of lightning looked like a weapon of some sort. If the creatures had intelligence— It would be amusing to test the limits of their minds, and the power of the weapon they were using. . . .

He watched a moment longer, his breath quickening. His mighty shoulders hunched forward. Then with one shrug he cast off the hampering garment of gossamer and laughed deep in his throat and lunged smoothly forward into the open doorway of the screen. He went naked and weaponless, his eyes blazing scarlet. This was all that made life worth living. Danger, and beauty beyond danger. . . .

Darkness spun around him. He shot forward through dimensionless infinity along a corridor of his own devising.

The girl leaned back on her metal bench and crossed one beautiful long leg over the other, stirring the sequined folds of her gown into flashing motion.

"How much longer, Paul?" she asked.

The man glanced over his shoulder and smiled.

"Five minutes. Look away now—I'm going to try it again." He reached up to slip a curved, transparent mask forward, closing his pleasant, dark face away from the glare. The girl sighed and shifted on the bench, averting her eyes.

The laboratory was walled and ceiled in dully reflecting

metal, so that the blue-green blur of her gown moved as if in dim mirrors all around her when she changed position. She lifted a bare arm to touch her hair, and saw the reflections lift too, and the pale blur that was her hair, shining ashes of silver and elaborately coiffed.

The murmur of well-oiled metal moving against metal told her that a lever had been shifted, and almost instantly the room was full of golden glare, like daylight broken into hissing fragments as jagged as lightning. For a long moment the walls quivered with light and sound. Then the hissing died, the glare faded. A smell of hot metal tainted the air.

The man sighed heavily with satisfaction and lifted both hands to pull the mask off. Indistinctly behind the glass she heard him say:

"Well, that's done. Now we can—"

But he never finished, and the helmet remained fixed on his shoulders as he stared at the wall they were both facing. Slowly, almost absentmindedly, he pushed aside the glass across his face, as if he thought it might be responsible for the thing they both saw. For above the banked machinery which controlled the mechanism he had just released, a shadow had fallen upon the wall. A great circle of shadow. . . .

Now it was a circle of darkness, as if twilight had rushed timelessly into midnight before them as they watched, and a midnight blacker than anything earth ever knew. The midnight of the ether, of bottomless spaces between worlds. And now it was no longer a shadow, but a window opening upon that midnight, and the midnight was pouring through. . . .

Like smoke the darkness flowed in upon them, dimming the glitter of machinery, dimming the girl's pale hair and pale, shining shoulders and the shimmer of her gown until the man looked at her as if through veil upon veil of falling twilight.

Belatedly he moved, making a useless gesture of brushing the dark away with both hands before his face.

"Alanna—" he said helplessly. "What's happened? I—I can't see—very well—"

He heard her whimper in bewilderment, putting her own hands to her eyes as if she thought blindness had come suddenly upon them both. He was too sick with sudden dizziness to move or speak. This, he told himself wildly, must be the blindness that foreruns a swoon, and his obedient mind made the floor seem to tilt as if the faintness and blindness were inherent in himself, and not the result of some outward force.

But before either of them could do more than stammer a little, as their minds tried desperately to rationalize what was happening into some weakness of their own senses, the dark was complete. The room brimmed with it, and sight ceased to exist.

When the man felt the floor shake, he thought for an unfathomable moment that it was his own blindness, his own faintness again, deceiving his senses. The floor could not shake, as if to a ponderous tread. For there was no one here but themselves—there could not be great footfalls moving softly through the dark, making the walls shudder a little as they came. . . .

Alanna's caught breath was clear in the silence. Not terror at first; but surprised inquiry. She said, "Paul— Paul, don't—"

And then he heard the beginning of her scream. He heard the beginning, but incredibly, he never heard the scream's end. One moment the full-throated roundness of her cry filled the room, pouring from a throat stretched wide with terror; the next, the sound diminished and vanished into infinite distances, plummeting away from him and growing thin and tiny while the echo of its first sound still rang through the room. The impossibility of such speed put the last touch of nightmare upon the whole episode. He did not believe it.

The dark was paling again. Rubbing his eyes, still not

sure at all that this had not been some brief aberration of his own senses, he said, "Alanna—I thought—"

But the twilight around him was empty.

He had no idea how long a while elapsed between that moment and the moment when he stood up straight at last, facing the wall upon which the shadow still lay. In between there must have been a period of frantic search, of near hysteria and self-doubt and reeling disbelief. But now, as he stood looking up at the wall upon which the shadow still hung blackly, drawing into itself the last veils of twilight from the corners of the room, he ceased to rationalize or disbelieve.

Alanna was gone. Somehow, impossibly, in the darkness that had come upon them a Something with great silent feet that trod ponderously, shaking the walls, had seized her in the moment when she said, "Paul—" thinking it was himself. And while she screamed, it had vanished into infinite distances out of this room, carrying her with it.

That it was impossible he had no time to consider. He had time now only to realize that nothing had passed him toward the door, and that the great circle upon the wall before him was—an entrance?—out of which Something had come and into which Something must have retreated again— and not alone. . . .

And the entrance was closing.

He took one step toward it, unreasoning and urgent, and then stumbled over the boxed instrument which he had been testing just before insanity entered the room. The sight and feel of it brought back his own sanity a little. Here was a weapon; it offered a grip upon slipping reality to know that he was not wholly helpless. Briefly he wondered whether any weapon at all would avail against That which came in impossible darkness on feet that made no sound, though their tread shook the foundations of the building. . . .

But the weapon was heavy. And how far away from the

parent machine would it work? With shaking fingers he groped for the carrying handle. He staggered a little, lifting it, but he turned toward the end of the room where the great circle drank in the last of its twilight and began imperceptibly to pale upon the wall. If he were to follow, to take That which had gone before him by surprise, he must go swiftly. . . .

One glance at the lever of the parent machine, to be sure it was thrown full over, for the weapon itself drank power from that source alone—if it would drink power at all in the unfathomable distances to which he was going. . . . One last unbelieving glance around the room, to be quite sure Alanna was really gone—

The lower arc of the circle was a threshold opening upon darkness. He could not think that he would pass it, this flat shadow upon the flat and solid wall, but he put out one hand uncertainly and took a step forward, and another, bent to the weight of the box he carried. . . .

But there was no longer any weight. Nor was there any light nor sound—only wild, whirling motion that spun him over and over in the depths of his blindness. Spun interminably—spun for untimed eons that passed in the flash of an eye. And then—

"Paul! Oh, Paul!"

He stood reeling in a dim, round room walled with strange designs he could not quite focus upon. He had no sense that was not shaken intolerably; even sight was not to be relied upon just now. He thought he saw Alanna in the dimness, pale hair falling over her pale, shining shoulders, her face distorted with bewilderment and terror. . . .

"Paul! Paul, answer me! What is it? What's happened?"

He could not speak yet. He could only shake his head and cling by blind instinct to the weight that dragged down upon one arm. Alanna drew her bare shoulders together under the showering hair and hugged herself fearfully, the creamy arms showing paler circles where her fingertips pressed them hard. Her teeth were chattering, though not from cold.

"How did we get here?" she was saying. "How did we get here, Paul? We'll have to go back, won't we? I wonder what's happened to us? The words were almost aimless, as if the sound of speech itself were more important to her now than any sense of what she was saying. "Look behind you, Paul—see? We came out of—there."

He turned. A great circle of mirror rose behind him on the dim wall, but a mirror reversed, so that it reflected not themselves, but the room they had just left.

Clearer than a picture—he looked into it—his laboratory walls shining with dull reflections, his batteries and dials, and the lever standing up before them that meant the heavy thing he carried would be deadly—perhaps. Deadly? A weapon in a dream? Did they even know that the Something which dwelt here was inimical?

But this was ridiculous. It was too soon yet to accept the fact that they were standing here at all. In reality, of course, they must both be back in the laboratory, and both of them dreaming the same strange dream. And he felt, somehow, that to treat all this as a reality would be dangerous. For if he accepted even by implication that such a thing could be true, then perhaps—perhaps. . . . Could acceptance make it *come* true?

He set his weapon down and rubbed his arm dazedly, looking around. Words did not come easily yet, but he had to ask one question.

"That—that thing, Alanna. What was it? How did you—"

She gripped her own bare arms harder, and another spasm of shuddering went over her. The blue-green sequins flashed chilly star-points from her gown as she moved. Her voice shook too; her very mind seemed to be shaking behind the blank eyes. But when she spoke the words made approximate sense. And they echoed his own thought.

"I'm dreaming all this, you know." Her voice sounded

far away. "This isn't really happening. But—but *something* took me in its arms back there." She nodded toward the mirrored laboratory on the wall. "And everything whirled, and then—" A hard shudder seized her. "I don't know. . . ."

"Did you see it?"

She shook her head. "Maybe I did. I'm not sure. I was so dizzy—I think it went away through that door. Would you call it a door?" Her little breath of laughter was very near hysteria. "I—I felt its feet moving away."

"But what was it? What did it look like?"

"I don't know, Paul."

He closed his lips on the questions that rushed to be asked. Here in the dream, many things were very alien indeed. Those patterns on the wall, for instance. He thought he could understand how one could look at something and not be sure at all what the something was. And Alanna's heavy spasms of shuddering proved that shock must have blanked her mind protectively to much of what had happened. She said:

"Aren't we going back now, Paul?" And her eyes flickered past him to the pictured laboratory. It was a child's question; her mind was refusing to accept anything but the barest essentials of their predicament. But he could not answer. His first impulse was to say, "Wait—we'll wake up in a minute." But suppose they did not? Suppose they were trapped here? And if the Thing came back. . . . Heavily, he said:

"Of course it's a dream, Alanna. But while it lasts I think we'll have to act as if it were real. I don't want to—" The truth was, he thought, he was afraid to. "But we must. And going back wouldn't do any good as long as we go on dreaming. *It* would just come after us again."

It would come striding through the dream to drag them back, and after all people have died in their sleep—died in their dreams, he thought.

He touched the unwieldy weapon with his toe, thinking silently, "This will help us—maybe. If anything can, it will.

And if it won't—well, neither will running away." And he glanced toward the high, distorted opening that must be a doorway into some other part of this unimaginable, dream-created building. It had gone that way, then. Perhaps they should follow. Perhaps their greatest hope of waking safely out of this nightmare lay in acting rashly, in following with the weapon before it expected them to follow. It might not guess his own presence here at all. It must have left Alanna alone in the dim room, intending to return, not thinking to find her with a defender, or to find the defender armed. . . .

But was he armed? He grinned wryly.

Perhaps he ought to test the weapon. And yet, for all he knew, the Thing's strange, alien gaze might be upon him now. He was aware of a strong reluctance to let it know that he had any defense against it. Surprise—that was important. Keep it a secret until he needed a weapon, if he ever did need one. Very gently he pressed the trigger of the lens that had poured out lightnings in the faraway sanity of his laboratory. Would it work in—a dream? For a long moment nothing happened. Then, faintly and delicately against his palm he felt the tubing begin to throb just a little. It was as much of an answer as he dared take now. Some power was there. Enough? He did not know. It was unthinkable, really, that he should ever need to know. Still—

"Alanna," he said, "I think we'd better explore a little. No use just standing here waiting for *it* to come back. It may be perfectly friendly, you know. Dream creatures often are. But I'd like to see what's outside."

"We'll wake up in a minute," she assured him between chattering teeth. "I'm all right, I think, really. Just—just nervous." He thought she seemed to be rousing from her stupor. Perhaps the prospect of action—any action—even rashness like this, was better for them both than inactivity. He felt surer of himself as he lifted the heavy weapon.

"But Paul, we can't!" She turned, half-way to the door, and faced him. "Didn't I tell you? I tried that before you came. There's a corridor outside, with knives all over the floor. Patterns of them, sharp-edged spirals and—and shapes. Look." She lifted her sparkling skirt a little and put out one foot. He could see the clean, sharp lacerations of the leather sole. His shoulders sagged a bit. Then:

"Well, let's look anyhow. Come on."

The corridor stretched before them, swimming in purple distances, great gothic hollows and arches melting upon arches. There were things upon the walls. Like the patterns in the room behind them, many were impossible to focus upon directly, too different from anything in human experience to convey meaning to the brain. The eye perceived them blankly, drawing no conclusions. He thought vaguely that the hall looked like a museum, with those great frames upon the walls.

Beside the door another tall frame leaned, empty. About six feet high, it was deep enough for a man to lie down in, and all around its edges an elaborate and beautiful decoration writhed, colored precisely like Alanna's blue-green gown. Interwoven in it were strands of silver, the color of her pale and shining hair.

"It looks like a coffin," Alanna said aimlessly. Some very ugly thought stirred in Paul's mind. He would not recognize it; he pushed it back out of sight quickly, but he was gladder now that he had brought this lightning-throwing weapon along.

The hall shimmered with strangeness before them. So many things he could not quite see clearly, but the razor-edged decorations of the floor were clear enough. It made the mind reel a little to think what utter alienage lay behind the choice of such adornment for a floor that must be walked upon—even in a dream. He thought briefly of the great earth-shaking feet in the darkness of his laboratory. Here in the dream they walked this knife-edged floor. They must.

But how?

The spirals of the pattern lay in long loops and rosettes. After a moment, eyeing them, he said, "I think we can make it, Alanna. If we walk between the knives—see, there's space if we're careful." And if they were not careful, if they had to run. . . . "We've got to risk it," he said aloud, and with those words admitted to himself for perhaps the first time an urgency in this dream, risk and danger. . . .

He took a firmer grip upon his burden and stepped delicately into the hollow of a steely spiral. Teetering a little, clutching at his arm to steady herself, Alanna came after him.

Silence—vast, unechoing hollows quivering with silence all around them. They advanced very slowly, watching wide-eyed for any signs of life in the distances, their senses strained and aching with the almost subconscious awareness of any slightest motion in the floor that might herald great feet ponderously approaching. But That which had opened the doorway for them had gone now, for a little while, and left them to their own devices.

Paul carried the lens of his weapon ready in his free hand, the lightest possible pressure always on its trigger so that the tubing throbbed faintly against his palm. That reassurance that contact still flowed between his faraway laboratory and this unbelievable hall was all that kept him forging ahead over the razory mosaics.

They went slowly, but they passed many very strange things. A tremendous transparent curtain swung from the vaulted ceiling in folds as immovable as iron. They slipped through the little triangle of opening where the draperies hung awry, and a shower of fiery sparkles sprang out harmlessly when they brushed the sides. They passed a fountain that sent up gushes of soundless flame from its basin in the center of the corridor floor. They saw upon the walls, in frames and without them, things too alien to think about clearly. That very alienage was worrying the man. In dreams one rehearses the stimuli of the past, fears and hopes and memories. But how *could* one dream of things like these? Where in any human past could such memories lie?

They skirted an oval stone set in the floor, the metal patterns swirling about it. They were both dizzy when they looked directly at it. Dangerous dizziness, since a fall here must end upon razor edges. And once they passed an indescribable something hanging against a black panel of the wall, that brought tears to the eyes with its sheer loveliness, a thing of unbearable beauty too far removed from human experience to leave any picture in their minds once they had gone past it. Only the emotional impact remained, remembered beauty too exquisite for the mind to grasp and hold. And the man knew definitely now that this at least was no part of any human memory, and could be in itself no dream.

They saw it all with the strange clarity and vividness of senses sharp with uncertainty and fear, but they saw it too with a dreamlike haziness that faded a little as they went on. To the man, a terrible wonder was dawning. Could it, after all, be a dream? Could it possibly be some alien reality into which they had stumbled? And the import of that frame outside the door they had left—the frame shaped like a coffin and adorned with the colors of Alanna's gown and hair. . . . Deep in his mind he knew what that frame was for. He knew he was walking through a museum filled with lovely things, and he was beginning to suspect why Alanna had been brought here too. The thing seemed unthinkable, even in a dream as mad as this, and yet—

"Look, Paul." He glanced aside. Alanna had reached up to touch a steel-blue frame upon the wall, its edges enclosing nothing but a dim rosy shimmer. She was groping inside it, her face animated now. No thought had come to her yet about that other frame, evidently. No thought that from this dream neither of them might ever wake. . . .

"Look," she said. "It seems empty, but I can *feel* something—something like feathers. What do you suppose—"

"Don't try to suppose," he said almost brusquely. "There isn't any sense to any of this."

"But some of the things are so pretty, Paul. See that—that snowstorm ahead, between the pillars?"

He looked. Veiling the hallway a little distance away hung a shower of patterned flakes, motionless in midair. Perhaps they were embroideries upon some gossamer drapery too sheer to see. But as he looked he thought he saw them quiver just a little. Quiver, and fall quiet, and then quiver again, as if—as if—

"Paul!"

Everything stopped dead still for a moment. He did not need Alanna's whisper to make his heart pause as he strained intolerably to hear, to see, to feel. . . . Yes, definitely now the snowstorm curtain shook. And the floor shook with it in faint rhythms to that distant tremor—

This is it, he thought. *This is real.*

He had known for minutes now that he was not walking through a dream. He stood in the midst of impossible reality, and the Enemy itself came nearer and nearer with each great soundless footfall, and there was nothing to do but wait. Nothing at all. It wanted Alanna. He knew why. It would not want himself, and it would brush him away like smoke in its juggernaut striding to seize her, unless his weapon could stop it. His heart began to beat with heavy, thick blows that echoed the distant footsteps.

"Alanna," he said, hearing the faintest possible quiver in his voice. "Alanna, get behind something—that pillar over there. Don't make a sound. And if I tell you—*run!*"

He stepped behind a nearer pillar, his arm aching from the weight of his burden, the lens of it throbbing faintly against his palm with its promise of power in leash. He thought it would work. . . .

There was no sound of footfalls as the rhythm grew stronger. Only by the strength of those tremors that shook the floor could he judge how near the Thing was drawing. The pillar itself was shaking now, and the snowstorm was convulsed each time a mighty foot struck the floor soundlessly. Paul thought of the knife-edged patterns which those feet were treading with such firm and measured strides.

For a moment of panic he regretted his daring in coming to meet the Thing. He was sorry they had not stayed cowering in the room of the mirror—sorry they had not fled back down the whirling darkness through which they came. But you can't escape a nightmare. He held his lensed weapon throbbing like a throat against his palm, waiting to pour out lightning upon—what?

Now it was very close. Now it was just beyond the snowstorm between the pillars. He could see dim motion through their veil. . . .

Snow swirled away from its mighty shoulders, clouded about its great head so that he could not see very clearly what it was that stood there, tall and grotesque and terrible, its eyes shining scarlet through the veil. He was aware only of the eyes, and of the being's majestic bulk, before his hand of its own volition closed hard upon the pulse of violence in his palm.

For one timeless moment nothing happened. He was too stunned with the magnitude of the thing he faced to feel even terror at his weapon's failure; awe shut out every other thought. He was even a little startled when the glare of golden daylight burst hissing from his hand, splashing its brillance across the space between them.

Then relief was a weakness that loosened all his muscles as he played the deadliness of his weapon upon the Enemy, hearing the air shriek with its power, seeing the stone pillars blacken before those lashes of light. He was blinded by their glory; he could only stand there pouring the lightnings forth and squinting against their glare. The smell of scorched metal and stone was heavy in the air, and he could hear the crash of a falling column somewhere, burned through by the blast of the flame. Surely *it* too must be consumed and falling. . . . Hope began to flicker in his brain.

It was Alanna's whimper that told him something must still be wrong. Belatedly he reached up to close the glass visor of the mask he still wore, and by magic the glare ceased to blind him. He could see between the long, writhing whips of light—see the pillars falling and the steel patterns of the floor turn blue and melt away. But he could see it standing between those crumbling pillars now. . . .

He could see it standing in the full bath of the flames, see them splash upon its mighty chest and sluice away over its great shoulders like the spray of water, unheeded, impotent.

Its eyes were darkening from crimson to an angry purple as it lurched forward one ponderous, powerful stride, brushing away the sparks from its face, putting out a terrible arm. . . .

"Alanna—" said the man in a very quiet voice, pitched below the screaming of the flame. "Alanna—you'd better start back. I'll hold it while I can. You'd better run, Alanna. . . ."

He did not know if she obeyed. He could spare no further attention from the desperate business at hand, to delay it—to hold it back even for sixty seconds—for thirty seconds—for one breath more of independent life. What might happen after that he could not let himself think. Perhaps not death—perhaps something far more alien and strange than death. . . . He knew the struggle was hopeless and senseless, but he knew he must struggle on while breath remained in him.

There was a narrow place in the corridor between himself and it. The lightning had weakened one wall already. He swung it away from the oncoming colossus and played the fire screaming to and fro upon blackened stones, seeing mortar crumble between them and girders bending in that terrible heat.

The walls groaned, grinding their riven blocks surface against surface. Slowly, slowly they leaned together; slowly they fell. Stone dust billowed in a cloud to hide the final collapse of the corridor, but through it the scream of lightnings sounded and the shriek of metal against falling stone. And then, distantly, a deeper groaning of new pressure coming to bear.

The man stood paralyzed for a moment, dizzy with an unreasonable hope that he had stopped the Enemy at last, not daring to look too closely for fear of failure. But hope and despair came almost simultaneously into his mind as he watched the mass of the closed walls shuddering and resisting for a moment—but only for a moment.

With dust and stone blocks and steel girders falling away from its tremendous shoulders, it stepped through the ruined arch. Jagged golden lightnings played in its face, hissing and screaming futilely. It ignored them. Shaking off the debris of the wall, it strode forward, eyes purple with anger, great hands outstretched.

And so the weapon failed. He loosed the trigger, hearing its shriek die upon the air as the long ribbons of lightning faded. It was instinct, echoing over millenniums from the first fighting ancestor of mankind, that made him swing the heavy machine overhead with both hands and hurl it into the face of the Enemy. And it was a little like relinquishing a living comrade to let the throb of that fiery tubing lose contact with his palm at last.

Blindly he flung the weapon from him, and in the same motion whirled and ran. The knife-edged floor spun past below him. If he could hit a rhythm to carry him from loop to empty loop of the pattern, he might even reach the room at the end of the passage— There was no sanctuary anywhere, but unreasoning instinct made him seek the place of his origin here. . . .

Ahead of him a flutter of blue-green sequins now and then told him that Alanna was running too, miraculously keeping her balance on the patterned floor. He could not look up to watch her. His eyes were riveted to the spirals and loops among which his precarious footing lay. Behind him great feet were thudding soundlessly, shaking the floor.

The things that happened then happened too quickly for the brain to resolve into any sequence at all. He knew that the silence which had flowed back when the screaming lightnings died was suddenly, shockingly broken again by a renewed screaming. He remembered seeing the metal patterns of the floor thrown into sharp new shadows by the light behind him, and he knew that the Enemy had found the trigger he had just released, that his weapon throbbed now against an alien hand.

But it happened in the same instant that the doorway of the entrance room loomed up before him, and he hurled himself desperately into the dimness after Alanna, knowing his feet were cut through and bleeding, seeing the dark blotches of the tracks she too was leaving. The mirror loomed before them, an unbearable picture of the lost familiar room he could not hope to enter again in life.

And all this was simultaneous with a terrifying soundless thunder of great feet at his very heels, of a mighty presence suddenly and ponderously in the same room with them, like a whirlwind exhausting the very air they gasped to breathe. He felt anger eddying about him without words or sound. He felt monstrous hands snatch him up as if a tornado had taken him into its windy grasp. He remembered purple eyes glaring through the dimness in one brief instant of perception before the hands hurled him away.

He spun through empty air. Then a howling vortex seized him and he was falling in blindness, stunned and stupefied, through the same strange passageway that had brought him here. Distantly he heard Alanna scream.

There was silence in the dim, round room in the center of the treasure house, except for a muffled howling from the screen. He who was master here stood quietly before it, his eyes half shut and ranging down the spectrum from purple to red, and then swiftly away from red through orange to a clear, pale, tranquil yellow. His chest still heaved a little with the excitement of that minor fiasco which he had brought upon himself, but it was an excitement soon over, and wholly disappointing.

He was a little ashamed of his momentary anger. He should not have played the little creatures' puny lightnings upon them as they fell down the shaft of darkness. He had misjudged their capacity, after all. They were not really capable of giving him a fight worth while.

It was interesting that one had followed the other, with its little weapon that sparkled and stung, interesting that one fragile being had stood up to him.

But he knew a moment's regret for the beauty of the blue-and-white creature he had flung away. The long, smooth lines of it, the subtle coloring. . . . Too bad that it had been worthless because it was helpless too.

Helpless against himself, he thought, and equally against the drive of its own mysterious motives. He sighed.

He thought again, almost regretfully, of the lovely thing he had coveted hurtling away down the vortex with lightnings bathing it through the blackness.

Had he destroyed it? He did not know. He was a little sorry now that anger for his ruined treasures had made him lose his temper when they ran. Futile, scuttling little beings —they had cheated him out of beauty because of their own impotence against him, but he was not even angry about that now. Only sorry, with vague, confused sorrows he did not bother to clarify in his mind. Regret for the loss of a lovely thing, regret that he had expected danger from them and been disappointed, regret perhaps for his own boredom, that did not bother any longer to probe into the motives of living things. He was growing old indeed.

The vortex still roared through the darkened screen. He stepped back from it, letting opacity close over the surface of the portal, hushing all sound. His eyes were a tranquil yellow. Tomorrow he would hunt again, and perhaps tomorrow. . . .

He went out slowly, walking with long, soundless strides that made the steel mosaics sing faintly beneath his feet.

WE GUARD
THE BLACK PLANET!

by

HENRY KUTTNER

The stratoship dropped me at Stockholm, and an air-ferry took me to Thunder Fjord, where I had been born. In six years nothing had changed. The black rocks still jutted out into the tossing seas, where the red sails of Vikings had once flaunted, and the deep roar of the waters came up to greet me. Against the sky Freya, my father's gerfalcon, was wheeling. And high on the crag was the Hall, its tower keeping unceasing vigil over the northern ocean.

On the porch my father was waiting, a giant who had grown old. Nils Esterling had always been a silent man. His thin lips seemed clamped tight upon some secret he never told, and I think I was always a little afraid of him, though he was never unkind. But between us was a gulf. Nils seemed—shackled. I realized that first when I saw him watching the birds go south before the approach of winter. His eyes held a sick longing that, somehow, made me uneasy.

Shackled, silent, taciturn, he had grown old, always a little withdrawn from the world, always, I thought, afraid of the stars. In the daytime he would watch his gerfalcon against the deep blue of the sky, but at night he drew the shades and would not venture out. The stars meant something to him. Only once, I knew, he had been in space; he never ventured beyond the atmosphere again. What had happened out there I did not know. But Nils Esterling came back changed, with something dead inside his soul.

I was going out now. In my pocket were my papers, the result of six years of exhausting work at Sky Point, where I had been a cadet. I was shipping tomorrow on the *Martius,* Callisto bound. Nils had asked me to come home first.

So I was here, and the gerfalcon came down wheeling, dropping, its talons clamping like iron on my father's gloved wrist. It was like a welcome. Freya was old, too, but her golden eyes were still bright, her grip still deadly.

Nils shook hands with me without rising. He gestured me to a chair. "I'm glad you came back, Arn. So you passed. That was good to hear. You'll be in space tomorrow."

"For Callisto," I said. "How are you, Nils? I was afraid—"

His smile held no mirth. "That I was ill? Or perhaps dying. No, Arn. I've been dying for forty years—" He looked at the gerfalcon. "It doesn't matter a great deal now. Except that I hope it comes soon. You'll know why when I tell you about—about what happened to me in space four decades ago. I'll try not to be bitter, but it's hard. Damned hard." Again Nils looked at the gerfalcon.

He went on after a moment, threading the cord through Freya's jesses. "You haven't much time, if your ship blasts off tomorrow. What port? Newark? Well—what about food?"

"I ate on the ferry, Dad—" I seldom called him that. He moved his big shoulders uneasily. "Let's have a drink." He summoned the servant, and presently there were highballs before us. I could not repress the thought that whiskey was incongruous; in the Hall we should have drunk ale from horns. Well, that was the past. A dead past now.

Nils seemed to read my thought. "The old things linger somehow, Arn. They come down to us in our blood. So—"

"*Waes hael,*" I said.

"*Drinc hael.*" He drained the glass. Knots of muscle bunched at the corners of his jaw. With a sudden, furious motion, he cast off the gerfalcon, the leash slipping through the jesses. Freya took to the air with a hoarse, screaming cry.

"The instinct of flight is in our race," Nils said. "To be free, to fight, and to fly. In the old days we went Viking because of that. Leif the Lucky sailed to Greenland; our ships went down past the Tin Isles to Rome and Byzantium; we sailed even to Cathay. In the winter we caulked our keels and sharpened our swords. Then, when the ice broke up in the fjords, the red sails lifted again. Ran called us—Ran of the seas, goddess of the unknown."

His voice changed; he quoted softly from an old poet.

*What is woman that you forsake
    her,
And the hearthstone, and the
    home-acre,
To go with the old gray Widow-
    maker . . . .*

"Aye," said Nils Esterling, a lost sickness in his eyes. "Our race cannot be prisoned, or it dies. And *I* have been prisoned for forty years. By all the hells of all the worlds!" he whispered, his voice shaking. "A most damnable prison! My soul turned rotten before I'd been back on Earth a week. Even before that. And there was no way out of my prison; I locked it with my own hands, and broke the key.

"You never knew about that, Arn. You'll know now. There's a reason why I must tell you—"

He told me, while the slow night came down, and the borealis flamed and shook like spears of light in the polar sky. The Frost Giants were on the march, for a sudden chill blew in from the fjord. Overhead the wind screamed, like the trumpet cries of Valkyries.

Far beneath us surged the sea, moving with its sliding, resistless motion, spuming against the rocks. Above us, the stars shone brightly.

And on Nils' wrist, where it had returned, the gerfalcon Freya rested, drowsy, stirring a little from time to time, but content to remain there.

It had been thus forty years and more ago, Nils said, in his youth, when the hot blood went singing through his veins, and the Viking spirit flamed within him. The seas were tamed.

The way of his ancestors was no longer open to him. But there were new frontiers open—

The gulfs between the stars held mysteries, and Nils signed as A. B. on a spaceship, a cranky freighter, making the Great Circle of the trade routes. Earth to Venus, and swinging outward again to the major planets.

The life toughened him, after a few years.

And in Marspole North, in a *satha*-dive, he ran into Captain Morse Damon, veteran of the Asteroid War.

Damon told Nils about the Valkyries—the guardians of the Black Planet.

He was harsh and lean and gray as weathered rock, and his black stare was without warmth. Sipping watered *satha*, he watched Nils Esterling, noting the leatheroid tunic worn at cuffs and elbows, the frayed straps of the elasto sandals.

"You know my name."

"Sure," Esterling said. "I see the newstapes. But you haven't been mentioned for a while."

"Not since the Asteroid War ended, no. The pact they made left me out in the cold. I had a guerilla force raiding through the Belt. In another year I could have turned the balance. But after the armistice—"

Damon shrugged. "I'm no good for anything but fighting. I kept a ship; they owed me that. The *Vulcan.* She's a sweet boat, well found and fast. But I can't use her unless I sign up with the big companies. Besides, I don't want to do freighting. The hell with that. I've been at loose ends, blasting around the System, looking for—well, I don't know what. Had a shot or two at prospecting. But it's dull, sinking assay shafts, sweating for a few tons of ore. Not my sort of life."

"There's a war on Venus."

"Penny-ante stuff. I'm on the trail of something big now. On the trail of—" he smiled crookedly—"ghosts. Valkyries."

"Mars isn't the place, then. Norway, on Earth—"

Damon's gaze sharpened. "Not Norway. Space. Valkyries, I said—women with wings."

Esterling drank *satha,* feeling the cold, numbing liquor slide down his throat. "A new race on some planet? I never heard of winged humans."

"You've heard of Glory Hole and Davy Jones' Locker. Mean to say you've been in space three years and never heard of the Valkyries—the Black Planet?"

Esterling put down his glass gently. How did Damon know that he'd been a spaceman for three years? Till now he had thought this merely a casual acquaintance, two Earthmen drinking together on an alien world. Now—

"You mean the legend," he said. "Never paid much attention. When a ship cracks up in space, the crew go to the Black Planet after they die. Spaceman's heaven."

"Yeah. A legend, that's all. When wrecks are found, all

the bodies are found in 'em—naturally! But the story is that there are winged women—call them Valkyries—who live in an invisible world somewhere in the System."

"You think they exist?"

"I think there's truth behind the legend. It isn't merely a terrestrial belief. Martians, Vesuvians, Callistans—they all have their yarns about winged space-women."

Esterling coughed in the smoky atmosphere. "Well?"

"Here it is. Not long ago I met up with an archeologist, a guy named Beale. James Beale. He's got a string of degrees after his name, and for ten years he's been going through the System, checking up on the Black Planet, collecting data all over the place. He showed me what he had, and it was plenty convincing. It added up. A scrap of information from Venus, a story from beyond Io. Legends mostly, but there were facts too. Enough to make me believe that there's an invisible world somewhere in space."

"How invisible?"

"I don't know. Beale says it must be a planet with a very low albedo—or something of the sort. It absorbs light. The winged people live on it. Sometimes they leave it. Maybe they have ships, though I can't tell about that, of course. So we have the legends. Beale and I are going to the Black Planet."

"All right," Esterling said. "It sounds crazy enough, but you could be right. Only—what do you expect to find there?"

Damon smiled. "Dunno. Excitement, anyhow. Beale's sure there are immense sources of power on the black world. I don't suppose we'll lose anything on the deal. Hell, I'm fed up with doing nothing, knocking around the System waiting for something to happen—and it never does. I'm not alive unless I'm fighting. This is a fight, in a way."

"Well?"

"Want a job?"

"You short-handed?"

"Plenty. You look strong—" Damon reached across the table and squeezed the other's biceps. His face altered, not much, but enough to convince Esterling of what he already suspected.

"Okay, Damon." He rolled up his sleeve, revealing an arm-bracelet of heavy gold clasped about his upper arm. "Is this what you're after?"

The captain's nostrils distended. He met Esterling's stare squarely.

"You want the cards on the table?"

"Sure."

Damon said, "I just got back from Norway, on Earth. I went there to look you up. Beale found out about that bracelet."

Esterling nodded. "It's an heirloom. Belonged to my great-grandmother, Gudrun. I dont know where she got it."

"It has an inscription. A copy of it was made about a hundred years ago for the Stockholm Museum. Beale ran across that copy. He can read Runic, and the bracelet carries an inscription—"

"I know."

"Do you know what it means?"

"Something about the Valkyries. Part of an old *Edda*, I suppose."

Damon made a noise deep in his throat. "Not quite. It gives the location of the Black Planet."

"The hell it does!" Esterling removed the bracelet and examined it carefully. "I thought it was merely symbolism. The rune doesn't mean anything."

"Beale thought it did. He saw the copy, I said, and it was incomplete. But he found enough to convince him that the complete inscription gave the location of the Black Planet."

"But why—"

"How should I know? Maybe the winged people visited Earth once, maybe somebody found the Black Planet by accident and remembered his space-bearings. He wrote it down where he'd have it safely—on an arm-bracelet. Somehow your great-grandmother got it."

Esterling stared at the golden band. "I don't believe it."

"Will you sign on with me, as supercargo, to look for the Black Planet? You can use a job, by the looks of your clothes."

"Sure I can. But a job like that—"

"Talk to Beale, anyway. He'll convince you."

Esterling grimaced. "I doubt that. However, I suppose I can't lose." He looked again at the bracelet. "Okay, I'll see him."

Damon rose, tossing coins on the stained metalloy table. Esterling finished his *satha*, conscious that the treacherous Martian distillate was affecting him. *Satha* did that. It gave you a deceptive cold clarity that disguised its potency. Martians could take it, with their different metabolism; but it was dangerous to Earthmen.

It was doubly dangerous for Esterling now. He walked beside Damon along the curving street, the ornate, fragile-seeming buildings of Marspole North towering above him—the ones that were not in ruins. It was possible to build tall towers on Mars, because of the slight gravity-pull, but the frequent quakes that shook the ancient planet often brought down those towers in crashing wreckage.

Near the spaceport a man was waiting, thin, dwarfish, and with a pinched, meager face. He was fingering a scrubby mustache and shivering with cold in his thin whites.

"You kept me waiting long enough," he said complainingly, his voice a high-pitched whine. "I'm nearly frozen, drat it. Is he Esterling?"

Damon nodded. "Yeah. Esterling—Beale. He's got the bracelet."

Beale's fingers fluttered at his mouth. "Heavens, that's a relief. We've been tracking you all over the System, man.

A week ago we learned you'd shipped out of Io for Mars-pole North, so we came here by fast express to wait for you. I suppose the captain's told you about the Black Planet."

Esterling was feeling a little sick in the icy air. He had a moment's qualm, wondering if Damon had doped his drinks. Automatically his hand went to his belt, but he'd pawned his gun that morning.

Damon said, "You talk to him. I'll attend to the ship." He slipped off into the shadows.

Beale peered up at the Norseman. "Would you mind letting me see the bracelet? Thanks . . . ." He blinked near-sightedly at the golden band. The two moons gave little light, and Beale took out a tiny flashlight. His breath hissed out.

"Good heavens, Mr. Esterling, you can have no idea what this means to me. That copy in the Stockholm museum was incomplete, you know. Some of the runes were illegible. But this—"

"It tells where to find this—this black world? I'm a little drunk, but the whole yarn sounds crazy to me."

Beale blinked. "No doubt. No doubt. The legends about the Valley of Kings in Egypt seemed crazy till the tombs were finally discovered. The legend of the Valkyries—the flying women—is extremely widespread in space. There are clues . . . I reasoned by induction. It added up. I'm firmly convinced that there is such a planet, and that a hundred thousand years ago the winged people visited our own world. They left traces. Perhaps they've died out by now, but their artifacts remain."

"So?"

"I picked these up on Venus. They were found floating free in space. What do you make of them?" Beale fumbled in his pockets and drew out a bit of bone and a thin, pencil-like rod.

Esterling examined them with puzzled interest.

"It looks like a human shoulder-blade—or part of it."

"Yes, of course! But the extension—the prolongation! The osseous base for a wing, man! Notice the ball-and-socket arrangement, and the grooves where tendons have played, tendons strong enough to move wings."

"A freak?"

"No scientist would agree with you," Beale said shortly, and put the bone back in his pocket. "Look at the rod."

Esterling could make nothing of it. "Is it a weapon?"

"A weapon without power, at the moment. I took it apart. It's based on an entirely different principle from anything we've known. Atomic quanta-release, perhaps. I don't know. But I mean to find out, and there's only one place where I can do that."

The Norseman rubbed his jaw. "So the clue's on my bracelet. And you want me to join you, eh?"

"We're short-handed. There are difficulties—" Beale shivered again, glancing toward the dark spaceport. "I am a poor man, and it takes much money to outfit a ship."

"I thought Damon had a boat—the *Vulcan*."

Before Beale could answer, a faint whistle came out of the dark. The scientist caught his breath. "All right," he said. "Come on." He gripped Esterling's arm and urged the big man toward the field.

A ship loomed there, dull silver in the light of the double moons. Silhouetted against the entrance port was Damon, waving. Beale said, "Hurry up," in a tight voice, and started to run.

Satha had dulled Esterling's senses—or Damon had drugged his liquor. He sensed something amiss, but a heavy, languid blanket lay over his mind, making thought an intolerable effort. He let himself be guided toward the ship.

Damon reached down, seized his hand, and drew him up. The man was remarkably strong, for all his slight build. Esterling, off balance, went lurching against a bulkhead, and brought up sharply against the wall of the lock. He turned in time to see Beale clambering up, spider-like.

Footsteps sounded. A man in port officer's uniform came racing across the field, his voice raised in a shout. Esterling saw Beale turn, biting his lips nervously, and draw a gun. He shot down from the air-lock, the bullet striking the officer squarely between the eyes.

The shock of that sobered Esterling abruptly. But before he could move, Damon thrust him back into the ship. In the distance the faint wail of a siren began.

Beale said, "Drat it!" and came scrambling into the cabin. The valves slid shut with a dull thud. Esterling, his body numb with liquor or drugs, took a step forward. "What the devil—"

Damon snapped, "Watch him, Beale! I've got to blast off."

The scientist's gun leveled at Esterling. Beale licked his lips. "Good heavens," he burst out. "Why does everything always go wrong . . . . Don't move, Mr. Esterling."

Damon had eased himself into the control seat. He spoke briefly into the mike, and then stabbed at the rocket jet buttons. The floor pressed hard against Esterling's feet.

Beale reached up and gripped a strap. "Hold on," he commanded. "That's right. We haven't time to take a smooth orbit out. They'll be after us—"

"They are after us," Damon said dryly. Esterling stole a glance at the visiplate. Marspole North was dropping away below, and a patrol ship was taking off with a burst of red rocket-fire. The ground swung dizzily as Damon played the controls.

Esterling said, "Obviously, this isn't your ship, Captain."

"Of course not," Beale snapped. "But we had to get one. They don't guard the spaceports. Damon picked up a dozen drifters and armed them—enough to take care of the skeleton crew. So—"

"So you killed the crew. I get it."

Without turning, Damon said, "Right. And we're manned

by drunken roustabouts who don't know a jet from an escape valve. You'll come in handy, Esterling—You're an A. B."

The ship lurched sickeningly. The plates were red-hot in the atmosphere, and the visiplate was useless now. But speed was necessary to provide escape velocity. The hull was strong enough, Esterling knew; there was no danger through friction. The real peril lay in the patrol ship.

Damon grunted. "This is a fast boat. Once we're beyond the gravity-pull, we'll be safe. Nobody can catch us. Now—"

He jammed on more power. The red flare on the visiplate faded. They were beyond the atmosphere.

The patrol vessel was visible, specks of light flaming from its sides. Beale grimaced. "Magnetic torpedoes, eh? We—we'll be killed, Damon. Did we have to take such chances?"

Then it happened. The *Vulcan* seemed to stop in midcourse, a grinding, shaking vibration jolting through its hull. Esterling felt the floor drop away beneath him. He was slammed against the wall, the breath going out of his lungs in an agonizing rush. He saw Beale still clinging to the strap, his lean body jerking and tossing like a puppet on wires. Damon was hurled forward against the instrument board. He pushed himself half erect, blood streaming from a pulped face. Somehow he was still alive. His fingers went out toward the buttons.

Beale was screaming, "Torpedo! The air—"

Damon cursed him thickly, indistinctly. He dashed the blood from his eyes and peered at the visiplate. Under his swift hands the ship lurched again, jolted, and leaped forward like an unleashed greyhound.

It seemed faster now.

"Any leaks?" Damon asked quietly.

Beale was clutching the strap, eyes closed, face gray.

Esterling hesitated a moment and then made a circuit of the control cabin, listening at the doors and valves for any betraying hiss of air.

"Try a cigarette," Damon said. "Got one? Here." He extended a blood-stained pack.

Esterling watched the smoke curl out of his nostrils. The only draft was toward the ventilator system, so that was all right. He nodded briefly.

Damon's black eyes were like glacial ice.

He indicated the mike.

"Been trying to raise the men. They were in the bow. No answer. Suppose you put on a suit and check up, eh?"

"Okay," Esterling said. He went to a locker and took out a regulation spacesuit, slipped into it with the ease of familiarity. "What about the patrol boat?"

"We're losing it."

Beale dropped down to a sitting position on the floor-plates, gripping his gun with both hands. He was praying in a low whisper, but interrupted himself to mumble, "Take off the rockets, Mr. Esterling. We don't want you to leave us."

The Norseman compressed his lips, but a glance at the gun muzzle, aimed directly at his heart, made him nod with sardonic resignation. He shrugged out of the rocket harness and let it drop to the floor.

He went out through the hull hatch, Beale handling the levers. Already Mars was far behind, a dull red ball against the black sky. The magnetic soles on his boots held him firmly against the hull, and Esterling clumped laboriously toward the bow. If he had his rocket harness. . . .

Without it, the ship's gravitation prisoned him. He could not escape. Where was the patrol boat?

He could not locate it among the star-points. Well, it scarcely mattered now. He was in for it. Breath misted the face-plate of his helmet, and he turned on the heater coils.

Esterling felt a little sick when he reached the place where the bow had been. The entire nose of the ship had been blown off. Fragments of scrap and parts of bodies were plastered against the hull, covered by a treacly black fluid which Esterling recognized as rocket fuel. He paused on the jagged edge of the gap, peering down into the hole that had been blasted out of the ship. After a moment he took a deep breath and swung into the darkness.

Ten minutes later he returned to the control cabin and stripped off his suit. Beale was still praying. Damon was at the controls, mopping at his face with a crimson handkerchief. He looked up.

"Well? What damage?"

"Nobody's left alive but us three."

"What damage to the ship?" Beale shrilled. "Good heavens, man, that's the important thing!"

Esterling grinned unpleasantly. "Did you know the *Vulcan* carried a full cargo of rocket fuel?"

"What of it?" Beale asked.

Damon turned sharply, a cold rage in his eyes. He showed his teeth in a snarl.

"*Damn!*" The oath exploded from him.

"Yeah," Esterling said. "The nose of the ship is blown off, and the inside bulkheads won't stand atmospheric friction. When we hit air again, the plates will get plenty hot. Rocket fuel won't explode without heat and oxygen, so we're safe as long as we're in space. But the minute we touch atmosphere, we go up like a rocket."

"Good heavens!" Beale gasped, fingers fluttering at his lips. "Damon, we've got to unload that fuel!"

The captain snorted. "In space? We can't. The ship's gravity would pull it right back again."

"Then we've got to land on an airless planet and unload it!"

Damon pointed at the visiscreen. "The patrol boat's

following our jets. We're faster, but the minute we slow down, they'll be on our tail. Nope. We've just got to keep going till we lose the patrol. After that—"

"Yes. I suppose so. We'll head out, eh?"

"It's the safest course. We'll jet toward Pluto."

Esterling lit a cigarette. "You're spacetight. You can't dodge the patrol. Why not call it a day and send out a white jet?"

Beale shook his head. "We can't do that. Once we reach the Black Planet we'll be safe."

"We'd better be," Damon said. "Just to make you feel better, I might as well tell you the *Vulcan's* washed up. Our bow tubes are gone. We can make a crash landing, with spacesuits, but we can't take off again. You still think we'll find spaceships on the black world?"

"Yes. Yes, indeed. The winged people visited Earth, as well as other planets, in the past. It's a gamble, of course, but—"

"It's a gamble we've got to take." Damon looked at Esterling sardonically. "Want a gun?"

"Eh?"

"Here." The captain tossed over a compressed-air automatic. "I don't know what we'll find on the Black Planet, but it may be trouble. You won't use that blaster on us, anyway. D'you think the patrol would believe we'd kidnaped you?"

Esterling slowly holstered the weapon. "I suppose not. But you're taking a chance."

"I don't think so. We'll split with you on whatever we find on the black world. According to Beale, that'll mean big money. Enough to buy off the law. Try any tricks, and the best you can expect is a patrol trial, with the cards stacked against you. Hell, keep the gun," Damon finished, with a careless shrug. "You're no fool. You'll play along."

"Yeah," Esterling said. "There's not much else I can do, I guess."

Damon chuckled.

Crippled, broken, a deadly time-bomb, the *Vulcan* thundered on into the eternal night of the void. The Asteroid Belt lay behind, with its flickering glare-dance of sunlight on the tiny worlds. Immense Jupiter grew larger, a pearly globe with a scarlet wound raw upon its surface—and Jupiter faded and dwindled.

Ringed Saturn was on the other side of the System, but Uranus watched them from the visiplate. They were beyond the Life Zone now. It was too cold, too far from the sun, for life to exist except under artificial conditions. Here and there on frigid moons a few space domes were spotted, outposts of lonely pioneers. But there were not many. Uranus was the borderline, the invisible wall beyond which it was not safe to venture.

The deadly emptiness of the interstellar wastes had reached in with fingers of fiery cold and touched the worlds that swung too far from the sun. They were accursed. Stones from ruined cities had been found here, artifacts so old that no remotely human race could have built them. The freezing tides of space and time, pulsing in eonlong beats, had swept up and buried them, and receded for a little while.

He had never been this far out. In the long weeks on the *Vulcan* a change came upon Nils Esterling, a blood heritage that fought its way to the surface and brought out all the latent mysticism of his race. He was plumbing uncharted seas, as his forefathers had done, and something deep within the man, atavistic and powerful, woke to life.

There's a legend that spacemen get their souls frozen on their first voyage. Esterling had been away from Earth for only a few years, but those years had been deadly ones. Planetary voyages are gruelling, racking jobs for the men who work the ships, and, on the far-flung, exotic worlds of the System, there is nothing akin to the green meadows and blue oceans of Earth. The red ochre of Mars blasts the vision; the stinging yellow fogs of Venus creep into your pores; the shifting rainbow light of Callisto shocks your nerves into jolting madness. Men do not live long in space—no! So, while they live, they make the most of the little they possess.

There are flaming brews from Blueland moss, distilled and potent with dreams. There is cold, stealthy *satha*, and there is the sweet *minga*-liqueur they make in Ednes, on Venus. There is *segir*-whiskey that turns the mind into red fire. There is absinthe from Earth and Fruit o' Worlds made by the dark monks of Io. And there are drugs. The sins of all the Systems are at the call of those who can pay.

Nils had gone down that dark path, for there was little choice. In a few years he had grown cold, reckless, embittered. He had tasted the exultation of space flight, and after that Earth would have seemed dull. Ahead of him lay more years, alternating periods of arduous voyages and wild sprees. Nothing else. In the end, death, and space burial.

The life had toughened him, building a harsh shell under which the old idealism had died to an ember. But now—there was a difference.

Three thousand years before his ancestors had gone Viking, their red-sailed ships driving out from the Northland fjords. Recklessly they had pushed on into unknown seas. The lure of mysteries, of exploration, drove them on. That touched Nils Esterling now.

The patrol ship had been lost long since. They were utterly alone, in an emptiness almost inconceivable to the human mind. The cold, motionless brilliance of the stars merely enhanced their isolation. Day after day the ship roared on through the void, and nothing changed; the sun remained a small yellow star, and the Milky Way lay across the dark sky like Bifröst Bridge that reaches to Asgard. Bifröst, the Bright Rainbow, across which the Valkyries thunder, bearing the souls of warriors fallen in battle.

Legend was not far from fact in this inhuman place, the airless void where man penetrated only by suffrance, venturing in tiny ships that a meteor could destroy easily. Nils Esterling felt the mysticism of far places stealing into his soul. He had felt thus before, once in the Euphrates Valley, where the Garden of Eden had been created; and again on Easter Island, facing the silent carved titans whose origins are hidden by the past.

There were gateways and barriers, he thought—walls built to keep intruders from venturing too far. Man had not conquered space. He had reached the nearer worlds, but beyond, in the vastness of the galaxies, lay mysteries. Closer even than that! A black planet, rolling majestically, invisible, on the edge of the System, holding its secrets . . . .

What were those secrets?

Sometimes skepticism came back, and Esterling sneered at his own credulity. How could a planet have remained undiscovered through the ages, beyond the orbit of Pluto?

It would have to be invisible.

But even as long ago as the Twentieth Century astronomers had suspected the existence of a trans-Plutonian world, one so far out from the sun that its influence was negligible, a world unseen, lost in the incredible immensity of space.

Yes. The Black Planet could exist.

Beale spent hours on abstruse calculations. He had figured dead reckoning by the runes on Esterling's bracelet, and Damon changed the course accordingly. The little scientist peered into the visiplate, using the telescopic attachment, but he could catch no glimpse of his goal.

"It must be invisible," he said. "That's a good sign."

Esterling stared at him. "Why?"

"In the plan of nature nothing is normally invisible, at least nothing of planetary size. That means the camouflage was created artificially. Physicists have speculated about the possibility of a negasphere—"

"I've seen dead-black planetoids," Damon broke in. "You never saw them till you were within a few hundred miles."

"Planetoids are small. And their presence could be detected by occlusion. An artificial negasphere would have the property of warping light-ray. Dwarf stars can draw light toward them, you know. A negasphere could bend it away—around the planet. The world wouldn't hide any stars with its bulk."

They watched the visiplate, but there was nothing there except the frozen rivers of stars in the night sky.

Monotonously time dragged on. There was neither sunrise nor sunset; they ate when hungry, slept when tired. Always the doomed ship fled on into the darkness. Until—

There was no warning. One moment they were in empty space; the next, Damon, at the controls, cried out harshly and cut the jets. The screen flamed white. A bell began to ring shrilly.

"What is it?" Beale hurried toward Damon, leaning over the captain's shoulder. He gasped. Esterling pushed him aside, eying the visiplate.

On the field a world was visible, huge, luminous, distinctly limned against the misty background of the stars. It had sprung out of nothingness. But it was not black. It blazed with cold, swirling radiance, tides of living light rolled across it.

"The Black Planet," Damon said. "But—"

Beale's voice was shrill with excitement. "There *was* a negasphere! We went through it without realizing. Of course! It isn't a tangible barrier; it's just a hollow shell of darkness around the planet. Out here, on the edge of the System—" He was silent, staring at the immense jewel-world that lay before them.

Esterling said, "We're in atmosphere. Look at those stars—misty, see? We can't stay with the ship."

Damon put the *Vulcan* at automatic controls, circling inward in a narrowing spiral. The alarm bell was still ringing.

"Yeah. We'd better get into our suits. Come on!"

They struggled with the fastenings. A jolting shock wrenched the vessel. Esterling snapped his helmet shut, looked to see that he had his rocket harness and gun, and lumbered toward the lock, awkward in the heavy space-boots. He swung open the valve.

On the lips of empty space he paused, looking down. Far beneath him the shining planet lay. He could not gauge its size. There were fewer stars now; the nega-sphere did not seem to block their light, but the atmos-phere did. There was an instant of sickening giddiness before he stepped out.

Then he was hurtling down, and panic clutched at his throat. Instinctively he pressed the stud that activated his rocket-harness, and his flight was arrested. Two figures shot past him, grotesque in their suits, Beale and Damon. They were gone.

He dropped again; there was still a long way to fall, and he did not wish to exhaust his fuel. The *Vulcan* slowly passed him, its tubes firing spasmodically, driving it down to destruction. From the smashed bow a tongue of flame licked up. There was oxygen in this atmosphere, then.

A Viking funeral for the dead men on the ship, Ester-ling thought. Against the blackness of the sky red fire blazed suddenly. It was like a beacon—

Struck by a new thought, he glanced down. The flames would certainly attract attention, if there was any life on the Black Planet. But what life could exist on that pearly, shining globe, seething with luminous tides?

Still he fell. The *Vulcan* blazed, red against the dark. How many spacemen had watched similar sights, watched their vessels crack up while they remained alone in space, without hope of rescue? No marooned sailor could ever have felt one-tenth of the utter desolation that pressed in from the void. The seas of Earth were wide, but the seas of space had no shores.

He could not see Beale or Damon. What would happen when he reached the world below? Would those shining tides swallow him? There could be no life there!

Emptiness, and falling, and an hypnotic languor that dulled Esterling's brain.

Across the sky the Milky Way flamed. Bifröst, where the Valkyries rode, the spear-maidens of Asgard. The Valkyries—

Wings beat soundlessly past him.

For a timeless second a face looked into Esterling's. The blood drummed in his temples. Hallucination, he thought. For she could not exist!

Her hair was corn-yellow, her eyes blue as the southern ocean. No curve of her slender body was hidden by the single gossamer garment she wore, and in all his life Esterling had never seen a girl half so lovely.

Nor half so strange!

Pinions lifted from her shoulders; wings, shining with coruscating light, upheld her in emptiness. She was winged!

One moment the girl hung there, her gaze probing into Esterling's. Then a touch of elfin malice came into the blue eyes. She made a quick gesture—and Esterling was swung off balance by an abrupt tug at his harness. Still falling, he revolved slowly in midair, in time to see another girl, almost a duplicate of the first, holding his rocket harness.

She had ripped it away—and Esterling was falling free, with nothing to half his plunge to the glowing world beneath!

His mouth was dry with sudden panic; he wrenched out his gun. Apparently the winged girls knew the meaning of weapons. The one holding the harness let it drop, and in perfect unison they dived toward Esterling. Handicapped as he was by his bulky suit, he had little chance. A hand gripped his arm. The gun was forced up and back. Falling through space, he could get no leverage, no way of exerting his strength.

Helpless, he fought the Valkyries.

It was useless, as he knew from the start. They were in their own element, agile, strong, deft. In the end he let them tear the gun from him, a suicidal hopelessness overcoming him. But the girls did not wish him to die, it seemed. Their arms wrapped about him, while the great pinions pulsed and beat. Esterling's fall slowed.

Far below, the planet grew larger. The tides of light swept across its surface. It filled half the sky. The *Vulcan*, still afire, plunged down and was swallowed by the luminous glow.

The world grew concave, then flat. Perspective changed. The sphere no longer hung in the void; it was an immense, seething ocean beneath. On that glowing sea were islands—and they drove with the mighty tides like ships.

Cities were built on the isles, fragile-seeming, with a curious architecture unlike anything Esterling had seen before. There was no regular pattern. Some of the islands were huge, others tiny. But all were garden places, spotted with clusters of towers and minarets that were like lustrous jewels.

The Hesperides—the Isles of the Blessed. Oceans of living light washed those strange shores. Across the rolling, seething seas the islands moved majestically, flotsam of a lost planet.

Toward one of them Esterling dropped, a prisoner of the Valkyries.

He saw above the towers a myriad darting shapes, flying with graceful, easy movements. The winged people! Nor were they all women; there were men among them, their wings stronger, darker.

Walls lifted above Esterling. He was being carried down a shaft. There was an instant of dizzying confusion, during which he was half-blinded by wings flailing and beating about him. Then he felt the strong arms relax.

Solid ground was under his feet. He stood on a little

platform of some plastic, blue-tinted substance. Behind him a passageway gaped in the wall. From his feet the pit dropped down to unknown depths.

The Valkyries alighted beside him. He felt slim fingers fumbling with his helmet, and, too late, made a gesture to halt the girl. The face-plate swung back. The air of the new world rushed into his lungs.

One breath told him that there was no danger. It was pure, fresh, and sweet, with a subtle tingling exhilaration that was almost intoxicating. Blue eyes laughed into Esterling's.

"*D'rn sa asth'neeso.*" The words were meaningless, but the gesture that accompanied them was significant. Esterling hesitated. A Valkyrie slipped past him, folded her wings like a cloak about her. She moved into the depths of the passage.

"*Iyan sa!*"

He followed, the other girl at his heels. A tapestry was flung aside, and he found himself in an apartment, obviously a sleeping-chamber, though not built for humans. The walls were transparent as glass.

He was, apparently, in one of the tallest towers. Beneath him lay the city. Beyond that, a luxuriance of rainbow forest, and, farther away, the blazing turmoil of the sea of light. The winged people swooped and glided among the towers.

The Valkyrie Esterling had first seen came closer. She murmured a few liquid, trilling syllables, and her companion vanished. Then, smiling fearlessly up into Esterling's eyes, she tapped the chest of his spacesuit and made a movement of inquiry.

His voice sounded harsh in the silence.

"Yeah. I don't need this, I guess." Gratefully he unburdened himself of the awkward overall garment and helmet.

The girl touched her breast. "Norahn." She repeated it. "Norahn—Norahn."

"Norahn," Esterling said. Her name? He imitated her gesture. "Nils."

There was a scuffle behind them. A group of Valkyries appeared from beyond the curtain, among them two struggling figures—Beale and Damon. They paused at sight of Esterling. Damon snapped open his helmet.

"What's this? Did they get your gun, too?"

"Take it easy," Esterling said. "They're friendly. Our being alive now proves that."

Damon grunted and began to remove his suit. Beale, his lips moving silently, did the same. The Valkyries drew back, as though waiting.

"Norahn—" Esterling said, rather helplessly. The girl smiled at him.

"Vanalsa inio."

She pointed to the door. A Valkyrie entered, carrying a great basket loaded with fruits, unfamiliar to the Earthmen. Norahn picked up a scarlet globe and bit into it, afterward offering it to Esterling.

The taste was strange, but acidly pleasant. Damon grunted, squatted on the floor, and began to eat. Beale was more hesitant, sniffing at each fruit warily before he tried it, but soon the three men were gorging themselves. It was a welcome change from space rations. They scarcely noticed when the Valkyries slipped out.

Only Norahn remained. She touched the red sphere Esterling was eating and said, *"Khar. Khar."*

"Khar. Norahn."

His mouth full, Beale mumbled, "A good sign. They're taking the trouble to teach us their language. Good heavens, I still can't quite believe this. A whole race of flying people—"

"Khar, Nils. *Khar."*

Time did not exist on the world of the Valkyries. The floating islands drifted with the shining tides, borne by an unchanging current that swept around the world. What the strange sea was Esterling never learned. It was not water, though one could bathe in it. The winged folk swooped down, dipped below the surface, and came up with glowing star-drops limning their bodies. Radio-activity, perhaps. Or some less understandable source of power, the alien force that had made the Black Planet unlike any other in the System.

It had come from outside, Norahn said, after they had learned to speak her tongue. In the old days, beyond the memory of the winged people, the planet had revolved around another sun, light-years away. That had been the age of science. There was no need for science now, though the tools still remained.

Beale's eyes brightened.

"We have no records, no memories. It was too long ago. There was a war, I think, and our people fled, moving this world like a ship. Across space we went. Long ago we visited the planets of this System. They had life but—that life was not intelligent. And we were afraid our ene-mies would follow and destroy us. So we made the nega-sphere, to hide ourselves from those who might pursue. We waited. The years passed. The centuries passed, and the ages. And we changed."

Norahn's wings swept wide. "Science was forgotten; we had no need for it. We fly. We *fly!*" Briefly her eyes were luminous with ecstasy. "It is decadence, perhaps, but we ask nothing more from the universe. It has been very long since any of us ventured beyond the negasphere. Indeed, it is forbidden. A curse falls on all who leave this world."

"A curse? What—"

"I do not know that. There have been some who ven-tured out in ships, but they did not return. The life is good here. We have our wings, and our cities. When we drift near the Darkness, we migrate."

Esterling said, "I don't understand. What is the dark-ness?"

"You will soon know. The tides bring us near to it now,

and soon we must find another island. You will see—"

It was a wall of blackness looming upon the horizon. A monstrous pile of cloudy dark, lit luridly by red flashes sparking intermittently through the gloom. The isle swept on toward it—and the bird-people made ready to depart.

"No life can exist in the Darkness," Norahn said. "The only land on this world are the floating isles, and they follow the tide. While they are on the lightside, we can dwell on them. When they enter the Darkness, we find another isle, till they have half-circled the planet and emerge once more."

Esterling stared at the great cloud. "What about your cities? Aren't they harmed?"

"No, we find everything as we left it. Our wise men say there is a certain radiation in the Darkness that destroys life—just as there are radiations here, in the sea, that give us power, and make us winged."

"How—' '

"I do not know. There are only legends." Norahn shrugged. "It does not matter. In a few hours we must leave for another isle. Be ready."

Esterling would never forget that strange migration across the glowing sea. Like a cloud the winged people rose, carrying the few belongings they needed—there were not many. Two Valkyries supported Esterling; others took charge of Beale and Damon. Their great wings carried them easily above the ocean.

Behind them the deserted islet drifted on into the Darkness.

Looking back, Esterling felt a tiny chill strike through him. His Norse blood thrilled to sudden warning. He thought of Jotunheim, the place of night, where the Frost Giants wait their time to break forth against the Aesir . . . .

The new isle was like the first, though larger, and with a greater expanse of forest. And the life was unchanged. The three Earthmen took little part in it; without wings,

they were handicapped. The existence of the winged
people went on without touching them, though Esterling
was not so far withdrawn as the others. He did not chafe.
He was content to watch, and to talk with Norahn; to see
her gliding above the shining sea.

Norahn told them they were prisoners. "If you can call
it that, when the freedom of our world is yours. But you
cannot leave. In the past, ships from your System have
sometimes crashed here, and men have survived. Not for
a long time, though. We treated them well. We took them
with us to safety when the isles reached the Darkness—
and in time they died. You will remain here, too."

"Why?" Damon asked.

"You would bring down the rest of your people upon
us. We are happy; we have passed the Age of Science, and
no longer need it. We are perfectly adapted to our environment. But we have great sources of power here. Your race
would want that power. Our planet would be ruined for
us. You would take our islands to build huge, ugly machines. Nor could we fight. We have forgotten how."

"You must have some weapons," Beale said.

"Perhaps—but we do not need them. We have hidden
our world; we guard it against intrusion—that is our greater
safety. We could not fight, nor do we wish to. Ages ago all
that died out of our race, soon after our science reached
its peak and froze there. All we need lies ready to our
hand, without further effort on our part."

"But the machines—" Beale persisted. "Don't they ever
break down? Don't they ever need repair?"

Norahn shrugged her shining wings. "They are so simple
a child could make repairs. That was the last interest that
held our scientists, so legend says—they worked until no
further need remained for invention, and then they worked
to simplify. Even one of you, who never saw a food-maker
or a *noyai*-loom before, could repair it in a few minutes
if it broke down. No, we have no need any longer for
weapons or invention or anything except—flight." Her

great wings lifted away from her body and quivered a little. "It tires me to be still and talk, even to you, Nils. I shall be back." She dropped from the tower and was gone into the cool, pearly light.

Beale said, "They have spaceships here, then." His voice was eager. "That's obvious, or Norahn wouldn't have bothered to tell us we were prisoners. And we could fly them if we could find them. I wonder where—"

"We'll find out," Damon told him.

Then the incredible happened. For a long time Esterling had been conscious of a curious sensation centering around his shoulder-blades. But he did not realize its significance till the day when, stripped to the waist, he was shaving before an improvised mirror. Damon, lounging by the balcony, said something in a surprised voice.

"Eh?" Esterling scraped at his cheek. "What's up?"

Instead of answering, Damon called for Beale. The scientist came out of an adjoining room, rubbing his eyes.

"Look at Esterling's back," the captain said. "Do you—"

Beale caught his breath. "Good heavens! Don't turn around, man; let me see."

"What is it?" Esterling squirmed before the mirror.

"Something's growing on your shoulder-blades. I'll be damned!" Damon murmured. "It can't be. *Norahn!*"

The girl's slim figure appeared above the balcony. "*Estan'ha?* Oh!" She leaped lightly to the floor and ran forward. "Be still, Nils." He felt her cool hand touch his back.

A queer, tingling excitement was pulsing within Esterling. Even before Norahn spoke, he guessed the truth.

"Wings," she said. "Yes—that is how they grow. From the buds, slowly expanding till they reach full size."

Damon had stripped off his shirt and was at the mirror. "Funny," he muttered. "I haven't got 'em. Have you, Beale?"

The scientist blinked. "Of course not. I haven't any

such recessive characteristics in my background. Nor have you."

Esterling looked at him. "What d'you mean?"

"The answer's obvious, isn't it? I'd wondered how the bracelet, with its rune about the Black Planet, came into your possession. It belonged to your great-grandmother, didn't it?"

"Gudrun. Yes. But—"

"What do you know about her?"

"Damned little," Esterling said. "She was supposed to be blonde, with blue eyes, and very lovely. There was some mystery about her. She didn't live long, and the bracelet was given to her son."

"There was space-travel in your great-grandmother's day," Beale said. "And Norahn said some of her people used to leave this world in their ships. They never came back. It's pretty obvious where Gudrun came from, isn't it?"

"She—she had no wings."

"Wings can be amputated. They're apparently a recessive characteristic, handed down to you from your great-grandmother."

Esterling was trembling a little. "Then why should they grow now? Why wasn't I born with them?"

Beale nodded toward the window, beyond which the shining sea rolled. "There are certain radiations on this planet—radiations that don't exist elsewhere in the System. You were born with wing-buds on your back. But they needed the right kind of environment to develop. That particular radiation exists here. If you'd never come to this world, you'd never have grown wings."

Norahn smiled happily into Esterling's eyes.

"Soon you can fly, Nils! I will show you the way—"

It was like recovering sight after being blind from birth. Flight, to Nils Esterling, unfolded vistas he had never known. The trick of it came with surprising ease. After the wings had reached their full development, the supporting muscles grew stronger, too. He never forgot that first flight. It was not long, but the feeling of complete and absolute freedom, the abrupt and easy checking of his fall, sent the blood singing through his veins. Flight was a heady drunkenness. The wine of it was stronger than any liquor Esterling had ever tasted.

And Norahn taught him, as she had promised.

He understood now the intoxication the winged people felt.

Earthly humanity had dropped from Esterling. He was one of the winged people now. Flight was his heritage, the high, keen delight of utter freedom, not bound by dimensions.

The islet swept on inexorably toward the Darkness.

It was time for the migration again. The winged folk rose and sped away, in search of a new home. Beale and Damon delayed, however. They were determined to remain with the island when it entered the Darkness.

At the window-opening Norahn watched the sky, where the great blackness grew momentarily more menacing. "It is dangerous. You will die."

Damon grunted. "The radiation might not harm us. And I'd like to know what's in the Darkness. Beale thinks—"

"Don't be a fool," Esterling said roughly. "You know damned well you can't live where the winged people can't. I can't stop you from committing suicide, I suppose. But what can you hope to gain by staying with the island?"

Illogically, Beale and Damon persisted in their arguments—persisted, while the Darkness grew nearer. Norahn's two companions grew more and more uneasy. At last they took flight, white-faced at their closeness to the barrier of the dark.

Esterling watched them go. "Okay," he said. Maybe Norahn and I can carry you. Make up your minds. Because we're leaving too—right now!"

Damon capitulated with surprising suddenness. "All

right. I suppose we'll have to. If you won't wait till we get nearer to the Darkness."

"We're near enough. You'll have to forget your curiosity, Beale. Norahn, can you call back some of your people to help?"

She shook her head. "They are too far. They will not remain on the isle when it drifts near the Darkness. But I can carry the little man easily."

"Okay. Get on my back, Damon. That's it. Lock your legs around my waist. Now—"

The wings were powerful. Beale was a small man, and Damon no giant. Esterling and Norahn dropped from the balcony, flung their pinions wide, and swooped up, gaining altitude. The islet slid away beneath them.

They flew on above the shining sea. Far in the distance was a smudge that showed where the bird-people were, in a close band.

"Listen," Damon said, into Esterling's ear, "those people have spaceships, don't they?"

"They used to."

"Where are they?"

"On some of the islands. None we've ever lived on, though."

"But you've seen them."

"From above—yeah."

"So have I. Once, when they carried us off to visit another island. I know where they are from here, allowing for tidal drift." There was a pause. Damon went on, "How'd you like to get off this world?"

Esterling smiled a little. "Funny. I've never thought of that. This place—I like it here."

"Well, I don't. How about dropping us where we can get at a spaceship?"

"One of theirs, you mean? Not a chance. For one thing, you couldn't fly it. For another, what about fuel? Remember, they haven't used the ships for ages."

"Oh, yes they have. Norahn told us about how some

of them go out into space and never return. And about how simple everything here is to operate. I'll gamble on the fuel. My guess is it's there ready—that's how machinery on this world seems to operate. And if the ship's that simple—well, I can handle anything that flies."

"And you'd be back with an army, wouldn't you? Norahn was right, Damon. This world should be kept isolated. The people here are happy."

"Happy, hell! Beale!" Damon's voice was sharp. Now!"

Esterling saw the scientist, a dozen yards away, move quickly. There was a gun in his hand. He pressed its muzzle against Norahn's temple. Simultaneously the Norseman felt a cold ring of steel touch his own temple.

"Take it easy," Damon said quietly. "Don't try any stunting. I can fire before you can drop me. So can Beale."

Esterling's face was white. "It's all right," he said, his voice unsteady. "Just keep on, Norahn."

"Yeah," Damon seconded. "Keep on. But in a different direction. You're going to take us to a spaceship, Esterling, or you and Norahn get your heads blown off."

"Where'd you get the guns?" he asked.

"Where they'd been hidden," Damon said. "I've been planning this for some time. I couldn't buck the whole gang of you, but I figured if I could get you and Norahn alone—"

"Yeah," Esterling said. "Yeah."

It was a long flight. Wing muscles were tired and aching when an islet grew in the distance from a tiny speck to a broad expanse. Beale shouted something and pointed.

Damon said into Esterling's ear, "I can see ships down there. No winged people, though. I guess they stay away from anything that reminds them of science. Go down— easy."

Obediently Esterling glided down the slopes of shining air, Norahn beside him. The silvery, torpedo-shaped rows of ships grew larger. Damon whistled at their design.

"I'll bet they're plenty fast!"

Esterling landed lightly. Damon leaped from his back, gun ready, waiting till Norahn and Beale were down.

"Keep your gun out," he said to the scientist. "I want to check up on this ship."

Its lock was childishly simple. In a moment he had vanished into the interior. The others waited tensely. Presently Beale reappeared, smiling.

"I was right. Simple instructions and controls. Anybody could operate who could astrogate. And there's plenty of fuel. Now, Esterling, what about going with us?"

The Norseman looked at Norahn.

"No," he said. "I'm staying."

Beale bit at his thin lips. "Drat it," he mumbled. "Damon, we should take some proof back with us—"

"We've got the ship."

"Sure. But when we bring men back here, it'll help to know as much as possible about the winged people. Perhaps they can't fight, but they've inherited weapons. We've never been able to locate them. Now Norahn could give us plenty of information—"

Esterling yelled, "Norahn! Get out of here! Quick!" He jumped Damon, his fist striking at the captain's gun. There was a rush of footsteps behind him, and something crashed down on his head with sickening force. Weakness ran like water through his body. He scarcely felt Damon's fist jolt against his jaw.

Dimly he heard Norahn scream. There was the thud of a valve closing, and then a fiery blast of rockets and a shriek of cleft air. Esterling, flat on his face, groaned weakly and tried to rise. It was useless.

A black speck dwindled in the sky.

"Norahn!" he said hoarsely. *"Norahn—"*

Somehow Esterling dragged himself to his hands and knees. He was blind and sick with pain, and his skull felt as though it had been fractured. But there was another spaceship looming through the trees, and he had to reach it—

Somehow he did. He never knew how. Somehow he stumbled along shining corridors and found an instrument board that swam before his eyes. Afterward he knew that he must have done the requisite things his reflexes were trained to do on any ship that plies the spaceways. He must have closed the valves and fallen into the astrogater's seat and found the proper instruments ready to his fumbling hands. But it was sheer will-power that did it.

When his head cleared the starry emptiness of space filled the visiplate before him. Already he was through the negasphere. Norahn's world had vanished. And for an instant he remembered the curse that was said to fall upon all natives who left that world.

After that was eternity. Esterling could not leave the controls; he scarcely dared glance away from the visiplate. And a throbbing, blazing ache inside his skull pounded at his brain.

Damon fled sunward. Esterling followed doggedly. They reached the orbit of Pluto.

And now at last, slowly, by infinite degrees, the fleeing ship grew larger in the visiplate.

Esterling manipulated the controls with dizzy recklessness. Now they were almost together, the hunter and the pursued. And now—now—

With a surprisingly light impact he crashed his ship against Damon's, and without pausing to see the results, turned to the rack where the spacesuits hung.

It was while getting into the suit that he noticed for the first time what had happened to his wings. The great shimmering pinions that had carried him over the glowing seas of Norahn's world were colorless—limp.

Out in the void, he kicked himself across to the other ship. He didn't head for the entrance lock; Damon would be expecting that move. Instead, Esterling drew himself, hand over hand, to the emergency escape hatch in the bow. He levered it open.

Beale was waiting for him.

Esterling looked to see that the bow compartment was airtight, the door sealed. Norahn was in this ship, and he had to be careful. But the valve was tight.

Beale fired. The bullet went through Esterling's suit and shoulder as he lurched aside. But it was only a flesh wound. He plugged the tear in the suit by bunching the fabric together with one hand, and with the other he reached back and opened the escape hatch.

Beale was not wearing an air-helmet.

He managed one more shot before his breath was wrenched out of his lungs, but the bullet went wild, spattering against metal. The blasting gust of wind racing out of the hatch pulled Beale with it, smashing him against Esterling. The scientist's finger clawed frantically at the other's suit.

Beale slid down, his eyes glaring, his tongue protruding. Esterling looked at the dead man without emotion.

He closed the hatch behind him, opened the door to the rest of the ship, and quickly removed the encumbering suit and helmet. Already fresh air had replaced the vacuum. Esterling picked up Beale's gun and stepped across the threshold.

Four strides took him to another door. He thrust it open.

He was facing Damon. In a corner of the control cabin lay Norahn, bound. Her wings were—withered.

Damon fired. The bullet struck Esterling somewhere. He took a step forward. Norahn was crying, very softly, like a hurt child.

Damon whispered, "Get back. Stay where you are. I'll—"

He thrust the gun forward, his finger contracting on the trigger. Esterling threw his own weapon straight at the other's face as he sprang. His right hand found Damon's gun-wrist. His left touched the corded muscles of a throat.

Norahn was crying, bitterly, hopelessly—

"I killed him," my father said. "With my hands. But he died only one death."

Breakers crashed beneath us in Thunder Fjord. The sky had grown light. Freya, the gerfalcon, hooded and asleep, stirred on Nils Esterling's shoulder.

I looked out at the dark sea. "You couldn't go back?"

"No. Those wings would never grow again. Only on the Black Planet could they ever have grown. Once withered—" he made a hopeless gesture—"Norahn and I were earth-bound. It was the legendary curse that fell on any of her folk who left that world. And—and she had been born to flight."

The sun's rim loomed on the horizon. Nils stared up into the burning rays.

"She wouldn't let me take her back. The Black Planet is for those with wings. Not for the earthbound. I brought her to Earth, Arn. I brought her here. She died when you were born. Scarcely a year. . . . We had happiness, but it was bitter-sweet. For we had known flight."

Nils unhooded the gerfalcon. Freya moved, ruffled her feathers, blinking a golden eye.

"Flight," my father said. "To stop flying is to die. Norahn died in a year. And for over forty years I have been chained here, remembering. Arn—" he slipped something from his arm and dropped it into my hand—"this is yours now. You're going into space. Your heritage is out there, beyond the orbit of Pluto, where the isles of the winged folk drift on the bright tides of Norahn's world. It's your world as well. In you are the seeds of flight."

He looked at the gerfalcon. "I have no words to tell you of your heritage, Arn. You will never know, till you have wings. And then—"

Nils Esterling stood up, casting the gerfalcon free. Freya screamed harshly. Her wings beat the air. She circled, mounted, climbing the winds.

My father's glaze brooded on me as I slipped the golden bracelet on my arm. He dropped back into the chair, as though exhausted.

"That's all, I suppose," he said wearily. "It's time for you to go. And—I'll say good-by."

I left him there. He did not watch me go. Once I turned, far down the path above Thunder Fjord, and Nils Esterling had not moved. He was looking up at Freya, wheeling in the blue.

The next time I looked, the outthrust of the crag hid the Hall. All I could see was the empty sky, and the gerfalcon circling there on splendid wings.

THE

STRANGE FLIGHT

OF RICHARD CLAYTON

---

by

ROBERT BLOCH

Richard Clayton braced himself so that he stood like a diver waiting to plunge from a high board into the blue. In truth he was a diver. A silver spaceship was his board, and he meant to plunge not down, but up into the blue sky. Nor was it a matter of twenty or thirty feet he meant to go—instead, he was plunging millions of miles.

With a deep breath, the pudgy, goateed scientist raised his hands to the cold steel level, closed his eyes, jerked. The switch moved downward.

For a moment nothing happened.

Then a sudden jerk threw Clayton to the floor. The *Future* was moving!

The pinions of a bird beating as it soars into the sky— the wings of a moth thrumming in flight—the quivering behind leaping muscles; of these things the shock was made.

The spaceship *Future* vibrated madly. It rocked from side to side, and a humming shook the steel walls. Richard Clayton lay dazed as a high-pitched droning arose within the vessel. He rose to his feet, rubbing a bruised forehead, and lurched to his tiny bunk. The ship was moving, yet the terrible vibration did not abate. He glanced at the controls and then swore softly.

"Good God! The panel is shattered!"

It was true. The instrument board had been broken by the shock. The cracked glass had fallen to the floor, and the dials swung aimlessly on the bare face of the panel.

Clayton sat there in despair. This was a major tragedy. His thoughts flashed back thirty years to the time when he, a boy of ten, had been inspired by Lindberg's flight. He recalled his studies; how he had utilized the money of his millionaire father to perfect a flying machine which would cross Space itself.

For years Richard Clayton had worked and dreamed and planned. He studied the Russians and their rockets, organized the Clayton Foundation and hired mechanics, mathematicians, astronomers, engineers to labor with him.

Then there had been the discovery of atomic propulsion, and the building of the *Future*. The *Future* was a shell of steel and duraluminum, windowless and insulated by a guarded process. In the tiny cabin were oxygen tanks, stores of food tablets, energizing chemicals, air-conditioning arrangements—and space for a man to walk six paces.

It was a small steel cell; but in it Richard Clayton meant to realize his ambitions. Aided in his soaring by rockets to get him past the gravitational pull of Earth, then flying by means of the atomic-discharge propulsion, Clayton meant to reach Mars and return.

It would take ten years to reach Mars; ten years to return, for the grounding of the vessel would set off additional rocket-discharges. A thousand miles an hour—not an imaginative "speed of light" journey, but a slow, grim voyage, scientifically accurate. The panels were set, and Clayton had no need to guide his vessel. It was automatic.

"But now what?" Clayton said, staring at the shattered glass. He had lost touch with the outer world. He would be unable to read his progress on the board, unable to judge time and distance and direction. He would sit here for ten, twenty years—all alone in a tiny cabin. There had been no room for books or paper or games to amuse him. He was a prisoner in the black void of Space.

The earth had already faded far below him; soon it would be a ball of burning green fire smaller than the ball of red fire ahead—the fire of Mars.

Crowds had swarmed the field to watch him take off; his assistant Jerry Chase had controlled them. Clayton pictured them watching his shining steel cylinder emerging from the gaseous smoke of the rockets and rushing like a bullet into the sky. Then his cylinder would have faded away into the blue and the crowds would leave for home and forget.

But he remained, here in the ship—for ten, for twenty years.

Yes, he remained, but when would the vibration stop? The shuddering of the walls and floor about him was awful to endure; he and the experts had not counted on this problem. Tremors wrenched through his aching head. What if they didn't cease, if they endured through the entire voyage? How long could he keep from going mad?

He could think. Clayton lay on his bunk and remembered—reviewed every tiny detail of his life from birth to the present. And soon he had exhausted all memory in a pitifully short time. Then he felt the horrible throbbing all about him.

"I can exercise," he said aloud, and paced the floor; six steps forward, six back. And he tired of that. Sighing. Clayton went to the food-stores in the cabinet and downed his capsules. "I can't even spend any time eating," he wryly observed. "A swallow and it's over."

The throbbing erased the grin from his face. It was maddening. He lay down once more in the lurching bunk; switched on oxygen in the close air. He would sleep, then; sleep if this damned thrumming would permit. He endured the horrid clanking that groaned all through the silence; switching off the light. His thoughts turned to his strange position; a prisoner in Space. Outside the burning planets wheeled, and stars whizzed in the inky blackness of spatial Nothingness. Here he lay safe and snug in a vibrating chamber; safe from the freezing cold. If only the awful jarring would stop!

Still, it had its compensations. There would be no newspapers on the voyage to torment him with accounts of man's inhumanity to man; no silly radio or television programs to annoy him. Only this cursed, omnipresent vibration. . . .

Clayton slept, hurtling through Space.

It was not daylight when he awoke. There was no daylight and no night. There was simply himself and the ship in Space. And the vibration was steady, nerve-wracking in its insistent beating against the brain. Clayton's legs trembled as he reached the cabinet and ate his pills.

Then, he sat down and began to endure. A terrific feeling of loneliness was beginning to assail him. He was so utterly detached here—cut off from everything. There was nothing to do. It was worse than being a prisoner in solitary confinement; at least they have larger cells, the sight of the sun, a breath of fresh air, and the glimpse of an occasional face.

Clayton had thought himself a misanthrope, a recluse. Now he longed for the sight of another's face. As the hours passed he got queer ideas. He wanted to see Life, in some form—he would have given a fortune for the company of even an insect in his soaring dungeon. The sound of a human voice would be heaven. He was so *alone*.

Nothing to do but endure the jerking, pace the floor, eat his pills, try to sleep. Nothing to think about. Clayton began to long for the time when his nails needed cutting; he could stretch out the task for hours.

He examined his clothes intently, stared for hours in the little mirror at his bearded face. He memorized his body, scrutinized every article in the cabin of the *Future*.

And still he was not tired enough to sleep again.

He had a throbbing headache constantly. At length he managed to close his eyes and drift off into another slumber, broken by shocks which startled him into waking.

When finally he arose and switched on the light, together with more oxygen, he made a horrible discovery.

He had lost his time-sense.

"Time is relative," they had always told him. Now he realized the truth. He had nothing to measure time by—no watch, no glimpse of the sun or moon or stars, and no regular activities. How long had he been on this voyage? Try as he might, he could not remember.

Had he eaten every six hours? Or every ten? Or every twenty? Had he slept once each day? Once every three or four days? How often had he walked the floor?

With no instruments to place himself he was at a total loss. He ate his pills in a bemused fashion, trying to think above the shuddering which filled his senses.

This was awful. If he lost track of Time he might soon lose consciousness of identity itself. He would go mad here in the spaceship as it plunged through the void to planets beyond. Alone, tormented in a tiny cell, he had to cling to something. What was Time?

He no longer wanted to think about it. He no longer wanted to think about anything. He had to forget the world he left, or memory would drive him frantic.

"I'm afraid," he whispered. "Afraid of being alone in the darkness. I may have passed the moon. I may be a million miles away from Earth by now—or ten million."

Then Clayton realized that he was talking to himself. That way was madness. But he couldn't stop, any more than he could stop the horrible jarring vibration all around him.

"I'm afraid," he whispered in a voice that sounded hollow in the tiny humming room. "I'm afraid. *What time is it?*"

He fell asleep, still whispering, and Time rushed on.

Clayton awoke with fresh courage. He had lost his grip, he reasoned. Outside pressure, however equalized, had affected his nerves. The oxygen might have made him giddy, and the pill diet was bad. But now the weakness had passed. He smiled, walked the floor.

Then the thoughts came again. What day was it? How many weeks since he had started? Maybe it was months already; a year, two years. Everything of Earth seemed far away; almost part of a dream. He now felt closer to Mars than to Earth; he began to anticipate now instead of looking back.

For a while everything had been mechanical. He switched light on and off when needed, ate pills by habit, paced the floor without thinking, unconsciously tended the air system, slept without knowing when or why.

Richard Clayton gradually forgot about his body and the surroundings. The lurching buzz in his brain became a part of him; an aching part which told that he was whizzing through Space in a silver bullet. But it meant nothing more, for Clayton no longer talked to himself. He forgot himself and dreamed only of Mars ahead. Every throb of the vessel hummed, "Mars—Mars—Mars."

A wonderful thing happened. He landed. The ship nosed down, trembling. It eased gently onto the gassy sward of the red planet. For a long time Clayton had felt the pull of alien gravity, knew that automatic adjustments of his vessel were diminishing the atomic discharges and using the natural gravitational pull of Mars itself.

Now the ship landed, and Clayton had opened the door. He broke the seals and stepped out. He bounded lightly to the purple grass. His body felt free, buoyant. There was fresh air, and the sunlight seemed stronger, more intense, although clouds veiled the glowing globe.

Far away stood the forests, the green forests with the

purple growth on the lushly-rearing trees. Clayton left the ship and approached the cool grove. The first tree had boughs that bent to the ground in two limbs.

Limbs—limbs they were! Two green arms reached out. Clawing branches grasped him and lifted him upward. Cold coils, slimy as a serpent's, held him tightly as he was pressed against the dark tree-trunk. And now he was staring into the purple growth set in the leaves.

The purple growths were—*heads.*

Evil, purple faces stared at him with rotting eyes like dead toadstools. Each face was wrinkled like a purple cauliflower, but beneath the pulpy mass was a great mouth. Every purple face had a purple mouth and each purple mouth opened to drip blood. Now the tree-arms pressed him closer to the cold, writhing trunk, and one of the purple faces—a woman's face—was moving up to kiss him.

The kiss of a vampire! Blood shone scarlet on the moving sensuous lips that bore down on his own. He struggled, but the limbs held him fast and the kiss came, cold as death. The icy flame of it seared through his being and his senses drowned.

Then Clayton awoke, and knew it was a dream. His body was bathed with moisture. It made him aware of his body. He tottered to the mirror.

A single glance sent him reeling back in horror. Was this too a part of his dream?

Gazing into the mirror, Clayton saw reflected the face of an aging man. The features were heavily bearded, and they were lined and wrinkled, the once puffy cheeks were sunken. The eyes were the worst—Clayton did not recognize his own eyes any more. Red and deep-set in bony sockets, they burned out in a wild stare of horror. He touched his face, saw the blue-veined hand rise in the mirror and run through graying hair.

Partial time-sense returned. He had been here for years. Years! He was growing old!

Of course the unnatural life would age him more rapidly,

but still a great interval must have passed. Clayton knew that he must soon reach the end of his journey. He wanted to reach it before he had any more dreams. From now on, sanity and physical reserve must battle against the unseen enemy of Time. He staggered back to his bunk, as trembling like a metallic flying monster, the *Future* rushed on in the blackness of interstellar Space.

They were hammering outside the vessel now; their iron arms were breaking in the door. The black metal monsters lumbered in with iron tread. Their stern, steel-cut faces were expressionless as they grasped Clayton on either side and pulled him out. Across the iron platform they dragged him, walking stiffly with clicking feet that clanged against the metal. The great steel shafts rose in silvery spires all about, and into the iron tower they took him. Up the stairs—clang, clang, clang, pounded the great metal feet.

And the iron stairs wound round endlessly; yet still they toiled. Their faces were set, and iron does not sweat. They never tired, though Clayton was a panting wreck ere they reached the dome and threw him before the Presence in the tower room. The metallic voice buzzed, mechanically, like a broken phonograph record.

"*We—found—him—in—a—bird—oh—Master.*"

"*He—is—made—of—soft—ness.*"

"*He—is—alive—in—some—strange—way.*"

"*An—an—im—al.*"

And then the booming voice from the center of the tower floor.

"*I hunger.*"

Rising on an iron throne from the floor, the Master. Just a great iron trap, with steel jaws like those on a steamshovel. The jaws clicked open, and the horrid teeth gleamed. A voice came from the depths.

"*Feed me.*"

They threw Clayton forward in iron arms, and he fell into the trap-jaws of the monster. The jaws closed, champing with relish on human flesh. . . .

Clayton woke screaming. The mirror gleamed as his trembling hands found the light-switch. He stared into the face of an aging man with almost white hair. Clayton was growing old. And he wondered if his brain would hold out.

Eat pills, walk cabin, listen to the throbbing, put on air, lie on bunk. That was all, now. And the rest—waiting. Waiting in a humming torture-chamber, for hours, days, years, centuries, untold eons.

In every eon, a dream. He landed on Mars and the ghosts came coiling out of a gray fog. They were shapes in the fog, like slimy ectoplasm, and he saw through them. But they coiled and came, and their voices were faint whispers in his soul.

"Here is Life," they whispered. "We, whose souls have crossed the Void in death, have waited for Life to feast on. Let us take our feasting now."

And they smothered him under gray blankets, and sucked with gray, prickling mouths at his blood. . . .

Again he landed on the planet and there was nothing. Absolutely nothing. The ground was bare and it stretched off into horizons of nothingness. There was no sky nor sun, merely the ground; endless in all directions.

He set foot on it, cautiously. He sank down into nothingness. The nothingness was throbbing now, like the ship throbbed, and it was engulfing him. He was falling into a deep pit without sides, and the oblivion closed all about him. . . .

Clayton dreamed this one standing up. He opened his eyes before the mirror. His legs were weak and he steadied himself with hands that shook with age. He looked at the face in the glass—the face of a man of seventy.

"God!" he muttered. It was his own voice—the first sound he had heard in how long? How many years? For how long had he heard nothing above the hellish vibrations of this ship? How far had the *Future* gone? He was old already.

A horrid thought bit into his brain. Perhaps something

had gone wrong. Maybe the calculations were at fault and he was moving into Space too slowly. He might never reach Mars. Then again—and it was a dreadful possibility —he had passed Mars, missed the carefully charted orbit of the planet. Now he was plunging on into empty voids beyond.

He swallowed his pills and lay down in the bunk. He felt a little calmer now; he had to be. For the first time in ages he remembered Earth.

Suppose it had been destroyed? Invaded by war or pestilence or disease while he was gone? Or meteors had struck it, some dying star had flamed death upon it from maddened heavens. Ghastly notions assailed him—what if Invaders crossed Space to conquer Earth, just as he now crossed to Mars?

But no sense in worrying about *that*. The problem was reaching his own goal. Helpless, he had to wait; maintain life and sanity long enough to achieve his aims. In the vibrating horror of his cell, Clayton took a mighty resolve with all his waning strength. He *would* live and when he landed he would see Mars. Whether or not he died on the long voyage home, he would exist until his goal was reached. He would fight against dreams from this moment on. No means of telling Time—only a long daze, and the humming of this infernal spaceship. But he'd live.

There were voices coming now, from outside the ship. Ghosts howled, in the dark depths of Space. Visions of monsters and dreams of torment came, and Clayton repulsed them all. Every hour or day or year—he no longer knew which—Clayton managed to stagger to the mirror. And always it showed that he was aging rapidly. His snow-white hair and wrinkled countenance hinted at incredible senility. But Clayton lived. He was too old to think any longer, and too weary. He merely lived in the droning of the ship.

At first he didn't realize. He was lying on his bunk and

his rheumy eyes were closed in stupor. Suddenly he became aware that the lurching had stopped. Clayton knew he must be dreaming again. He drew himself up painfully, rubbed his eyes. No—the *Future* was still. It had *landed!*

He was trembling uncontrollably. Years of vibration had done this; years of isolation with only his crazed thoughts for company. He could scarcely stand.

But this was the moment. This was what he had waited for ten long years. No, it must have been many more years. But he could see Mars. He had made it—done the impossible!

It was an inspiring thought. But somehow, Richard Clayton would have given it all up if he could only have learned what time it was, and heard it from a human voice.

He staggered to the door—the long-sealed door. There was a lever here.

His aged heart pumped with excitement as he pulled the lever upward. The door opened—sunlight crept through—air rushed in—the light made him blink and the air wheezed in his lungs—his feet were moving out—

Clayton fell forward into the arms of Jerry Chase.

Clayton didn't know it was Jerry Chase. He didn't know anything any longer. It had been too much.

Chase was staring down at the feeble body in his arms.

"Where's Mr. Clayton?" he murmured. "Who are you?" He stared at the aged, wrinkled face.

"Why—it's Clayton! he breathed. "Mr. Clayton, what's wrong, sir? The atomic discharges failed when you started the ship, and all that happened was that they kept blasting. The ship never left the earth, but the violence of the discharges kept us from reaching you until now. We couldn't get to the *Future* until they stopped. Just a little while ago the ship finished shuddering, but we've been watching night and day. What happened to you, sir?"

The faded blue eyes of Richard Clayton opened. His mouth twitched as he faintly whispered.

"I—lost track of Time. How—how long was I in the *Future?*"

Jerry Chase's face was grave as he stared again at the old man and answered, softly.

"*Just one week.*"

And as Richard Clayton's eyes glazed in death, the long voyage ended.

WAKE FOR
THE LIVING

by

RAY BRADBURY

There was any amount of banging and hammering for a number of days along with deliveries of metal parts and oddments which Mr. Charles Braling took into his little workshop with feverish anxiety. He was a dying man, a badly dying man, and he seemed to be in a great hurry, between racking coughs and spitting, to piece together one last invention.

"What are you doing?" inquired his younger brother, Richard Braling. He had listened with increasing difficulty and much curiosity to that banging and rattling about, and now he stuck his head through the workroom door.

"Go far, far away and let me alone," said Charles Braling, who was seventy, trembly and wet-lipped most of the time. He trembled nails into place and trembled a hammer down with a weak blow upon a large timber and then stuck a small metal ribbon down into an intricate machine, and, all in all, was having a carnival of labor.

Richard looked on, bitter-eyed, for a long moment. There was a hatred between them. It had gone on for some years and now was neither better nor worse for the fact that Charlie was dying. Richard was delighted to know of the impending death, if he thought of it at all. But this busy fervor of his brother's stimulated him.

"Pray tell," he asked, not moving from the door.

"If you must know," snarled old Charles, fitting in an old thingumabob on the box before him, "I'll be dead in another week and I'm—I'm building my own coffin!"

"A coffin, my dear Charlie; that doesn't *look* like a coffin. A coffin isn't that complex. Come on now, what *are* you up to?"

"I tell you it is a coffin! An odd coffin, yes, but, nevertheless—" the old man moved his fingers around within the large box—"nevertheless a coffin!"

"But it would be easier to buy one."

"Not one like this! You couldn't buy one like this any place, ever. Oh, it will be a really fine coffin, all right."

"You're obviously lying." Richard moved forward. "Why, that coffin is a good twelve feet long. Six feet longer than normal size!"

"Oh, yes?" The old man laughed quietly.

"And that transparent top; who ever heard of a coffin lid you can see through? What good is a transparent lid to a corpse?"

"Oh, just never you mind at all," sang the old man heartily. "La!" And he went humming and hammering about the shop.

"This coffin is terribly thick," shouted the young brother over the din. "Why, it must be five feet thick; how utterly unnecessary!"

"I only wish I might live to patent this amazing coffin," said old Charlie. "It would be a God-send to all the poor peoples of the world. Think how it would eliminate the expense of most funerals. Oh, but, of course, you don't know how it would do that, do you? How silly of me. Well, I

shan't tell you. If this coffin could be mass-produced—
expensive at first, naturally—but then when you finally got
them made in vast quantities, ah, but the money people
would save."

"To hell with it!" And the younger brother stormed out
of the shop.

It had been an unpleasant life. Young Richard had always
been such a bounder he had never had two coins to clink
together at one time; all of his money had come from old
brother Charlie, who had the indecency to remind him of
it at all times. Richard spent many hours with his hobbies;
he dearly loved piling up bottles with French wine labels,
in the garden. "I like the way they *glint*," he often said,
sitting and sipping and sipping and sitting. He was the
man in the county who could hold the longest gray ash on
a fifty-cent cigar for the longest recorded time. And he knew
how to hold his hands so his diamonds jangled in the light.
But he had not bought the wine, the diamonds, the cigars—
no! They were all gifts. He was never allowed to buy anything himself. It was always brought to him and given to
him. He had to ask for everything, even writing paper. He
considered himself quite a martyr to have put up with
taking things from that rickety old brother for so long a
time. Everything Charlie ever laid his hand to turned to
money; everything Richard ever tried in the way of a
leisurely career had failed.

And now, here was this old mole of a Charlie whacking
out a new invention which would probably bring Charlie
additional specie long after his bones were slotted in the
earth!

Well, two weeks passed.

One morning the old brother toddled upstairs and stole
the insides from the electric phonograph. Another morning
he raided the gardener's greenhouse. Still another time he
received a delivery from a medical company. It was all
young Richard could do to sit and hold his long gray cigar
ash steady while these murmuring excursions took place.

"I'm finished!" cried old Charlie on the fourteenth morning, and dropped dead.

Richard finished out his cigar and, without showing his inner excitement, he laid down his cigar with its fine long whitish ash, two inches long, a real record, and arose.

He walked to the window and watched the sunlight playfully glittering among the fat beetle-like champagne bottles in the garden.

He looked toward the top of the stairs where dear old brother Charlie lay peacefully sprawled against the banister. Then he walked to the phone and perfunctorily dialed a number.

"Hello, Green Lawn Mortuary? This is the Braling residence. Will you send around a wicker, please? Yes. For brother Charlie. Yes. Thank you. Thank you."

As the mortuary people were taking brother Charles out in their wicker, they received instructions. "Ordinary casket," said young Richard. "No funeral service. Put him in a pine coffin. He would have preferred it that way— simple. Good-bye."

"Now!" said Richard, rubbing his hands together. "We shall see about this 'coffin' built by dear Charlie. I do not suppose he will realize he is not being buried in his 'special' box. Ah."

He entered the downstairs shop.

The coffin sat before some wide-flung French windows, the lid shut, complete and neat, all put together like the fine innards of a Swiss watch. It was vast, and it rested upon a long long table with rollers beneath for easy maneuvering.

The coffin interior, as he peered through the glass lid, was six feet long. There must be a good three feet of false body at both head and foot of the coffin, then. Three feet at each end which, covered by secret panels that he must find some way of opening, might very well reveal—exactly what?

Money, of course. It would be just like Charlie to suck his

riches into his grave with himself, leaving Richard with not a cent to buy a bottle with. The old tight-wad!

He raised the glass lid and felt about, but found no hidden buttons. There was a small sign studiously inked on white paper, thumb-tacked to the side of the satin-lined box. It said:

THE BRALING ECONOMY CASKET. Simple to operate. Can be used again and again by morticians and families with an eye to the future.

Richard snorted thinly. Who did Charlie think he was fooling?

There was more writing:

DIRECTIONS: SIMPLY PLACE BODY IN COFFIN.

What a fool thing to say. Put body in coffin! Naturally! How else would one go about it? He peered intently and finished out the directions:

SIMPLY PLACE BODY IN COFFIN—AND MUSIC WILL START.

"*It can't be!*" Richard gaped at the sign. "Don't tell me all this work has been for a—" He went to the open door of the shop, walked out upon the tiled terrace and called to the gardener in his greenhouse. "Rogers!" The gardener stuck his head out. "What time is it?" asked Richard.

"Twelve o'clock, sir," replied Rogers.

"Well, at twelve-fifteen, you come up here and check to see if everything is all right, Rogers," Yes, sir," said the gardener. Richard turned and walked back into the shop. "We'll find out—" he said, quietly.

There would be no harm in lying in the box, testing it. He noticed small ventilating holes in the sides. Even if the lid were closed down there'd be air. And Rogers would be up in a moment or two. Simply place body in coffin—and music will start. Really, how naive of old Charlie. Richard hoisted himself up.

He was like a man getting into a bathtub. He felt naked and watched over. He put one shiny shoe into the coffin, and crooked his knee and eased himself up and made some little remark to nobody in particular; then he put in his other knee and foot and crouched there, as if undecided about the temperature of the bath-water. Edging himself about, chuckling softly, he lay down, pretending to himself; "for it was fun pretending that he was dead, that people were dropping tears on him, that candles were fuming and illuminating and that the world was stopped in mid-stride because of his passing. He put on a long pale expression, shut his eyes, holding back the laughter in himself behind pressed, quivering lips. He folded his hands and decided they felt waxen and cold.

Whirr! Spung! Something whispered inside the box-wall. *Spung!*

The lid slammed down on him!

From outside, if one had just come into the room, one would have imagined a wild man was kicking, pounding, blathering and shrieking inside a closet! There was a sound of a body dancing and cavorting. There was a thundering of flesh and fists. There was a squeaking and a kind of wind from a frightened man's lungs. There was a rustling like paper and a shrilling as of many pipes simultaneously played. Then there was a real fine scream. Then—silence.

Richard Braling lay in the coffin and relaxed. He let loose all his muscles. He began to chuckle. The smell of the box was not unpleasant. Through the little perforation he drew more than enough air to live comfortably on. He need only push gently up with his hands, with none of this kicking and screaming, and the lid would open. One must be calm. He flexed his arms.

The lid was locked.

Well, still there was no danger. Rogers would be up in a minute or two. There was nothing to fear.

The music began to play.

It seemed to come from somewhere inside the head of the coffin. It was fine music. Organ music, very slow and melancholy, typical of Gothic arches and long black tapers. It smelled of earth and whispers. It echoed high between stone walls. It was so sad that one almost cried listening to it. It was music of potted plants and crimson and blue-stained glass windows. It was late sun at twilight and a cold wind blowing. It was a dawn with only fog and a far away fog-horn moaning.

"Charlie, Charlie, Charlie, you old fool, you! So this is your odd coffin!" Tears of laughter welled into Richard's eyes. "Nothing more than a coffin which plays its own dirge. Oh, my sainted grandma!"

He lay and listened critically, for it was beautiful music and there was nothing he could do until Rogers came up and let him out. His eyes roved aimlessly; his fingers tapped soft little rhythms on the satin cushions. He crossed his legs, idly. Through the glass lid he saw sunlight shooting through the French windows, dust particles dancing on in. It was a lovely blue day with wisps of clouds overhead.

The sermon began.

The organ music quieted and a gentle voice said:

"We are gathered together, those who loved and those who knew the deceased, to give him our homage and our due—"

"Charlie, bless you, that's *your* voice!" Richard was delighted. A mechanical, transcribed funeral, by God! Organ music and lecture, on records! And Charlie giving his own oration for himself!

The soft voice said, "We who knew and loved him are grieved at the passing of—"

"What was *that?*" Richard raised himself, startled. He didn't quite believe what he had heard. He repeated it to himself just the way he had heard it:

"We who knew and loved him are grieved at the passing of Richard Braling."

That's what the voice had said.

"Richard Braling," said the man in the coffin. "Why, *I'm* Richard Braling,"

A slip of the tongue, naturally. Merely a slip. Charlie had

meant to say, *Charles* Braling. Certainly. Yes. Of course. Yes. Certainly. Yes. Naturally. Yes.

"Richard was a fine man," said the voice, talking on. "We shall see no finer in our time."

"My name, *again!*"

Richard began to move above uneasily in the coffin.

Why didn't Rogers come?

It was hardly a mistake, using that name twice. Richard Braling. Richard Braling. We are gathered here. We shall miss . . . We are grieved. No finer man. No finer in our time. We are gathered here. The deceased. Richard Braling. *Richard* Braling.

Whirrr! Spunng!

Flowers! Six dozen bright blue, red, yellow, sun-brilliant flowers leaped up from behind the coffin on concealed springs!

The sweet odor of fresh-cut flowers filled the coffin. The flowers swayed gently before his amazed vision, tapping silently on the glass lid. Others sprang up, and up, until the coffin was banked with petals and color and sweet odors. Gardenias and dahlias and petunias and daffodils, trembling and shining.

"Rogers!"

The sermon continued.

". . . Richard Braling, in his life, was a connoisseur of great and good things. . . ."

The music sighed, rose and fell, distantly.

". . . Richard Braling savored of life as one savors of a rare wine, holding it upon the lips. . . ."

A small panel in the side of the box flipped open. A swift bright metal arm snatched out. A needle stabbed Richard in the thorax, not very deeply. He screamed. The needle shot him full of a colored liquid before he could seize it. Then it popped back into a receptacle and the panel snapped shut.

"Rogers!"

A growing numbness. Suddenly he could not move his fingers or his arms or turn his head. His legs were cold and limp.

"Richard Braling loved beautiful things. Music. Flowers," said the voice.

"Rogers!"

This time he did not scream it. He could only think it. His tongue was motionless in his anaesthetized mouth.

Another panel opened. Metal forceps issued forth on steel arms. His left wrist was pierced by a huge sucking needle.

His blood was being drained from his body.

He heard a little pump working somewhere.

". . . Richard Braling will be missed among us. . . ."

The organ sobbed and murmured.

The flowers looked down upon him, nodding their bright-petaled heads. Six candles, black and slender, rose up out of hidden receptacles and stood behind the flowers, flickering and glowing.

Another pump started to work. While his blood drained out one side of his body, his right wrist was punctured, held, a needle shoved into it, and the second pump began to force formaldehyde into him.

Pump, pause, *pump*, pause, *pump*, pause, *pump*, pause.
The coffin moved.

A small motor popped and chugged. The room drifted by on either side of him. Little wheels revolved. No pallbearers were necessary. The flowers swayed as the casket moved gently out upon the terrace under a blue clear sky.

Pump, pause. *Pump*, pause.

"Richard Braling will be missed by all his. . . ."

Sweet soft music.

Pump, pause.

"Ah, sweet mystery of life, at last . . ." Singing.

"Braling, the gourmet . . ."

"Ah, I know at last the secret of it all. . . ."

Staring, staring, his eyes egg-blind, at the little card out of the corners of his eyes: THE BRALING ECONOMY CASKET.

Directions: *Simply place body in coffin—and music will start.*

A tree swung by overhead. The coffin rolled gently through the garden, behind some bushes, carrying the voice and the music with it.

"Now it is the time when we must consign this part of this man to the earth. . . ."

Little shining spades leaped out of the sides of the casket.

They began to dig.

He saw the spades toss up dirt. The coffin settled. Bumped, settled, dug, bumped, and settled, dug, bumped and settled again.

Pump, pause, *pump*, pause, *pump*, pause, *pump*, pause.

"Ashes to ashes, dust to dust. . . ."

The flowers glistened and waved. The box was deep. The music played.

The last thing Richard Braling saw was the spading arms of the Braling Economy Casket reaching up and pulling the hole in after it.

"Richard Braling, Richard Braling, Richard Braling, Richard Braling, Richard Braling. . . ."

The record was stuck.

Nobody minded. Nobody was listening.

BEFORE EDEN

by

ARTHUR C. CLARKE

I guess," said Jerry Garfield, cutting the engines, "that this is the end of the line." With a gentle sigh, the underjets faded out; deprived of its air-cushion, the scout-car *Rambling Wreck* settled down upon the twisted rocks of the Hesperian Plateau.

There was no way forward; neither on its jets nor its tractors could S.5—to give the *Wreck* its official name—scale the escarpment that lay ahead. The South Pole of Venus was only thirty miles away, but it might have been on another planet. They would have to turn back, and retrace their four-hundred-mile journey through this nightmare landscape.

The weather was fantastically clear, with visibility of almost a thousand yards. There was no need of radar to show the cliffs ahead; for once, the naked eye was good enough. The green auroral light, filtering down through clouds that had rolled unbroken for a million years, gave the scene an underwater appearance, and the way in which all distant objects blurred into the haze added to the impression. Sometimes it was easy to believe that they were driving across a shallow sea-bed, and more than once Jerry had imagined that he had seen fish floating overhead.

"Shall I call the ship, and say we're turning back?" he asked.

"Not yet," said Dr. Hutchins. "I want to think."

Jerry shot an appealing glance at the third member of the crew, but found no moral support there. Coleman was just as bad; although the two men argued furiously half the time, they were both scientists and therefore, in the opinion of a hard-headed engineer-navigator, not wholly responsible citizens. If Cole and Hutch had bright ideas about going forward, there was nothing he could do except register a protest.

Hutchins was pacing back and forth in the tiny cabin, studying charts and instruments. Presently he swung the car's searchlight towards the cliffs, and began to examine them carefully with binoculars. Surely, thought Jerry, he doesn't expect me to drive up there! S.5 was a hover-track, not a mountain goat. . . .

Abruptly, Hutchins found something. He released his breath in a sudden explosive gasp, then turned to Coleman.

"Look!" he said, his voice full of excitement. "Just to the left of that black mark! Tell me what you see."

He handed over the glasses, and it was Coleman's turn to stare.

"Well I'm damned," he said at length. "You were right. There *are* rivers on Venus. That's a dried-up waterfall."

"So you owe me one dinner at the Bel Gourmet when we get back to Cambridge. With champagne."

"No need to remind me. Anyway, it's cheap at the price. But this still leaves your other theories strictly on the crackpot level."

"Just a minute," interjected Jerry. "What's all this about

rivers and waterfalls? Everyone knows they can't exist on Venus. It never gets cold enough on this steam-bath of a planet for the clouds to condense."

"Have you looked at the thermometer lately?" asked Hutchins with deceptive mildness.

"I've been slightly too busy driving."

"Then I've news for you. It's down to 230, and still falling. Don't forget—we're almost at the Pole, it's wintertime, and we're sixty thousand feet above the lowlands. All this adds up to a distinct nip in the air. If the temperature drops a few more degrees, we'll have rain. The water will be boiling, of course—but it will be water. And though George won't admit it yet, this puts Venus in a completely different light."

"Why?" asked Jerry, though he had already guessed.

"Where there's water, there may be life. We've been in too much of a hurry to assume that Venus is sterile, merely because the average temperature's over five hundred degrees. It's a lot colder here, and that's why I've been so anxious to get to the Pole. There are lakes up here in the highlands, and I want to look at them."

"But *boiling* water!" protested Coleman. "Nothing could live in that!"

"There are algae that manage it on Earth. And if we've learned one thing since we started exploring the planets, it's this—wherever Life has the slightest chance of surviving, you'll find it. This is the only chance it's ever had on Venus."

"I wish we could test your theory. But you can see for yourself—we can't go up that cliff."

"Perhaps not in the car. But it won't be too difficult to climb those rocks, even wearing thermosuits. All we need do is walk a few miles towards the Pole; according to the radar maps, it's fairly level once you're over the rim. We could manage in—oh, twelve hours at the most. Each of us has been out for longer than that, in much worse conditions."

That was perfectly true. Protective clothing that had been designed to keep men alive in the Venusian lowlands would have an easy job here, where it was only a hundred degrees hotter than Death Valley in midsummer.

"Well," said Coleman. "You know the regulations. You can't go by yourself, and someone has to stay here to keep contact with the ship. How do we settle it this time—chess or cards?"

"Chess takes too long," said Hutchins, "especially when you two play it." He reached into the chart table and produced a well-worn pack. "Cut them, Jerry."

"Ten of spades. Hope you can beat it, George."

"So do I. Damn—only five of clubs. Well, give my regards to the Venusians."

Despite Hutchins' assurance, it was hard work climbing the escarpment. The slope was not too steep, but the weight of oxygen gear, refrigerated thermosuit and scientific equipment came to more than a hundred pounds per man. The lower gravity—thirteen percent weaker than Earth's—gave a little help, but not much, as they toiled up screes, rested on ledges to regain breath, and then clambered on again through the submarine twilight. The emerald glow that washed around them was brighter than that of the full moon on Earth. A moon would have been wasted on Venus, Jerry told himself; It could never have been seen from the surface, there were no oceans for it to rule—and the incessant aurora was a far more constant source of light.

They had climbed over two thousand feet before the ground levelled out into a gentle slope, scarred here and there by channels that had clearly been cut by running water. After a little searching, they came across a gulley wide and deep enough to merit the name of river-bed, and started to walk along it.

"I've just thought of something," said Jerry after they had travelled a few hundred yards. "Suppose there's a storm up ahead of us? I don't feel like facing a tidal wave of boiling water."

"If there's a storm," replied Hutchins a little impatiently, "we'll hear it. There'll be plenty of time to reach high ground."

He was undoubtedly right, but Jerry felt no happier as they continued to climb the gently-shelving water-course. His uneasiness had been growing ever since they had passed over the brow of the cliff and had lost radio contact with the scout-car. In this day and age, to be out of touch with one's fellowmen was a unique and unsettling experience. It had never happened to Jerry before in all his life; even aboard the *Morning Star,* when they were a hundred million miles from Earth, he could always send a message to his family and get a reply back within minutes. But now, a few yards of rock had cut him off from the rest of mankind; if anything happened to them here, no one would ever know, unless some later expedition found their bodies. George would wait for the agreed number of hours; then he would head back to the ship—alone. I guess I'm not really the pioneering type, Jerry told himself. I like running complicated machines, and that's how I got involved in spaceflight. But I never stopped to think where it would lead, and now it's too late to change my mind.

They had travelled perhaps three miles towards the Pole, following the meanders of the river-bed, when Hutchins stopped to make observations and collect specimens. "Still getting colder!" he said. "The temperature's down to 199. That's far and away the lowest ever recorded on Venus. I wish we could call George and let him know."

Jerry tried all the wavebands; he even attempted to raise the ship—the unpredictable ups and downs of the planet's ionosphere sometimes made such long-distance reception possible—but there was not a whisper of a carrier-wave above the roar and crackle of the Venusian thunderstorms.

"This is even better," said Hutchins, and now there was real excitement in his voice. "The oxygen concentration's way up—fifteen parts in a million. It was only five back at the car, and down in the lowlands you can scarcely detect it."

"But fifteen in a *million!*" protested Jerry. "Nothing could breathe that!"

"You've got hold of the wrong end of the stick," Hutchins explained. "Nothing does breathe it. Something *makes* it. Where do you think Earth's oxygen comes from? It's all produced by life—by growing plants. Before there were plants on Earth, our atmosphere was just like this one— a mess of carbon dioxide and ammonia and methane. Then vegetation evolved, and slowly converted the atmosphere into something that animals could breathe."

"I see," said Jerry, "and you think that the same process has just started here?"

"It looks like it. *Something* not far from here is producing oxygen—and plant life is the simplest explanation."

"And where there are plants," mused Jerry, "I suppose you'll have animals, sooner or later."

"Yes,' said Hutchins, packing his gear and starting up the gulley, "though it takes a few hundred million years. We may be too soon—but I hope not."

"That's all very well," Jerry answered. "But suppose we meet something that doesn't like us? We've no weapons."

"And we don't need them. Have you stopped to think what we look like? Obviously any animal would run a mile at the sight of us."

There was some truth in that. The reflecting metal foil of their thermosuits covered them from head to foot like flexible, glittering armor. No insects had more elaborate antennae than those mounted on their helmets and back-packs, and the wide lenses through which they stared out at the world looked like blank yet monstrous eyes. Yes, there were few animals on Earth that would stop to argue with such apparitions; but any Venusians might have different ideas.

Jerry was still mulling this over when they came upon the lake. Even at that first glimpse, it made him think not of the life they were seeking, but of death. Like a black mirror, it lay amid a fold of the hills; its far edge was hidden in the eternal mist, and ghostly columns of vapor swirled and danced upon its surface. All it needed, Jerry told himself, was Charon's ferry waiting to take them to the other side—or the Swan of Tuonela swimming majestically back and forth as it guarded the entrance to the Underworld. . . .

Yet for all this, it was a miracle—the first free water that men had ever found on Venus. Hutchins was already on his knees, almost in an attitude of prayer. But he was only collecting drops of the precious liquid to examine through his pocket microscopes.

"Anything there?" asked Jerry anxiously.

Hutchins shook his head.

"If there is, it's too small to see with this instrument. I'll tell you more when we're back at the ship." He sealed a test-tube and placed it in his collecting-bag, as tenderly as any prospector who had just found a nugget laced with gold. It might be—it probably was—nothing more than plain water. But it might also be a universe of unknown, living creatures on the first stage of their billion-year journey to intelligence.

Hutchins had walked no more than a dozen yards along the edge of the lake when he stopped again, so suddenly that Garfield nearly collided with him.

"What's the matter?" Jerry asked. "Seen something?"

"That dark patch of rock over there. I noticed it before we stopped at the lake."

"What about it? It looks ordinary enough to me."

"I think it's grown bigger."

All his life, Jerry was to remember this moment. Somehow he never doubted Hutchins' statement; by this time he could believe anything, even that rocks could grow. The sense of isolation and mystery, the presence of that dark and brooding lake, the never-ceasing rumble of distant storms and the green flickering of the aurora—all these had done something to his mind, had prepared it to face the incredible. Yet he felt no fear; that would come later.

He looked at the rock. It was about five hundred feet away, as far as he could estimate. In this dim, emerald light it was hard to judge distances or dimensions. The rock—or whatever it was—seemed to be a horizontal slab of almost black material, lying near the crest of a low ridge. There was a second, much smaller, patch of similar material near it; Jerry tried to measure and memorize the gap between them, so that he would have some yard-stick to detect any change.

Even when he saw that the gap was slowly shrinking, he still felt no alarm—only a puzzled excitement. Not until it had vanished completely, and he realized how his eyes had tricked him, did that awful feeling of helpless terror strike into his heart.

Here were no growing or moving rocks. What they were watching was a dark tide, a crawling carpet, sweeping slowly but inexorably towards them over the top of the ridge.

The moment of sheer, unreasoning panic lasted, mercifully, no more than a few seconds. Garfield's first terror began to fade as soon as he recognized its cause. For that advancing tide had reminded him, all too vividly, of a story he had read many years ago about the army ants of the Amazon, and the way in which they destroyed everything in their path. . . .

But whatever this tide might be, it was moving too slowly to be a real danger, unless it cut off their line of retreat. Hutchins was staring at it intently through their only pair of binoculars; he was the biologist, and he was holding his ground. No point in making a fool of myself, thought Jerry, by running like a scalded cat, if it isn't necessary.

"For heaven's sake," he said at last, when the moving carpet was only a hundred yards away and Hutchins had not uttered a word or stirred a muscle. "What *is* it?"

Hutchins slowly unfroze, like a statue coming to life.

"Sorry," he said. "I'd forgotten all about you. It's a plant, of course. At least I suppose we'd better call it that."

"But it's *moving!*"

"Why should that surprise you? So do terrestrial plants. Ever seen speeded-up movies of ivy in action?"

"That still stays in one place—it doesn't crawl all over the landscape."

"Then what about the plankton plants of the sea? *They* can swim when they have to."

Jerry gave up; in any case, the approaching wonder had robbed him of words.

He still thought of the thing as a carpet—a deep pile one, ravelled into tassels at the edges. It varied in thickness as it moved; in some parts it was a mere film; in others, it heaped up to a depth of a foot or more. As it came closer and he could see its texture, Jerry was reminded of black velvet. He wondered what it felt like to the touch, then remembered that it would burn his fingers even if it did nothing else to them. He found himself thinking, in the light-headed nervous reaction that often follows a sudden shock: "If there *are* any Venusians, we'll never be able to shake hands with them. They'd burn us, and we'd give them frost-bite."

So far, the thing had shown no signs that it was aware of their presence. It had merely flowed forward like the mindless tide that it almost certainly was. Apart from the fact that it climbed over small obstacles, it might have been an advancing flood of water.

And then, when it was only ten feet away, the velvet tide checked itself. On the right and the left, it still flowed forward; but dead ahead it slowed to a halt.

"We're being encircled," said Jerry anxiously. "Better fall back, until we're sure it's harmless."

To his relief, Hutchins stepped back at once. After a brief hesitation, the creature resumed its slow advance and the dent in its front line straightened out.

Then Hutchins stepped forward again—and the thing

slowly withdrew. Half a dozen times the biologist advanced, only to retreat again, and each time the living tide ebbed and flowed in synchronism with his movements. I never imagined, Jerry told himself, that I'd live to see a man waltzing with a plant. . . .

"Thermophobia," said Hutchins. "Purely automatic re-action. It doesn't like our heat."

"Our heat!" protested Jerry. "Why, we're living icicles by comparison."

"Of course—but our suits aren't, and that's all it knows about."

Stupid of me, thought Jerry. When you were snug and cool inside your thermosuit, it was easy to forget that the refrigeration unit on your back was pumping a blast of heat out into the surrounding air. No wonder the Venusian plant had shied away.

"Let's see how it reacts to light," said Hutchins. He switched on his chest-lamp, and the green auroral glow was instantly banished by the flood of pure white radiance. Until Man had come to this planet, no white light had ever shone upon the surface of Venus, even by day. As in the seas of Earth, there was only a green twilight, deepening slowly to utter darkness.

The transformation was so stunning that neither man could check a cry of astonishment. Gone in a flash was the deep, sombre black of the thick-piled velvet carpet at their feet. Instead, as far as their lights carried, lay a glazing pattern of glorious vivid reds, laced with streaks of gold. No Persian prince could ever have commanded so opulent a tapestry from his weavers, yet this was the accidental product of biological forces. Indeed, until they had switched on their floods, these superb colors had not even existed, and they would vanish once more when the alien light of Earth ceased to conjure them into being.

"Tikov was right," murmured Hutchins. "I wish he could have known."

"Right about what?" asked Jerry, though it seemed almost

a sacrilege to speak in the presence of such loveliness.

"Back in Russia, fifty years ago, he found that plants living in very cold climates tended to be blue and violet, while those from hot ones were red or orange. He predicted that the Martian vegetation would be violet, and said that if there were plants on Venus they'd be red. Well, he was right on both counts. But we can't stand here all day—we've work to do."

"You're sure it's quite safe?" asked Jerry, some of his caution reasserting itself.

"Absolutely—it can't touch our suits even if it wants to. Anyway, its moving past us."

That was true. They could see now that the entire creature—if it was a single plant, and not a colony—covered a roughly circular area about a hundred yards across. It was sweeping over the ground, as the shadow of a cloud moves before the wind—and where it had rested, the rocks were pitted with innumerable tiny holes that might have been etched by acid.

"Yes," said Hutchins, when Jerry remarked about this. "That's how some lichens feed; they secrete acids that dissolve rock. But no questions, please—not till we get back to the ship. I've several lifetimes' work here, and a couple of hours to do it in."

This was botany on the run. . . . The sensitive edge of the huge plant-thing could move with surprising speed when it tried to evade them. It was as if they were dealing with an animated flap-jack, an acre in extent. There was no reaction—apart from the automatic avoidance of their exhaust-heat—when Hutchins snipped samples or took probes. The creature flowed steadily onwards over hills and valleys, guided by some strange vegetable instinct. Perhaps it was following some vein of mineral; the geologists could decide that, when they analyzed the rock samples that Hutchins had collected both before and after the passage of the living tapestry.

There was scarcely time to think or even to frame the

countless questions that their discovery had raised. Presumably these creatures must be fairly common, for them to have found one so quickly. How did they reproduce? By shoots, spores, fission, or some other means? Where did they get their energy? What relatives, rivals or parasites did they have? This could not be the only form of life on Venus—the very idea was absurd, for if you had one species, you must have thousands. . . .

Sheer hunger and fatigue forced them to a halt at last. The creature they were studying could eat its way around Venus—though Hutchins believed that it never went very far from the lake, as from time to time it approached the water and inserted a long, tube-like tendril into it—but the animals from Earth had to rest.

It was a great relief to inflate the pressurized tent, climb in through the airlock, and strip off their thermosuits. For the first time, as they relaxed inside their tiny plastic hemisphere, the true wonder and importance of the discovery forced itself upon their minds. This world around them was no longer the same; Venus was no longer dead—it had joined Earth and Mars.

For life called to life, across the gulfs of space. Everything that grew or moved upon the face of any planet was a portent, a promise that Man was not alone in this universe of blazing suns and swirling nebulae. If as yet he had found no companions with whom he could speak, that was only to be expected, for the light-years and the ages still stretched before him, waiting to be explored. Meanwhile, he must guard and cherish the life he found, whether it be upon Earth or Mars or Venus.

So Graham Hutchins, the happiest biologist in the Solar System, told himself as he helped Garfield collect their refuse and seal it into a plastic disposal bag. When they deflated the tent and started the homeward journey, there was no sign of the creature they had been examining. That was just as well; they might have been tempted to linger for more experiments, and already it was getting uncomfortably close to their deadline.

No matter; in a few months they would be back with a team of assistants, far more adequately equipped and with the eyes of the world upon them. Evolution had labored for a billion years to make this meeting possible; it could wait a little longer.

For a while nothing moved in the greenly glimmering, fogbound landscape; it was deserted by man and crimson carpet alike. Then, flowing over the windcarved hills, the creature reappeared. Or perhaps it was another of the same strange species; no one would ever know.

It flowed past the little cairn of stones where Hutchins and Garfield had buried their wastes. And then it stopped.

It was not puzzled, for it had no mind. But the chemical urges that drove it relentlessly over the polar plateau were crying: Here, here! Somewhere close at hand was the most precious of all the food it needed—phosphorous, the element without which the spark of life could never ignite. It began to nuzzle the rocks, to ooze into the cracks and crannies, to scratch and scrabble with probing tendrils. Nothing that it did was beyond the capacity of any plant or tree on Earth —but it moved a thousand times more quickly, requiring only minutes to reach its goal and pierce through the plastic film.

And then it feasted, on food more concentrated than any it had ever known. It absorbed the carbohydrates and the proteins and the phosphates, the nicotine from the cigarette ends, the cellulose from the paper cups and spoons. All these it broke down and assimilated into its strange body, without difficulty and without harm.

Likewise it absorbed a whole microcosmos of living creatures—the bacteria and viruses which, upon an older planet, had evolved into a thousand deadly strains. Though only a very few could survive in this heat and this atmosphere, they were sufficient. As the carpet crawled back to the lake, it carried contagion to all its world.

Even as the Morning Star *set course for her distant home,* Venus *was dying. The films and photographs and specimens that Hutchins was carrying in triumph were more precious even than he knew. They were the only record that would ever exist of Life's third attempt to gain a foothold in the Solar System.*

Beneath the clouds of Venus, the story of Creation was ended.

MOTHER

---

by

PHILIP JOSE FARMER

Look, mother. The clock is running backwards."

Eddie Fetts pointed to the hands on the pilot room dial, always set on Central Standard Time because the majority of the research expedition thought it would remind them of their home state, Illinois, whenever they looked at it. When staryachting, one time was as good as another.

Dr. Paula Fetts said, "The crash must have reversed it."

"How could it do that?"

"I can't tell you. I don't know everything, son."

"Oh!"

"Well, don't look at me so disappointedly. I'm a pathologist, not an elecronicist."

"Don't be so cross, mother. I can't stand it. Not now."

He walked out of the pilot room. Anxiously, she followed him. Burying the crew and her fellow scientists had been very trying for him. Spilled blood had always made him

485

dizzy and sick; he could scarcely control his hands enough to help her sack the scattered bones and entrails. He had wanted to put the corpses in the nuclear furnace, but she had forbidden that. The Geigers amidships were ticking loudly, warning that there was an invisible death in the stern.

The meteor that struck the moment the ship came out of Translation into normal space had probably wrecked the engine-room. So she had understood from the incoherent highpitched phrases of a colleague before he fled to the pilot room. She had hurried to find Eddie. She feared his cabin door would still be locked, as he had been making a tape of the *Heavy Hangs the Albatross* aria from Gianelli's *Ancient Mariner*.

Fortunately, the emergency system had automatically thrown out the locking circuits. Entering, she had called out his name in fear he'd been hurt. He was lying half-unconscious on the floor, but it was not the accident that had thrown him there. The reason lay in the corner, released from his lax hand: a quart free-fall thermos, rubber-nippled. From Eddie's open mouth charged a breath of rye that not even chlorophyll pills had been able to conceal.

Sharply, she had commanded him to get up and onto the bed. Her voice, the first he had ever heard, pierced through the phalanx of Old Red Star. He struggled up, and she though smaller, had thrown every ounce of her weight into getting him up and onto the bed.

There she had lain down with him and strapped them both in. She understood that the lifeboat had been wrecked also, and that it was up to the captain to bring the yacht down safely to the surface of this chartered but unexplored planet, Baudelaire. Everybody else had gone to sit behind the captain, strapped in their crashchairs, unable to help except with their silent backing.

Moral support had not been enough. The ship had come in on a shallow slant. Too fast, though. The wounded motors had not been able to hold her up. The prow had taken the brunt of the punishment. So had those seated in the nose.

Dr. Fetts had held her son's head on her bosom and prayed out loud to her God. Eddie had snored and muttered. Then there was a sound like the clashing of the gates of doom—a tremendous bong as if the ship were a clapper in a gargantuan bell tolling the most frightening message human ears may hear—a blinding blast of light—and darkness and silence.

A few moments later Eddie began crying out in a childish voice, "Don't leave me to die, mother! Come back! Come back!"

Mother was unconscious by his side, but he did not know that. He wept for a while, then he lapsed back into his rye-fogged stupor—if he had ever been out of it—and slept. Again darkness and silence.

It was the second day since the crash, if "day" could describe the twilight state on Baudelair. Dr. Fetts followed her son wherever he went. She knew he was very sensitive and easily upset. All his life she had known it and had tried to get between him and anything that would cause trouble. She had succeeded, she thought, fairly well until three months ago when Eddie had eloped.

The girl was Polina Fameux, the ash blonde long-legged actress whose tridi image, taped, had been shipped to all stars where a small acting talent and a large and shapely bosom were admired. Since Eddie was a well known Metro baritone, the marriage made a big splash whose ripples ran around the civilized Galaxy.

Dr. Fetts had felt very bad about the elopement, but she had, she knew, hidden her grief very well beneath a smiling mask. She didn't regret having to give him up; after all, he was a full-grown man, no longer her little boy; but, really, aside from the seasons at the Met and his tours, he had not been parted from her since he was eight.

That was when she went on a honeymoon with her second husband. And then they'd not been separated long, for Eddie had gotten very sick, and she'd had to hurry back and take care of him, as he had insisted she was the only one who could make him well.

Moreover, you couldn't count his days at the opera as being a total loss, for he vised her every noon and they had a long talk—no matter how high the vise bils ran.

The ripples caused by her son's marriage were scarcely a week old before they were followed by even bigger ones. They bore the news of the separation of the two. A fortnight latter, Polina applied for divorce on the grounds of incompatibility. Eddie was handed the papers in his mother's apartment. He had come back to her the day he and Polina had agreed they "couldn't make a go of it," or, as he phrased it to his mother, "couldn't get together."

Dr. Fetts was, of course, very curious about the reason for their parting, but, as she explained to her friends, she "respected" his silence. What she didn't say was that she had told herself the time would come when he would tell her all. Eddie's "nervous breakdown" started shortly afterwards. He had been very irritable, moody, and depressed, but he got worse the day a so-called friend told Eddie that whenever Polina heard his name mentioned, she laughed loud and long. The friend added that Polina had promised to tell someday the true story of their brief merger.

That night his mother had to call in a doctor.

In the days that followed, she thought of giving up her position as research pathologist at De Kruif and taking up all her time to help him "get back on his feet." It was a sign of the struggle going on in her mind that she had not been able to decide within a week's time. Ordinarily given to swift consideration and resolution of a problem, she could not agree to surrender her beloved quest into tissue regeneration.

Just as she was on the verge of doing what was for her the incredible and the shameful: tossing a coin, she had been vised by her superior. He told her she had been chosen to go with a group of biologists on a research cruise to ten preselected planetary systems.

Overjoyed, she had thrown away the papers that would turn Eddie over to a sanitorium. And, since he was quite famous, she had used her influence and his good name to get the government to allow him to go along. Ostensibly, he was to make a survey of the development of opera on planets colonized by Terrans. That the yacht was not visiting any colonized globes seemed to have been missed by the bureaus concerned. But it was not the first time in the history of the government that its left hand knew not what its right was doing.

Actually, he was to be "rebuilt" by his mother, who thought of herself as being much more capable of setting him up again than any of the prevalent, A, F, J, R, S, K, or H therapies. True some of her friends reported amazing results with some of the symbol-chasing techniques. On the other hand, she knew two close companions who had tried them all and had gotten no benefits from any of them.

After all, she decided, she was his mother; she could do more for him than any of those "alphabatties"; he was flesh of her flesh, blood of her blood. Besides, he wasn't so sick. He just got awfully blue sometimes and made theatrical but insincere threats of suicide or else just sat and stared into space. But she could handle him.

So now it was that she followed him from the backward running clock to his room. And saw him step inside, look for a second, and then turn to her with a twisted face.

"Neddie is ruined, mother. Absolutely ruined."

She glanced at the piano. It had torn loose from the wall-racks at the moment of impact and smashed itself against the opposite wall. To Eddie, it wasn't just a piano; it was Neddie. He had a pet name for everything he contacted for more than a brief time. It was as if he hopped from one appellation to the next, like an ancient sea sailor who felt lost unless he were close to the familiar points of the shore-line. Otherwise, Eddie seemed to be drifting helplessly in a chaotic ocean, one that was anonymous and amorphous.

Or, analogy more typical of him, he was like the night-clubber who feels submerged, drowning, unless he hops from table to table, going from one well known group of faces to the next, and avoiding the featureless and unnamed dummies at the strangers' tables.

He did not cry over Neddie. She wished he would. He had been so apathetic during the voyage. Nothing, not even the unparalled splendor of the naked stars nor the inexpressible alienness of strange planets had seemed to lift him very long. If he would only weep or laugh loudly or display some sign that he was reacting violently to what was happening. She would even have welcomed his striking her in anger or calling her bad names.

But no, not even during the gathering of the mangled corpses, when he looked for a while as if he was going to vomit, would he give way to his body's demand for expression. She understood that if he were to throw up, he would be much better, for it would, as it were, have gotten rid of much of the psychic disturbance along with the physical.

He would not. He had kept on raking flesh and bones into the large plastic bags and kept a fixed look of resentment and sullenness.

She hoped now that the loss of his piano would bring the big tears and the racked shoulder. Then she could take him in her arms and give him sympathy. He would be her little boy again, afraid of the dark, afraid of the dog killed by a car, seeking her arms for the sure safety, the sure love.

"Never mind, baby," she said. "When we're rescued, we'll get you a new one."

"When—!"

He lifted his eyebrows and sat down on the bed's edge. "What do we do now?"

She became very brisk and efficient.

"The ultrad was set working the moment the meteor struck. If it's survived the crash, its still sending SOS's. If not, then there's nothing we can do about it. Neither of us knows how to repair it.

"However, it's possible that in the last five years since this planet was chartered, other expeditions may have landed here. Not from Earth, but from some of the colonies. Or from nonhuman globes. Who knows? It's worth taking a chance. Let's see."

A single glance was enough to wreck their hopes about the ultrad. It had been twisted and broken until it was no longer even recognizable as the machine that sent swifter-than-light waves through the no-ether.

Dr. Fetts said with false cheeriness, "Well, that's that! So what? It makes things so easy. Let's go into the storeroom and see what we can see."

Eddie shrugged and followed her. There she insisted that both take a panrad. If they had to seperate for any reason, they could always communicate and also using the DF's—the direction finders built within it—locate each other. Having used them before, they knew the instruments' capabilities and how essential they were on scouting or camping trips.

The panrads were lightweight cylinders about two and a half feet high and eight inches in diameter. Crampacked, they had the mechanisms of two dozen different utilities. They never ran out of power, because their batteries could be recharged from the body electricity of their own owners, and they were practically indestructible and worked under almost any conditions, even under water or in extreme cold or heat.

Dr. Fetts insisted they handcuff their left wrists to the cylinders as long as they were outside the yacht. That way, they couldn't drop them and thus have no chance of keeping in touch. Eddie thought such precaution was ridiculous, but he said nothing.

Keeping away from the side of the ship that had the huge hole in it, they took the panrads outside. The long wave bands were searched by Eddie while his mother moved the dial that ranged up and down the shortwaves. Neither really expected to hear anything, but their quest was better than doing nothing.

Finding the modulated wave-frequencies empty of any significant noises, he switched to the continuous waves. He was startled by a dot-dashing.

"Hey, mom! Something in the 1000 kilocycles! Unmodulated!"

"Naturally, son," she said with some exasperation in the midst of her elation. "What would you expect from a radio-telegraphic signal?"

She found the band on her own cylinder. He looked blankly at her. "I know nothing about radio, but that's not Morse."

"What? You must be mistaken!"

"I—I don't think so."

"Is it or isn't it? Good God, son, make up your mind fast about something you should be sure of."

She turned the amplifier up. Though it wasn't necessary, she cocked her head to listen. As both of them had learned Galacto-Morse through sleeplearn techniques, she checked him at once.

"You're right. What do you make of it?"

His quick ear pounced on the pulses.

"No simple dot and dash. Four different time-lengths."

He listened some more.

"They've got a certain rhythm, all right. I can make out definite groupings. Ah! That's the sixth time I've caught that particular one. And there's another. And another."

Dr. Fetts shook her ash-blonde head. She could make out nothing but a series of zzt-zzt-zzt's. There was a rhythm to it, she admitted, but even after trying hard to identify certain units, she didn't recognize them when they repeated. Well, she shrugged, she was as tone-deaf and non-musical as they came. Eddie took after his father in that trait.

He glanced at the DF needle.

"Coming from NE by E. Should we try to locate?"

"Naturally," she replied. "But we'd better eat first. We don't know how far away it is, or what we'll find there. While I'm getting a hot meal ready, you get our field trip stuff ready."

"O.K.," he said with more enthusiasm than he had shown for a long time.

When he came back he ate all of the large dish his mother had prepared on the unwrecked galley stove.

"You always did make the best stew," he said.

"Thank you. I'm glad you're eating again, son. I am surprised. I thought you'd be sick about all this."

He waved vaguely, but energetically.

"The challenge of the unknown, you know. I have a sort of feeling this is going to turn out much better than we thought. Much better."

She came close and sniffed his breath. It was clean, innocent even of stew. That meant he'd taken chlorophyll, which probably meant he'd been sampling some hidden rye. Otherwise, how explain his reckless disregard of the possible dangers? It wasn't like his normal attitude.

She said nothing, for she knew that if he tried to hide a bottle in his clothes or field sack while they were tracking down the radio signals, she would soon find it. And take it away. He wouldn't even protest, merely let her lift it from his limp hand while his lips swelled with resentment.

They set out. Both wore knapsacks and carried cuffed panrads. He had slung a gun over his shoulder, and she had snapped onto her sack her small black bag of medical and lab supplies.

High noon of late autumn was topped by a weak red sun that barely managed to make itself seen through the eternal double-layer of clouds. Its twin, an even smaller blob of lilac, was setting on the northwestern horizon. They walked in a sort of bright twilight, the best that Baudelaire ever achieved. Yet, despite the lack of light, the air was too warm. That was a phenomenon common to certain planets behind the Horsehead Nebula, one being investigated but as yet unexplained.

The country was hilly and had many deep ravines. Here and there were prominences high enough and steepsided enough to be called embryo mountains. Considering the roughness of the land, however, there was a surprising amount of vegetation. Pale green, red, and yellow bushes, vines, and little trees clung to every bit of ground, horizontal or vertical. All had comparatively broad leaves that turned with the sun in hopes to catch the most of the light.

From time to time, as the two Terrans strode noisily through the forest, small multi-colored insect-like and mammal-like creatures scuttled from hiding place to hiding place. Eddie decided to unsling his gun and carry it in the crook of his arm. Then, after they were forced to scramble up and down ravines and hills and fight their way through thickets that became unexpectedly tangled, he put it back over his shoulder, where it hung from a strap.

Despite their exertions, they did not tire fast. They weighed about twenty pounds less than they would have on Earth, and, though the air was thinner, it was, for some unknown reason, richer in oxygen.

Dr. Fetts kept up with Eddie. Thirty years the senior of the twenty-three year old, she passed even at close inspection for his older sister. Longevity pills took care of that. However, he treated her with all the courtesy and chivalry that one gave one's mother and helped her up the steep inclines, even though the climbs did not appreciably cause her deep chest to demand more air.

They paused once by a creek bank to get their bearings.

"The signals have stopped," he said.

"Obviously," she replied.

At that moment the radar-detector built into the panrad began a high ping-ping-ping. Both of them automatically looked upwards.

"There's no ship in the air."

"It can't be coming from either of those hills," she pointed out. "There's nothing but a boulder on top each. Tremendous rocks."

"Nevertheless, it's coming from there, I think. Oh! Oh! Did you see what I saw? Looked like a tall stalk of some kind being pulled down behind that big rock."

She peered through the dim light. "I think you were imagining things, son. I saw nothing."

Then even as the pinging kept up, the zzting started again. But after a burst of noise, both stopped.

"Let's go up and see what we shall see," she said.

"Something screwy," he commented. She did not answer.

They forded the creek and began the ascent. Halfway up, they stopped to sniff puzzled at a gust of some heavy odor coming downwind.

"Smells like a cageful of monkeys," he said.

"In heat," she added. If he had the keener ear, hers was the sharper nose.

They went on up. The RD began sounding its tiny hysterical gonging. Nonplused, Eddie stopped. The DF indicated the radar pulses were not coming from the top of the hill up which they were going, as formerly, but from the other hill across the valley. Abruptly, the panrad fell silent.

"What do we do now?"

"Finish what we started. This hill. Then we go to the other."

He shrugged and then hastened after her tall slim body in its long-legged coveralls. She was hot on the scent, literally, and nothing could stop her. Just before she reached the bungalowsized boulder topping the hill, he caught up with her. She had stopped to gaze intently at the DF needle, which swung widely before it stopped at neutral. The monkey-cage odor was very strong.

"Do you suppose it could be some sort of radio-creating mineral?" she asked, disappointedly.

"No. Those groupings were semantic. And that smell . . . ."

"Then what—?"

He didn't know whether to feel pleased or not because she had so obviously and suddenly thrust the burden of responsibility and action on him. Both pride and a curious shrinking affected him. But he did feel exhilarated. Almost, he thought, he felt as if he were on the verge of discovering what he had been looking for for a long time. What the object of his search had been, he could not say. But he was excited and not very much afraid.

He unslung his weapon, a two-barreled combination shotgun and rifle. The panrad was still quiet.

"Maybe the boulder is camouflage for a spy outfit," he said. He sounded silly, even to himself.

Behind him, his mother gasped and screamed. He whirled and raised his gun, but there was nothing to shoot. She was pointing at the hilltop across the valley, shaking, and saying something incoherent.

He could make out a long slim antenna seemingly projecting from the monstrous boulder crouched there. At the same time, two thoughts struggled for first place in his mind: one, that it was more than a coincidence that both hills had almost identical stone structures on their brows, and two, that the antenna must have been recently stuck out, for he was sure that he had not seen it the last time he looked.

He never got to tell her his conclusions, for something thin and flexible and manifold and irresistible seized him from behind. Lifted into the air, he was borne backwards. He dropped the gun and tried to grab the bands of tentacles around him and tear them off with his bare hands. No use.

He caught one last glimpse of his mother running off down the hillside. Then a curtain snapped down, and he was in total darkness.

Before he could gather what had happened, Eddie sensed

himself, still suspended, twirled around. He could not know for sure, of course, but he thought he was facing exactly the opposite direction. Simultaneously, the tentacles binding his legs and arms were released. Only his waist was still gripped. It was pressed so tightly that he cried out with pain.

Then, boot-toes bumping on some resilient substance, he was carried forward. Halted, facing he knew not what horrible monster, he was suddenly assailed—not by a sharp beak or tooth or knife or some other cutting or mangling instrument—but by a dense cloud of that same monkey perfume.

In other circumstances, he might have vomited. Now his stomach was not given the time to consider whether it should clean house or not. The tentacle lifted him higher and thrust him against something soft and yielding—something fleshlike and womanly—almost breastlike in texture and smoothness and warmth, and its hint of gentle curving.

He put his hands and feet out to brace himself, for he thought for a moment he was going to sink in and be covered up—enfolded—ingested. The idea of a gargantuan amoeba-thing hiding within a hollow rock—or a rocklike shell—made him writhe and yell, and shove at the protoplasmic substance.

But nothing of the kind happened. He was not plunged into a smothering and slimy featherbed that would strip him of his skin and then his flesh and then either dissolve his bones or reject them. He was merely shoved repeatedly against the soft swelling. Each time he pushed or kicked or struck at it. After a dozen of these seemingly purposeless acts, he was held away, as if whatever was doing it was puzzled by his behavior.

He had quit screaming. The only sounds were his harsh breathings and the zzzts and pings from the panrad. Even as he became aware of them, the zzzts changed tempo and settled into a recognizable pattern of bursts—three units that crackled out again and again.

"Who are you? Who are you?"

Of course, it could just as easily have been, "What are you?" or "What the hell!" or "Nov smoz ka pop?"

Or nothing—semantically speaking.

But he didn't think the latter. And when he was gently lowered to the floor, and the tentacle went off to only-God-knew-where in the dark, he was sure that the creature was communicating—or trying to—with him.

It was this thought that kept him from screaming and running around in the lightless and fetid chamber, brainlessly, instinctively seeking an outlet. He mastered his panic and snapped open a little shutter in the panrad's side and thrust in his righthand index finger. There he poised it above the key and in a moment, when the thing paused in transmitting, he sent back, as best he could, the pulses he had received. It was not necessary for him to turn on the light and spin the dial that would put him on the 1000 kc. band. The instrument would automatically key that frequency in with the one he had just received.

The oddest part about the whole procedure was that his whole body was trembling almost uncontrollably—one part excepted. That was his index finger, his one unit that seemed to him to have a definite function in his otherwise meaningless situation. It was the section of him that was helping him to survive—the only part that knew how—at that moment. Even his brain seemed to have no connection with his finger. That digit was himself, and the rest just happened to be linked to it.

When he paused, the transmitter began again. This time the units were unrecognizable. There was a certain rhythm to them, but he could not know what they meant. Meanwhile, the RD was pinging. Something somewhere in the dark hole had a beam held tightly on him.

He pressed a button on the panrad's top, and the built-in flashlight illuminated the area just in front of him. He saw a wall of reddish-gray rubbery substance and on the wall a roughly circular and light grey swelling about four feet in diameter. Around it, giving it a Medusa appearance, were coiled twelve very long and very thin tentacles.

Though he was afraid that if he turned his back to them, the tentacles would seize him once more, his curiosity forced him to wheel about and examine with the bright beam his surroundings. He was in an egg-shaped chamber about thirty feet long, twelve wide, and eight to ten high in the middle. It was formed of a reddish-grey material, smooth except for irregular intervals of blue or red pipes. Veins and arteries, obviously.

A door-sized portion of the wall had a vertical slit running down it. Tentacles fringed it. He guessed it was sort of iris and that it had opened to drag him inside. Starfish-shaped groupings of tentacles were scattered on the walls or hung from the ceiling. On the wall opposite the iris was a long and flexible stalk with a cartilaginous ruff around its free end. When Eddie moved, it moved, its blind point following him as a radar antenna pursues the thing it is locating. That was what it was. And unless he was wrong, the stalk was also a C.W. transmitter-receiver.

He shot the light on around. When it reached the end farthest from him, he gasped. Ten creatures were huddled together facing him! About the size of half-grown pigs, they looked like nothing so much as unshelled snails; they were eyeless, and the stalk growing from the forehead of each was a tiny duplicate of that on the wall. They didn't look dangerous. Their open mouths were little and toothless, and their rate of locomotion must be slow, for they moved, like a snail, on a large pedestal of flesh—a foot-muscle.

Nevertheless, if he were to fall asleep, they could overcome him by force of numbers, and those mouths might drip an acid to digest him, or they might carry a concealed poisonous sting.

His speculations were interrupted violently. He was seized, lifted, and passed on to another group of tentacles. He was carried beyond the antenna-stalk and toward the snail-beings. Just before he reached them, he was halted, facing the wall. An iris, hitherto invisible, opened. His light shone into it, but he could see nothing but convolutions of flesh.

His panrad gave off a new pattern of dit-dot-deet-dats. The iris widened until it was large enough to admit his body, if he were shoved in headfirst. Or feetfirst. It didn't matter. The convolutions straightened out and became a tunnel. Or a throat. From thousands of little pits emerged thousands of tiny and razor sharp teeth. They flashed out and sank back in, and before they had disappeared thousands of other wicked little spears darted out and past the receding fangs.

Meat-grinder effect.

Beyond the murderous array, at the end of the throat, was a huge pouch of water, a veritable tank. Steam came from it, and with it an odor like that of his mother's stew. Dark bits, presumably meat, and pieces of vegetables floated on the seething surface.

Then the iris closed, and he was turned around to face the slugs. Gently, but unmistakably, a tentacle spanked his buttocks. And the panrad zzzted a warning.

Eddie was not stupid. He knew now that the ten creatures were not dangerous unless he molested them. In which case he had just seen where he would go if he did not behave.

Again he was lifted and carried along the wall until he was shoved against the light grey spot. The monkey-cage odor, which had died out, became strong again. Eddie identified its source with a very small hole which appeared in the wall.

When he did not respond—he had no idea yet how he was supposed to act—the tentacles dropped him so unexpectedly that he fell on his back. Unhurt by the yielding flesh, he rose.

What was the next step? Exploration of his resources. Itemization: The panrad. A sleeping-bag, which he wouldn't need as long as the present too-warm temperature kept up.

A bottle of Old Red Star capsules. A free-fall thermos with attached nipple. A box of A-2-Z rations. A Foldstove. Cartridges for his double-barrel, now lying outside the creature's boulderish shell. A roll of toilet paper. Toothbrush. Paste. Soap. Towel, Pills; chlorophyll, Hormone, vitamin, longevity, reflex, and sleeping. And a thread-thin wire, a hundred feet long when uncoiled, that held prisoner in its molecular structure a hundred symphonies, eighty operas, a thousand different types of musical pieces, and two thousand great books ranging from Sophocles and Dostoyevsky and Hammet and Henry Miller to the latest bestseller. It could be run off inside the panrad.

He inserted it, thumbed a designated spot, and spoke, "Eddie Fetts's recording of Puccini's *Che gelida manina*, please."

And while he listened approvingly to his own magnificent voice, he zipped open a can he had found in the bottom of the sack. His mother had put into it the stew left over from their last meal in the ship.

Not knowing what was happening, yet, for some reason, sure he was, for the present, safe, he munched meat and vegetables with a contented jaw. Transition from abhorrence to appetite sometimes came easily for Eddie.

He cleaned out the can and finished up with some crackers and a chocolate bar. Rationing was out. As long as the food lasted, he would eat well. Then, if nothing turned up, he would. . . But then, somehow, he reassured himself as he licked his fingers, his mother, who was free, would find some way to get him out of his trouble.

She always had.

The panrad, silent for a while, began signaling. Eddie spotlighted the antenna and saw it was pointing at the snail-beings, which he had, in accordance with his custom, dubbed familiarly. Sluggos he called them.

The Sluggos crept towards the wall and stopped close to it. Their mouths, built on the tops of their heads, gaped like so many hungry young birds. The iris opened, and two lips formed into a spout. Out of it streamed steaming-hot water and chunks of meat and vegetables. Stew! Stew that fell exactly into each waiting mouth.

That was how Eddie learned the second phrase of Mother Polyphema's language. The first message had been, "What are you?" This was, "Come and get it!"

He experimented. He tapped out a repetition of what he'd last heard. As one, the Sluggos—except the one then being fed—turned to him and crept a few feet before halting, puzzled.

Inasmuch as Eddie was broadcasting, the Sluggos must have had some sort of built-in DF. Otherwise they wouldn't have been able to distinguish between his pulses and their Mother's.

Immediately after, a tentacle smote Eddie across the shoulders and knocked him down. The panrad zzzted its third intelligible message: "Don't ever do that!"

And then a fourth, to which the ten young obeyed by wheeling and resuming their former positions.

"This way, children."

Yes, they were the offspring, living, eating, sleeping, playing, and learning to communicate in the womb of their mother—the Mother. They were the mobile brood of this vast immobile entity that had scooped up Eddie as a frog scoops up a fly. This Mother. She who had once been just such a Sluggo until she had grown hog-size and had been pushed out of her Mother's womb. And who, rolled into a tight ball, had freewheeled down her natal hill, straightened out at the bottom, inched her way up the next hill, rolled down, and so on. Until she found the empty shell of an adult who had died. Or, if she wanted to be a first class citizen in her society and not a prestigeless *occupée*, she found the bare top of a tall hill—or any eminence that commanded a big sweep of territory—and there squatted.

And there she put out many thread-thin tendrils into the soil and into the cracks in the rocks, tendrils that drew sustenance from the fat of her body and grew and extended downwards and ramified into other tendrils. Deep underground the rootlets worked their instinctive chemistry; searched for and found the water, the calcium, the iron, the copper, the nitrogen, the carbons, fondled earthworms and grubs and larvae, teasing them for the secrets of their fats and proteins; broke down the wanted substance into shadowy colloidal particles; sucked them up the thready pipes of the tendrils and back to the pale and slimming body crouching on a flat space atop a ridge, a hill, a peak.

There, using the blueprints stored in the molecules of the cerebellum, her body took the building blocks of elements and fashioned them into a very thin shell of the most available material, a shield large enough so she could expand to fit it while her natural enemies—the keen and hungry predators that prowled twilighted Baudelaire—nosed and clawed it in vain.

Then, her evergrowing bulk cramped, she would resorb the hard covering. And if no sharp tooth found her during that process of a few days, she would cast another and a larger. And so on through a dozen or more.

Until she had become the monstrous and much reformed body of an adult and virgin female. Outside would be the stuff that so much resembled a boulder, that was, actually, rock: either granite, diorite, marble, basalt, or maybe just plain limestone. Or sometimes iron, glass, or cellulose.

Within was the centrally located brain, probably as large as a man's. Surrounding it, the tons of the various organs: the nervous system, the mighty heart, or hearts, the four stomachs, the microwave and longwave generators, the kidneys, bowels, tracheae, scent and taste organs, the perfume factory which made odors to attract animals and birds close enough to be seized, and the huge womb. And the antennae—the small one inside for teaching and scanning the young, and a long and powerful stalk on the outside, projecting from the shelltop, retractable if danger came.

The next step was from virgin to Mother, lower case to uppercase as designated in her pulse-language by a longer pause before a word. Not until she was deflowered could she take a high place in her society. Immodest, unblushing, she herself made the advances, the proposals, and the surrender.

After which, she ate her mate.

The all-around clock in the panrad told Eddie he was in his thirtieth day of imprisonment when he found out that little bit of information. He was shocked, not because it offended his ethics, but because he himself had been intended to be the mate. And the dinner.

His finger tapped, "Tell me, O Mother, what you mean."

He had not wondered before how a species that lacked males could reproduce. Now he found that, to the Mothers, all creatures except themselves were male. Mothers were immobile and female. Mobiles were male. Eddie had been mobile. He was, therefore, a male.

He had approached this particular Mother during the mating season, that is, midway through raising a litter of young. She had scanned him as he came along the creekbanks at the valley bottom. When he was at the foot of the hill, she had detected his odor. It was new to her. The closest she could come to it in her memorybanks was that of a beast similar to him. From her description, he guessed it to be an ape. So she had released from her repertoire its rut stench. When he seemingly fell into the trap, she had caught him.

He was supposed to attack the conception-spot, that light gray swelling on the wall. After he had ripped and torn it enough to begin the mysterious workings of pregnancy, he would have been popped into her stomach-iris.

Fortunately, he had lacked the sharp beak, the fang, the claw. And she had received her own signals back from the panrad.

Eddie did not understand why it was necessary to use a mobile for mating. A Mother was intelligent enough to pick up a sharp stone and mangle the spot herself.

He was given to understand that conception would not start unless it was accompanied by a certain titillation of the nerves—a frenzy and its satisfaction. Why this emotional state was needed, Mother did not know.

Eddie tried to explain about such things as genes and chromosomes and why they had to be present in highly-developed species in order to have differences and selections of favorable characteristics and open the gates to evolutionary changes.

Mother did not get it.

Eddie wondered if the number of slashes and rips in the spot corresponded to the number of young. Or, if in any way, say, there were a large number of potentialities in the heredity-ribbons spread out under the conception-skin. And if the haphazard irritation and consequent stimulation of the genes paralleled the chance combining of genes in human male-female mating. Thus resulting in offspring with traits that were both joinings and dissimiliarities of their parents'.

Or did the inevitable devouring of the mobile after the act indicate more than an emotional and nutritional reflex? Did it hint that the mobile caught up scattered gene-nodes, like hard seeds, along with the torn skin, in its claws and tusks, that these genes survived the boiling in the stew-stomach, and were later passed out in the feces? Where animals and birds picked them up in beak, tooth, or foot, and then, seized by other Mothers in this oblique rape, transmitted the heredity-carrying agents to the conception-spots while attacking them, the nodules being scraped off and implanted in the skin and blood of the swelling even as others were harvested? Later, the mobiles were eaten, digested, and ejected in the obscure but ingenious and never-ending cycle? Thus ensuring the continual, if haphazard, recombining of genes, chances for variations in off-spring, opportunities for mutations, and so on?

Mother pulsed that she was nonplused.

Eddie gave up. He'd never know. After all, did it matter?

He decided not and rose from his prone position to request water. She pursed up her iris and spouted a tepid quartful into his thermos. He dropped in a pill, swished it around till it dissolved, and drank a reasonable facsimile of Old Red Star. He preferred the harsh and powerful rye, though he could have afforded the smoothest. Quick results were what he wanted. Taste didn't matter, as he disliked all liquor tastes. Thus he drank what the Skid Row bums drank and shuddered even as they did so, renaming it Old Rotten Tar and cursing the fate that had brought them so low they had to gag such stuff down.

The rye glowed in his belly and spread quickly through his limbs and up to his head, chilled only by the increasing scarcity of the capsules. When he ran out—then what? It was at times like this that he most missed his mother.

Thinking about her brought a few large tears. He snuffled and drank some more and when the biggest of the Sluggos nudged him for a back-scratching, he gave it instead a shot of Old Red Star. A slug for Sluggo. Idly, he wondered what effect a taste for rye would have on the future of the race when these virgins became Mothers.

At that moment he was rocked by what seemed a wonderful lifesaving idea. These creatures could suck up the required elements from the earth and with them duplicate quite complex molecular structures. Provided, of course, they had a sample of the desired substance to brood over in some cryptic organ.

Well, what easier to do than give her one of the cherished capsules? One could become any number. Those, plus the abundance of water pumped up through hollow underground tendrils from the nearby creek, would give enough to make a master-distiller green!

He smacked his lips and was about to key her his request when what she was transmitting penetrated his mind.

Rather cattily, she remarked that her neighbor across the valley was putting on airs because she, too, held prisoner a communicating mobile.

The Mothers had a society as hierarchical as table-protocol in Washington or the peck-order in a barnyard. Prestige was what counted, and prestige was determined by the broadcasting power, the height of the eminence on which the Mother sat, which governed the extent of her radar-territory, and the abundance and novelty and wittiness of her gossip. The creature that had snapped Eddie up was a Queen. She had precedence over thirty-odd of her kind; they all had to let her broadcast first, and none dared start pulsing until she quit. Then, the next in order began, and so on down the line. Any of them could be interrupted at any time by Number One, and if any of the lower echelon had something interesting to transmit, she could break in on the one then speaking and get permission from the Queen to tell her tale.

Eddie knew this, but he could not listen in directly to the hilltop-gabble. The thick pseudo-granite shell barred him from that and made him dependent upon her womb-stalk for relayed information.

Now and then Mother opened the door and allowed her young to crawl out. There they practiced beaming and broadcasting at the Sluggos of the Mother across the valley. Occasionally that Mother deigned herself to pulse the young, and Eddie's keeper reciprocated to her offspring.

Turnabout.

The first time the children had inched through the exit-iris, Eddie had tried, Ulysses-like, to pass himself off as one of them and crawl out in the midst of the flock. Eyeless, but no Polyphemus, Mother had picked him out with her tentacles and hauled him back in.

It was following that incident that he had named her Polyphema.

Thus, he knew she had increased her own already power-ful prestige tremendously by possession of that unique thing—a transmitting mobile. So much had her importance grown that the Mothers on the fringes of her area passed on the news to others. Before he had learned her language, the entire continent was hooked-up. Polyphema had become a veritable gossip columnist; tens of thousands of hill-crouchers listened in eagerly to her accounts of her deal-ings with the walking paradox: a semantic male.

That had been fine. Then, very recently, the Mother across the valley had captured a similar creature. And in one bound she had become Number Two in the area and would, at the slightest weakness on Polyphema's part, wrest the top position away.

Eddie became widely excited at the news. He had often daydreamed about his mother and wondered what she was doing. Curiously enough, he ended many of his fantasies with lip-mutterings, reproaching her almost audibly for hav-ing left him and for making no try to rescue him. When he became aware of his attitude, he was ashamed. Neverthe-less, the sense of desertion colored his thoughts.

Now that he knew she was alive and had been caught, probably while trying to get him out, he rose from the lethargy that had lately been making him doze the clock around. He asked Polyphema if she would open the entrance so he could talk directly with the other captive. She said yes. Eager to listen in on a conversation between two mobiles, she was very co-operative. There would be a mountain of gossip in what they would have to say. The only thing that dented her joy was that the other Mother would also have access.

Then, remembering she was still Number One and would broadcast the details first, she trembled so with pride and ecstasy that Eddie felt the floor shaking.

Iris open, he walked through it and looked across the valley. The hillsides were still green, red, and yellow, as the plants on Baudelaire did not lose their leaves during winter.

But a few white patches showed that winter had begun. Eddie shivered from the bite of cold air on his naked skin. Long ago he had taken off his clothes. The wombwarmth had made garments too uncomfortable; moreover, Eddie, being human, had had to get rid of waste products. And Polyphema, being a Mother, had had periodically to flush out the dirt with warm water from one of her stomachs. Everytime the tracheae-vents exploded, streams that swept the undesirable elements out through her door-iris, Eddie had become soaked. When he abandoned dress, his clothes had gone floating out. Only by sitting on his pack did he keep it from a like fate.

Afterwards, he and the Sluggos had been dried off by warm air pumped through the same vents and originating from the mighty battery of lungs. Eddie was comfortable enough—he'd always liked showers, anyway—but the loss of his garments kept him from escaping. If he were to, he would soon freeze to death outside unless he found the yacht quickly. And he wasn't sure he remembered the path back.

So now, when he stepped outside, he retreated a pace or two and let the warm air from Polyphema flow like a cloak from his shoulders.

Then he peered across the half-mile that separated him from his mother, but he could not see her. The twilight state and the dark of the unlit interior of her captor quite hid her.

He tapped, in Morse, "Switch to the talkie, same frequency." Paula Fetts did so. She began asking him, frantically, if he were all right.

He replied he was fine.

"Have you missed me terribly, son?"

"Oh, very much."

Even as he said this, he wondered, vaguely, why his voice sounded so hollow. Despair at never again being able to see her, probably.

"I've almost gone crazy, Eddie. When you were caught I ran away as fast as I could. I had no idea what horrible monster it was that was attacking us. And then, halfway down the hill, I fell and broke my leg. . . ."

"Oh, no, mother!"

"Yes. But I managed to crawl back to the ship. And there, after I'd set it myself, I gave myself B.K. shots. Only, my system didn't react like it's supposed to. There are people that way, you know, and the healing took twice as long.

"But when I was able to walk, I got a gun and a box of Blasto. I was going to blow up what I thought was a kind of rock-fortress, an outpost for some kind of extee. I'd no idea of the true nature of these beasts. First, though, I decided to reconnoiter. I was going to spy on the boulder from across the valley. And I was trapped by this thing.

"Listen, son. Before I'm cut off for any reason, let me tell you not to give up hope. I'll be out of here before long and over to rescue you."

"How?"

"If you remember, my lab kit holds a number of carcinogens for field work. Well, you know that sometimes a Mother's conception-spot, torn up during mating, instead of begetting young, goes into cancer—the opposite of pregnancy. I've injected a carcinogen into the spot and a beautiful carcinoma has developed. She'll be dead in a few days."

"Mom! You'll be buried in that rotting mass!"

"No. This creature has told me that when one of her species dies, a reflex opens the labia. That's to permit their young—if any—to escape. Listen, I'll—"

A tentacle coiled about him and pulled him back through the iris, which shut.

When he switched back to C.W., he heard, "Why didn't you communicate? What were you doing? Tell me! Tell me!"

Eddie told her. There was a silence that could only be interpreted as astonishment. After she'd recover her wits, she said, "From now on, you will talk to the other male through me."

Obviously, she envied and hated his ability to change wavebands, and, perhaps, had a struggle to accept the idea.

It was outré.

"Please," he persisted, not knowing how dangerous were the waters he was wading in, "please let me talk to my mother di—"

For the first time, he heard her stutter.

"Wha-wha-what? Your Mo-Mo-Mother?"

"Yes. Of course."

The floor heaved violently beneath his feet. He cried out and braced himself to keep from falling and then flashed on the light. The walls were pulsating like shaken jelly, and the vascular columns had turned from red and blue to gray. The entrance-iris sagged open, like a lax mouth, and the air cooled. He could feel the drop in temperature in her flesh with the soles of his feet.

It was some time before he caught on.

Polyphema was in a state of shock.

What might have happened had she stayed in it, he never knew. She might have died and thus forced him out into the winter before his mother could escape. If so, and he couldn't find the ship, he would die. Huddled in the warmest corner of the egg-shaped chamber, Eddie contemplated that idea and shivered to a degree the outside air couldn't account for.

However, Polyphema had her own method of recovery. It consisted of spewing out the contents of her stew-stomach, which had doubtless become filled with the poisons draining out of her system from the blow. Her ejection of the stuff was the physical manifestation of the psychical catharsis. So furious was the flood that her foster son was almost swept out in the hot tide, but she, reacting instinctively, had coiled tentacles about him andth e Sluggos. Then she followed the first upchucking by emptying her other three waterpouches, the second hot and the third lukewarm and the fourth, just filled, cold.

Eddie yelped as the icy water doused him.

Polyphema's irises closed again. The floor and walls gradually quit quaking; the temperature rose; and her veins and arteries regained their red and blue. She was well again. Or so she seemed.

But when, after waiting twenty-four hours, he cautiously approached the subject, he found she not only would not talk about it, she refused to acknowledge the existence of the other mobile.

Eddie, giving up the hopes of conversation, thought for quite a while. The only conclusion he could come to, and he was sure he'd grasped enough of her psychology to make it valid, was that the concept of a mobile female was utterly unacceptable.

Her world was split into two: mobile and her kind, the immobile. Mobile meant food and mating. Mobile meant —male. The Mothers were—female.

How the mobiles reproduced had probably never entered the hillcrouchers' minds. Their science and philosophy were on the instinctive body-level. Whether they had some notion of spontaneous generation or amoeba-like fission being responsible for the continued population of mobiles, or they'd just taken for granted they "growed," like Topsy, Eddie never found out. To them, they were female and the rest of the protoplasmic cosmos was male.

That was that. Any other idea was more than foul and obscene and blasphemous. It was—unthinkable.

So that Polyphema had received a deep trauma from his words. And though she seemed to have recovered, somewhere in those tons of unimaginably complicated flesh a bruise was buried. Like a hidden flower, dark purple, it bloomed, and the shadow it cast was one that cut off a certain memory, a certain tract, from the light of consciousness. That bruise-stained shadow covered that time and event which the Mother, for reasons unfathomable to the human being, found necessary to mark KEEP OFF.

Thus, though Eddie did not word it, he understood in the cells of his body, he felt and knew, as if his bones were prophesying and his brain did not hear, what came to pass.

Sixty-six hours later by the panrad clock, Polyphema's entrance-lips opened. Her tentacles darted out. They came back in, carrying his helpless and struggling mother.

Eddie, roused out of a doze, horrified, paralyzed, saw her toss her lab kit at him and heard an inarticulate cry from her. And saw her plunged, headforemost, into the stomach-iris.

Polyphema had taken the one sure way of burying the evidence.

Eddie lay face down, nose mashed against the warm and faintly throbbing flesh of the floor. Now and then his hands clutched spasmodically as if he were reaching for something that someone kept putting just within his reach and then moving away.

How long he was there, he didn't know, for he never again looked at the clock.

Finally, in the darkness, he sat up and giggled, inanely, "Mother always did make good stew."

That set him off. He leaned back on his hands and threw his head back and howled like a wolf under a full moon.

Polyphema, of course, was dead-deaf, but she could radar his posture, and her keen nostrils deduced from his body-scent that he was in a terrible fear and anguish.

A tentacle glided out and gently enfolded him.

"What is the matter?" zzted the panrad.

He stuck his finger in the keyhole.

"I have lost my mother!"

"?"

"She's gone away, and she'll never come back."

"I don't understand. *Here I am.*"

Eddie quit weeping and cocked his head as if he were listening to some inner voice. He snuffled a few times and wiped away the tears, slowly disengaged the tentacle, patted it, walked over to his pack in a corner, and took out the bottle of Old Red Star capsules. One he popped into the thermos; the other he gave to her with the request she duplicate it, if possible. Then he stretched out on his side, propped on one elbow, like a Roman in his sensualities, sucked the rye through the nipple, and listened to the medley of Beethoven, Moussorgsky, Verdi, Strauss, Porter, Casals, Feinstein, and Waxworth.

So the time—if there were such a thing there—flowed around Eddie. When he was tired of music or plays or books, he listened in on the area hook-up. Hungry, he rose and walked—or often just crawled—to the stew-iris. Cans of rations lay in his pack; he had planned to eat on those until he was sure that—what was it he was forbidden to eat? Poison? Something had been devoured by Polyphema and the Sluggos. But sometime during the music-rye orgy, he had forgotten. He now ate quite hungrily and with thought for nothing but the satisfaction of his wants.

Sometimes the door-iris opened, and Billy Greengrocer hopped in. Billy looked like a cross between a cricket and a kangaroo. He was the size of a collie, and he bore in a marsupalian pouch vegetables and fruit and nuts. These he extracted with shiny green, chitinous claws and gave to Mother in return for meals of stew. Happy symbiote, he chirruped merrily while his many-faceted eyes, revolving independently of each other, looked one at the Sluggos and the other at Eddie.

Eddie, on impulse, abandoned the 1000 kc. band and roved the frequencies until he found that both Polyphema and Billy were emitting a 108 wave. That, apparently, was their natural signal. When Billy had his groceries to deliver, he broadcast. Polyphema, in turn, when she needed them, sent back to him. There was nothing intelligent on Billy's part; it was just his instinct to transmit. And the Mother was, aside from the "semantic" frequency, limited to that one band. But it worked out fine.

Everything was fine. What more could a man want? Free food, unlimited liquor, soft bed, air-conditioning, showerbaths, music, intellectual works (on the tape), interesting conversation (much of it was about him), privacy, and security.

If he had not already named her, he would have called her Mother Gratis.

Nor were creature comforts all. She had given him the answers to all his questions, all. . . .

Except one.

That was never expressed vocally by him. Indeed, he would have been incapable of doing so. He was probably unaware that he had such a question.

But Polyphema voiced it one day when she asked him to do her a favor.

Eddie reacted as if outraged.

"One does not—! One does not—!"

He choked and then he thought, how ridiculous! She is not—

And looked puzzled, and said. "But she is."

He rose and opened the lab kit. While he was looking for a scalpel, he came across the carcinogens. Without thinking about it, he threw them through the half-opened labia far out and down the hillside.

Then he turned and, scalpel in hand, leaped at the light grey swelling on the wall. And stopped, staring at it, while the instrument fell from his hand. And picked it up and stabbed feebly and did not even scratch the skin. And again let it drop.

"What is it? What is it?" crackled the panrad hanging from his wrist.

Suddenly, a heavy cloud of human odor—mansweat—was puffed in his face from a nearby vent.

"? ? ? ?"

And he stood, bent in a half-crouch, seemingly paralyzed. Until tentacles seized him in fury and dragged him towards the stomach-iris, yawning mansized.

Eddie screamed and writhed and plunged his finger in the panrad and tapped, "All right! All right!"

And once back before the spot, he lunged with a sudden and wild joy; he slashed savagely; he yelled. "Take that! And that, P . . ." and the rest was lost in a mindless shout.

He did not stop cutting, and he might have gone on and on until he had quite excised the spot had not Polyphema interfered by dragging him towards her stomach-iris again. For ten seconds he hung there, helpless and sobbing with a strange mixture of fear and glory.

Polyphema's reflexes had almost overcome her brain. Fortunately, a cold spark of reason lit up a corner of the vast, dark, and hot chapel of her frenzy.

The convolutions leading to the steaming, meat-laden pouch closed and the foldings of flesh rearranged themselves. Eddie was suddenly hosed with warm water from what he called the "sanitation" stomach. The iris closed. He was put down. The scalpel was put back in the bag.

For a long time Mother seemed to be shaken by the thought of what she might have done to Eddie. She did not trust herself to transmit until her nerves were settled. When she did, she did not refer to his narrow escape. Nor did he.

He was happy. He felt as if a spring, tight-coiled against his bowels since he and his wife had parted, was now, for some reason, sprung. The dull vague pain of loss and discontent, the slight fever and cramp in his entrails and apathy that sometimes afflicted him, were gone. He felt fine.

Meanwhile, something akin to deep affection had been

lighted, like a tiny candle under the drafty and overtowering roof of a cathedral. Mother's shell housed more than Eddie; it now curved over an emotion new to her kind. This was evident by the next event that filled him with terror.

For the wounds in the spot healed and the swelling increased into a large bag. Then the bag burst and ten mouse-sized Sluggos struck the floor. The impact had the same effect as a doctor's spanking a newborn baby's bottom; they drew in their first breath with shock and pain: their uncontrolled and feeble pulses filled the ether with shapeless SOS's.

When Eddie was not talking with Polyphema or listening in or drinking or sleeping or eating or bathing or running off the tape, he played with the Sluggos. He was, in a sense, their father. Indeed, as they grew to hog-size, it was hard for their female parent to distinguish him from her young. As he seldom walked any more, and was often to be found on hands and knees in their midst, she could not scan him too well. Moreover, something in the heavywet air or in the diet had caused every hair on his body to drop off. He grew very fat. Generally speaking, he was one with the pale, soft, round, and bald offspring. A family likeness.

There was one difference. When the time came for the virgins to be expelled, Eddie crept to one end, whimpering, and stayed there until he was sure Mother was not going to thrust him out into the cold, hard, and hungry world.

That final crisis over, he came back to the center of the floor. The panic in his breast had died out, but his nerves were still quivering. He filled his thermos and then listened for a while to his own baritone singing the *Sea Things* aria from his favorite opera, Gianelli's *Ancient Mariner*. Suddenly he burst out and accompanied himself, finding himself thrilled as never before by the concluding words.

And from my neck so free
The Albatross fell off, and sank
Like lead into the sea.

Afterwards, voice silent but heart singing, he switched off the wire and cut in on Polyphema's broadcast.

Mother was having trouble. She could not precisely describe to the continent-wide hook-up this new and almost inexpressible emotion she felt about the mobile. It was a concept her language was not prepared for. Nor was she helped any by the gallons of Old Red Star in her bloodstream.

Eddie sucked at the plastic nipple and nodded sympathetically and drowsily at her search for words. Presently, the thermos rolled out of his hand.

He slept on his side, curled in a ball, knees on his chest and arms crossed, neck bent forward. Like the pilot room chronometer whose hands reversed after the crash, the clock of his body was ticking backwards, ticking backwards . . .

In the darkness, in the moistness, safe and warm, well fed, well loved.